"DON'T MOVE," HE COMMANDED FROM THE DOORWAY

"Do not," he added, his voice dropping even lower, stroking her jittery insides, "hide your body from me." And his hot gaze ran down the length of her again. She was utterly beautiful. Though she was half-hidden behind that damnable towel, Zach could see the back of her, and hot blood roared like a torrent through his body. She looked ethereal, bathed in soft blue twilight that shimmered around her, cloaking her skin like a gossamer veil.

"Take down the towel," he growled.

Statue-still, Katherine felt her heart beat a staccato rhythm in her chest. He was like a dark god, tall and formidable, his intense masculinity a palpable force. The firelight warmed his bare flesh, rippling over the bronze glow of his shoulders, etching intriguing shadows into his hard, handsome face.

He was the epitome of masculinity . . . and power.

Smoke Eyes

Maureen Reynolds

BANTAM BOOKS

NEW YORK · TORONTO · LONDON · SYDNEY · AUCKLAND

SMOKE EYES

A Bantam Fanfare Book / December 1992

FANFARE and the portrayal of a boxed "ff"
are trademarks of Bantam Books,
a division of Bantam Doubleday Dell Publishing Group, Inc.

ISBN 0-553-29501-2

Published simultaneously in the United States and Canada

Bantam Books are published by Bantam Books, a division of Bantam Doubleday Dell Publishing Group, Inc. Its trademark, consist-
ing of the words "Bantam Books" and the portrayal of a rooster, is
Registered in U.S. Patent and Trademark Office and in other countries. Marca Registrada. Bantam Books, 666 Fifth Avenue, New
York, New York 10103.

PRINTED IN THE UNITED STATES OF AMERICA

RAD   0 9 8 7 6 5 4 3 2 1

Smoke
Eyes

One

Colorado, 1888

"Doc! Doc Flynn!"

The frantic male voice and thundering of fists on her front door jolted Dr. Katherine Flynn from the depths of deep sleep. Startled, she jumped and promptly knocked her forehead against the headboard. "Ouch!" she muttered, rubbing the tender spot.

The knocking continued over the man's shouts. "Doc Flynn! *Please!*"

"Coming," Katherine mumbled sleepily. She shoved herself upright, until she was sitting back against the pillows, and tried to force her eyes open. She should be accustomed to this by now—abrupt awakenings at odd hours of the night—but she'd had a long day and couldn't shake her dazed, disoriented feeling.

"For the love of Mike, Doc! Doc, are you there?"

"Coming!" Katherine called again, more loudly, though she doubted the man could hear anything but his own violent pounding on the door. Lord, he was apt to smash his fist right through the wood. She pushed the covers aside and slid from the bed. Her bare feet touched the cold wooden floor and she shivered, groping for her wrapper.

"Doc! Please!"

"Please!" a shrieking voice echoed from the kitchen. Katherine grinned, recognizing Clarabelle's voice. The yellow-and-green parrot had been a Christmas gift from the town eccentric, old Birdie McDowell, and the pet was both a delight and a bane to Katherine. As Katherine struggled to pull her wrapper on, the bird called out to whoever was pounding on the door.

"What?"

The knocking ceased.

"Who's there?" Clarabelle screeched.

"It's me!" the man said. "Louis Robinson."

"Please!" the bird squawked.

Katherine giggled. "Quiet, Clarabelle!"

"Why?" Clarabelle shot back. "Why?"

The pounding resumed, and Katherine stumbled out of her room toward the front door. With all the racket one would think she'd be fully alert, but she still couldn't keep her eyes open and groped blindly across the front room. She blundered into the rocking chair one of her patients had left in the center of the room, stubbing her big toe. She gasped and grabbed it, and called herself a featherbrain.

"Featherbrain," Clarabelle repeated.

"Blast it, Clarabelle, will you hush!"

"Well, what do you want? What do you want?" Clarabelle retorted.

Louis proceeded to shout his business through the door, and Katherine slapped a palm against her forehead. "Quiet!" she cried to the chattering bird. She pulled open the door and poked her head around the edge of it, careful to hide her body from Louis's view. The big red-faced townsman stood blinking at her, his mouth hanging open. He looked thoroughly confused as he removed his hat and held it against his barrel chest. "Well, Doc, howse I'm s'posed to tell you what happened if yer tellin' me to be quiet?"

She smiled apologetically. "That wasn't me talking, Louis, that was Clarabelle."

The man's brow furrowed. "Huh?"

Katherine sighed. Not everyone knew she owned a parrot. Obviously Louis was one of the unenlightened. "My parrot, Louis. She mimics folks—speaks like a human."

Louis's face cleared. "Well, I'll be."

Katherine waited for him to digest this bit of information while the gusty cold March air swept up her thin flannel nightgown. Judging by the pearl-gray light outdoors it wasn't the middle of the night as she had originally thought, but closer to dawn.

"Well, gosh, Doc, that bird sounds jes like you."

"I suppose," she murmured dryly. "Now what brings you here at this hour, Louis?"

He tightened his grip on his hat and frowned. "Gosh, Doc, I'm real sorry 'bout wakin' you but there's been a murder." At Katherine's horrified expression, he stumbled on, his words running together in a garbled stream. "Yup, dammit, down at the whorehouse— Nellie's. You know Richard Waters, he's been kilt! Stabbed to death right in the act—bled all over that little filly, Dusty—she was kilt too." He stopped, out of breath, and shuddered. "God, what a mess!" He paused again, catching the grim tightening of her lips. "Sorry, Doc, sorry to be the one to have to give you the bad news. But the sheriff needs you down there right quick."

Even in the pale light Louis could see a shadow darkening Doc's enormous gray eyes. She was the most caring doctor he'd ever run into. Truth be told, it bothered him that she was female, but she made up for that by the way she cared so about folks—made all her patients feel like family. Though she had only been practicing in town for six months, the townsfolk were drawn to her as if to a beacon of light. She was quick-witted and lively, brimming with gentleness and laughter. Youngsters and old folk especially gravitated toward her, and she strove to make everyone feel important. None of her patients felt slighted; she gave the wealthiest and the poorest equal attention. She was precious, a gift to the town. She was also the most intoxicatingly beautiful woman Louis had ever seen. As if to make up for delivering her such grim news, he slid his battered hat back on and said, "I'll walk you over to Nellie's, Doc."

Katherine gave him a terse nod, already shutting the door, then hurried back to her bedroom. She dressed hastily, piled her thick hair atop her head in a careless knot, plunged her arms into her wool coat, and grabbed her black medical bag. As she dashed out the front door, she called good-bye to Clarabelle.

"Does that bird care whether or not you say good-bye?" Louis asked as they hurried over the crunchy snow to Nellie's.

Katherine shrugged, casting Louis a jaunty grin. "It makes *me* feel better for some odd reason," she explained, catching her breath as the sharp Colorado air funneled into her lungs.

He grinned back at her, then frowned as they crossed Fisher Road and swung left toward Main Street. "Sorry fer you to have to see this, Doc."

She patted his forearm reassuringly. "Don't worry, Louis, I've seen this sort of thing before. It's never pleasant, and so very hard to understand, but I'm a doctor, and I must often tend to these . . . tragedies." Louis only grunted in response, and she had to smile. "Now *you*," she teased, "can only have this firsthand knowledge if you were visiting Nellie's. You'd best be careful," she warned gently, "for there's a potion a doctor can administer to a man so that he doesn't leave his wife's bed to visit trollops."

Louis flushed purple. He began to stammer. "But—but my wife . . . she *wants* me to enjoy the whores! She says she's tired of carryin' younguns year after year. We got seven of 'em, you know!"

"I know," Katherine murmured, sighing inwardly. Louis probably spoke the truth, but she warned him about giving his wife the pox. He shrugged and said he didn't sleep with his wife anymore, and his expression told her to mind her own business. Katherine said nothing more, and waved to Noah Epson, owner of the dry goods store, as they passed him on Main Street.

"Well, hullo, and good morning to you, Doc!" Noah called. "Ah, it's a pleasure to see such a beautiful face first thing in the morning!"

Katherine smiled, but Louis hurried her on, his big hand cupping her elbow. She caught sight of the town's schoolmarm, Miss Emilee Harris, and called out to her too. The teacher just kept her head bent against the gusty wind as she headed toward the schoolhouse on the north side of town. It was always a challenge to get the teacher to smile, and Katherine shook her head, remembering her own childhood teacher's good sense of humor.

She sobered when they approached Nellie's. The distant blue mountains, hazy in the pink-gray predawn light, served as backdrop for the two-story bordello. She glanced at Louis and swallowed. "Thank you, Louis, for seeing me across town. I guess you can go on home now." He was reluctant to leave the action, though, and she had to give him a little nudge before he grunted and turned away.

Katherine took a deep breath, hefted her bag against her thigh, and stepped inside. The warm front room smelled of whiskey and stale smoke and the damp heat of male bodies, and she wrinkled her nose. As her eyes adjusted to the dim light, she caught sight of Nellie sitting at one of the round wooden tables nursing a bottle of whiskey. Ashen-faced, her gray-blond hair straggling from her usually perfect coiffure, she did not even glance up as Katherine walked over to her.

"Nellie." Katherine removed the bottle from her grip and sat down across from the stunned madam. Reaching across the table, she took Nellie's hand and squeezed it gently.

Nellie stared at their hands with unseeing eyes. "Dusty was my littlest one, Doc. I don't see why she had to come to such a gruesome end. She never did no one no harm." She let out a sad, shuddering breath, as if she had been crying for a long time. But Katherine could see by the wet glitter in her eyes that she had not shed a tear. "She was an orphan when I took her in an' I tole her she'd never have to worry 'bout where her next meal would be comin' from."

She reached for the whiskey bottle, but Katherine kept it firmly in her grasp. Nellie gave a tired little smile, then narrowed her eyes so that Katherine could see all the harsh lines in her haggard face. "To see her like that, bleedin' like a stuck pig unner that bastard ..."

Katherine felt another presence behind her and turned to look over her shoulder at the town deputy, Tom Greene. He stood on the second step from the landing, slowly twirling his hat in his hands as he observed the two women.

"Tom," Katherine said in greeting.

He nodded once. "Sheriff wants you upstairs."

She squeezed the older woman's plump fingers again and stood. "If you drink the whiskey, Nellie, you'll feel much worse later than you do now."

Nellie smiled grimly. "Aw, Doc, yer a sweet one, you are, to be worryin'. But I wanna forget for a little while. I kin take care o' myself." Her voice cracked when she added, "Ya might wanna take a swig yerself before you head up there." Katherine shook her head, grabbed hold of her medical bag, and trudged up the stairs. As she followed Tom down the dim, narrow upstairs hall, their footsteps were muffled by the carpeted floor. From behind the door of one of the rooms she could hear a woman's soft crying. She glanced at the wallpaper with its faded roses, the wall sconces, the brass numerals on the girls' doors, unwilling to look at the door Tom had pushed open at the end of the hall, where the murder scene awaited her.

She braced herself for the worst and found it—an assault on her senses. Though she was a doctor and had faced many gruesome scenarios, the two naked, entwined corpses on the bed jarred her to her core. For a paralyzed moment she stood in the doorway, her vision blurred. Then it sharpened acutely, focusing on Richard Waters, prominent businessman in town, slumped facedown over Dusty, the frail little blonde whose throat had been slashed. The knife was still buried in Waters's back, the jeweled handle glinting oddly in the dawn light. A puddle of blood stained the white sheets and dripped in a maddening rhythm to the wooden floor. Numbed, Katherine stared at the red pool seeping into the floorboards. The overwhelming stench of death permeated the close air, and her stomach turned.

She tightened her lips. "Open the window, Tom," she said to the deputy. He'd been staring out of it, still twirling his hat, looking as if he'd rather be anywhere in the world but in that room. Dutifully he pushed up the bottom half of the window and propped it open with a stick. The fresh, frost-nipped air swept into the room, cleansing it. Katherine shut the door behind her and strode over to the bed. As she set her bag on the night table, she glanced at the sheriff. "Good morning, Sheriff."

Sheriff Bates, a thickset man with a ruddy face and shrewd brown eyes, watched her unbuckle her bag and dig through it. "Mornin', Doc," he mumbled. He continued watching her as she wrapped a cloth around her hands and pulled the knife from Waters's back. The action made a thick, sucking sound, and he felt the back of his throat swell. "A goddamn disgrace, ain't it?"

Katherine did not answer. Her movements were calm, clinical, professional. Her keen gaze swept over the bodies as she held the knife aloft for Sheriff Bates to take. He did, wiping the blade clean with his handkerchief. He handed it to Tom, who stuffed it into his back pocket.

"Unusual dagger," Katherine said, rounding the bed to get a better view of the wound. "And even more unusual that the killer left it in Mr. Waters's back."

Bates grunted. Damn smart woman, this female sawbones, he thought. Though her capabilities earned her his utmost respect, she also discomfited him with her knowledge, her almost mystical powers. He owed her a lot. She'd saved his little girl's life last fall, doctoring her through three days and two nights of raging fever. But it made the back of his neck itch to think she could be smarter than any man in town.

He cleared his throat. Her comment deserved a response at least. "Yer right about that, Doc. That dagger is a collector's piece if I ever saw one."

She gave him a sidelong glance that put him on the defensive, and he ran a hand through his gray hair. "The way I figure it is the killer left in a hurry—maybe heard footsteps in the hall—and fled. That's why the knife was still in Waters's back."

"Hmmm . . ." Katherine frowned. She tried to roll Richard Waters off Dusty, but he was too heavy. "Help me with this, please, Tom."

Tom forced himself forward. He grabbed hold of the naked Waters and rolled him over. Waters's mouth and eyes were wide open, and Katherine squeezed her own shut for a moment as she heard Tom swear. When she opened them again, Tom was at the window, the sheriff's face was grim, and she had to draw in a deep, steadying breath as she continued her examination.

"There is no discoloration," she said. "No more than two hours have passed since the murder. Judging by the angle of the knife the killer is right-handed."

The sheriff shifted as he watched Katherine begin to tidy up.

"I wonder," she went on, "if the murderer was after Waters or Dusty."

Bates was stunned. *That* possibility hadn't even crossed his mind. He'd assumed Waters was the target. Damn the doc for planting that seed! Now he'd have to think this through a lot more thoroughly. There were probably plenty of folks who would have liked to kill the unconscionable Waters, but a whore? Waters seemed the more likely intended victim. He had been a prominent but corrupt banker who'd lived on exclusive Mulberry Street with a beautiful wife and an incorrigible sixteen-year-old son. Bates had often brought the boy in for fighting and drinking and other unruly behavior, and he'd always thought it was sad to see the son following the path of the father. But maybe someone *had* wanted to kill Dusty, and Waters had just been in the way. . . .

He cleared his throat again and scratched the back of his head, feeling mighty uneasy under the doc's questioning stare. But he tried to look nonchalant. "Sure," he said, "I thought of that." He saw by the flicker of amusement in Doc's eyes that she didn't believe him. She was packing up her bag again, and he felt he needed to say something to prove he had a clear slant on this case. "I even thought it could have been a drifter passin' through town. I sure as hell don't know who in Newberry would own such a fancy knife as that. Lookit the handle—all gems an' goldlike."

Katherine was washing her hands at the copper basin on the washstand. Just by her bland expression he could tell she had her own thoughts on this murder, and he itched to ply her with questions. But he had an enormous quantity of pride, and he'd be damned if he'd ask a woman's opinion on any matter, even if she was a doctor.

She turned and smiled encouragingly at him. "I'm sure you'll conduct a thorough investigation, Sheriff."

Now how she could say that—as if she knew something he didn't—and make him feel incompetent, while she was bestowing the loveliest of smiles on him, stumped the sheriff. He tugged on one ear as she continued in that soft voice of hers that could both mesmerize and galvanize at once. "You can bring the bodies to my lab for autopsies anytime today. I'll leave the lab door unlocked. I have to run an errand to the apothecary, but after that I have office hours from noon to four o'clock. I will, of course, report my findings as soon as the autopsies are completed." She lifted her medical bag off the night table, and the weight of it had her listing to one side. "Has anyone informed Mrs. Waters and her son?"

"We were on our way over there shortly. It ain't going to be pleasant to tell her her husband got killed in a whore's bed."

Katherine grimaced. It would be just like the sheriff to frame the news in such an inelegant way. "Umm . . . perhaps I can stop there on my way home and break the news."

The sheriff looked relieved. "Well, thanks, Doc. I sure appreciate that."

Her gaze drifted to the taciturn Tom. "Good day, Tom, Sheriff. I better hurry down to the Waters's home before the news reaches them first. Word of a scandal has a way of spreading as fast as a prairie fire."

Without waiting for either of them to open the door, she strode from the room. Walking quickly, she left the bordello and stepped into the sparkling day. She struck out across town, which was beginning to stir as merchants opened their shops and men performed their early morning chores. Children were spilling out of whitewashed houses with their books and tin dinner pails, on their way to school. Her gaze scanned Mike Owens's eatery, which boasted fine food and drink, skipped past the dress shop and bootery, the little white church with its tall steeple, Mrs. Smith's confectionery shop, where the smell of spices drifted on the crisp morning air. Clean, prosperous Newberry, she thought, now sullied by a disgraceful murder. The town would be in an uproar when word leaked out—and it would, rapidly. People would panic; men would fear for their wives and daughters. And, of course, Nellie's business would plummet.

The sun's glare hurt Katherine's eyes. The snow was powerfully bright, the sky a deep cerulean blue—such stark contrasts to the ghastly colors of death in the bordello she left behind.

She headed for Mulberry Street and the gracious two-storied white house where she would relate her news, where the lives of its inhabitants would be changed forever.

By midmorning the town was abuzz with news of the murder. The daily paper had published a special edition to carry the story, and the article was a mix of fact, speculation, and innuendo. **"PROMINENT BANKER AND DOXY STABBED TO DEATH IN NELLIE'S BORDELLO,"** the headline blared. "Early this morning, when most of the residents of Newberry were sound asleep in the comfort of their homes, Richard Waters, prominent banker, husband, and father, was found stabbed to death in Nellie's bordello with his doxy beneath him. . . ."

It was all there, every scandalous detail. Shocking! the townspeople said to one another. Horrifying! The news traveled like brush fire, searing the streets, whisking past doorways and through businesses.

On her way to the apothecary later that morning, Katherine was stopped by several folks who wanted to talk about it, but she dismissed the gossip with a word or two and moved on. It hadn't been pleasant to deliver the news to Francine Waters, and the regal blond woman's reaction had been, to Katherine, disturbing. She'd been forced to tell Francine on her doorstep, for Francine had not invited her in. She hadn't even opened the door all the way, but Katherine had seen the Waters boy, Toby, standing behind his mother. He was tall, pale, and thin, harsh-faced with his fists clenched menacingly. As Katherine spoke, the boy's face had darkened, but Francine's had remained unchanged. She had gazed at Katherine with huge violet eyes, her face like cold white marble. When Katherine was finished, she had said in a barely audible voice, "Thank you," and closed the door.

Katherine had stood on the step for several minutes, staring at the paneled door, stunned that the woman could appear so unruffled. No shock, no grief, no emotion had been revealed, and Katherine had left the house confused, wondering how a woman could possess such enormous composure.

She'd gone home, bathed, and dressed in a crisp white lawn blouse and a skirt of forest green. Bundled up in her wool coat, hood, and mittens, she'd started off for the apothecary. With all the people stopping her along the way, she worried she wouldn't make it home by noon to begin her office hours.

Finally she reached the apothecary, and as she pulled open the door a little bell tinkled. The pungent scent of herbs and medicines tickled her nostrils, and she heard the familiar sounds of men spitting tobacco juice into a box of sand at the back of the store. Often, loiterers came in from the cold to share a yarn by the warmth of the potbellied stove. They were as much a part of the shop as the glass carboys and bottles that crammed the shelves behind the counter.

They greeted her, then shifted around and leaned toward her, eager to divulge their gossip and to learn what she knew.

"Hey, Doc, hear about the murder?"

"Of course," she said, and stepped toward the counter as her eyes adjusted to the dimmer light of indoors. Brilliant early spring sunlight cascaded through the glass window at the front of the shop. It warmed the wide-planked floorboards and glinted off the colored liquids in the glass containers on the shelves. Warm, cozy, familiar, the shop was a haven from the cold. Katherine inhaled deeply, proud that she was co-owner of the shop with the man behind the counter, George Watson.

"Well, Doc, what've ya heard?" one of the men asked.

She smiled at them as if they were children asking for licorice whips. "I'm sure nothing you don't already know."

As she swept off her hood, she inadvertently silenced them, for it took the men's breath away just to look at her. Sometimes it was hard for them to remember she was a doctor. She was incredibly beautiful, with a face so fine-boned it could have been etched from porcelain. All her features were flawless, but her most striking and captivating feature was a pair of sooty-lashed pure gray eyes that dominated her face.

Paying no attention to the men's stares, Katherine smiled at George and plunked her heavy medical bag on the counter. "What have you for me today, George?" she asked.

He grinned and gestured to the bottles he'd unloaded on the counter. "Shipment from the East, Doc. A couple of weeks late, but when a blizzard strikes you know how hard it is for the trains to get through."

"Yes. Will you have that crate of medicine ready for me in the morning before I head out to the reservation?" She made the thirty-five-mile drive south to the Arapaho reservation once a month. She knew that none of the townsfolk understood why she administered to the Arapaho, but neither did she bother to explain.

George nodded. "Yep, sure will." He'd do anything for the doc. There was rumor that she had Indian blood in her, but she didn't look like a breed. Only the warm, golden cast to her skin hinted at a possibility of mixed blood, but most folks in Newberry chose to overlook it. She was the damn finest doc that had ever graced the town, and if she withdrew her services it would be a damned shame. "It'll be ready first thing in the morning. Hey, Doc, ain't that somethin' about the killin'?"

"It's something all right," Katherine said, moving down the counter to inspect the shipment. The sight of various hard-to-find drugs—compounds and powders and packets of medicine—stirred her physician's blood. She studied the labels and set bottles aside for someone to carry to her home later, where she would measure them out.

"Aw, c'mon, Doc," one of the idlers by the stove called out. "You gotta have more information about this thing than we do!"

She swept her amused glance over them. "Honestly," she said, flipping her hands up in a careless gesture, "it's all in the paper—"

The door burst open, severing her words. Accompanied by a gust of howling March wind, in tumbled little Birdie McDowell. Aptly named, she was frail and sparrowlike, her faded red hair orangey now with age—and the hair dye she put in it—her eyes a brilliant, glittering green. Flinging her back against the door, she pressed till it was shut and the wind reduced to a mere whine that seeped underneath. She rested there, spread-eagled, to catch her breath.

Her bonnet, tilted askew, was covered with lace and flowers made of chiffon. Birdie regularly ordered merchandise from stores back East, and Katherine guessed the hat was her latest catalogue purchase. When Birdie caught sight of Katherine, her bright eyes narrowed until they were mere green slits.

"Ha!" she cackled merrily. "You, lass, are just the gal I want to see."

Oh, no, Katherine thought, her mind searching for an excuse to make a hasty departure. Birdie was renowned for her endless, aimless chatter to which one could hardly respond. She darted an appealing glance to George, who muttered something about fetching another shipment as he exited to the back of the shop.

Birdie stepped forward, primping and setting her hat in place. Her little pointed face grew animated, her eyes snapping brightly. "There's a stranger in town— saw him a half hour ago—and he is the most handsome devil I've clapped these old eyes on this side of Eire!" Placing a gnarled hand on Katherine's arm, she gasped as if she'd been struck just now with a revelation, when Katherine knew it had been her thought all along. "He'd be perfect for you, missy. *Perfect.*"

Katherine almost laughed aloud, and would have if Birdie hadn't been serious. She was always on the lookout for a husband for Katherine, who had no use or desire for one. As she looked down into Birdie's unblinking eyes, she struggled to keep a straight face. Birdie had once confided to Katherine that she had been a prostitute in San Francisco, and even now she was a painted woman with her heavily rouged cheeks, kohled eyes, and the rice powder she dabbed on her wrinkled, elfin face.

"Birdie," Katherine said in a reasonable tone, "how can you think he's perfect for me when you don't even *know* this person? He could be—"

"Ah!" Birdie cut her off. "He's got t'be Irish, he does. *Got* to be." If a person could claim even a drop of Irish blood, then he was simply and unconditionally acceptable to Birdie McDowell. She snapped her fingers. "I'm sure of it! It's in the man's walk—in his shoulders—" She strutted across the floor, the tiny woman comically mimicking the walk of a big swaggering stranger. All the men around the stove had ceased their spitting and gossiping to watch her. Even George emerged from the back of the shop, his eyes bugging behind his spectacles at the outrageous scene. Katherine swallowed her laughter again and thought the best course to take was to steer Birdie onto a more neutral subject.

"Is that a new bonnet, Birdie?" she asked.

Birdie stopped her prancing to preen before Katherine. Smiling happily, she nodded. "Yes." She touched a dangling blue feather and her smile spread, her face creasing in myriad wrinkles like a crumpled paper bag. "Do you like it?" Without waiting for Katherine's answer, she leaned forward and whispered conspiratorially, so none of the men could hear—though none of them were in the least bit interested any longer— "When I wear this hat men can't keep their eyes off me."

I'll bet, Katherine thought, hiding her amusement. Her gaze traveled over the outlandish bonnet, its brim bent from the punishing wind. "What," she asked with a poker face, "will you order next?"

Birdie grinned. "Funny you should ask, little lassie, 'cause I plan t' order one fer you too."

Katherine blinked. "One what?" she asked warily.

Birdie glanced sidelong at the cluster of idlers by the stove and leaned even closer to Katherine. But her voice sounded as loud as a rifle shot in the suddenly quiet shop. "A bathing costume."

Katherine was flabbergasted. "A what?"

"You heard me." Gleefully, Birdie rocked back on her heels. "You need one for spring to swim in the creek. We'll have a good time frolicking in our bathing costumes in Olson's Creek, won't we, missy?"

"I—" Katherine was stunned. Not only was the image of Birdie in a bathing costume ludicrous, but the idea of her and Katherine 'frolicking' made Katherine shake her head as if to clear it.

Birdie swung around suddenly and stared at the men. "Ha!" She pointed an accusing finger at a man who'd grown interested in their conversation. "You suddenly have ears like a fox, do you, Thaddeus Clay?"

The young man went scarlet and began to stammer as Birdie advanced on him, wagging her finger. "I d-dunno wh-what yer talkin' about, ma'am."

She went right up to his face and placed one hand on her hip, thrusting it toward him in a provocative fashion. "Why, yes, you do, honey. We were talking about bathing costumes, and yer eyes would bug right outta that empty head if you were to see me and that little filly in such a getup, wouldn't they now?"

The men's guffaws shook the shop, and poor Thaddeus's face turned the color of a plum. Katherine's own face flushed, but she forgot her embarrassment when the door burst open. Tom, the deputy, spilled over the threshold, the cold wind shunting into the shop behind him. He squinted as his eyes adjusted to the dark interior, and Katherine gasped. There was a purple knot over his left eye and a thread of blood oozed from his split bottom lip.

"Tom!" she cried. "What happened to you?"

He focused on her and said hoarsely, "The sheriff wants you right quick down at the jailhouse." He was panting, as if he'd run all the way from there. The men in the back of the shop stood up, tobacco and papers fluttering from their laps to the floor. "We got us a suspect," he added.

"Who?" everyone asked at once.

"Stranger . . . drifter, just like the sheriff said, Doc."

Katherine reached for her medical bag on the counter. "But why does the sheriff need me at the jail?" she asked.

Tom pressed a thumb to his split lip. "He took a swing at me—and the sheriff—one swing—and lookit the damage. He's a big sonuva—" He swallowed, remembering his manners, then continued rapidly, "It took four men to bring him in, and I still had to clunk him one on the head." His Adam's apple bobbed. "Only thing . . . he's threatenin' a lawsuit."

"Lawsuit?" Birdie squawked. "He doesn't sound like yer *regular* drifter to me."

Katherine wondered what a "regular" drifter was, but she kept her attention on Tom. "Why a lawsuit?"

Tom looked petrified, as if he had come face to face with Lucifer. Poor Tom, she thought. He'd had a most trying day, and it was not even eleven o'clock. "Well, when I clunked him one on the head, I knocked it open." He passed a shaky hand through his hair. "I didn't mean to, but he was this wild—anyway, he was bleedin' and swearin' and demandin' we let him loose—that if we lock him up and with his head split open to boot, then he'd sue. But we got him in the cell and the sheriff wants you to come patch him up."

"Gawd a'mighty!" one of the loiterers cried. "We gotta see this!"

And the whole crowd of them spilled out of the shop after Katherine and the deputy, heading for the jail.

Two

They hiked in single file to the jail, jabbering excitedly up the front steps and clumping behind Katherine and Tom. When she entered the jail, Katherine gasped at the sight of the sheriff with his gun trained on the prisoner in the first cell. She did not even let her gaze slide toward the prisoner, keeping it fixed on the gun instead.

"Good Lord, Sheriff!" she said. "Is that necessary?"

"He's dangerous, Doc. An animal! Lookit what he did to Tom there."

"He can't hurt you behind bars," Katherine said. Though she had not yet looked at the prisoner, she could feel his presence, big and dark and menacing. She sensed his gaze on her, and though she had distinctly heard him shouting obscenities before she entered the jailhouse, he was curiously quiet now. She felt a waiting stillness in the air, as if they'd caged a tiger that was getting ready to pounce.

Suddenly, behind her, Birdie gasped in shock. "It's him! The stranger I saw earlier this morning!"

Katherine looked over her shoulder at her friend and saw her face drained of all color but for the two bright spots of rouge on her cheeks. Katherine arched an eyebrow and murmured drolly, "Perfect for me, hmmm, Birdie?"

Birdie flapped her arms and sputtered, but Katherine turned back to the sheriff. "Let me into the cell so I can see if he needs suturing, Sheriff."

The sheriff jerked the pistol toward the keys hanging on the wall behind the desk, and Tom went to fetch them.

"You so much as *look* at her crossways," the sheriff warned the prisoner, "an' I'll blow yer head clear off."

"Well, now, Sheriff"—the stranger's deep, raspy drawl made Katherine's breath catch—"you'd have one dead suspect on your hands if you did that . . . and the real killer would still be on the loose."

The sheriff pulled back the trigger, and Katherine heard the sharp click of a cartridge. The prisoner made a low sound in his throat, and she turned to him in time to see him whirl around and stare out the small barred window at the rear of the cell. He was tall and lean with incredibly wide shoulders packed with iron muscle. Even beneath the fabric of his rough striped shirt she could see those hard muscles shift and ripple. Awed by the size of him, she let her gaze drift over his broad back, down to his lean waist, and lower, to where his black trousers clung to his form so intimately she could see the slight hollows in his tight, hard buttocks. A strange sensation flickered through her, and she quickly looked up at his rock-hard profile. He continued to stare out the window, as if oblivious to the people around him, his long fingers wrapped around a window bar. The man was riveting.

Tom unlocked the door and, with the sheriff muttering something behind her, Katherine stepped into the cell. The prisoner ignored her.

"Drifter, all right," she heard the sheriff say. "Didn't drift fast enough."

Katherine wanted desperately to hush him, for she could scarcely hear her own voice over the sudden violent thudding of her heart. "Sir," she said, "would you please come sit on the bunk so I can tend to you?"

Slowly, he turned to face her. Because the light was behind him, she could not make out his features, but there was no denying his mocking tone. "Sir?" he repeated. "Have you forgotten, madam, that I am in this cell because I've been accused of murder?"

Katherine turned briskly to set her bag on the bunk and open it. She heard his booted heels strike the stone floor—once, twice—then he was beside her, and she could smell him, earthy and male.

With trembling fingers she rummaged through her bag while the big stranger settled himself on the bunk, long legs sprawled wide. "Tom," she said, glancing his way, "would you fetch me some water? I need to wash his cut."

"Sure thing," Tom muttered, obviously terrified the ominous-looking prisoner would lunge for him and crush his throat in his big powerful hands. After all, *he'd* been the one to smash the cutthroat's head open.

Katherine removed her coat and laid her instruments on a rickety chair. When Tom brought her the basin of water, she put it down and wrung out a clean cloth. She turned to the prisoner, and her heart stopped. Somehow she had ended up standing between his wide-spread legs. If she moved left or right she would brush his hard inner thighs, and if she jumped backward—which her instincts clamored for her to do—she would be making a scene over a trivial matter. And he was not about to move.

She glanced at his face, still shadowed in the poorly lit cell. Quickly she averted her eyes to the opened skin under a lock of thick black hair, matted with blood. As she moved closer to him she could almost feel his amused gaze on her face. She ignored it and pushed his hair aside to reveal the wound near his temple, still trickling blood. She pressed the cold cloth to the cut and said tautly, "You'll need a stitch or two."

He said nothing, but all the while she was aware that he watched her face with a quiet intensity. She kept her own eyes lowered as she swiftly threaded a needle with a length of catgut. Stepping close again, she applied a burning disinfectant to his skin that would have made most men howl. This one didn't even flinch. He did speak, though. His deep, dark voice sounded like a rusty file sawing against metal, and a peculiar warmth raced up her spine.

"Was that part of my sentence, Doc?"

Katherine almost giggled. So the vicious murderer had a sense of humor, did he? She lifted the needle and told him to keep still. As the needle pierced his skin he grunted. "These parts don't grant a man a fair trial?" he asked. "They just accuse him and deem these tiny little tortures upon him to prepare him for the final hanging?"

Katherine's mouth began to tremble. "Do not," she warned in a whisper, "make me laugh."

"Another threat? Will it cost me an eye?"

A bubble of laughter escaped her, and the towns-folk began to whisper.

"Now you've done it," he said with mock solemnity. "They're getting ready for a lynching."

As if there was some truth to his words, the sheriff cleared his throat and growled, "Stranger!"

The prisoner ignored him. He waited patiently for Katherine to finish suturing him, and she began to feel unaccountably nervous. Though the cell was dank, the man radiated a virile heat that enveloped her. His scent was warm and musky—male. As her slender fingers moved nimbly over the wound, her heart thudded hard in the base of her throat. It was odd, she thought, that his skin was so deeply tanned this time of year. He must have drifted from some warmer climate. Curious, she chanced a surreptitious peek at his face, and her breath caught before she quickly looked away. He was fatally handsome. His mouth was hard and sensual, his nose bold and proud with a slight hook just below the bridge, his black brows harsh slashes over eyes she dared not meet.

When she was finished she knotted the last stitch and pushed the hair back off his temple. The gesture was meant to keep the wound clean, but it suggested an intimacy that made her jerk her hand back.

"I—" she began, then looked into his eyes. They were black as pitch and delved into her so deeply, she felt a tug in her belly. His eyes drooped a little at the corners, giving him a hooded, sensual look. They were intense, compelling eyes—eyes a woman would never forget.

Katherine frowned. There was something naggingly familiar about the man, but she couldn't know him. She would have remembered such a powerful, ruggedly male creature.

She dipped the cloth in the water again, wrung it

out, and began to sponge off the blood. His face was harsh-planed and angular, as if chiseled from rock, and her hand trembled as it moved down his hard cheekbone, his long jaw, and along his warm neck where blood had trickled. He sat stone-still through her ministrations, yet her heart pounded violently. She dared another glance at his arresting eyes, and they warmed on her.

A faint trace of cynical humor lit their depths as he teased, "Are you going to tell that inept excuse for a lawman to take his gun off my head, Smoke Eyes?"

Katherine jolted as if someone had put a cattle prod to her flesh. Her eyes rounded like two silver dollars. The needle dropped from her nerveless fingers as she stared at the man as if she'd seen a ghost. And she may as well have, she thought, her breath quickening. She blinked, then peered closely at his solemn face, her gaze running over his rugged features as if he might vanish in a moment. *Smoke Eyes.* Only the folks she'd grown up with knew her by her Arapaho name.

With her heart in her throat, she lifted a hand and touched her fingers to his jaw. Black eyes, black hair. A hard, handsome face. She'd known a boy that fit that description, and had last seen him eleven years ago. Her mouth was suddenly dry, her throat aching as she opened her mouth to whisper one disbelieving word. "Zach?"

She knew it was he when he smiled. That slow, dazzling, one-sided smile that creased his lean cheek with a deep groove that had been there as long as she'd known him. For a shocked second she stood immobile, staring at him, her right hand pressed to her throat. The pulse in its hollow knocked about wildly. She closed her eyes, as if unable to witness the sight of him after all these years, then opened them. Joyous wonder swept through her, and being a spontaneous soul, she flung her arms around his neck and hugged him tightly.

"Zach! Zach Fletcher!" she exclaimed. "My God, it's been so many years!"

Tears dampened her eyes as the townsfolk stood agape behind her. She felt Zach's big hand at the small of her back as he pulled her against his broad chest, hugging her even tighter. "Now this is more of the welcome I had in mind," he murmured in her ear.

The intimacy in his rough voice prodded her to drop her arms and step back. They were adults now, she thought. She couldn't be throwing herself at him even if they were old friends. Unable to contain her excitement, though, she grasped his big hands in hers and squeezed them.

"You're so big!" she said, and he laughed, the sound appealingly masculine. She'd last seen him when he was sixteen, just before he ran off to sea. He had been a hard, sullen youth then, as restless as a wild animal. He was a man now, and though his ruggedly chiseled face carried a hint of his tumultuous past, the laugh creases at the corners of his eyes testified to his sense of humor. Poignant emotion gripped her throat, making it ache. With a bittersweet pang she remembered that he had never said good-bye.

"Zach," she said softly, "what are you doing here? Why have you come to Newberry?"

Affection warmed his eyes. He lightly rubbed his thumbs over her knuckles, creating tingles across her skin. "I've come to see an old friend, of course." His eyes crinkled at the corners. "Doc Butler told me I'd be surprised when I saw the changes in you, but, honey, I didn't expect anything like this." His gaze drifted to her mouth and lingered there. She didn't notice as her excitement peaked again, and she let out a little squeal.

"You saw Cody? Did you see Tess too?"

He grinned. "Yep. But can we find somewhere else to reminisce? I want to have a few private moments with you . . . and not in a jail cell."

She laughed. "Isn't this just like you to wind up in jail as soon as you hit town?"

Her heart jumped in her throat as he rose suddenly, his long powerful body unfolding with a smooth, animal grace. He dominated the small cell with his towering height and broad shoulders. A corner of his mouth lifted in a slow smile, and her pulses jumped when she caught the lazy, hypnotic gleam in his eyes. His hard arm encircled her waist, startling her, and he pulled her close against him.

"You've hardly given me a proper hello, minx," he murmured huskily, then his mouth came down on hers. Zach meant it to be one quick, hard kiss, but as soon as their bodies fused, the heat that seared between them was combustible. She was all soft, feminine curves against his hard body. The contrast sent his senses rocketing, and he drew her even tighter to him.

The kiss was rapid, crushing, but hot, open-mouthed. A luscious, insidious warmth curled inside Katherine, sweet and heavy. Oblivious to her surroundings, to the murmurings of the folks behind them, she melted into his solid length, her hands gripping the powerful muscles of his shoulders. The heat of him, fierce and wild, seeped into her, running rampantly through her weak body, branding her with his unforgettable stamp. She could feel his raw power in every pore, smell his delicious masculine scent, and it filled her head, intoxicating her. She had never felt anything like this before.

He made a gruff sound and ran his tongue over her bottom lip with one swift erotic stroke. She stiffened, shocked at the intimacy, yet pulsating waves of heat continued washing over her, bathing her in the flame.

She made a small sound against his open mouth, and suddenly the room seemed to explode. The townsfolk screamed and Zach instinctively shoved Katherine behind him.

"What the hell?" He was breathing hard, his eyes narrowed.

The sheriff stood in the center of the room looking sheepish. He'd been so stunned by the sight of the prisoner kissing Katherine, he'd forgotten the gun in his hand. The more passionate the kiss had become the more pressure he had put on the trigger. The gun had gone off, the bullet ricocheting off the floor. The townsfolk were either ducking behind the desk or lying stomach-flat on the floor, their arms covering their heads.

Bates waved the gun. "What the hell to *you*, mister! Who do you think you are kissin' the doc like that? Doc, get out of there. That's a dangerous criminal you're hidin' behind!"

Katherine stepped out from behind the shield of Zach's body, her eyes wide, cheeks flushed. "For heaven's sake, Sheriff, put that fool thing away! Zach is an old friend. He's harmless." Though he wasn't really, she thought. A slight frown wrinkled her brow as she slipped into her coat. "Sheriff, you must free this man."

Bates was dumbfounded. *"What?"*

She met his glower with a cool stare. "What evidence have you to keep this man in jail?"

The sheriff began to sputter, and she waited patiently, her arms folded across her chest. "Why, he *looks* like trouble, don't he?"

Katherine could not believe her ears. When Bates read her expression he changed his tactic. "Why, I hauled him in because he was hanging around Nellie's brothel!"

Katherine almost laughed. That was nothing new.

Zach had frequented brothels since his youth. "Well, then, Sheriff, you may as well arrest half the men in this town for 'hanging around' the brothels. And if Zach killed Richard Waters and Dusty, the *last* place you should find him is anywhere *near* Nellie's!"

The townsfolk nodded their agreement.

"Makes perfect sense, Sheriff," one man said, then clamped his mouth shut when the sheriff glowered at him.

Bates turned his fierce stare back on Zach. "He's a drifter, Doc."

"Like hell," Zach muttered.

Katherine rested a hand on Zach's hard forearm. "He came to see me, Sheriff. We've known each other since childhood. And the murder weapon certainly does not belong to him. Right, Zach?"

His eyes flicked her way. "I don't even know what the murder weapon is."

Bates was incensed. He'd thought he'd had a sure— and easy—resolution, and it turned out he could have a lawsuit instead. He wanted this man to be the murderer. But the doc was defending him. And the townsfolk, now rising cautiously to their feet, were siding with her. He was going to get *some* satisfaction out of this thing!

"Doc," he blustered, "I demand this man apologize to you for taking liberties!"

Actually, Zach hadn't taken liberties, Katherine admitted to herself. She'd allowed him that one long, burning kiss. Flustered, her cheeks stained with hot color, she turned away to gather up her instruments and stuff them into her bag.

"Oh, Sheriff," she said lightly, "it was just a kiss between old friends." Then why, she wondered, did she feel so jittery? Her mouth still tingled, and his taste lingered tantalizingly on her sensitive lips. She ran her tongue over them, then stopped when she caught Zach's stare on her. She chased away the shiver that raced up her spine and flashed him a grin. "I'm ready if you are," she said, fighting the curious yet powerful attraction she felt for him. It was silly, she reasoned, that she should be so shaken by a kiss from Zach. He'd always had a seductive nature and it would be natural for him to greet a woman—old friend or not—with a kiss. But did he run his tongue over every woman's lips, as he had hers? It seemed a highly familiar way to greet someone. But it was more than likely habit with Zach. Really, she was making too much of this!

He grinned back at her and slung his wool peacoat over one shoulder, ready to follow her out of the cell. But the click of the gun's cartridge stopped them both. Zach's smile faded as he met the sheriff's gaze. The sheriff flinched, but he stood his ground.

"Where the hell do you think yer going, mister?"

Zach's mouth curled in a lethal smile. "You're a mighty brave man with that gun in your hand, Sheriff." His gaze flicked to the gun and back up to the sheriff's red face. "Go ahead," he said in a dangerously soft voice. "Shoot. If you don't kill me it'll be one more liability against you. If you do kill me you'll probably go to trial for shooting an unarmed and innocent man. I know the doc here will vouch for that."

"Sheriff, for heaven's sake!" Katherine said. "I'm in this cell too. Please put the gun away. Zach is innocent of this crime!"

Slowly and reluctantly Bates holstered his gun. "Has he ever been in trouble with the law?" he demanded.

Katherine swallowed a nervous giggle. Zach had been a hell-raiser back in Harper City, Kansas. "Sheriff," she said, stepping from the cell, "*I've* been in trouble with the law."

"You!" the sheriff exclaimed, and the townsfolk expressed their vociferous doubts.

"It's true," she said, turning to look at Zach as he came out of the cell behind her. "Isn't it, Zach? Wasn't I the worst little rapscallion you ever knew?"

He grinned down at her. "The worst."

She made a face at him. He didn't have to be *so* quick to agree.

"Well, tell us about it, Doc," George Watson said.

They swarmed around her—all but the sheriff and Tom, who kept a respectful distance from Zach—and Katherine laughingly waved away their avid questions as she headed for the door. "Some other time," she promised them. "I have office hours today, and I promised to visit Clara Peterson before I start."

Cyrus Blake pulled open the door for her, and she stepped outside. Behind her the group of townsfolk parted for the formidable-looking stranger. There was an edge of menace to his graceful walk, and the way he'd turned up the collar of his peacoat made him look even more dangerous. Everyone in the room shivered, not from the cold, but from the aura of dark power he emanated.

"Mister."

Zach stopped, and the townsfolk froze as he regarded them all in cool, speculative silence. The sheriff had intended to give him one last parting shot, but found his voice paralyzed in his throat. Tom spoke for him.

"Don't go too far."

Zach's jaw tightened. "My lawyer," he said through clenched teeth, "will be contacting you."

He left the jail to their fearful, hushed murmurings, and stepped out to the blessed sunny day. He was surprised to find Katherine already striding away, slush splashing her high-buttoned shoes and the hem of her coat. He had to grin as he watched her struggle with her heavy bag.

"Hey!" he called. "Wait up! Where are you off to in such a hurry?"

She glanced over her shoulder at him. "I can't wait. I have to visit a sick patient. You have to catch up!"

She knew he would. She watched him vault lightly from the jailhouse steps and hit the ground with the easy grace of a wildcat. When he reached her, he wasn't even out of breath. He flashed her a grin, the sun glinting off his straight white teeth.

"How did you do that?" he asked.

"What?"

"When the sheriff asked if I'd ever been in trouble with the law, you charmed him completely, making it sound like law-breaking could be a part of anyone's past—even a respectable doctor's."

She shrugged. "Sheriff Bates was just being incredibly stubborn."

Zach snorted his disdain. "This town is governed by an incompetent!"

"Are you really going to sue him?"

He smiled again that devilish smile that made her insides jump curiously, crazily. She didn't understand her reaction to a smile that had in the past only made her want to share in his mischief. Now, it seemed, Zach's stunning grin held much more than mischief.

"That depends," he said mildly, "on how I feel tomorrow. That gun-wielding jackass should pay some penalty for trying to rob a man of every damned shred of pride he possesses."

Katherine laughed. "Oh, I doubt if he did that, Zach. If I remember correctly, you are possessed of a *huge* dose of pride."

He cast her a wry look as they cut across Dobson Road and headed for Main Street. "The sheriff is a bit jumpy about this murder," she went on. "To him it was a logical arrest given the fact that you're a stranger and were loitering near Nellie's."

Though her tone was lighthearted and teasing, Zach looked annoyed, his brows lowering in a frown. Katherine marched stoutly along, crossing the street and narrowly missing being hit by a cutter. Its horses' hooves spattering mud and snow on the hem of her dark skirt. She had no time to shake it off before Zach caught her around the waist and lifted her onto the slick boardwalk.

"For God's sake, Smoke Eyes," he said as he set her down in front of the general store. "You nearly got yourself killed."

He stood only inches from her, regarding her with an admonishing look, as a father would a wayward child. It both exasperated and amused Katherine that he could so easily step back into his role of her protector.

"Zach, really," she said, pushing her way past him. "I've been crossing roads for years by myself with nary a mishap."

"Pure luck," Zach muttered, and caught his breath as her light, musical laughter lit the cold air. "Listen," he said, touching her arm. "I wasn't hanging around Nellie's brothel. I was hunting for you, Smoke Eyes. I just arrived two hours ago. As soon as I checked into the hotel, I asked the hotel clerk where you lived. Since I couldn't find you there I thought I'd look around town. A prostitute approached me and I asked her if she knew where you were. That's when the sheriff came up behind me, grabbed me in a choke hold, and proceeded to abuse the power of his office by throwing a perfectly innocent citizen in jail."

"Oh, Zach, what a reception!" Katherine rounded the corner to Second Street and gasped as the wind hit her full force. She glanced up at his strong profile and felt a strange quickening in her belly. "It's so good to see you again," she murmured, unable to tell if he'd heard. "How long are you here for?" she asked, raising her voice.

She saw the muscles tighten in his jaw and he suddenly looked grim. "Few days."

"Well, hullo, Doc!"

They looked up to confront a ruddy-cheeked old man with a shock of thick white hair.

"Hello, Sam," Katherine said.

The wind whistled down the road, blowing snow and whipping her skirts around her legs. Sam was oblivious to the discomfort and launched into a long, detailed account of his daily life for the past two weeks. He talked about his dog, his wife, his limited supplies, his fall off the woodpile and why he was on it in the first place. There had been no reason to call her, he assured Katherine. He'd only bruised an elbow. He went on and on, even about how supper the night before had affected his stomach. Katherine listened to every word. But when Sam paused to take a deep breath, she interrupted his monologue by gently placing her hand on his arm.

"Sam, this is all very interesting, but I'm on my way to see Clara, and I have to hurry to make office hours."

"Oops! Sorry," he said cheerfully. He tipped his hat and was on his way. The Peterson house was across the street, and squinting against the glare of the sun and snow Katherine could see little Bobby Peterson waiting for her on the front porch. She waved to him.

"Smoke Eyes," Zach said before she could take another step. But someone else called her from across the road.

"Doc!" a boy of about ten hollered.

She looked past Zach to see red-haired Tommy

Bates standing in front of the dry goods store. She guessed he was on his way home from school to eat lunch. "Hello, Tommy."

"Black Jack is fine now—all healed up!"

"Good! Now you take care of him. See that he doesn't move around too much for a while."

The boy grinned and scampered down the boardwalk, sliding and skidding on the ice. Katherine continued on to the Peterson home, unaware of Zach staring at her. All the people in the town seemed enamored of her, he thought. Did she charm everyone so effortlessly? It was a marvel. The little hellion he'd known back in Kansas had evolved into an incredibly lovely and enchanting woman. He stood and watched her walk away, his gaze following the alluring curves of her slender body, the gentle sway of her hips. He felt his own body stir uncontrollably, and cursed its base reaction. Frowning, he strode after her, catching up in two long strides.

"Who's Black Jack?" he asked. "An old pirate washed up to town?"

She flashed him a grin. "Tommy's dog," she said. "He ate an old shoe and suffered a horrid bellyache, but I gave him some medicine and evidently it worked."

They had reached the Petersons' front yard. Little Bobby ran into the house to tell his mother the doctor was here.

"Smoke Eyes." Zach touched her shoulder to stop her, turning her toward him so he could look down into her face. "Do you have to be in such a hurry?"

Katherine smiled ruefully. "Yes, I do."

His eyes seemed to burn into her, then they turned disconcertingly tender. A light shiver danced up her spine. "Let me look at you a minute, darlin'."

She shivered again as he trailed a long finger across

her high cheekbone, then along the length of her jaw. She felt the tip of his finger touch her bottom lip, the rough skin rasping gently, and fought the strange quiverings deep inside her. His finger drifted down her throat to where the pulse jumped in its hollow, and his eyes glittered with darkening intensity.

"Your face," he said in a voice gruff with emotion, "is a masterpiece."

Katherine couldn't breathe. For years men had paid homage to her beauty, but none had ever stirred her as Zach's words did.

His eyes, she thought, were devastating. Heavy-lidded and with thick dark lashes, they were deceptively lazy, yet smoldered with a steady-burning flame. An ever-simmering promise of seduction emanated from him, and she guessed few women on earth could resist his potent power.

He had changed, she realized, her gaze running over his compelling face. He had always been hard, but now he was more so. A brutal strength was stamped into his features and big body as certain as the color of his coppery skin. His penetrating gaze sparked a heat in her blood that thrummed vibrantly through her veins. She didn't understand it, and tried desperately to shake off her disturbing reaction to him—an old friend.

Drawing in a shaky breath, she managed to smile. "Are you waxing poetic, Zach?"

Zach studied her face, the way the light played over it. Her skin was peach-colored and just as soft. A tawny flush colored her cheekbones, and he could see the faint freckles that dusted her dainty nose. He let his gaze drift over her fragile jawline, her small, determined chin, and he grinned as he remembered her stubborn streak, which no sane person would dare tangle with.

He sobered again as his gaze fixed on her mouth—

long and lush with an upper lip as full and silk-soft as her bottom lip. Again he felt that kick in his groin and gritted his teeth, fighting the powerful surge of desire. Damn, but his body had a mind of its own! Still . . . he could not look away from her exquisite face, wanting only to brush each inch of it with kisses. Her face was more fine-boned than some of the Oriental women he had known on his travels. And her hair! She'd piled the magnificent mane upon her head in a careless knot, and the sunlight gilded all its subtle, glorious hues of gold and wine, warm bronze and chestnut red. A simple, practical style, but she still projected an elegance that made his throat ache.

At last his gaze locked on hers, and his stomach muscles tightened. Her eyes. Great, overwhelming eyes framed with long, silky black lashes. Their effect on him was like a punch in the gut; he was no more immune to them now than he'd been at sixteen. She only had to lock those gorgeous, soul-searching eyes on him and all the hardness in him melted.

She startled him by reaching up to place one hand alongside his neck, under his collar, where his skin was warm. He was gripped with the most incredible urge to put his own hands around her waist and pull her against him. Her eyes glimmered up at him like silver.

"Zach," she said softly, "I have a very busy day. I'm afraid we'll have to postpone our visit."

He squelched a curious surge of disappointment, and his voice sounded harder than he'd intended. "When can we get together, Smoke Eyes? We have a lot to catch up on, and I'm sure you want to hear about Doc Butler and Tessa."

"Of course," Katherine said, and wondered at the strange breathlessness that assailed her each time her gaze met his. She edged her chin up as if to gather her wits. "I want to hear everything—all about your travels, your home, your life."

"Then how about eight o'clock this evening? Can you meet me for dinner in the hotel dining room?"

She smiled with real pleasure. "I haven't had a dinner out in ages. That would be splendid!"

"Good." He gave her that riveting half smile, and his teeth gleamed against his weathered tan. "I owe you at least that much for springing me out of jail."

She laughed. "I'm sure you would have 'sprung' yourself without my help—one way or another."

His answering laugh was short and husky, and she felt again that odd tightening in her stomach. Their gazes locked, and only when the Petersons' front door slammed did either look away. Katherine turned to go inside.

"See you at eight, Smoke Eyes."

She looked back at him. He stood with wide-spread legs and his scuffed leather boots planted solidly on the slushy ground, as if he were bracing himself against the brisk Colorado wind. Across the short distance his eyes probed her. She shuddered against the effect of his virile masculinity.

"Zach," she said, and though she strove for a light tone, her voice was taut, sharp with emotion. "You must call me Katherine now."

Without another word she walked away, Zach's intense gaze burning like a brand on her back as she climbed the porch steps and slipped into the house.

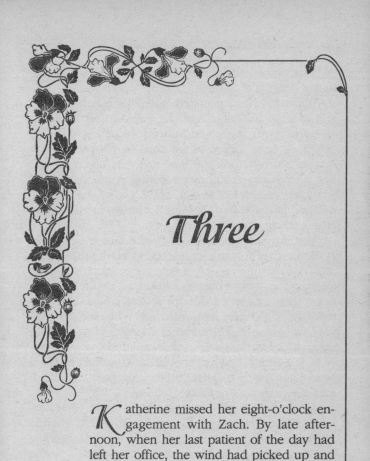

Three

Katherine missed her eight-o'clock engagement with Zach. By late afternoon, when her last patient of the day had left her office, the wind had picked up and the sky had darkened to a steely gray. She'd hurried out to her lab to perform the autopsies on Dusty and Richard Waters, and before she'd finished soft, fat snowflakes had begun to float down. Later, as she was tidying up the lab, she heard the thunder of horses' hooves. Craning her neck toward the window, she saw through the thickly falling snow a rancher swing down off his horse and race toward her house.

She yanked open the lab door and called to the frantic man. "I'm here!"

With one hand clamped upon his hat, he turned and ran toward her. "Doc!" he panted, and his voice was so hoarse she could scarcely hear him. "It's my boy! He's been kicked in the head by his horse!"

She scarcely took the time to thrust her arms into her coat. Her stableboy, a young Arapaho named Shadow, readied her mount, and together she and the rancher galloped away toward his home, more than an hour's distance.

The boy was unconscious by the time they arrived at the ranch. He had been kicked in the forehead and, remarkably, suffered only a mild concussion. Katherine cleaned and shaved the boy's head and put in thirty sutures, then monitored him for several hours. The Carters offered to board her for the night, but she declined when their son regained consciousness and showed no signs of being comatose. She explained to the concerned parents that he should be fine except for a headache, and gave Mrs. Carter some powders to administer to him as needed.

Mr. Carter offered her a ride back in his sleigh, using her horse, Hippocrates, as one of the team. He told his wife he might rent a room at the hotel, depending on the ferocity of the storm, and if she needed him to send a hand. During the ride Katherine, bundled under a thick buffalo robe, finally had time to reflect on the day. It had been a long and tiring one, and she leaned back to enjoy the smooth ride home, tilting her face up to the black heavens and the powdery snow. Zach, she thought. *Zach*.

They had been such good friends back in Kansas. Both rebels, both desperately aching for love. He had been a reckless and brave youth, abandoned at six by his mother, left alone for months at a time while his father drifted. Because he had knocked about most of his young life, by sixteen he was lawless and untamed, and hated restraint of any sort. In that way they had been acutely alike. Her own parents had died of typhoid fever and she had been living with her Arapaho grandfather in a shanty on the Kansas prairies. He had let her run wild and free, and when Miss Tessa Amesbury, the schoolteacher, had finally lured her into the classroom, she and Zach had befriended each other.

Katherine shook her head and laughed to herself. Oh, how they'd tormented poor Tessa! Their pranks had rivaled each other's, and they were forever embroiled in fisticuffs with the other children who taunted and scorned them—especially her. And often, she thought as her chest ached with a heavy emotion, Zach had defended her from those unkind, sometimes merciless children, so that soon the bullies learned to keep a respectful distance from his fists. *She* had been the only soft spot in rough Zach. But even she had not been able to stop him from leaving.

They'd shared secrets and cigarettes and unspoken pacts that had run as deep as her Arapaho blood. They'd even shared their dreams—his to go to sea, hers to become a physician. It was why, when he left, that she had expected some warning, or at least a good-bye. But he had gone abruptly, when Harper City had been plagued by diphtheria, and shortly afterward her grandfather had died. She hadn't even been able to tell him *that*. His departure, coupled with the loss of her grandfather, had broken her heart, and she'd cried for days. After the longest while she'd realized Zach was never coming back, not even to take her with him as she had so childishly hoped he would. So she did as she'd always done when life had dealt her a cruel blow. She put up her chin and moved forward.

She'd wanted to go to medical school, and as difficult as that was for a woman, she was determined. Under Miss Amesbury's and Dr. Butler's tutelage she excelled in her studies and graduated with a straight A average. She had too much pride to admit that some of her drive stemmed from Zach's pursuit of his own dream and her desire not to be bested. Never mind that he hadn't written her one letter; Zach was not the writing sort. And she had learned, as time went on, not to take his abrupt departure personally, for that was the way he had always conducted his affairs— unceremoniously, detached, *alone*.

And now he'd come back, more than six feet of muscle-packed power and hot, raw sexuality. Katherine shuddered, remembering his kiss. In all her years at medical school—in all her *life*—she had never run across a man as potent as Zach Fletcher. He burned with energy and radiated a compelling magnetism that could sear a woman's soul. Katherine had been kissed plenty in medical school, and though she'd found those kisses, and the suitors, mildly pleasant, they were nothing compared to the scorching heat of Zach's kiss. She felt branded. Even in the frigid night air, her cheeks grew hot at the memory.

She pressed her mittened hands to her face. Her reaction to the kiss was silly! She'd always felt so comfortable with Zach—he'd saluted her fiery spirit and mischievous streak—but now she was disturbed. Perhaps she needed to find another man who kissed just as well.

She leaned forward. "Mr. Carter!"

"Eh?" He cocked an ear in her direction.

"If you're going to the hotel, could you bring me there? I need to take care of some business."

"Sure thing, Doc."

She did, after all, owe Zach the courtesy of an explanation. Mr. Carter would most likely wait for her while she whisked up to the front desk and left the message that she'd had an emergency.

It was nearly ten-thirty when they glided into town, and the wind was gusting powerfully. Half of the coal-oil lamps that lit Main Street had been snuffed out. The others flickered fitfully. Mr. Carter pulled up before the hotel, and the lantern over its porch cast a yellow light on the glittering snow. After he helped Katherine down, she made her way up the icy-slick steps and into the warmth of the hotel lobby. She sighed with relief and pulled off her mittens. Blue Benson, the hotel clerk, caught sight of her and his owlish eyes widened in surprise.

"Hey, Doc!"

She smiled and walked toward the front desk, shaking the snow from her coat, her muffler, and her hair.

"Someone sick, Doc?" Blue asked.

She stamped the snow from her feet. "Quite a storm," she said. "I'd hoped the blizzards might be through for the year."

Blue shrugged. "Never know what to expect." He watched her place her muffler around her shoulders. "Well, who's sick?"

"No one, actually, Blue. I came by to leave a message for Zach Fletcher."

Blue looked like he'd swallowed a goose egg. Katherine hid her amusement while she waited for him to regain his composure. "You socializing with that scoundrel?"

She was startled. "How do you know he's a scoundrel?" she asked, not denying that he was.

Blue rubbed his bald pate, flustered. "Well, for Pete's sake, Doc, he terrified the sheriff, busted up a couple of men, just cuz they were doing their duty."

She should have known word would travel quick. "I hardly think," she said in a lightly chiding tone, "that splitting Zach's skull open was in the line of duty. He was only defending himself."

Blue took in a quick breath. "Are you speaking up for that stranger, Doc?"

She laughed. "He's hardly a stranger, Blue. We've known each other for years, and he came to Newberry to visit me."

Blue gaped at her. "Well, I'll be. No one told me that."

"I'm not surprised," she murmured, and turned when Mr. Carter came in, stomping his feet loudly.

"It's brutal out there," he said. "Doc, I covered the horses while we wait, and Blue, I think I'm gonna need to rent a room."

"One left," Blue said, handing him the key. "Folks are sleeping in cuz of the storm."

Katherine leaned forward over the desk. "Let me leave my message for Zach so I won't keep Mr. Carter waiting," she said, but Blue told her that Zach was still in the dining room.

Her eyes widened. "He waited all this time?"

Blue grinned. "I don't blame him." He sobered, realizing he might have overstepped his boundary. "Well, you better hurry, Doc. The dining room closes in ten minutes."

"I'll be right back," she told Mr. Carter, and left the two men to gossip while she hurried toward the dining room. Surely, she thought, Zach would have turned in for the night. He'd waited for her over two hours!

She heard the murmuring of diners and the subdued clinking noises of china and silver before she reached the dining room doorway. Smoothing a hand over her hair, she glanced down at her damp wool coat and wet shoes. She must look a mess! She peeked around the corner and saw the room still half crowded with people. And her heart stood still when she spotted Zach.

He was seated at a corner table, staring at the bottle of beer before him, his long legs extended and crossed at the ankles. He wore a somber, brooding expression. What was wrong? she wondered. He seemed unaware of his surroundings as he studied his beer, eyebrows drawn low, his features troubled and harsh. Though he lounged back in his chair, his big body pulsated with power, a dangerous, seductive quality that took her breath away. There was no doubt about it, she thought. She was inexorably drawn to him.

Alarm jackknifed through her. "No," she whispered, her heart pounding heavily. She must fight this attraction, must continue to regard Zach as an old friend. For he was. She was certain that countless women were attracted to him. Yet, because he *was* her friend it troubled her to feel her own pulses scramble out of control when she merely looked at him, or even thought about him.

She steeled herself against the strange tension that buzzed in her stomach and took a step forward. Zach looked up, his eyes drilling a path to her from across the room. She stopped. The penetrating warmth of his gaze tingled on her skin. He nodded to her, and she started toward him on shaky legs, wishing desperately that he would take those very unsettling eyes off her.

But Zach watched Katherine walk toward him. Wet and weary, she looked like the bedraggled urchin he'd known in Harper City. Only she was a woman now. And she was exquisite. Silky tendrils of her glorious red hair had escaped the knot on her head and they framed her flushed, striking face. As she approached, her eyes were locked with his, and they shimmered like diamonds. Every muscle in his body tightened, and he frowned, shifting in his chair. It shook him to realize he felt something completely elemental for her, and he knew he absolutely should *not* act on that feeling. This was Smoke Eyes, his friend. She would most likely scorn him if she even suspected how his body responded to her, and what he was thinking. He almost smiled then, for he was now imagining her walking toward him naked. Hell, he was only human. And a man couldn't be hung for his thoughts.

By the time she reached him the room was abuzz and several heads had turned toward them.

"Smoke Eyes," he said as he stood. "What happened?"

She smiled tiredly. "I'm sorry, Zach, I never imagined you'd wait for me all this time. I had an emergency—had to travel several miles out to a ranch and I just got back."

"I figured it was something like that." He stared down at her. "It was considerate of you to come tell me." He slipped a broad hand under her elbow and drew her close to him. "I really need to talk to you, Smoke Eyes. Are you too worn-out to talk now?"

Confusion flickered through her. He'd said he *needed* to talk to her, not *wanted* to. She'd thought their dinner was to be purely a social occasion, but judging by the harsh lines about his eyes and mouth, she was certain it was meant to be more. He waited, his face taut, lips compressed. She drew in a deep, shaky breath, and though she was exhausted, she nodded.

"I'm a little worn around the edges, but I have time." She glanced out the window beside her where driving snow and needles of ice slashed the glass. "But the dining room is closing and—"

"Do you think we could rent you a room for the night? The storm's getting rough and it would make it easier for you."

"Blue just rented out the last one," she said ruefully.

Zach scowled. "Well, then we have only one other option." He grinned suddenly. "Actually, we have two, but I don't think you want to share a room with me." When he saw a pink blush crawl up her cheeks, his grin broadened. "Guess not." He curled an arm around her shoulders, drawing her to him. Katherine's heart hammered like a jackrabbit's under his touch; she could smell the tangy scent of his cologne, feel the compelling heat of his hard body as it brushed hers, and her heart continued to thrust frantically against her ribs.

"Zach," Katherine whispered. She was keenly aware of the many pairs of eyes on them, and even more aware of the heat and temptation of his hard body as it brushed against hers. But Zach seemed oblivious of the attention he aroused in the other diners, or of how her heart was hammering. He guided her through the dining room, ignoring the craning necks and gawking stares of the townsfolk.

"I'll get my coat and drive you to your place," he said as he led her out to the lobby. Blue and Mr. Carter were still there talking, and they stopped to look at them. Before she could protest, Zach was taking the stairs two at a time. She watched his broad back and shoulders, the movement of his tight buttocks and long legs, until he was gone from view.

"Is it true he's suing the sheriff, Katherine?"

The man who spoke stood so close to her, she nearly jumped a foot off the floor.

She clapped a hand over her pounding heart and faced a tall, good-looking man with wavy auburn hair and blue-green eyes. "Jim!" He was a banker who'd just recently moved from Denver and was, she knew, very taken with her. They'd often attended the Saturday night social together, but she regarded him only as a friend. "He's an old friend of mine, Zach Fletcher."

"I know who he is."

She ignored Jim's surly mood and started toward Mr. Carter. "Mr. Carter, Zach is going to bring me home. You can turn in now if you'd like, and I sure do appreciate the ride out here. I'll have my stableboy take care of your horse and you can come get him in the morning, weather permitting."

Mr. Carter nodded. "Anything you say, Doc."

Despite his words, she could tell by his expression that he was uneasy about letting her go off with Zach. She had no doubt Blue had just filled him in on the details of Zach's arrest, and Zach did look like a roughneck. She patted his arm reassuringly.

"Don't worry. I've known him for years."

Mr. Carter grunted and looked toward the staircase. "Here he is now."

Katherine turned to see Zach coming down the stairs with that loose-limbed cocky gait of his, his coat slung over one shoulder. He afforded the men only a quick glance before resting his warm gaze on her. She quickly introduced him. He gave the three men a terse nod, then turned his attention to her again. "Ready?"

She tied her muffler around her neck and smiled. "As ready as I'll ever be."

"I dunno," Blue said from behind them, "if you should brave the storm, Doc."

"Oh, Blue," she said, tucking her hair under her hood. "I'm not that far away—just a couple of streets over." She turned as Zach's big hand touched the small of her back, guiding her toward the doors.

"It's the man, not the storm I worry about her braving," came Jim's taunting voice. "After all, he was thrown in jail this morning."

Katherine felt Zach's body tense, felt his hand drop away from her back. He turned slowly to confront Jim, his expression so hard, it looked chipped from ice. His cold gaze flashed to Blue and Mr. Carter, who'd both backed up a couple of steps, then sliced back to Jim. Jim blanched, but his lips tightened and he clenched his fists.

"*Thrown* in jail," Zach said tightly, "is a damn accurate way to phrase the incident." The cold chill in his eyes issued a deadly warning. "Next time you got something to say, mister, don't say it to my back. That's what most folks call a yellowbelly."

Jim's face burned scarlet, and his voice was loud with embarrassed fury. "Are you calling me a yellowbelly?"

Zach's gaze raked insultingly over him. "Well, right now," he drawled, "you look more like a rooster than anything else."

Jim sprang for him, but Blue and Mr. Carter were prepared for this and jumped between the two men, holding Jim off. He hadn't a chance, they figured, up against the rough-looking stranger.

"No fightin'!" Blue yelled. "Mr. Lowell, Mr. Fletcher, go to Murphy's saloon if it's brawling you're lookin' for!"

Katherine tugged on Zach's arm. "Come on," she said softly. She knew he was itching for a fight, and he could have easily plastered Jim to the wall with one swipe of his fist. "It's getting late." She turned to Jim, her eyes beseeching him. "Jim, you must apologize. Zach is a guest in town and he was treated unfairly."

It seemed impossible for Jim to turn any redder, but he did. His face became the color of geraniums. "Like hell!" he shouted, shaking off Blue and Mr. Carter. When he caught Katherine's crestfallen expression, though, he was immediately repentant. "Excuse my language, Katherine, but he was damned insulting! Excuse my language again."

Jim was doubly incensed that he'd earned no sympathy from Katherine. He straightened his clothing and found, much to his disturbance, that the tall, broad-shouldered stranger had already turned his back on him, dismissing him as if he were no more than a pesky fly.

"All buttoned up, Doc?" Zach asked Katherine when they reached the door. He leaned forward to squint through one of the windows that framed the door. The banshee wind screamed and the snow swished thickly against the glass. Katherine shivered but had no chance to balk as Zach's big hand engulfed hers and he pulled open the door. He tugged her with him out into a great gust of howling wind and stinging snow. " 'Bye Blue, Mr. Carter!" she called. But the door slammed on her words, and she was swallowed up in the great white world of the night.

"How many jealous beaux of yours am I gonna have to fight off while I'm in town?" Zach shouted over the wind. He tipped the man who'd watched the horses, then put a strong arm around Katherine to help her down the snow-covered hotel steps.

"At least a dozen!" she teased, then gasped as she lost her balance. She hung tight to Zach's coat, and he leaned down to scoop her up into his arms. He ignored her wriggle of protest and plunked her into the sleigh. "Sit tight," he said, "and get under that buffalo robe."

She did, and the warmth of the thick robe was luscious. Zach swung himself up easily, taking the reins in his gloved hands. "Direct me!" he shouted, and she did. The sleigh sped off, its runners squeaking in the snow. They flew toward her home, the wind in their faces, making it difficult to talk. But Katherine was oh-so-aware of Zach's solid thigh pressed intimately to hers, so she could feel his muscles shift and flex as he moved. He was so big, so wide-shouldered, that he blocked some of the wind, and the contact of his warm body brought her a delicious thrill. She wondered if he felt the thrill too, then told herself she must stop this strange, almost feverish reaction to him. She must! But how could one stanch feelings?

They coasted up to her stable where Shadow leaped out and took the reins. Without hesitation, Zach once again swept her up into his arms and strode toward her house. In the front yard her shingle banged wildly in the wind. Despite her indignant struggles and the awkward weight of her medical bag, he managed to get them both up the porch steps. He let her out of his arms to open the door, and they both stumbled over the threshold into the house, which had become chilled in her absence. Zach kicked the door closed behind them, shutting out the driving wind and snow, and Katherine moved swiftly to light a kerosene lantern on a nearby table.

When she turned, she was startled to see how close Zach stood to her. The lamplight danced across his harsh features, licking bronze flames over his dark skin. Her heart began to pump heavily. He was all man. Even in this chilly room, his heat and his power were staggering. He was breathing hard, snowflakes melting in his raven black hair, and studying her with that unsettling probing intensity.

Her trembling fingers went to her throat, and she glanced toward the fireplace, not knowing where to rest her gaze. She glanced back to him and gave him a little smile. "Well, we made it," she said with false brightness, and rubbed her arms nervously. He continued to watch her, almost somberly. She swallowed, then her smile turned teasing. "Though you didn't have to carry me," she continued, embarrassed that he did. "I could have managed myself."

He grinned crookedly. "I don't know, mite. I thought a few times there the wind was going to pick you up and sweep you away to the mountains."

She blushed. Reference to her small stature embarrassed her, and she wished folks just wouldn't notice her less than average size. Flustered, she turned away to hang her coat on the wood peg by the door. "Would you build a fire, Zach? I'll go get us something to eat." She turned to face him. "Are you hungry?"

She could have kicked herself as soon as she'd asked him, for her innocent words seemed to carry a double entendre. The fire in his eyes burned more fiercely for a moment, then he grinned. When he spoke, his rich, rumbling voice created more shivery goose bumps upon her skin.

"Naw," he said. "I ate while I was waiting for you at the hotel."

She smiled. "I've never known you to turn down a meal. You always had the appetite of a grizzly, and now the size to match it!"

Something flickered across his face, but the dark emotion vanished as quickly as it had appeared. She could not know that he had missed a lot of meals of late, that his appetite had diminished, absorbed as he was with the problem that pressed in on him every day, the problem that had driven him halfway across the country to her in the hopes that she might help him. He felt drained from the pressure of it, and for the first time in his life unable to control a situation, frustrated and tense that he could not. But for now, he shoved the worry to the back of his mind, knowing he could deal with it later.

He reached out and chucked Katherine under her chin, his smile crinkling the corners of his eyes. "And you, little one, maybe should have eaten a lot more. You're no bigger than a mustard seed."

Her face flamed, and she pushed his hand away. "I'll go make some tea to warm us up."

"Stay with me a minute while I build a fire."

Katherine's heart jumped in her chest. She watched as he shrugged his coat off and hung it on the peg beside hers. Their sleeves touched, and the sight was oddly intimate, as if Zach hung his coat there regularly. As if he belonged there.

She tore her gaze away from the coats to find something even more disturbing. Zach was down on one knee, stacking kindling in the grate, and she saw his white cambric shirt had come loose from the waistband of his dark trousers in back. If she lifted it, she wondered, would his back be as darkly tanned as his face and hands? Her breathing quickened and her pulse began to beat abnormally fast.

What was wrong with her? She *needed* that tea, if only to calm her rioting nerves! Yet she stayed, studying the spread of his great shoulders, the rippling of his muscles under his clothes as he worked. Against the stark white collar of his shirt, his hair was blacker than the devil's own, and she longed to reach out and touch the soft thickness—just once.

She shuddered, and moved to stand beside him. The paper and kindling caught, and for a moment they both stared at the gold-scarlet fire, feeling the delicious heat warm them. Finished with his task, Zach stood. He was so close to Katherine, their bodies almost touched. The air between them heated, sizzling like the fire.

Suddenly Zach laughed, and Katherine turned to look at him. "Do you remember," he asked, "the time we almost razed half of Harper City?"

She laughed with him, rocking back a little on her heels. "I remember. We'd been playing poker in 'our' shack—that old run-down abandoned shanty—and drinking that bottle of beer you'd stolen from your father. And smoking 'weed,' as you used to call it." She shook her head and folded her arms across her chest as she looked back into the flames. "The beer made us drowsy and we left a cigarette burning as we fell asleep. Thank heavens for the snowstorm that night or we might have gone up in smoke."

Zach laughed again. "I thought the doc was gonna tan our hides but good that night." He shoved his hands into the back waistband of his trousers, remembering how angry Cody had been when the sheriff had hauled them both to his door. "But he just let us sleep at his place and gave us the sternest talking-to I'd ever got in my life." He grinned at her. "He told me I was a bad influence on you, Smoke Eyes."

Her eyes danced. "Funny, he told me *I* was a bad influence on *you.*"

They laughed together.

"And then he made us rebuild what we'd burned down," Zach said.

"As if anyone used that old shack but us!" she added.

"The doc was the closest thing to a father I ever had," Zach admitted, his eyes sobering as his gaze drifted back to the fire. His own father had been a drifter, a drinker, a man who'd leave his young son alone to fend for himself. But the times he came home sober and talked, dreaming aloud, Zach always hoped he'd stay that way. He never did. Just when things would go right for a while—they'd build on a claim, or Pa would hold down a good job—the old man would go on a drinking binge again and leave. Zach came to believe there was something about him that made folks want to leave him. Even his mother had abandoned him, left him at the poorhouse in New York City when he was six. He had never really known her, but he'd always wanted to find her and ask her why. Why?

Dr. Cody Butler was the only man who'd thought the young Zach had some worth. He'd encouraged Zach's strong interest in the sea and shipping, and had man-to-man talks with him in his lab at night when there was no one about to interfere. But Zach had always been a loner, always one to take charge and never bend to authority. When he was sixteen, he'd known it was time to leave for sea.

So he'd gone. And had left behind the three people in the world that meant so much to him. He found it hard to believe that one of them was standing beside him right now. Quickening his blood. Making everything in him pound, every muscle in him tighten as his instincts screamed out to leave this thing alone. But how could he? He wanted her. It was certainly nothing new for him to desire a woman, but this was Smoke Eyes, a childhood friend and not a woman to take lightly. She had not been a *child* to take lightly, and even after so many years, she'd left an imprint on his soul. He'd thought of her often as he traveled, her memory like a tiny flame, a piece of her spirit. He'd always felt guilty about the way he'd left her, but she would have clung to him and begged him to take her with him, and that would have been impossible. He'd had to get on with the business of becoming a man. Sometimes, he'd learned, a man had to be cruel to be kind. And he'd known Cody and Tess would take care of her. It wasn't as if he'd really abandoned her.

He'd often wondered, though, what kind of woman she had become. He'd never had any doubt she would become a successful physician, if that was truly what she wanted. He could remember her doctoring wounded animals out on the prairie, collecting herbs, and reading medical journals she had stolen from Cody's lab. Her grandfather had taught her how to mix potions, taught her their magical, medicinal purposes. But Zach had also wondered if she'd gotten sidetracked, fallen in love and married. When he'd stopped in Kansas on his way to her and learned that she hadn't, his curiosity had been pricked. He'd known her as a fiesty child, with a temper as fiery as her hair. But he'd also known the deep sensitivity she carried inside her—sometimes more of an affliction to her than a cherished quality—and her compassion for others, even those who'd obstracized her. Yes, there had been many layers and facets to Smoke Eyes when she was young. And now, he thought achingly, there were even more as a woman.

Dangerous as it was, he wanted to explore this new, uncharted territory. Unwise as it might be to succumb to the potent attraction he felt for her, he couldn't shut out the fierce wanting that hammered through his body. Reckless, dauntless, he'd courted danger all his life, meeting it head-on, conquering it, finding it again. The danger of making love to a woman like Smoke Eyes was nearly irresistible. But he did have a conscience, and it was, at the moment, making a damn nuisance of itself.

She was very close. Her fragrance—the evocative, mingled scents of fruit and spice upon her skin, like the crushed petals of orange and apple blossoms, deliciously warmed by clove and fragrant vanilla—drifted between them to torment him. He closed his eyes, clenching his jaw against the yearning to touch her, to kiss her. Turning to look at her, he felt a stab in his gut when he saw that she had been watching him too. The firelight flickered over the clean lines of her finely drawn face and scattered bronze glints across her eyes, like the sun on water. Her lips, soft as pink rose petals, were slightly parted and his heart pounded like the crash of a wild surf upon a rough shore. He ached to kiss her, ached from the inside out as hot blood roared through his body. *Need.* In the past weeks he had been so numb with despair, he'd forgotten the keen, spiky ache of desire that had been with him almost as far back as he could remember. Women. He took them and left them without an afterthought. They had loved him for it, and they had learned. Just once had he made the mistake of taking an inexperienced woman. After her, he had bedded only sophisticated women, and only to fulfill a need.

But he could not remember ever feeling this pounding ache, drumming through his blood like hot needles, the wanting so abrupt, so intense, it left a sharp taste in his mouth. And he knew, by the way her eyes had widened and by the soft mist that had come into them, that she was as intensely aware of him as he was of her. How many times had this beautiful woman fallen in love? At the moment she looked alarmed and very uncertain.

The storm howled around the snug house. Snow and ice lashed at the windows but between them there burned only a thick, sultry jungle heat. The air was charged, crackling, like a summer sky before a storm. And though animal instincts fired his blood, Zach clamped down on his feral impulses and dragged his gaze from hers, shoving his fists deep into his trousers pockets.

Wishing desperately for a smoke or a drink, he forced himself to look around the rustic room, with its warm, burnished autumn colors, autumn-warm like Smoke Eyes. It was dominated by the huge stone-slab fireplace built right into the wood-beamed wall. Scattered over the varnished oak floorboards were vibrant-colored rugs, and the rough-hewn furniture was inviting and comfortable. Her desk was stacked high with medical books and journals, and her diplomas hung above it. He imagined her over the years, head bent over her studies, plunging herself into her work as she always did, with her entire, indomitable spirit.

Behind her, the mantel was crammed with woven

baskets, wood whittlings, clay pottery, even a tiny potted flowering cactus. He reached for a miniature wood warrior, his long fingers tightening around it.

"Your grandfather made this, didn't he?"

Katherine nodded. Words were clogged in her throat, and she could only watch Zach as he surveyed her home. She shivered as he spoke, his deep, rumbling voice stirring up memories.

"Your grandfather taught me how to whittle," he said. "Remember when I used to go up to see you and watch him whittle, and you'd get bored and skip off?" The elderly man and Smoke Eyes had lived in a tarpaper shack. Zach had found her grandfather fascinating with his silver plaited hair, weathered brown face, and gnarled old hands.

"I remember," Katherine murmured.

"It was a pastime I took with me to sea. Sorry to learn he died so soon after I left."

She forced herself to meet his eyes. She had wanted to die then too, but now she smiled sadly. "He was an old man," she said.

"Yes, but he was your family."

She swallowed. Zach had been her family too.

He nudged her playfully and his smile turned teasing. "But I heard you got yourself adopted by the Lyndons."

Katherine made a wry face. "I guess you caught up on a lot when you visited Cody and Tess." She held her hands out to the fire, warming them. "At first I wasn't happy about living with Mary and Tim, because I wanted to stay with Tess. But in the end it worked out for the best. Cody and Tess got married, and I think I would have been in the way."

She shook her head, laughing softly. "I was a trial. But Mary and Tim were very good to me, and Cody and Tess were always there. Somehow they understood my contrary nature. If it weren't for them I'd never have gone on to medical school. They helped me raise the money so I could attend Geneva Medical College in New York, and they both came out for my graduation. That had been the first time in all those years I'd seen them. And it was good that I did, for I didn't have the opportunity to stop in Harper City on my way here. I write to them as often as I can."

She looked up at him, her eyes aglow. "It really is so good to see you again, Zach." Her expression turned sympathetic as her gaze ran over his drawn face, the weariness and strain etched into the lines about his eyes and mouth. Impulsively she reached up to lay her palm on his cheek, and she felt a muscle jump under her hand. She drew her hand back as if scorched. Yet Zach's eyes continued to hold hers, and there was no shielding herself from their burning intensity. She felt oddly exposed, as if he could see deep inside her, to her vulnerable soul. She felt weak-kneed and wondered if he knew how violently her heart pounded. He stood so close, she could see herself reflected in his black irises.

She turned away and forced calmness into her voice. "You seem troubled," she said. "Let's go into the kitchen and I'll make some tea and we can talk out there."

"Sure," Zach said easily, though his troubles weren't the kind he could just blurt out. And he had learned, in just the little time he'd spent with Smoke Eyes, that a wholly different kind of trouble might have started. He needed to know.

"But first," he said, smiling down at her, "I want you to show me your place—the operating room—all of it." And without waiting for her to answer, he turned and walked out of the room.

It took Katherine a moment to realize he'd left, and

she hurried after him, reaching the hallway in time to see him walk down it in that loose, long-legged saunter that made her mouth go dry. She ran her moist palms down the sides of her skirt, then took in a quick breath as he passed the operating room and turned, neat-as-you-please, straight into her bedroom.

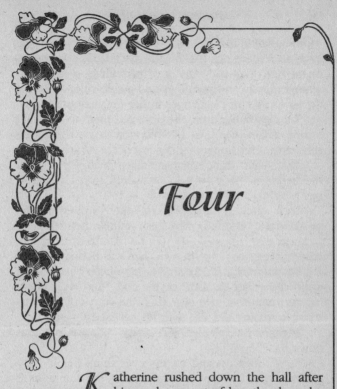

Four

Katherine rushed down the hall after him and was out of breath when she reached the doorway. She stopped to inhale deeply, hoping to give the appearance of supreme calm. "What are you doing?" she asked, her heart pounding frantically as he lit the china lamp on her bureau. The room glowed with soft rose-gold light.

He glanced at her. "I'm taking a tour of your house," he said almost absently, and reached to touch the camisole she'd left at the foot of her bed.

Katherine shivered as if he'd touched her skin. He stood in her feminine bedroom radiating that strangely compelling heat, his presence so intense against the soft backdrop, it bordered on savage. Big and dark and masculine—even amid white organdy and perfumes and gentle colors—Zach's power would forever linger in her imagination.

She closed her eyes, then opened them to find him staring at her, warming her blood with his simmering sensuality. Her fingers tightened on the doorjamb.

"But"—her voice went suddenly high—"you're in my bedroom." She wished he would stop looking at her personal items so intensely.

Zach cocked an eyebrow, then smiled as he watched the becoming pink flush stain Katherine's face. "I know that," he said. Though he tried to appear only mildly interested, everything in him was rioting, confusing his judgment. He forced his gaze from her, looking again at the lacy camisole on the bed. "And an interesting bedroom it is." He picked up the ivory-colored garment, caressing the silk with his callused fingers.

"Please, Zach," she said softly. "Please put that down."

He glanced up and let his eyes drink her in. She stood in the doorway holding tight to the frame, as if the house would blow away if she let go. From behind her the firelight cast a red-gold aura around her. She looked like a dream at dawn, when a man had no control over the primal urgings of his body. The quick charge of heat bolted down his body again, tightening all his muscles. He wanted to take her now, to follow her down on this big, inviting bed and explore all her curves and hollows. He wanted to look at her body in the lamplight, to trace every inch of her peachy-gold skin with his tongue, to touch it with his hands and learn her texture. More, he wanted to hear the soft sounds she would make as he loved her, wanted her to say his name as he came into her. He wanted this woman he'd known as a child, and wanted her to want him, too, even if it ruined everything that had ever been between them.

Her camisole drifted from his fingers back down to the bed. It surprised him that she'd wear such a sensual piece of clothing under her practical skirt and blouse . . . and then again it didn't surprise him. She'd always been a series of contrasts, and this was just another. The woman, he wanted to explore the woman she had become.

"Come here," he said quietly, but she shook her head. A faint smile touched his lips and he went on the prowl, circling the room, touching things, while she stood motionless, as if mesmerized.

The four-poster was covered with a patchwork quilt of muted blues and rose and cream. The washstand held a china washbowl, pitcher, and a tray of fragrant French milled soaps. Against one wall stood a cherry-wood armoire with one door open. Zach swallowed hard as his gaze roved other lace and silk garments, and he could imagine the whisper of them upon her bare skin.

Suddenly Katherine rushed past him like a racing locomotive and slammed the armoire door shut. She leaned back with her palms flat against the panels and glowered up at him. "You are *not* permitted to scrutinize my undergarments!"

He laughed softly. "Well, hell, honey," he drawled. "You can't stop a man from lookin'."

Her cheeks were fiery red, her eyes snapping. She guarded the armoire doors as valiantly as a knight would his castle. "And I want you out of my bedroom!"

"Sure, Smoke Eyes," he said mildly, and moved toward her dresser. "In a minute." He uncapped a bottle of perfume and sniffed it.

"And my name is Katherine." Her ire was up now.

He was bold and arrogant and taking unmentionable liberties. So what if they were old friends? Obviously he was a man and she was a woman and they were in her bedroom. It was simply not proper. "And put that down," she added for good measure.

But Zach only lifted his eyebrows at her, amused. He focused on the scattered objects upon her dresser—the silver hairbrush, scented caches, a small framed photograph of Tessa and Cody. There was also jewelry made of handwrought silver, arrowheads, a little turquoise, colorful beads and shells strung in strands and belts. He touched the beads with one finger. "Wampum," he said, looking at her again. She was rubbing her arms nervously, unsure of what to say, what to do. "Cold, darlin'?" he asked.

She stopped rubbing her arms. "I—yes, actually. I'm very cold. It's time I brewed that tea."

She rushed past him again, but he caught her. It didn't even seem that he had moved—he was still leaning back against her dresser—but before she could blink his hand closed around her wrist like a steel trap, and he tugged her so that she fell against him.

He was so hot! Their bodies touched everywhere—every throbbing pulse point, hard muscle to pliant curve. Tiny explosions popped and spurted up and down Katherine's spine, dancing through her veins. She could feel his sexual invitation seeping into her, infusing her with vibrant energy. He shifted only slightly, and the hard plane of muscles against her felt like oak slabs, except he was warm and intensely alive. Her cheeks burned at the intimacy of their position.

Her gaze flew to his, and she could not draw breath. "Zach . . ." He was watching her from under his thick lashes, and she knew, by the predatory gleam in his eyes, that he was going to kiss her. And she couldn't let that happen.

She wriggled against him, then stilled as the flame in his eyes intensified. He smiled faintly, and she dropped her gaze.

"Look at me," he said in a low voice.

She felt a thrill run the length of her body and met his eyes once more. Their centers burned with black heat. His crooked smile made wild drums beat inside her.

"I'm going to kiss you again," he said.

Her heart took flight. Their breaths, warm and shallow, mingled on the air. "I know," she whispered.

"Do you want me to?"

"Of course not." But her voice, thick and husky, lacked conviction.

His sensual mouth hardened. "You will," he promised, and brushed his lips across hers. She jerked against him, but he held the intention of the kiss, his mouth but a pulse beat away from hers. "Did you like that kiss in the jail?"

Her heart was beating so fiercely, she thought she might faint. His body was fused to hers, its heat burning through their clothing and making her weak. He smelled of musk and wind. "I ... didn't want to."

His laugh fired her blood. Against her, she could feel the pounding of his heart, hammering the same eager rhythm as her own. "It was a mistake—"

He crushed her words with his mouth, almost as if he knew that kissing her could be a mistake too. But his kiss was hungry, hot, practiced. Katherine lost her breath, her will, and every desire to fight him. He was sweeping her away into a pulsing, wet, wild wind that swirled deep inside her, through her, and up into him. He thrust his tongue deep into her mouth, filling her with such explosive sensation, she moaned softly and went limp in his arms. He withdrew and plunged his tongue again in a passionate, dancing rhythm that ripped through her body, tugging deep in her loins.

Zach made a gruff sound and pulled her tighter against him, as if he couldn't get close enough. He took and took from her lush, soft mouth, exploring its texture. He ran his tongue across her full bottom lip, and heard her sigh. He pressed his mouth harder on hers, wanting to get inside her, deeper, deeper. He kissed her longingly, ferociously, as if she were the only woman in all the world.

Mindlessly Katherine followed his lead, unable to resist the demanding strokes of his tongue. Wild, shivery streaks of desire washed through her, and she shuddered as his groan filled her mouth. She felt the rumbling, primal growl deep in her belly where liquid surges pulled low. She never could have imagined a kiss could feel like this! Such savage sensation and vast, almost violent longing. She didn't understand the empty ache that throbbed between her legs, the desperate need to press against him, the craving for more. She did want more, and she knew that Zach was the only man who would ever be able to fulfill that want. He seemed to know precisely what she needed at the exact instant. He played her like a musical score, one moment fiercely, the next exquisitely tender. She was consumed, burning in the torrid flame of his kiss, of him.

He pulled the pins from her hair, and the heavy mass cascaded over her shoulders. Tearing his lips from hers, he pressed fierce kisses all along her throat, then back up to the hollow behind her ear.

"I'm burning, drunk on you, honey," he murmured, his low voice scattering pinpricks of sensation over her skin. Then his mouth covered hers again, and he kissed her with such passion and tenderness, she felt herself dissolving into him.

He bent her back over his arm and quickly, expertly, unbuttoned her blouse. Through her chemise she felt the hot rasp of his finger as he ran it down the valley between her breasts. Suddenly she stiffened, then struggled against him like a wild creature. Breaking free, she spun away to grip the dresser, and over her ragged breathing she heard Zach's harsh curse. He was breathing hard, too, dragging in labored breaths as if he had run a long distance.

"How could you?" she cried, whirling around to glare at him through rising tears. She groped at the front of her blouse, clutching it closed. "How could you do this to *us*? We're *friends*, or were—"

Zach tore a hand through his hair, waiting for his body to cool, but it seethed with pulsating passions that hammered in his blood, his loins. She stood proudly before him, so self-righteous, her eyes defiant, her small chin trembling with fury. She was so beautiful, and so fierce, and he almost smiled. But tears filled her eyes, and he felt his throat tighten.

"Smoke Eyes," he said, reaching toward her in entreaty. She backed away, to the far side of the dresser, still clutching the edge. His lips tightened. "Listen, darlin' . . ." He tried to go on, but he was having a hard time keeping his gaze from her mouth, softly swollen from his kiss. She looked wild and wanton, her red hair tumbling in glorious disarray down her shoulders and back, and a wild-rose color staining her cheekbones. How could he possibly calm himself? He shoved his hand through his hair again and drew a deep breath. "Yes, we were friends—but that was a long time ago and we were young then." He let his gaze run down to her partially opened bodice. She stiffened; he lifted his eyes to hers again. "We've changed."

"Yes," she said in a taut voice. "We've changed. We have our own lives now, and surely you will be returning to yours very soon. When? Tomorrow? The next day? How foolish of you to have started this"—and she swept a hand over her breasts, her eyes flashing—"when nothing, absolutely nothing, can come of it!"

He sprang forward so fast, she let out an alarmed cry. He caught her upper arms and pulled her hard against him. His eyes narrowed, he glared down at her. *"This,"* he said between his teeth, shaking her a little, "started the moment we set eyes on each other in the jail." His voice sounded raw, and he was still breathing heavily. "Something *already* has come of it, and the heat is pounding in me, a goddamn ache that won't let go. *Nothing* is going to put the fire out but you, honey."

His rough voice poured over Katherine, steeping her in eroticism. She tried to pull free but he held tight. He made a harsh sound, like a growl, and she saw the taut muscles working in his rigid jaw.

"That kiss," he went on, "was fire, sugar. And it was out of control." His voice dropped even lower, rumbling in a caress both smooth and coarse, making her shiver and melt inside. "And I know you feel it too."

"No!"

"Yes!" He shook her again, his intense gaze delving so deep into her, it seared her soul. "Do you want me to prove it again?"

Trembling fury poured through her, and she struggled against him. "Stop!" To kiss him again would be torment. He spoke the truth, of course, and she was terrified of the wild rush of longing his hard words had unleashed in her. Everything in her leapt toward him. She wanted to feel his tongue in her mouth again, filling it with long, deep strokes. She wanted to press her hands to his powerful back again and feel the muscles ripple. Yet she wanted to escape him too. An alarming thought flashed into her mind, and she abruptly asked, "Are you married?"

His jaw tightened, and her alarm bloomed into full-tilt panic. She didn't think she could bear it if he was married.

"Are you?" she demanded.

"No," he said in a hard, flat voice.

She almost cursed the relief that flooded her, and she tipped her chin up, bravely meeting his slightly mocking stare. "I know you're used to taking what comes your way, Zach." Her chin edged even higher. "But I am not for the taking."

His face turned hard as granite, and his hands tightened around her arms until she cried out. He leaned closer to her, his mouth just a whisper away from her own. "Then we, little one, are going to have a battle on our hands because I"—his gaze flicked to her lips, which she nervously moistened with her tongue—"am a very determined man." His voice was soft and drawling, a direct contrast to the power of his steely fingers that kept her still. "And I do aim to 'take' you"—he let his ardent gaze wander to her mouth again—"with me."

Her brows drew together in a frown. "Wh-what?" How could she even think straight with his handsome face so close, his earthy male scent permeating the air between them? She fought the shiver that chased up her spine, wishing she could run from the intensity in his gaze. But she saw, too, the harsh lines of weariness on his face.

"I want you to come home with me, Smoke Eyes."

Stunned, completely confused now, she stared up at him. When she saw an odd flash of emotion in his eyes, she had to look away, as if she'd seen something too intimate.

"Zach, I—" Her eyes met his again, and she shook

her head. "Surely, you're joking." When she saw he did not share her humor, she frowned again. "Why would I do such a thing? I just can't up and leave. I have a practice here. I—"

She stopped, deciding he was toying with her, and flashed him a teasing smile. "As nice as it might be to see your home, sir, I think the residents of Newberry would be rather at a loss without a doctor."

She saw his facial muscles tighten, and tried again. "Very well. *Why* do you so desperately want me to see your home? Is it a mansion in the South? A villa in France?" When his brows lowered, she shrugged lightly. "No? Hmmm . . . A castle in Scotland?" His heavy scowl grew blacker. "No? Goodness, Zach, where *do* you live? I would hope some land I've never been before, for then I'd be delighted to visit. This summer after I've made plans for a temporary replacement. Why are you glowering at me?"

As she stared up at him, she realized he was suffering some inner pain, and she gentled her voice. "What is it, Zach?"

"It's not my home I want you to come see." His voice was hoarse, his eyes bleak and haunted. "I want you to see my son."

For a moment Katherine gasped at him, unable to absorb the cold shock of his words. She felt the coiled tension in his body, the pressure of his powerful fingers biting into her arms. She saw pain flash across his tight features—a harsh sorrow, a kind of desperate agony that cut at her heart.

"He's eight years old," he went on in that awful, jagged voice. "And he's very ill. Stomach tumor." He bit out the words like they were shards of glass cutting his vitals. It was good, Katherine thought numbly, that his hands still held her, for her knees had gone watery and threatened to buckle. "Three very fine physicians have all given the same diagnosis. He needs surgery. But the risks are great." He released her then, and she sagged down on the edge of the bed, staring up at him dazedly.

"You have a *son*?" That was the first shock. The second was that the boy was dying, the third was that Zach was asking her to administer to him. *Oh, my God*, she thought, and watched him rake tense fingers through his hair. He swore softly, crudely, and she knew she wasn't making it any easier on him.

"Dammit, this is not the way I'd intended to tell you." He paced the room, taking long, quick strides and rubbing the muscles at the back of his neck. He gave a harsh bark of a laugh that made her jump. "But there doesn't seem to be any *delicate* way to inform you of these facts."

He had a *son*. Katherine looked away from him to her hands. If he had a son, then there was a mother. Where was she? How did Zach feel about her? She wasn't his wife, she must be his mistress. Did she know that Zach continued to prowl after other women even after she had borne his son? Was he one of those sailors with a woman in every port? Hot emotion poured through her—embarrassment, disappointment, and yes, even hurt—that he could kiss her as he just had while he kept another woman. Humiliation burned in her. How dare he treat her so lightly. She swiftly looked up at him. He was watching her with those keen hawk eyes, his hard mouth compressed in a grim line.

"She's dead," Zach said tersely. He let out his breath between his teeth. He was making a complete mess of the situation! He hunkered down before her, grasping her wrists and staring into her eyes. "I know this is a shock for you, sugar, and I know it might seem farfetched and unreasonable that I ask you to come home with me—" The muscles in his jaw flexed; she was staring at him as if he were demented. He quickly straightened, and his voice was clipped now.

"Let me start at the beginning." He walked to the window and leaned both hands on the sill, staring out into the storm. "I met Laura in London. She was a nice girl—not rich, not poor. I'd been a long time at sea and when we met she was living a rather grim life—taking care of an ailing mother and living with her grandfather in his London town house. I met her in Hyde Park one afternoon and we struck up a conversation. She was lonely and without hope she would ever be able to leave her mother and therefore find a husband. I liked Laura but was never in love with her. We got on fine, explored London together, and *she* fell in love with me." He swallowed. "Well, being a typical selfish bastard I took advantage of that. On my next trip to London—two years later—I learned I'd fathered a son. There was no doubt he was mine. He favors me. Besides, Laura wasn't the type of woman who'd bed men casually. Her family had been horrified that she'd bedded one at all. But they took the boy under their wing, and I, learning how much Laura loved me, turned heel and visited my son, Drew, only three times in all these years."

When he heard Katherine's stifled gasp, he frowned darkly and turned to face her. "I was never proud of that, dammit, but I knew Drew was in good hands. I couldn't have married Laura. She would have tried to tie me down, and in the end I would have made her very unhappy. I was never a letter writer, so I didn't even correspond except to send her money. I became a sea captain—a wealthy one," he added without conceit, "and was able to send them enough so that Drew would have the best."

He expelled a ragged breath and rubbed his eyes with one hand, letting his thumb and forefinger rest on the bridge of his nose. "One day I received a letter from Drew's great-grandfather informing me that Laura had had an accident. She'd taken a fall from her horse and she was dead. The great-grandfather was distraught, and the boy"—Zach swallowed heavily—"was like a ghost. He'd just stay in his room, play with his soldiers, not even eat. He was lonely and depressed and I thought the least I could do was bring him home with me. Though at the time I didn't know he was sick."

He turned again to stare out at the black, pitiless night. The wind howled, a cold, lonesome sound, and shook the house. He thought of the boy—hollow-eyed, listless, detached from life as if he, too, was waiting for death to seize him and carry him away from this world of unbearable pain. Zach clamped his jaw, biting down on the image that had haunted him for weeks now. Then he heard Katherine's calm, professional voice like a balm.

"How long have you known about the tumor?"

He looked over his shoulder at her, studying her. Straightening, he shoved his fists into his trousers pockets, and his mouth tightened into a bitter line. "Several weeks now. At first I thought he was just pale and ill from the loss of his mother, but as time wore on I realized it was something more. Most of the time I live in Marblehead, Massachusetts, but after we left England, we stopped first at my second home on a small tropical island in the Caribbean. I thought the sun and beaches would do him good. That home is like paradise, and for a while Drew thrived, but he'd lost his appetite and his stomach was swelling. It was there on the island I realized he was physically sick. My physician examined him and diagnosed a tumor. I didn't want to believe him, of course, and I had two other diagnoses in Marblehead. They all agree."

"And he will die if he's not operated on," Katherine surmised correctly.

Zach's gaze was hard. "And might even if he is."

She watched him, feeling as though the bottom of her stomach had dropped out. "Why me?" she whispered. "If you have doctors there willing and competent to operate on him, then why have you come all this way for me?"

He dropped down onto the window seat, leaning forward to brace his forearms on his knees. The raw pain in his face caused an awful tightness to swell in Katherine's chest. "Drew just lies in bed all day. He refuses to speak, hasn't spoken a word for a month, except once, to voice a request. He doesn't even play with his soldiers anymore, doesn't read, doesn't do anything but look up at the ceiling, or out the window, like he'll find some answer out there, in the sea." In the faint lamplight his expression looked even more grave. "The one time he spoke he asked for you."

Katherine's eyes widened. "Me?" She didn't understand. "Zach, what do you mean? How—"

"I told him about you—us, when we were young. I thought sharing stories of my past could help Drew and me get to know each other. I told him about our pranks in Harper City—and about the places I've seen and been since, but most of the time he wanted to hear about you, Smoke Eyes."

For the first time since he'd spoken of the boy, a faint trace of humor warmed Zach's gaze. "Drew was intrigued by that name, and your Arapaho blood. I told him about how you used to heal injured creatures by tying sticks to broken limbs, or doctoring with herbs and potions and little chants your grandfather had taught you. I guess maybe he envisions you as some sort of mystical, magical creature and—" sweat broke out on his brow, and his jaw went rigid—"and he's got it in his mind somehow that only *you* can heal him."

Katherine was suddenly cold and shaking. She folded her arms across her chest and swallowed hard to dissolve the knot in her throat. "Zach, I—but that's silly. The other physicians—"

"The other physicians will *not* operate on him as he is. They are extremely concerned about his weakened state, and tell me that he needs fortifying before they will administer to him. But the main reason they won't operate is because of Drew's depressed state of mind. He seems to have lost the will to live. They say they will not even consider operating until his state of mind has improved. They give him about a month—to either improve or deteriorate further." He stared straight at her. "I know it might sound unreasonable to you, but children are not pragmatic and I'm desperate, desperate enough to come halfway across the country and beg you."

Looking at him, Katherine could feel his despair as if it were her own. Emotions washed over her, and she felt almost sick as conflicting feelings warred inside her. She opened her mouth to speak, to tell him that it really was *not* practical for her to travel east with him, but he continued, his voice curiously hoarse.

"You should have seen his eyes light up when I told him I was coming to see you, see if you would be able to come back with me. It was the only sign of life he's shown since Laura died."

His words, his tone, touched something deep inside her, and Katherine glanced away from his hard, handsome face, those far-seeing black eyes that pulled at her, making her feel things she did not want to feel. Uncertainty ate at her as she tried to will away the awful sinking sensation in her middle, the knot of emotion that tightened around her heart as she thought of his son, the entire wretched situation. But she couldn't fathom the idea of traveling east, leaving her practice for an undetermined length of time, or—most unsettling of all—living in Zach's home. The very idea made her tremble, and she leapt to her feet. She had to move, get away from him, had to think. She pressed her clammy palms to her feverish cheeks and blurted out, "I—I'm going to make some tea."

"What the hell?"

She heard Zach swear, but she was already on her way to the kitchen. He couldn't know that tea soothed her when she was distraught, and she felt like gulping down huge quantities of the stuff. She whisked in to the kitchen and clattered and banged the stove lids as Clarabelle squawked and scolded her. Once the stove was lit, she spooned tea into the teapot, then whirled to get the cups. Her heart hit her throat when she saw Zach. With one shoulder propped against the doorframe, his arms crossed over his broad chest, he was watching her carefully. She shrugged and reached for the cups.

"I never got us that tea, and chamomile tea is just the thing on a stormy night."

She glanced at him and swallowed when she met his brooding gaze. For a numbing moment she stared at him, then catapulted herself back into action, spinning around to fetch the sugar. But Zach was suddenly behind her; she could feel his heat. When he put his hands on her shoulders, tension sizzled between them. He turned her gently around to face him.

"Smoke Eyes," he murmured, and his deep voice was tender.

Katherine was lost. She could bear anything from him but tenderness. "Don't touch me," she pleaded.

"You don't have to give me answers now," he said, his voice even quieter. He began to stroke her cheek with one rough thumb, and she arched away from him, alarm sparking through her.

"I said don't touch me!" she exclaimed, and the kettle began to scream. She spun to get it, and Clarabelle shrieked at all the commotion. Zach looked both amused and exasperated, and Katherine's hands shook as she poured the hot water into the teapot. "Is that why you kissed me, Zach?" she asked, keeping her back to him. "Did you think your fatal charm would work magic on me, as I'm sure it has on countless women? That it could persuade me to come home with you? A bribe of sorts? One good turn deserves another?" She regretted her words as soon as they were out. They sounded snide and cold, and she could *feel* the iron control he exerted to keep from pouncing on her.

"I didn't *think* at all." His drawling, sarcastic words made her cheeks burn. He made it sound as if she were a hussy, that *her* charms had seduced *him*.

Glancing at him, she caught the dark amusement in his eyes and put her chin up. "Then why don't we forget the entire episode—pretend the kiss never happened?" The humor in his eyes turned to downright laughter, and she had to look away.

"You know that kiss had nothing to do with Drew," he said. "I wanted to kiss you very badly then, and I want to kiss you very badly now."

She whirled on him, eyes narrowed. "I told you I want to forget the kiss."

He smiled. "Try."

Katherine knew she would never be able to forget. Their eyes caught and held—hers flashing with temper, his amused. But suddenly her gaze wavered. She sighed and rubbed her eyes wearily. "You've placed a huge responsibility on me."

"I know that." His voice was somber, low.

She leaned her forehead against the cupboard and

closed her eyes, suddenly overwhelmed with fatigue. "I don't see how I can leave Newberry, Zach. I have my patients, and the reservation, and—"

"Don't give me an answer yet, Smoke Eyes. Think about it. At least sleep on it."

Yes, sleep sounded wonderful. "Katherine," she said weakly, rolling her head to look at him.

He frowned, puzzled. "What?"

"I told you to call me Katherine. You must. Here."

He glanced around the room as if looking for eaves-droppers. "There's no one here but you and me, darlin'."

The endearment sent ripples of pleasure over her skin, and she clenched her fists against the turbulent emotions he aroused in her. But, as if Clarabelle disa-greed, she made a rude sound, renting the air with a loud belch. Katherine closed her eyes in embarrass-ment, but Zach threw back his head and laughed, the sound rich and full-throated. As if encouraged, Clarabelle came forth with another rude noise, then the voice of the town cobbler, who must have come out to the kitchen to share his troubles with her. "What am I gonna do about my wastin' manhood, awk?"

Zach stared at Katherine in disbelief. "What th—"

She held up her hands. "Please," she said. "No foul language in here. Clarabelle repeats everything. Obvi-ously."

"Hmmm. Where did you get her?"

"She was a Christmas present from Birdie McDowell."

Zach lifted a dark brow. "Birdie McDowell?"

"She's one of the folk who followed me into the jail this morning. An older woman with a painted face, or-ange hair?"

"Ah."

"Yes." She laughed. "Actually, Clarabelle is good company."

Zach chose not to comment on the eccentricity of a woman named Birdie and a bird named Clarabelle. For a long moment, he contemplated Katherine, then asked, "Do you get lonely here, Smoke Eyes?"

"The parrot," she warned, "could end up repeating that name. And no." She poured the tea. "I'm too busy to get lonely."

She picked up her teacup and blew out the lamp. Zach watched as her lithe, shadowy figure glided up to him in the dim light. Her thick waving tresses spilled over her shoulders and cascaded down her graceful back, and he had to shove his hands into his pockets to keep from touching even one curl.

"I'm going to bed now," she said.

Her words roused fiery images in his mind. He felt his gut tighten and his loins swell. He fought to end the screaming urges in his body once and for all.

"Will you be all right?" she asked, looking up at him through the shadows.

An odd emotion tightened in his chest. As annoyed and upset as she'd been with him, she still worried. He smiled. "I'll be fine."

"And I'll see you tomorrow?"

"First thing," he promised. "And I'll let myself out."

Katherine hesitated, then murmured, "Good night."

"Good night."

She felt his gaze on her back until she stepped over the threshold of her bedroom and closed the door behind her. She quickly drank her tea—which did not calm her—then stripped and slid on her flannel nightgown. She dove into bed, where she lay burning for Zach in the frigid night.

Five

The sun blazed brilliantly into her chilly room the next morning. Katherine felt deliciously warm under her thick quilt, though the tip of her nose was cold. She stretched, then opened her eyes. She felt rejuvenated, refreshed. There had been no late-night calls, no disrupted sleep. Of course, anyone who might have wanted to reach her would have been thwarted by the storm.

The storm. . . . Her gaze went to the frosted windowpane, where sunlight made dazzling silvery patterns against the glass. She could hear the occasional creaking of a tree bough, but could not hear the wind. It was almost as if there had been no storm, but, oh, there had been. A firestorm. Zach.

She closed her eyes, wanting to blot out the image of his rakishly handsome face, but it danced behind her eyelids, teasing her. She drew in a quick, shallow breath and felt her breasts grow tight, her nipples harden. Hugging her arms to her chest, she stared at the ceiling, trying to will away the feelings and sensations that whipped through her. Though she had suggested to Zach that they forget the kiss, pretend it'd never happened, she knew there would be no forgetting. He'd branded her with his mouth and body as surely as if he owned her.

He had a son. She swallowed the lump that surfaced in her throat. Alone now, she could think without Zach's dark, unsettling stare on her. What, she wondered, was his son like? And what had his mother been like? How desolate Drew must feel. How alone. He had no siblings, and was living with a stranger of a father . . . and he was desperately ill. Poor baby, she thought. Poor little boy. Something hitched in her chest, and she fought the emotion. Still, her natural compassion for people tugged deep. She pushed the bedcovers aside and climbed out of bed, scowling and rubbing her nose. How unfair of Zach to expect this feat of her! Yet she had to admit she would take drastic measures if she were in the same situation.

Her brow furrowed with frustration, she glanced at the clock. Half past ten! "Oh, my Lord!" she cried, and winced when her bare feet touched the icy floorboards. She was late already. She should have been on her way to the reservation by now. Leaving her wrapper behind, she hurried to the kitchen to light the stove and heat some water for her bath. Halfway there she came up short at the sight of her colorful Arapaho blanket—the one her mother had woven years ago—thrown haphazardly over the front room sofa. Strange, she didn't remember leaving it out. Peering closer, she detected the unmistakable form of a long male body beneath it. Zach!

She crept forward, noticing other evidence that he'd stayed the night. His worn leather boots stood by the door, and his clothes were thrown over the back of a chair. His clothes! Her gaze swerved back to him. Naked. The man had stayed the night in her house without a stitch of clothing on—and without, she would bet, a thought for her reputation!

Stunned, she stood over him, ready to wake him and send him, with blistering words, on his way. But she got mesmerized by the swath of curly black hair that covered his wide chest. Her knees went watery and her stomach trembled. As if the sight was too disturbing, she brought her gaze up to his face. Even in repose Zach exuded that compelling strength and vivid masculinity. He was a man born to dominate, and even as he slept she was drawn to him.

With his hair tumbling over his forehead, he looked dashing. His face was nicked with a few small scars, adding a rakishness to his considerable appeal. She wanted to touch him, and had to catch herself from stepping forward and putting her hands on his hard, angular face. Her heart pounded so violently, she could not hear herself breathe. Why, she wondered, did he have to be so damnably attractive? She didn't like this at all—these new feelings she harbored for Zach. She'd always felt so comfortable with him, but now she only felt uneasy. He wanted her, as a man wants a woman. And, to be truthful, what she felt for him was probably want too.

As if there was no help for it, her gaze was drawn to his beautiful body. The sunlight that filtered in through the shuttered window spilled over him, mak-

ing his skin gleam gold-brown. His body was as powerfully sleek and muscled as a cougar's, and she
guessed there was not an ounce of wasted flesh on
him. Her gaze drifted down over him, and she
regretted—for a moment—that the blanket covered
him.

How many women, she wondered, had Zach seduced with his potency and lazy, seductive charm?
How many women had run their hands over his
smooth, bronze flesh, the powerful muscles in his
shoulders and chest, as she longed to now?

Fighting the urge to slip the blanket back, she swept
her gaze back up to him—and gasped as it collided
with his gaze, black and wicked as a pirate's heart. He
smiled at her—and his rusty, early-morning voice broke
the silence.

"Had your fill, darlin'?"

Katherine lost her breath. She wanted to run, but
her feet seemed nailed to the floor.

"Now it's my turn," he drawled, and his gaze wan-
dered over her with such excruciating thoroughness,
she wanted to die. Heat flushed through her entire
body, and yet she stood like a statue, allowing him un-
forgivable liberties with just his incredible gaze.

Zach felt his gut tighten—and everything else. He
wanted her. He wanted to stretch her out beneath him
and bury himself in her. Her flaming auburn hair was a
violent shock of color against her pale yellow nightgown. And despite the flannel gown, he could make
out her breasts, firm and upthrusting, and her dusky,
puckered nipples. The gown even shaped itself to her
hips, and his gaze lingered at the juncture of her thighs.
Everything in him ached. With immense control he
brought his gaze to hers again and smiled.

"Did you come to serve me breakfast in bed,
darlin'?"

"I, uh—" Her fingers fluttered at her throat. "No."

She turned to bolt, but Zach was faster. He moved like a striking rattler, one arm lashing out and wrapping around her tiny waist. He pulled her down on top of him, holding her tight against him, against the thick bulge of his arousal. She squirmed and wiggled, and sweat broke out on his brow.

"Sure you did," he said. Boldly, he ran a hand over her sweetly rounded buttocks and up her spine, pinning her to him. "Or was it me you wanted for breakfast?"

Quickly he flipped her onto her back and half straddled her, his forearms braced on either side of her shoulders, his face just above hers. "Or perhaps"—he bent his head to touch his lips to hers—"we'll share breakfast." And he slid his damp tongue over her lips, feeling her gasp before he plunged his tongue inside her mouth, stroking deep. Almost before she could respond he withdrew, only to thrust inside again, hotter, harder, deeper. He searched her mouth with a demanding hunger, commanding her to follow his lead.

"Stop!" Katherine gasped, when he pulled away. She struggled beneath him, surging up against his tumescent manhood. He groaned, and she felt his harsh breathing near her ear. Her blood beat wildly, and swift currents of surging liquid pulled deep inside her, pooling between her thighs where his hard leg nestled. It felt wickedly good, dreadfully right. Dangerous, wild attraction. She wanted him, *wanted* him! Already he had taught her that. And there was no fighting the delicious pleasure that soared through her as he touched his tongue to the throbbing pulse behind her ear. But she tried. Again she bucked beneath him, hoping to squirm out from under his heavy body. She pushed her fists against the solid wall of his bare chest, and felt the shocking thrill of his crisp hair and warm skin. Her hands wanted to linger, but she writhed again, her knee angling up and almost maiming him.

He jerked aside to protect his groin. "Whoa, honey, you could cool a man's desire real quick making moves like that." And with a sudden move of his own that snatched her breath away, he whisked her atop him again, lifting her so that she dangled over him in mid-air.

"Put me down!" she yelled, humiliated.

He only grinned. "Hey, waif," he teased. "You weigh next to nothing." As if to prove it he pumped his arms once, twice, moving her up and down with ease.

Katherine was fuming. "Put me down, you scoundrel! Put me down!"

"Give me a good reason why." He was obviously enjoying himself immensely.

"I'm getting dizzy!" She put the back of her hand against her forehead and closed her eyes dramatically.

He laughed. "Not good enough."

Her eyes flew open. "You lied!" she fumed.

His brows lifted. "About what?"

"You said you would let yourself out last night!"

"I said I'd let myself out. I never said I was going to let myself out last night in the middle of a blizzard."

She gasped, and her eyes narrowed. "Ooh! You tricked me!"

His grin broadened. "If you keep wriggling around like that you're going to have an unfortunate fall."

She only wriggled more. "You tyrant—you took advantage! You deliberately set it up so you could spend the night!"

Zach cocked a brow higher. "But I didn't expect such a warm—" He looked at where her pulse jumped erratically in her throat, and he could feel the kick of his own pulse too. He wanted to run his fingers down the slender arch of her neck, knowing already that her skin was chamois-soft. It took colossal effort for him to tear his gaze from that tempting sight. "That is, such a *casual* welcome this morning."

"You're not welcome!"

"Ah, darlin', do you want me to prove you different?"

She was silent, staring down at him with wide eyes.

"Now," he went on, "if you had been a hospitable friend, you would have invited me to stay. You could then have avoided the surprise of finding me here. But since you didn't extend the invitation, I had to take matters into my own hands . . . so to speak."

"I *would* have asked you to stay if—"

He lifted a brow in mild inquiry. "If what?"

Katherine silently cursed him. Of course she would have asked him to stay if he hadn't kissed her with such scorching heat and penetrating thoroughness. She couldn't tell him that, couldn't tell him how deeply he had shaken her. But judging by the mocking glint in his eyes, he knew. She watched his smoldering gaze leave hers, then she heard his voice, coarse and gritty-rough.

"Well, darlin', will you look at that."

She glanced down and saw that the gaping front of her nightgown revealed her breasts. Her nipples were crimped tight and straining toward him, as if begging for the touch of his mouth upon them.

Her face grew scalding hot. Mortified, she squirmed to cover herself, but the nightgown was bunched up, trapped in his hands. He made a low sound and swiftly, before she could protest, lowered her to touch his lips to one warm, quivering breast. She gasped when he opened his mouth and pulled the rigid nipple deep inside. He sucked strongly, making her cry out as fire shot through her body.

"Zach!" She reached blindly for his hair, tangling it in her fingers. He broke away suddenly and cupped her breast in his warm palm, lifting it while his thumb traced a circle around the stiff nipple. Katherine moaned, torn between needing to stop him and wanting to beg for more. He seemed content just to watch as he almost idly stroked his thumb back and forth, back and forth, just a whisper of a caress across her turgid nipple.

"Your breasts," he whispered, "are beautiful." And he pushed one up so that her nipple popped into his mouth. He took the hardened peak between his tongue and teeth and sucked softly, tugging at her in a maddening rhythm that made her say things she did not know, could only hear.

As if she had willed it he moved to her other breast and opened his mouth wide, taking her inside. A soft sound erupted from her throat, and she grabbed his arms, her fingers gripping his hard biceps. Scalding blood pulsed through her body as she melted.

"Oh, Zach, Zach . . ." She had never felt anything so agonizingly sweet. He tugged her flesh even deeper into his mouth, then suddenly, swiftly, turned her under him. Her breasts were crushed beneath his chest, and his solid thigh nestled snugly between her legs again, creating both a pleasure and an unbearable ache. She tried to twist away—these new, swirling sensations were too much—but his mouth fastened hungrily on hers while his hands began a quest of her body.

She turned her head away, gasping for breath. "Zach, get off—"

But somehow his hand was skimming up her bare ribs to caress her breast again. He kissed her, his tongue delving deep into her mouth, forcing her to meet it with her own. She did, reveling in the intercourse, half her mind thinking there could never be anything so intimate as kissing.

When he tore his lips from hers, his breathing was as harsh and ragged as if he had been swimming underwater. His eyes were fever-bright. He bent his head to press hot kisses down the length of her throat, to where her pulse throbbed.

"Zach—" She arched beneath him, holding on to his broad shoulders.

"God, you smell good, darlin'. Good enough to eat." Zach lifted his head to look at her, to search her misty eyes. His heart almost stopped beating when he saw the passion there. "Damn your eyes," he said hoarsely but tenderly, smoothing the silky hair back off her temples. He leaned down to take her mouth again on a ride from innocence to decadence. He fondled her breast under her nightgown, squeezing it and lifting it, teasing her taut nipple between two fingers.

"Smoke Eyes," he whispered when he lifted his head again. His heart was slamming against his chest, and though he tried to slow his passion, it was no use. "We need to get this thing off you," he said, and began to pull at her nightgown.

Katherine struggled, panicked, but still she wanted just one more moment of his magic touch, his mouth upon her breasts. He had taken her outside herself into a world dark and white, where only fire and feeling ruled. She was caught in his spell, intoxicated with wonder, almost painfully aroused by even the subtlest of his movements, his caresses. She lay steeped in him, excited by his primitive male instincts that called to her own unruly instincts.

"Help me," he whispered, riding his palm up her bare hip.

She shoved his hand away. "Zach, no—" she began, but he took her hand and pressed it to the front of his body. So hot, so hard—so frightening.

She would never know what would have happened

if she hadn't heard the sharp rap at the front door. "Doctor!" someone called out, and tremendous shame and shock washed through her.

"Zach!" She pushed at his wide shoulders, urging him off her, but he had no intention of moving.

"Tell him to go away," he whispered in her ear. "Or I will." He lifted his head to look down at her, his face tight with restrained passion.

She met his eyes, her own frosty. "If you do not get off me this instant, I assure you, Zach Fletcher, that I will not even consider going east with you."

Zach stiffened, as rigid as rock. That she could fling *that* at him *now*! Ice washed through him, then anger, hot and fierce, flooding his body. With a crude oath he pushed away from her and sat up, swinging his long legs to the floor. Chest heaving, he raked a hand through his hair, watching her with narrowed eyes. She was beautiful, her rich hair spilling over her shoulders, her unbuttoned nightgown revealing the curve of her firm breasts. It infuriated him that he could not control the ache of his body, the pounding passion in his blood.

"Doctor!"

Katherine jumped. She felt tattered from the inside out, shaken, weak. "Coming!" she called. Smoothing her nightgown with trembling hands, she stood and walked on rubbery legs to the door. She could feel Zach's eyes on her as she opened the door a crack and poked her head out. Cold, fresh air swept into the room.

"Shadow!" she said, seeing her stableboy standing on the front porch. He was a tall, lean boy with nut-brown skin, shoulder-length black hair, and flashing dark eyes. He wore a red chamois shirt underneath his fringed buckskin jacket, denims, and moccasins, cutting a striking figure. Behind him she could see her sleigh hitched up and ready for their thirty-five-mile jaunt to the reservation.

"You're late, Doctor," he said, his serious black eyes searching hers. "I was worried about you, you know, with the storm."

She sighed. "It's sweet of you to worry about me, Shadow, but as you can see I'm fine. I just happened to sleep late."

"But you were with a stranger last night." He said this with real concern in his voice, not disrespect.

"An old friend," she assured him, then glanced to the small ormolu clock on her mantel. "It's past eleven," she murmured. "I think it's best if we get a much earlier start tomorrow. Why don't you go to the apothecary and bring back the supplies I had George set out? Then go to the general store. Zeke knows what I want. That way we'll have a head start in the morning."

Shadow grinned shyly. "Sure, Doctor." Always eager to please her, he bounded off the steps to the snow-covered ground, kicking up clumps of snow as he headed for the stable.

"Oh—and Shadow!"

He stopped and turned.

"Be sure to purchase some licorice whips for yourself." He ducked his head in answer, and she closed the door, smiling. When her eyes met Zach's, though, her smile faded. He sat on the edge of the sofa with the blanket draped over his groin, a poor excuse for cover. He was watching her, frowning, quietly intimidating without speaking a word. He rubbed a hand over his stubbled jaw, and even that simple gesture radiated danger. Nervously, she moistened her lips. The room was filled with a palpable tension neither of them could ignore. But Zach broke the tension when he lifted his brows and asked, "Shadow?"

She shrugged lightly, though she felt anything but light. "My stableboy. He's Arapaho . . . an orphan about fourteen years old I brought back with me from the reservation. He sleeps in the stable."

"And moves like a shadow."

She clutched the back of her gown. She wanted to button it up, but it would be silly after what they'd just shared. "Yes." It was best to move, she thought, and forced her legs forward. "And is completely loyal. Licorice whips are his favorite treat."

"And you are so proficient at doling out treats, aren't you, darlin'?"

His voice was deep, dark, stroking, and reached far down into her. She fought her instinctive shiver and, straightening her shoulders, resolved not to dignify his insulting comment with a response. She did not even acknowledge him with a look. Though her legs were jerky she managed to march past him. But his hand shot out and he caught the tail of her nightgown. Giving it one swift tug, he pulled her back between his legs to land on his hard thigh. She cried out and, for balance, caught him around the neck with one arm.

He grinned devilishly. "See what I mean?"

She squirmed to get free, but his heavily muscled arm was locked around her waist, holding her tight. There was no point in fighting him—he was too strong.

"Stop this instant!" she demanded as his mouth swooped down to capture hers. She turned her face aside so he missed, but he only laughed, relishing the game. When he saw the sheen of tears in her eyes, though, he straightened.

"Have I hurt you?" he asked with such tenderness, she felt like weeping. She'd much rather hold on to her anger than to feel this confusing tumult of emotions.

"No, I'm not hurt!" she exclaimed. "I'm furious! Let me go, Zach." She was uncomfortably aware of her thigh resting intimately against his warm crotch. But he seemed in no hurry to accommodate her.

"We have a matter to discuss."

"We have nothing to discuss but your boldness!" She pushed against his stone-hard chest. "You're as randy as a lion, Zach Fletcher, and believe you me, I have potions for men who have trouble controlling their sexual—energy!"

He threw back his head and laughed, the warm, vibrant sound filling the air. Katherine felt a quick catch in her vitals as he smiled at her. Lowering his head, he put his mouth close to her ear and murmured, "What other potions have you brewed, little witch, of a . . . er, sexual nature?"

She shoved her hand against his granite stomach, ignoring his grunt as he lost his breath. "You're incorrigible!" she scolded, and struggled to her feet. But he still had her nightgown in one hand and he held tight. Standing between his widespread knees, she stared down at him, wondering what the devil she was going to do with him. He smiled, as if daring her to try something. Their private world was shattered a moment later when someone rattled the front-door knob.

"Doc?" came a crotchety male voice, and another rattling of the doorknob. "Doc, you in there?"

Katherine rolled her eyes. "Sticks."

"I beg your pardon?" Zach asked.

"Sticks Howard, our town crank. He lives alone in a tumble-down house with about twenty cats. The cats eat more than he does. I suppose that's why his stomach is always acting up. Some folks say all he needs is a good woman to soothe his irascibility. But others say the only female in town who can match him in temperament is the schoolmarm."

Zach grunted. "How do you know it's him?"

"He never knocks."

As if to prove it, Sticks rattled the knob again. "Doc? If you're in there, I need some pepsin for my stomach. It's acting up."

"You'll have to come back in about an hour, Sticks!" she called. "I'm not dressed!"

"I'm sure *that* comment will keep him away," Zach drawled. "I'll bet he's trying to sneak a peek into this room to see if you really are dressed."

Katherine looked at the front window, and sure enough, Sticks's shadow slipped by it. "Sticks Howard," she yelled. "Get away from that window!" He straightened as if slapped between the shoulder blades and was gone. Indignant, she glanced back to Zach and caught the warm amusement that glimmered in his eyes. Then she felt his hand stealing up her midriff to her breast. She jumped back.

"Get dressed," she told him, "and be gone!" She paled as he started to rise, the blanket falling below his hipbones. "Not yet. Wait—" She broke off when he stood up all the way, the blanket dropping to the floor. Despite herself, her gaze ran up his hard, sinewy body, meeting his mocking smile. Cheeks scalding, she turned and fled to the kitchen.

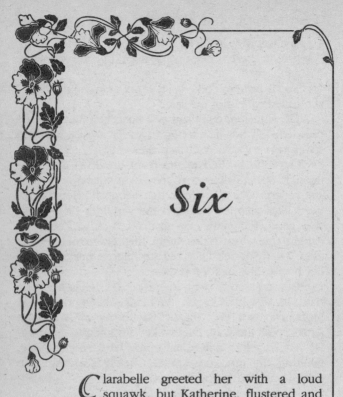

Six

Clarabelle greeted her with a loud squawk, but Katherine, flustered and shaky, ignored the bird and stuffed wood into the cast-iron range. "Damn his black eyes!" she muttered as she lit the fire.

She put the kettle on for her bath, then donning her coat and boots she dashed to the lean-to and dragged out her enamel tub. All the while she muttered and fretted and grumbled, wondering if she would have, *could* have stopped Zach if Shadow hadn't knocked on the door. What was this mindless, spiraling, sugar-sweet sensation that rose between her and Zach? How easy it was to sink into it, letting it drug, persuade, consume.

Closing her eyes she stopped in the center of the room and pressed her fingertips to her forehead. Heat washed through her as she remembered his hands upon her, his mouth. He had aroused her to the point of wanting to know more. Just his proximity made her burn and ache. She was terrified of her feelings, so new and uncontrollable. Yet *he* was experienced. He'd been experienced when he was but a youth in Harper City. In all these years, how many women had he left behind, how many hearts had he broken? Oh, it was all so unfair.

Clarabelle squawked and Katherine straightened. She grabbed the kettle and poured the steaming water into her bath, unaware that Zach lounged in the doorway, watching her as she kept up her fretful monologue.

"I suppose I *am* somewhat flattered that he finds me . . . attractive," she said to Clarabelle, reaching into the bureau drawer where she kept her linens. "But then Zach finds some attractive quality in every woman. He always has." She sighed and tossed a fluffy white towel on a chair. "Why do you suppose he looks at me so . . . intensely? It seems to mean he's going to kiss me."

He could wait, Zach decided. She was rare and fine and unspoiled, and she was not to be hurried. Watching her dash from one side of the kitchen to the other, muttering words he only half heard, he wished she were a woman he could seduce and then leave, without concern. But, he admitted, if she were that sort of woman, he probably wouldn't want her so badly. No, he thought, watching the way the sunlight sparked fire in her hair, he would wait until she was ready, and

then he would love her long and slow. In fact, he realized with a shock, he wanted to wait. It would be like
savoring the finest of wines. . . .

"Damn his black eyes!" Clarabelle screeched suddenly,

Katherine jumped, then grinned ruefully. "Yes, I
agree, Clarabelle," she said. "We females understand
each other. But we mustn't let *him* discover the impact
of—"

"Whose black eyes is that bird damning, little one?"

Katherine gasped and whirled. She was dismayed to
see Zach standing in the doorway, one shoulder
propped against the frame. He was wearing only his
trousers and his arms were crossed over his chest as he
surveyed her with a knowing look.

"Zach!" she exclaimed softly, wondering with embarrassment just how much he'd heard. "I thought you
were"—her gaze drifted to his bare, curly-haired
chest—"dressing."

"I stopped."

She managed to look into his amused eyes. "Why?"

He shrugged. "I want to know if you meant what
you said before your stableboy came to the door."

She frowned. "What did I say?"

An ironic smile touched the corners of his mouth.
"You said you wouldn't come east with me if I didn't
. . . ah, get off you."

She blushed and turned away to put the kettle on
for tea. And she knew that if she was reaching for tea
before her bath, then she was more troubled than
was healthy. "But you got off," she said to the tin of
tea.

"Does that mean you're going to come with me?"

"No." Oddly, the word clogged in her throat. Her
hands trembled as she spooned out the tea.

"I see. You haven't made up your mind yet." Actually, it seemed she had, but Zach would not take no for an answer. He'd simply allow her more time to get used to the idea. "Take as much time as you need. I still have several days before I have to head back, and I understand it's asking a lot for you to leave your practice and get a replace—"

"Zach!" She cut him off abruptly, spinning around, unable to listen any longer to the hurt in his hard, purposely toneless voice. When she turned and saw the dark flush on his face, the tension, she forced a tremulous smile to her lips. "You sprang this . . . news on me very late last night." He fixed his impenetrable eyes on her, and she found she could not deny him, yet. "I do need more time," she said wearily, then called herself a coward.

The tension eased out of his shoulders. "Truce?"

She drew in a shaky breath, hesitating. But how could she stay angry with him? Though he still emanated daunting heat and strength, he looked strangely vulnerable too. And after all, she and Zach had cared for each other long, long before now. Could he help it that he was an excessively male creature?

She smiled. "A truce," she said, "if you promise not to touch me."

He lifted a brow. Slowly, his gaze traveled over her, touching her everywhere, making her knees turn weak. "Did you know," he asked as he pushed away from the door frame and began to walk toward her, "that when you stand in the sunlight, I can see right through your gown?"

Hot blood leapt into her cheeks as he stopped inches in front of her. His wide palm cupped her chin, and he tilted her face up so he could see her eyes. "What more could a man ask for in the morning than to feast his eyes on such a beautiful body?" He trailed a finger over her full lower lip just before he angled his dark head to kiss her. But she pushed at his chest, feeling crisp hair and warm bare skin under her trembling fingertips.

"You didn't promise," she whispered, her heart pounding with both desire and alarm.

Amusement gleamed in his eyes. "And I'm not about to."

"Zach, you don't play fair."

"I never have."

She backed up a step, but he stalked her. Her mind searched frantically for a different approach. "You'll need salve on that cut."

He chuckled softly, seductively. "I never thanked you for stitching me up, sugar."

"No thanks needed," she said hastily, and backed right into Clarabelle's cage. The bird squawked, and at the same instant Katherine nearly fainted at the sight of a garishly painted face peering in at them from the window in the back door. "Birdie!" she gasped, and Clarabelle gasped too, as if recognizing the name.

Relieved at the distraction yet horrified at what Birdie must have witnessed, Katherine nearly stumbled over herself to get to the door. She flung it open, clutching the neck of her nightgown. Snow and wind flew into the cozy, warm kitchen. "Birdie McDowell, are you spying on me?"

Birdie looked insulted. She wore a lavender-and-pink hat jammed with an appalling concoction of flowers and birds, all of which bobbed when she tossed her head. "I beg your pardon, missy—and wouldn't if you weren't Irish!"

Katherine rolled her eyes. "Then why," she asked,

crossing her arms and tapping a bare foot, "were you peeking into my back window?"

Birdie cast a sly glance in Zach's direction, then she preened and pouted. "No one answered the front door. Your Injun feller told me you was in here, so I figured you were around back." She shrugged and touched her crimped orange hair, casting one more coquettish look at Zach. "But I didn't know you had a houseguest." She leaned forward and whispered, loud enough for Zach to hear, "And a very handsome, dashing houseguest at that!"

Flustered, Katherine started to explain. "Birdie, he was here for a visit last night—"

"I'll just bet he was. A very *long* visit, missy." She let her gaze skate meaningfully over Katherine's nightgown. "Did you both undress for this visit?"

Katherine went scarlet. She dared not glance at Zach, but could feel his amused gaze on her. "Birdie, obviously you are in perfect health, so may I ask why you're keeping me from my bath?"

Birdie's dyed eyebrows shot up. "He's going to watch you bathe?"

Katherine heard Zach's soft laughter behind her and gritted her teeth in frustration. Birdie was craning her neck to get a better look at him, one hand fluttering over her heart. "Are you Irish?" she asked him.

He shrugged.

"No matter," she said briskly. "I can spot an Irishman at twenty paces, and if I say you're Irish you are."

"Yes, ma'am," he drawled.

Birdie blushed and tapped Katherine on the arm. "Ooh," she cooed, "he's got manners! Ain't no one called me ma'am in a *very* long time."

Katherine clenched her teeth so hard, her jaw ached. "Birdie—"

"Ah, yes. Our poker game is tonight. Are ya comin', lass?"

"I can't. I have to head out to the reservation early."

"You always have one excuse after another," Birdie complained. "I wonder if you really know how to play poker at all!"

"She does," Zach said. Katherine closed her eyes and prayed she would soon wake up from this ridiculous dream. Here she stood in her nightgown in the middle of her kitchen discussing poker with an old woman and a half-naked man.

"What?" Birdie asked. "How do you know?"

"I taught her."

Birdie went all aflutter again and Katherine began to close the door. "We can talk later, Birdie."

"Wednesday night!" she cried. "Join our Wednesday night game! And bring Adonis with you!"

The door slammed on the last, but Katherine saw that Zach had heard her anyway. As if his supreme confidence had needed boosting!

"Poker?" he asked her.

She sighed. "For as long as I've been in Newberry, Birdie has been trying to persuade me to join her bi-weekly poker game." She picked up her towel and held it to her breasts, shielding them from his intrusive gaze. "Actually, it's a well-run operation with some of the local women sneaking out to a different house each game and telling their husbands—who visit the saloons and brothels—that they're participants in a literary circle. The husbands, eager to pursue their own night of gallivanting, buy the lie and let the wives go without protest." She shrugged and crossed the kitchen. "I don't even know who is in the group. But it might be fun, if I ever have the chance."

"Hmm." He watched her leave the kitchen and start down the hallway. "Hey, where are you going?"

"To get my wrapper, so you'll stop undressing me with your eyes. Grab a shirt, Captain, and meet me in my operating room."

They did, a few moments later. Zach got there first and was waiting for her, arms crossed over his chest as he leaned a hip against the table. As she'd requested he put his shirt on but had left it open with the shirttails out. He looked irresistible. Forcing her eyes away from his chest she went to the cabinet to fetch a jar of salve. "Ready?"

"I was just admiring your taste in decor," he said, and she turned to see he was looking at the skeleton in one corner.

"You like that?" she asked.

"Well, sure." He looked at her. "If you come across another one, could you save it for me?"

She laughed. "Male or female?"

"Female, of course."

"And that one? Can you tell me its gender?"

He grinned, the long groove cutting deep into his cheek. "Hell, anyone can see it's female."

Katherine was surprised. "How can you tell?"

"It would make a very short man."

"Well, you're right, but that's not generally a good measure." She went to the skeleton and touched its wide pelvic bones. "See? She's given birth. Men don't have these wide bones here. So the next time you're in the market for a skeleton, examine the bones carefully."

He shook his head. "This is a damn macabre topic, Smoke Eyes."

"You brought it up, Zach." She gestured to a chair. "You'll have to sit. I won't be able to apply this properly if I can't reach."

He lowered himself onto the chair and she stood in front of him, between his legs. Shrugging off the sense of déjà vu, she brushed his hair aside and cursed her trembling hands. "It's going to leave a scar, I think," she said, dabbing the salve on. She grinned at him. "What's one more?"

He grunted. "Is your home always like this?"

She pulled away to look at him. "What do you mean?"

"You could set up a social here. Don't you ever get any privacy?"

She shrugged and continued to apply the ointment. "A doctor's life is not her own. I like folks popping in any time. There's certainly never a dull moment. I suppose they're like my family since I don't have one of my own." The words were out before she could stop them. She hadn't meant to reveal so much to him, but when she glanced at his face and saw that he'd been studying her closely, she knew he'd already guessed. She stepped away, but he caught her by both wrists.

"Do you want one?" he asked softly.

"A family?" She smiled weakly. "No room in my life for a husband and babies. It would be a rare man to tolerate a doctor-wife, and the babies . . . Well . . ." In truth, she wanted babies, lots of babies, but it simply would never work. One needed a husband for babies and *that* arrangement would be intolerable. She loved her liberty above all things. She forced a jaunty grin to her lips. "Not to be," she said, then whisked away to set the jar of salve in the cabinet. "You," she added, "have got to go. My reputation will be in shreds if Birdie reveals what she saw this morning, and the later you leave the better chance someone has of seeing you."

He stood. "I'd like to come out to the reservation with you tomorrow."

Katherine's heart plummeted. She was hoping for a few days' reprieve from his dark, seductive power and keen eyes that watched her with the predatory quality of a hawk. "Why?"

"I'm curious. You always wanted to tend to your mother's people and I've never been to a reservation."

She wrinkled her nose. "Well, it's not an outing, but if you insist—"

"I don't." He walked over to her, and she had to tip her head back to meet his eyes. "I was hoping for an invitation." And he tapped her on the nose.

Flustered, she tried to ignore his affectionate touch. "You may accompany me if you keep your hands to yourself." At his cockeyed grin her lower lip thrust out in a pout. "You have to promise, Zach."

"I promise," he murmured. "Unless there's an emergency."

"Fair enough." She led him to the front door and he leaned down to kiss her cheek. Pleased by the tender gesture, she flushed. "Be here at dawn."

"What about today?" he asked as he buttoned his shirt.

"What *about* today?"

He quirked a brow. "Lunch? Dinner?"

She bit her lip to hide her smile. He looked so hopeful, she didn't want to say no. "We'll see. I'd really like to take that bath that's been waiting for me."

"Hmm. I'd like to see you take it too."

She ignored that. "I'll see you later."

He grabbed his coat and shrugged into it, while she peeked out the curtained window to see if any townsfolk were about. "Is the coast clear?"

The nautical expression puzzled her, but she deciphered it. "No one is about." As she swung the front door open, though, she saw what she'd missed from the window. The Gormen sisters—two of her dear friends—were standing on the front porch. When they saw Zach, they gasped in unison. He grinned down at them, pouring on that formidable charm, then loped off down the snowy road. They stared after him until he disappeared from view.

"Who was *that*?" wide-eyed Lisa asked, turning at last to Katherine.

Katherine tried to ignore the little stab at Lisa's obvious admiration for Zach. She'd never felt jealous over a man in her life, and it panged her that she did for Zach. "An old friend," she said casually.

Lisa and her sister Cynthia shared a meaningful look. "He doesn't look old to me," Lisa said. "In fact, he looks positively young and virile!"

"Is he married?" Cynthia asked.

A frown of annoyance flickered across Katherine's brow. "No. But he's not staying in town for long either."

Lisa poked her head in the door. "But he stayed here last night."

Katherine sighed as she invited them in. "There was a blizzard," she explained, as if they didn't know. "It would have been hazardous to send him home in the storm."

The sisters exchanged another knowing look, then they were inside in a flurry of wraps and chatter, stamping their feet on the mat by the door. The two women often reminded Katherine of china dolls, with their golden hair and wide clear blue eyes, and animated pretty faces. They were delightful women, and loved to share anecdotes and naughty tales with Katherine, all of them trying to top one another.

"I'm sure," Cynthia said as she hung up her coat, "he must be a very old friend if you didn't mind parading around in your nightgown in front of him."

Katherine's face flamed scarlet as the two sisters giggled. "I was not parading around!" she said, dismayed to realize that was exactly what she'd done. Strange, but the familiarity that had been established between her and Zach when they were younger had taken on another form. Oh, they were familiar all right, with much more than each other's personalities!

Her telltale blush made the two women break into fresh peals of laughter. "Well, he certainly didn't seem to mind, did he, Cynthia?" Lisa asked. "In fact, the way he was grinning, I think he *preferred* seeing the doctor in her nightgown."

"Stop, you two!" Katherine admonished, so flustered she tripped over the rug as she started walking backward to the kitchen. "I didn't realize you were such unmerciful teases!"

They laughed gleefully.

"You'll have to make yourselves comfortable in here for a few moments while I hurry and take my bath," she added when she reached the kitchen doorway. "I'll have to add more hot water as I'm sure what is in the tub has become cool by now."

"Oh. He kept you busy enough to ignore your bath, hmm?" Cynthia winked at her sister.

Katherine lifted her chin. "I refuse to listen to this any longer."

Lisa laughed. "All right, we'll stop . . . for now. But Katherine—"

She turned back to look at her friends.

"On our way here we learned that the sheriff has jailed a suspect for the murder of Richard Waters."

Katherine's heart pounded. "Who?"

"His son. Toby Waters."

"His son?" Katherine blanched. She thought of the pale, thin boy who had clenched his fists when she'd told him and his mother of his father's murder.

"The knife belongs to Toby," Cynthia said. "It really doesn't surprise me. That boy is a wild one."

Something didn't fit, though. Katherine didn't know what it was exactly, but she felt an inexplicable qualm run through her. She had to get to the jail as soon as possible.

Seven

Fortified by two strong cups of chamomile tea, Katherine hurried up the road toward the jail. The day was dazzling, clear and cold and dry with the sun shining, the snow sparkling. Lisa and Cynthia walked halfway with her, then they parted company. She was nearing the jail when she saw Zach stepping out of the telegraph office.

He was as magnificent as ever, all shoulders and long legs, wearing a red-and-black plaid wool shirt under his peacoat. His hair, brushed back off his forehead, shone like a raven's wing. She hadn't wanted to run into him again so soon, not with the memory of the things he'd done to her on the sofa that morning still bright and clear in her mind. Hoping for a peaceful respite to the churning emotions inside her, she stepped up her pace, only to hear him call out in that rough, husky voice that fired her nerves.

"Hey, Doc!"

She turned to watch him lope toward her. He flashed his brash pirate's smile, his white teeth so startling in his dark, handsome face. He looked much less weary than he had the day before. "You aren't avoiding me, are you?"

"What makes you say that?" she asked, but she heard the knowing in his chuckle.

He slipped a hand under her elbow as she continued on. "Had your bath?" he asked politely.

She looked up at him, startled. He wore his usual devilish grin. "Yes," she said.

Obviously, she thought, he'd bathed too—and shaved—for the clean scent of his shaving soap drifted to her, along with the warm musk smell of his body. Staring up at him like a smitten schoolgirl, Katherine felt hot and weak and wanted to run. Despite her wildly thrumming heart, she managed to ask, "Did you send a telegraph?"

His face sobered and he shoved his hands into his jacket pockets. "Yes. To home, to Dorrie, Drew's nanny. She sent a message to me as she did in Harper City, keeping me posted on Drew's condition."

Katherine swallowed. "Everything well?"

"As well as can be expected." He bit off the words, then ran a hand over his face. "I know he'll be waiting for word on your decision."

She felt a twinge of guilt and touched his arm gently. "Please, Zach. We talked about it this morning."

"I know," he said gruffly, and squinted out against

the sun glare. He was silent for a moment, then looked at her again. "So, what are we doing today?"

"We?" she asked, raising her brows.

He nodded, oddly serious.

"Well," she said, "I wouldn't think you'd want to, but I'm headed for the jail."

He swore softly and saw that the jailhouse was just ahead of them. "What the hell for?"

She grinned, her eyes twinkling with impish merriment. "Zach, don't tell me you're skittish about jailhouses now!"

He swore again, and she laughed delightedly. "Hell, no, I'm just afraid if I see that lamebrained sheriff again I might kill him."

"Speak of the devil," she murmured. Sheriff Bates had just stepped outside for a smoke. He stood on the top step rolling a cigarette, using his big belly as a shelf for the papers. When they blew away, he cursed, then cursed even louder when he saw Katherine and Zach.

"Hello, Sheriff!" Katherine called, deliberately putting herself between the two men as she climbed the jailhouse steps. "I heard you arrested a suspect."

"Think he got the right one this time, sugar?" Zach whispered to her, but loud enough for the sheriff to hear.

Bates's chest puffed up. "Damn right we do. Found the suspect's knife in his own father's back. And it ain't no secret the kid hated his pa, ain't no secret 't'all."

Zach frowned as he turned to Katherine. "His own *son?*"

"Toby's only a suspect." She glanced at the sheriff. "Right, Sheriff? I mean, innocent until proven guilty, correct?"

The sheriff grumbled something under his breath. "Doc, you come to make trouble?"

Katherine smiled sweetly. "Only if you think asking

questions is trouble." The sheriff *harumphed* and she continued. "I've come to talk to Toby."

Bates's small eyes widened. "What th—" He was visibly flustered and ran a hand over his hair. "Don't tell me yer going to try an' spring this one too!" He paled when Zach's icy black eyes narrowed on him.

Katherine was already walking past him, heading for the door. "I assume Tom is in there to let me into Toby's cell?"

"Aw, *I'll* let you in," Bates said, and hurried ahead of her, eager to put a distance between him and Zach.

The interior of the jailhouse was dank and dim. When Katherine's eyes adjusted to the fainter light, she saw Tom standing against a far wall, his gaze locked on Zach.

"Uh, Sheriff," was all he could manage, his Adam's apple bobbing in his throat. He still sported a swollen eye and a bruised lip.

Zach's gaze shifted from the sheriff to the cringing deputy, then back to the sheriff. "I think I'll wait outside," he said.

Both men looked relieved.

"Guess you should join him while I talk to Toby," Katherine said.

"But—but, Doc . . .," the sheriff stammered.

"It's only fair, don't you think, Sheriff, that Toby and I are granted some privacy." Peripherally, she saw Toby Waters in his cell watching them in his close, narrow way.

The sheriff grumbled something about waiting in the back room, but Tom, his gait hesitant, went to join Zach out front.

As the sheriff took the keys from the peg he threw Toby a hard look. "You pull anything, son, I'll have you tarred and feathered, unnerstand?"

Toby sneered at him and Katherine frowned. "Really, Sheriff," she murmured for his ears only, "what can he 'pull' with three men surrounding the jail?"

The sheriff turned to look at her. "Only two I can be sure of to help with the law."

Katherine was becoming exasperated with his attitude toward Zach. "Zach would guard me with his life."

Bates just grumbled some more. "He's got a mean temper."

"Only when provoked."

The sheriff started to scowl at her but couldn't meet her eyes. He hitched up his pants and went to unlock the cell. Then he paused. "I think I'll just let the two of you talk between bars. Much safer." He glanced at Katherine. "Doc, ten minutes. I'll be in the back room."

Both she and Toby watched him amble off, then Toby's harsh laughter brought Katherine's glance his way. He was looking at her, his pale eyes glittering queerly in his hard, angry face. "Incompetent old windbag, ain't he?"

The word *incompetent* surprised her. Obviously, she mused, he was a bright youth in a dire situation. She studied his tall, thin frame and thought of the previous morning, when she'd delivered the news of his father's murder. He hadn't looked shocked or frightened or grief-stricken then. Anger had been the only emotion she'd seen on his face. And it was the only emotion she saw now. "Is it true, Toby, that the knife in your father's back belongs to you?"

The boy looked bored. "Doc, what're you wastin' your time for?" His voice was a kind of nasal whine. "You know damn well the sheriff has me tried and convicted."

Even smarter than she realized. She knew Toby only from sight; she had seen him on the streets—an unlikable boy with a well-deserved infamous reputation. He drank liquor, bullied children, taunted old folks, and was a thief. His friends were drunkards, scoundrels, loafers, and wastrels. No one could understand it. His father had been the wealthiest man in Newberry, his mother quiet and gentle and beautiful. He was an only child and had everything a boy could want. He'd been behind bars before, jailed for misdemeanors, and seemed comfortable with his incarceration now.

But Katherine was not. She looked at him calmly and asked, "Did you kill your father, Toby?"

He flinched. The bald question stunned him, but he was quick to mask his shock. His upper lip lifted in his customary sneer. "You think I should admit to that? What if I did, Doc?" He shrugged his narrow shoulders. "What if I did?" He repeated it like a litany, with all the emotion gone out of his voice. "Maybe I had every reason in the world to kill him."

Though Katherine felt something cold slither through her, she kept her tone and gaze level. "That's not what I asked you." When his eyes narrowed, she repeated, "Did you kill your father?"

"What difference does it make who killed him? He's dead, isn't he?"

Cold words. Hollow words. He uttered them emptily, without a trace of bereavement. She watched him drop to his cot, hanging his head as he stared at the floor. Squelching the icy shudder that ran through her, she gripped the cell bars and forced herself to speak. "It does make a difference, Toby, if you hang for the murder of your father when someone else killed him."

He shrugged. She wished the sheriff had opened the cell door, for she wanted to shake some sense into the boy. But he looked as though he didn't care one way or another whether or not he died.

"Toby, Dusty was killed too."

He looked up, his pale eyes glittering, then he laughed harshly. "A whore! So, you saying I killed her too?"

"I'm not accusing you of anything. But I think it's important to realize that there were two murders committed."

"And you're trying to figure if the killer was after my father or the trollop." He sneered at her again. "Well, I don't know who killed him, but I do know my father deserved it."

Katherine felt as though he'd punched her in the chest. To feel that his own father deserved to be murdered! She could scarcely breathe, and shuddered as a slow, ugly smile spread across Toby's bony face.

"I wish I had, you know that, Doc? I wish I had killed him." He watched her, probably expecting her to gasp in shock.

She only asked softly, almost wonderingly, "Why, Toby? Why did you want him dead?"

He opened his mouth, then clamped it shut and stared at the floor once more. "I hated him," he whispered, his voice raw, pain-filled. He ducked his head lower, between his arms, but not before she glimpsed the twisted mask of torment on his face. "I don't want to talk about him, Doc."

"Toby, you have to. Please, I'll help you in any way I can."

He snorted his disdain. "Christ, are you naive!" He jerked his head up to glare at her. "Don't you understand? This town *wants* me to be the killer! The sheriff is only catering to their hopes. They hate me, just like they hated, but worshiped, my father, and now they're getting back at him through me."

"Toby, you're a smart boy. And I know you think this is a hopeless situation, but please, you must talk to me so I can help you. *Why* did you want your father dead?"

He looked away from her again. "Because of what he did to my mother."

Icy dread washed through Katherine. "What did he do?"

Toby clenched his fists, his teeth. His entire body went rigid. "He tortured her. He beat her, locked her up and kept her prisoner." His voice broke, but he straightened his hunched-over shoulders and continued talking to the floor. "I don't care what the law says, it isn't right. My father was smart and well-groomed and rich—you know how rich. He traveled all over the country—even to Europe—and impressed everyone. And when he smiled he could get *anyone* to do what he wanted. Except me."

He stopped, his fists clenched so tight his knuckles were bleached white. He was lost in his private horror, and Katherine could only grasp the cold steel bars, wanting to put her hand on his shoulder, comfort him. But Toby, she knew, would recoil from her touch. She watched him run both hands through his blond hair until the short curls stood up in tufts.

"Bastard," he whispered as if his throat hurt. "The bastard. He broke my ma. He broke her." He suddenly looked at her, and she sucked in her breath at the raw torment in his gaze. "He used to put a gun to her head and force her to bend to his will. Maybe the gun was loaded, maybe it wasn't, but God knows, it was enough of a threat. For a while—when I was very little—I remember her begging him to stop, to think of what he was doing to the boy—me. Poor Ma."

Toby buried his face in his hands. "I could never protect her. I hated myself for that. I still do. All those times we thought he'd changed—he'd be in a good mood for a while and buy us things—but later we realized it was just because he'd acquired another mistress and somehow that got him feeling generous. But those generous times were never for long. He'd start over again and it would be worse than before."

Toby ran his hands up and down his face and his shoulders shook, but he shed no tears. Katherine guessed he'd cried his last tears long ago. When he brought his hands down from his face, his eyes were almost colorless, haunted and bleak. He stared at her as if he'd forgotten she'd been standing there and had heard his story. The hard, cold look came over his face again, along with his leering, practiced smile.

"So, there you have it, Doc. My confession. Why I hated my father and wished him dead long before yesterday."

Katherine was silent, sickened and horrified by his story, his life. And his mother's. True, Toby was a shyster, and his story could have been fabricated, but to what purpose? Clearly he felt he had nothing to lose by his imprisonment, and he'd not once denied having killed his father. In fact, he had declared that he wished he *had* killed him.

"You didn't kill him," she said. Her words were firm and decisive, and she saw him jump. An odd sheen entered his eyes, almost like tears, but he swallowed hard and snorted, shattering the illusion.

"Doc, you're a fool."

"And I'm going to get you out of here."

He hung his head and rubbed the back of his neck. "A crazy fool," he added, but his tone lacked conviction.

Katherine was more certain than ever that he was innocent. "The murder weapon was yours."

"Doc, don't try to get me out. It's pointless."

"Who do you think got hold of your knife?"

He shrugged. "Anyone who knows me knows

about my knife collection. That one is a Viking dagger. It was my favorite. My father brought it back for me from Europe. I—" He dropped his head again, and she was startled to see that he looked shy. "I love history, and especially Viking history. Once I wrote a report on Viking weapons for Miss Harris, the schoolteacher, and I brought in some weapons to show the other pupils. They loved it and asked me all kinds of questions. But Miss Harris, the old sourpuss, failed me. Said the report wasn't in on time, though it was only a day late. Lots of kids handed in late reports and she only marked off one grade." He gritted his teeth and his skin pulled taut over his facial bones. "She doesn't like me much." He laughed shortly. "Not many folks do." A sudden wistful look crossed his face. "But that knife cost a damn fortune."

He looked at her again, and Katherine saw by the stark flash of vulnerability in his gaze that he recognized the fortune had signified much more than money. "So I don't know how you think you're going to spring me, Doc. All the evidence points to me. Who in the hell is going to believe my father was capable of such cruelty or deprived Ma and me of anything? Just look at our house and everything in it. He was too clever. And the knife *is* mine."

"Never mind all that," she said. "We won't make it easy on the sheriff, will we, Toby? He'll have to find the *real* killer. I'll make certain of it."

His mouth moved in a fractional smile. "Why, Doc? Why do you care a hang about me? I've never been nothing but trouble."

She grinned. "I was never anything but trouble either."

He hooted. "You?"

"Me. Now, Toby, you'll have to help me with this.

Do you know anyone who would want to kill your father?"

His face became shuttered again. "Lots of folks. But I won't name any names. Maybe it was just one of the other whores."

"But how would she have acquired your knife?"

He shrugged. "I could have left it anywhere."

"Did you carry it around with you?"

"No, not really." He ran a hand over his eyes. "Doc, I just don't know. Why don't you get that damned sheriff to ask these questions?"

"Perfect suggestion, Toby. I will." She turned toward the back room. "And, incidentally, I'm going to have that sourpuss schoolteacher send you your lessons."

"Lessons!" He looked appalled. "I haven't been to school in weeks!"

"A waste. You're a bright boy, Toby, and it's high time you did something with that brain other than saturating it with liquor."

He snorted as she disappeared around the corner to fetch the sheriff. She almost ran into him, for he was heading out of the back room. Before he could open his mouth she said, "He didn't do it."

"What?"

"Toby did not kill his father."

The sheriff looked badgered. "Aw, now, Doc, don't start this again."

"But he didn't. I'm sure of it."

Bates peered at her. "Have you become a sleuth all of a sudden?"

"You need to find out who else could have obtained Toby's knife, what the motive was, where Toby was at the time of the murder, and who would frame Toby."

"Frame!"

"That's right. The knife was left in Waters's back. For heaven's sake, Sheriff, that knife is so distinctive it didn't take you long to learn who owned it. Why would Toby set himself up like that?"

"Cuz he's the devil's own son. He likes the idea of shocking folks, and this is just another way to do that."

Though some doubt crept in, Katherine pushed it to the back of her mind. "The boy deserves a fair trial. More investigation is needed, Sheriff. Regardless of the fact that folks are relieved you've jailed him."

He scowled at her. "You know, Doc, you're becomin' a thorn in my side."

She didn't dispute that. "And I'm having the teacher send him his lessons."

His mouth fell open. *"What?"*

"That's right. He needs to keep up with his studies." She turned, starting to head out.

"This ain't a damn schoolroom!" he protested, following her.

"Your prisoner is sixteen years old. You'll have to make some accommodations." She hid her smile when he cursed.

"You know, Doc, if this goes to court, you'll have to testify in Denver."

She turned suddenly to look up at him. "From the start, Sheriff, I thought this looked like a frame, a setup. Now I'm positive." Though she wasn't, not entirely. But if she expressed any doubt about Toby's innocence, she would lose her credibility with the sheriff. She pressed her point. "It would be a worse crime than the murder itself to see that boy hang from the end of a rope when he's innocent."

Bates looked both angry and flustered. "Dammit, Doc! D'ya have to use such strong language? I'll give the kid a fair shake. I just think he did it, that's all."

"You thought Zach did it too."

Bates growled. "An' he still might have fer all I know." But he snapped his mouth shut when they rounded the corner and came into Toby's view.

"I'll have those lessons sent up later today!" she called to Toby, and both the sheriff and the boy grumbled. She said good-bye and opened the door to see both Zach and Tom at the bottom of the steps—shaking hands! Her eyes widened, then widened some more when she heard Zach's low, rough voice.

"Apology accepted. But don't let your boss know. I want him to feel some remorse for holding a gun on me and arresting me in the first place."

Tom grinned sheepishly. "Sure thing."

When Zach turned to Katherine, her heart jumped—again. "Ready, sugar?"

Katherine blushed at the endearment, avoiding Tom's knowing glance. They both jumped when the sheriff barked from inside the jailhouse. "Deputy!"

Tom was up the steps in one leap.

"Remember," Zach said, "tell him I'm rip-roarin' furious and plan to sue the entire town."

Tom laughed, then winced, pressing his thumb to his bruised lip. "And you'll deal with him in private."

Zach grinned. "Right."

Tom went into the jail trying to hide his smile. Katherine turned to Zach. "What mischief are you brewing now?" she asked.

"No more than Bates deserves. And it wasn't the deputy's fault he knocked my head open—he was just following an idiot's orders." He held her elbow as they walked away from the jail. "Did you make him mad?"

"I think I did."

"Good. And do you really think he's got the wrong suspect jailed—again?"

"Yes," she murmured, and told him Toby's story. Zach shook his head.

"I don't know, Smoke Eyes," he said, frowning. "Maybe you ought to let the sheriff handle this one."

She glared up at him. "How can you say that! How can I just leave Toby in there at the sheriff's mercy? The boy has no one to defend him. Even you just called the sheriff an idiot!"

Zach's lips tightened. He stopped to frown down at her, his hands resting on his lean hips. "He is an idiot, but that boy has a history. Let the deputy, at least, do his job. I'm sure he'll investigate even if Bates doesn't." He didn't say what was really gnawing at him—that Toby could keep her there, that she, compassionate soul that she was, could become so embroiled in this murder that it would keep her from traveling east with him. The very notion scared him spitless.

But Katherine was incensed. Her eyes flashed up at him. "I'm *not* sure Tom will investigate. You know he's the sheriff's lackey!"

"Ah. But don't you think the day is too beautiful to be wastin', darlin'?" His eyes softened, and he reached out to stroke her face. When she stepped back, confused and irritated, he only smiled at her. "Where are we going now, sweetheart?"

He was so good at this! Katherine thought. He could turn the tables so easily, so neatly, that she hadn't a leg left to stand on. All he had to do was touch her—with his gaze, his voice, his hands—and she melted. It terrified her. "I—" She swallowed, and his fingers drifted down her slender throat. She caught his wrist and sent him a pleading look. "Zach, please . . ."

"Please what, darlin'?"

She pushed his hand away again and glowered at him. "Please call me by my given name," she improvised, frowning with annoyance.

"I only asked you where we're headed next," he said, laughter lurking in his eyes and voice.

She lifted her small chin. It was time to take a stand. "*I'm* going to the schoolhouse to talk with the schoolteacher." Though she tried to make her voice firm and decisive, it seemed oddly soft and husky.

He smiled crookedly. "I asked where *we're* going, sweetheart."

She made a deliberate point of looking around, to both sides of her and behind her, then met his eyes again. "Funny, I don't see anyone here named Sweetheart." She lifted an eyebrow. "Do you?"

He laughed. "Ah, honey." His arm snaked around her waist, and he pulled her close. "There hasn't been a dull moment since I set eyes on you." He lowered his head and captured her mouth with his own, full and hard and wonderful. Breathless, Katherine pushed at his chest with her fist, but he had already stepped away, wicked amusement filling his eyes. He cast her that devilish grin. "God, you're beautiful."

She struggled to get her breath back. "Zach, you must stop this."

His faint smile was self-deprecating. "Far as I can tell, Smoke Eyes, I've hardly started anything . . . yet."

Katherine stood frozen under his compelling gaze. Then she heard a horse's soft whinny, a man call out to a neighbor, and the spell was broken. She whirled away.

"I'm going now," she said hastily.

"Then I'm going too," he said, falling into step beside her.

She stopped, sighing in defeat. "Since you're so intent on joining me, why don't you go back to my house and tell Shadow to hitch Hippo up to the sleigh. I have to ride out to Fish Walker's claim and check his son who has the croup. I can't see why you'd want to come along. It's boring, routine stuff."

"Who could resist wanting to see a man called Fish? Or a horse named Hippo?"

She bit her lip to hide her smile. "Short for Hippocrates."

"Ah." He slanted a glance at her. "And I have no intention of missing any opportunity to share close quarters with you, Smoke Eyes."

Her stomach cartwheeled. Rogue! she thought, but still she couldn't stop her flush of pleasure. She started off again toward the school. "If Shadow doesn't trust you with the sleigh, tell him to fetch me at the schoolhouse," she called over her shoulder.

Zach watched her walk away. His stomach muscles clenched tight, and before anything more could tighten, he strode off in the opposite direction.

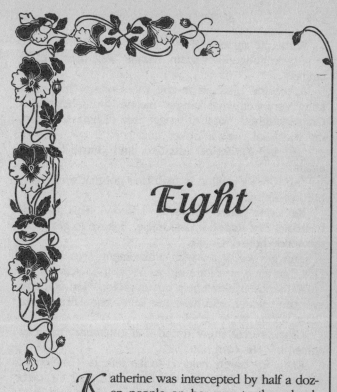

Eight

*K*atherine was intercepted by half a dozen people on her way to the schoolhouse, all expressing their relief at the arrest of Toby Waters.

"Don't surprise me none" seemed to be the favorite phrase among the townsfolk, and she found it difficult to keep her irritation in check. It was almost a relief when Gracie, one of the "girls" from Nellie's brothel, greeted her with, "Holy crow, Doc, would I like a man like that in my bed!" Gracie had caught sight of Zach with Katherine just minutes before, and she nudged Katherine with an elbow, grinning slyly. "How'd *you* get so lucky, eh?"

Katherine sighed. "He's a friend."

Gracie nudged her again. "Hmm? Well, friends can't tangle?"

Katherine blushed to the roots of her hair. She knew very well what "tangle" meant! Noting her blush, Gracie laughed. "Well, if ya get tired of him, send him my way. Gol', he's a looker, ain't he?"

"He is," Katherine admitted, and Gracie laughed again.

"An' I bet a stallion in bed. He's got that way about him, ya know?"

Katherine gritted her teeth. "I know." This was unbearable. She stepped past Gracie. "I have to get on to the schoolhouse, Gracie."

The girl eyed her with amusement. "No offense, Doc, but ain't ya a little old to be goin' to school?"

Katherine couldn't help but laugh too. "I'm going to visit the teacher, and have her send school lessons to Toby Waters while he's in jail."

Gracie's eyes grew round and solemn. "Ain't that somethin'? His own son . . ."

Katherine barely held on to her temper. How could people malign Toby, convict him, before all the facts were in? "I'm not so sure he did it," she said, and Gracie's eyes grew even rounder.

"Are you sayin' the killer's still runnin' loose?"

"I'm not saying anything but that Toby deserves a fair hearing like anyone else."

"Oh, I agree, Doc!" Gracie darted a quick look around. "You know," she whispered, leaning close to Katherine, "word in Nellie's is that the murderer might have been after Dusty. Folks get crazy ideas 'bout us girls, you know." Her face looked white and pinched. "We're all worried it could be one of us next."

Katherine searched the frightened girl's face. "Gracie, did Richard Waters visit Nellie's often?"

"Very often."

A new idea struck her. "And how did he treat the girls?"

"Well, he paid plenty, but I never did go for what he wanted in the bedroom. He liked to hurt women. You know. Tie them up and hurt them." She paled suddenly and shrank back. "Oh, no, Doc. It weren't one of us whores who killed him!"

She went on hurriedly, as if she feared Katherine might take her suspicions to the sheriff.

"You know, Waters had lots of paramours—lots of women in this town you might never suspect. He was a charmer, ooh, was he!" She guided Katherine under the eave of a building, into its shadow. "He used to tell us about them, about how he'd fool them and juggle two, three, and four women at a time. He'd take the younger ones to Denver or California or Washington. He was rich and important and women found him irresistible." She spoke earnestly, quickly, lest Katherine run off without hearing it all. "And he had plenty of enemies in business too. Ah, God, the things he used to tell us! Men hated him, but respected and admired him." She shook her blond head. "Seems to me there're more than just a handful of suspects the sheriff should be talkin' to. Even if the knife was his kid's."

"Mmm," Katherine murmured. She was convinced Gracie was speaking the truth. "Maybe you ought to tell the sheriff all this."

Gracie looked worried. "But if I do he'll want to question all of us, and I don't want any of us girls behind bars."

"I'm sure you don't. But he should question you all anyway, and if you're all innocent there's nothing to worry about, is there?"

"Mmm, I suppose. . . ."

Katherine smiled reassuringly at her. "You'll do fine,

Gracie. At least you'll let the sheriff know how many people could have wanted to kill Richard Waters." She stepped back out into the sunshine. "I really must hurry now. I've got to talk to the teacher and it looks like the children are out to recess." A glimmer of amusement lit her gaze. "I bet that's one woman Richard Waters didn't tangle with."

Gracie smirked and poked her shoulder. "And that's one bet you'd lose."

Katherine gasped. "Gracie! Surely you jest!"

Gracie shrugged. "Rumor had it that he courted her. I don't know what happened beyond that, Doc." She laughed. "It *is* a ridiculous picture now, ain't it? That lemon-puss and Richard Waters." She shrugged again. "But I dunno. He could make any woman feel beautiful."

Frowning, freshly disturbed, Katherine made her way to the schoolhouse. The children were having a snowball fight in the schoolyard and she smiled, memories of her own school days flooding her mind. Boys and girls called out to her, and she smiled and waved, then reached down to scoop up some snow and pack a snowball of her own. She couldn't resist. She hurled it at Tommy Bates, then dashed up the steps to the door, not caring in the least about her dignity. Inside, she paused for a moment, waiting for her eyes to adjust. When they did she saw Miss Harris staring reprovingly at her, her lips pinched tight. She had been at the blackboard, writing the primer spelling words, when Katherine's ungracious entrance interrupted her.

"Dr. Flynn," she said tautly.

Katherine felt reprimanded, felt hurtled back in time to when she'd been a less than exemplary student in Harper City. She swallowed her smile and kept a straight face as she nodded at Emilee Harris. "Miss Harris."

The teacher stiffened and began to fuss with books and papers on her desk. She watched Katherine walk toward her, and her hands stilled. Behind her round spectacles, her hazel eyes were humorless. "What can I do for you, Doctor?"

Katherine smiled at her, hoping for a smile in return, but it seemed the teacher did not know how to smile. "I've come to ask you to put some lessons together for Toby Waters. He's in jail, you know."

Miss Harris's mouth pinched even tighter. "Yes," she said, looking down her nose at Katherine. "I know."

Katherine scanned the blackboard, then the children's desks. Every item in the classroom was in perfect order. The floor was swept, the desks and heater polished till gleaming, and the air smelled of paper and chalk dust. Miss Harris, it seemed, ran a tight ship. She met the teacher's expressionless stare, then raised a brow. "Well? Will you have them ready by the end of the school day? The deputy will come down and pick them up."

Although her posture was already painfully erect, Miss Harris straightened even more. "I will not send lessons to that despicable boy."

Katherine's brows drew together. "You must. Sheriff's orders."

The teacher gave her a humorless smile. "That fool."

Did Bates have any inkling of the town's low opinion of him? Katherine wondered. She doubted it, but then, even if the sheriff knew, he would shrug the townspeople off as a collective bunch of ignoramuses.

She sighed and stepped back to perch on the edge of a desk. "Miss Harris," she said reasonably, "what possible objection could you have to sending Toby his lessons? You look like a dedicated teacher, and that boy is very bright. He needs to be reading and mastering skills that will get him through life."

"That boy," Miss Harris said as if she spoke of an offensive smell, "is beyond help. He hasn't been to school in weeks, Doctor, and before that he only came sporadically. He is one obnoxious young man, a disruptive, disorderly hellion who terrorized not only the younger students, but me." She fixed her glittering gaze on Katherine's face. "And don't," she added haughtily, "even attempt to flatter *me*. I am fully aware of how dedicated I am and I feel every student deserves a chance to succeed—within reason. Toby Waters is not within reason."

Hot anger swam through Katherine's blood, and she jumped to her feet. "I was not flattering you, Miss Harris, but merely stating what I thought was fact. I stand corrected. You are not the dedicated teacher I'd hoped. If you were, you would see just how bright and eager to learn Toby is. His family background is unfortunate and a strong reason for his behavior."

The teacher's fingers tightened around the spine of a book. "I beg your pardon, Doctor. Toby Waters is responsible for his own behavior. He comes from a solid and privileged background."

And his father courted you, Katherine thought, peering closer at the teacher, so close that Miss Harris shrank back. "Ah," she said softly, "you might think so. But I've heard quite a different story."

The teacher drew in a long, steady breath through her nostrils. "If you believe that boy, you've been fooled. He is a holy terror, and his father told me—" She cut herself off abruptly.

Katherine's eyes narrowed, and Miss Harris almost flinched at her disconcerting gaze. "You spoke to Richard Waters about Toby, Miss Harris?"

She bristled and puckered her lips. "Why, yes, of

course. He came to the school to discuss his son's behavioral problems in the classroom."

"Hmm. That's funny. It doesn't seem like Mr. Waters would have taken that sort of interest in his son."

Miss Harris gave her a superior look. "That goes to show you just how little you knew—anyone knew—about Richard."

"And you did, Miss Harris?"

She held her head high. "I knew him better than most. Does that surprise you, Doctor?"

Katherine shrugged. "Not really." Though it did. "I understand Richard Waters had a way with women."

"You understand nothing," she said angrily. "Our relationship was not a sordid one."

"I wonder if his wife thought that."

"His wife . . ." Her mouth quivered, and she closed her eyes. Katherine saw her hands tremble on the book she held. When she opened her eyes again, they looked glazed. "I know it might be hard to believe, Dr. Flynn, but I loved Richard Waters. He told me he and his wife had an understanding. They were free to live separate lives, but would stay married for the sake of that wretched boy. He would have left his wife if not for that boy."

Katherine stared at her. The unfortunate, misled woman actually believed that. "Miss Harris," she said softly, "I think Richard Waters was a master of deceit. He was a distinguished, successful man, but a cruel one, a twisted one." She continued to speak, even though Miss Harris shook her head. "You must know that he frequented brothels and had many mistresses."

Miss Harris made a choked sound and reached for her lace-trimmed handkerchief, then dabbed at her nose. "I loved him," she whispered, and Katherine felt her stomach turn in a sickening flop. How could one man hurt so many people? Watching Emilee Harris now, dabbing at her tears, she recalled Gracie's words. *He could make any woman feel beautiful.*

"I'm sorry he hurt you, Emilee," she said softly. "It's easy to fall for a man like that."

Emilee crushed her damp handkerchief in one hand and pressed her thin lips together. But her voice was still broken. "He told me lies . . . said I was the only one." The sound of children's voices, laughing and calling to one another in the schoolyard, floated into the classroom. The noise seemed to sober her. "Richard *was* special," she said, her voice stronger. "But all that is in the past now, isn't it?" She stuffed her handkerchief into her satchel. "Now I must call the children in. Their recess has been long extended." She sent Katherine an accusatory look.

Katherine bristled. How quickly the woman's moods could change! Well, she supposed the teacher felt she must maintain her prim image in order for her to gain respect. She let out a pent-up breath, and told Miss Harris that Tom would come by at the end of the day for Toby's lessons. The schoolteacher did not respond. She dismissed Katherine with an abrupt "Good day," and turned to continue writing on the board.

As soon as she stepped out into the sunlight, Katherine was pelted with snowballs. She let out a surprised shriek, then ducked and scooped up a handful of snow, slapping together her own weapon. But snowballs flew at her from every direction. They smacked her shoulders and back, arms and chest, and just as she was wiping snow from her eyelashes, she glanced ahead and saw Zach coasting up in her dashing red cutter.

She flew toward the sleigh, dodging snowballs and laughing with the children, even as snow slid inside her coat and down her back. "You little urchins!" she called. "I'll get you for this!"

The children merely came at her in full force, hurling their weapons indiscriminately. They rained down on Zach's head and shoulders too. "Holy—" he swore good-naturedly, as Katherine climbed into the sleigh and took shelter under the buffalo lap robe. "What the hell did you start, Smoke Eyes?"

The sleigh was off with a jolt. It sped over the glistening white snow as the children's laughter faded behind them. The wind was in their faces, and Katherine was tossed against Zach, gasping for breath while she wiped at the snow that clung to her hair. "Zach!" she said, still laughing. "Wrong way! You're going the wrong way!"

He glanced down at her and grinned, and Katherine thought that nothing could take her breath away like Zach's grin. He stopped the sleigh, wrapping the reins around the brake handle. Only then did she realize how intimately she was nestled against his warm, hard body. Her breath came light and shallow as her eyes locked on his. She glanced to his hair and saw the snow melting in it, making it glisten. Swallowing the ache in her throat she said huskily, "The other direction. You have to turn west." She caught a hint of laughter in his eyes.

"Your hand is on my thigh."

It was. She felt his muscles flex, and jerked her hand back as if stung. But it was too late. Zach's lips were on hers, his tongue curling into her mouth, stroking deep. She clung to his shoulders, shaking. She went weak and wild, her body scorching hot in the frigid day. Fire seared her veins, filling her with the sweet, sharp ache of desire.

His tongue danced against hers, its sensual, demanding thrusts somehow igniting her core. Waves of pleasure swept through her from her breasts to her loins as Zach went on kissing her, tasting her sweetness, as if he had all the time in the world.

She didn't fight him; she couldn't. She wound her arms around his neck and twined her fingers in his soft, thick hair. He groaned and released her mouth, but only to string fire kisses along the length of her throat and under her jaw. A purr of pleasure escaped her lips and she tipped her head back, allowing his heat, his flame, to consume her. She cupped his jaw, feeling his mouth move upon her skin, feeling his tongue taste her. She was melting, dissolving into him, nearly out of her mind with pleasure.

"Zach . . . Zach . . ."

"That's right, say my name, darlin'," he murmured, his voice thick with want. He nuzzled her throat again, then lifted his head to look down at her. She shuddered at the clear intention she read in his eyes, then her own eyes widened as she spotted something behind him. A thick cloud of smoke circled up in a dark column against the cornflower-blue sky.

"Fire!" she breathed, then she could smell it, could taste it in her mouth. Before she could direct him Zach slapped the reins, and the sleigh tore off over a hill. When they had cleared it Katherine gasped at the sight below. A tall clapboard house was on fire. Bright flame leapt toward the sky, and little black figures darted among the smoke.

"Oh, my God!" Katherine cried, jumping out of the sleigh before Zach could halt it.

"Smoke Eyes, get back here!"

She turned, smoke already smarting her eyes. "Zach," she said frantically, "this is the Duggans' house! They have seven children, at least half of them too young to attend school!"

He leapt out of the sleigh and grabbed her by the

shoulders. "Dammit, Smoke Eyes, get back in the sleigh!"

She couldn't. For as Zach swept past her, racing toward the flaming house, she looked up and saw two children standing at a window on the second floor, crying, calling, trapped.

Nine

Mrs. Duggan was screaming, a wailing infant in her arms, as she pointed up toward the second floor. "My babies!" she cried. She thrust the infant at Zach and charged toward her burning home.

"Goddammit!"

Zach glanced at the two toddlers and an old man standing by him, then shouted for Katherine who was running after Mrs. Duggan. The infant was squalling wildly, kicking his tiny legs, and Zach didn't know a damn thing about infants. In two loping strides he caught up to Katherine and thrust the baby at her. "Christ!" he muttered, glowering fiercely at her. "I told you to stay—"

"Zach!" she shouted, drawing the baby to her breast and gasping for clean air. "There're two children on the second floor—"

He was off like a shot, and reached Mrs. Duggan at the flaming door. She was hysterical. He hauled her backward, kicking and screaming, and he shook her roughly.

"Goddammit," he swore again. "You're no use to these kids dead." His words were cold and hard, but they sobered the woman. He jerked loose and left her sobbing in the snow, and Katherine went to her. The three other children—the toddlers who'd been standing by their grandfather—ran to her, hanging on her clothes, crying. Smoke stung Katherine's eyes and they filled with water. But she could still see Zach smashing a first-floor window with his elbow, then hauling himself in, headfirst. He was engulfed in smoke and flame.

She looked away from the inferno. "C'mon!" she shouted over the roaring din to the others. "Let's get to the barn!" She was afraid the children were inhaling too much smoke. They were coughing, and the baby was whimpering, too distraught to wail now. Mrs. Duggan stood frozen, though, watching, waiting.

"C'mon, Mrs. Duggan!" Katherine tugged on the woman's arm, then gave up. She herded the children and the old man into the safety of the barn. Once they were there, she told them to stay put and went to fetch water from the well. She ran smack into Zach at the barn door. His face was streaked with smoke and sweat.

"The ladder!" he said hoarsely. The grandfather pointed to it. Zach grabbed it and ran back to the house. He propped the ladder beneath the window where the children still stood. Katherine forgot the water as she watched him, fear gripping her.

He scampered up the ladder, taking three rungs at a time, and at the top he yelled something to the boy, then broke the window. Smoke billowed out, and for a moment she lost sight of him. When she saw him again he was halfway down the ladder with one of the children. Still a few feet from the ground, he dropped the boy to his mother, who fell with him to her knees, sobbing hysterically for the other. But that son would not come out. Zach was at the top of the ladder again, and Katherine could hear him coughing, see him shield his face from the intense heat with his arm. Every time he tried to climb in, the heat drove him back. Faintly, she could hear the child wailing.

At that moment, the Duggans' oldest child, ten-year-old Nan, came running toward the house, yelling for her puppy. "He's in there! In there!" she screamed, pointing up at the second floor. Sure enough Katherine could hear it, a kind of tortured yip.

Up at the top of the ladder, Zach realized he was going to have to go in after the boy and, apparently, a dog. He grasped the windowsill, cutting one hand on a piece of broken glass, and pulled himself inside the inferno.

Smoke engulfed him, and beyond it he could see orange flames darting, leaping, surrounding everything. Hot ash and cinders fell on him, stinging and burning his skin. He crawled through the thick curtain of gray-black smoke, groping for the boy. When he found him, a few feet away, he snagged him around the waist and started back toward the window. The child was coughing, and Zach thought that was a good sign, though he himself was coughing so hard, he could hardly move. He pushed the boy up onto the sill, shouting for him to grab the ladder and climb down. The boy understood.

Zach waited a moment to make sure he would get down all right, then went back for the dog.

The house seemed ready to crumble; the floor was giving way beneath him. He grabbed the whining puppy and crawled back to the window as fast as he could. Coughing uncontrollably, barely able to see through the smoke and the tears pouring from his eyes, he pulled himself over the sill, gingerly feeling for the ladder with his feet. When he felt it solidly beneath him, he started down, the dog under his arm.

He would have made it if the puppy hadn't suddenly panicked and struggled to get free. Swearing, Zach tried to tighten his grip on the dog, and when he did he threw himself off balance. He grabbed for the ladder, but nothing was there. And then he was falling and he could hear Smoke Eyes screaming. . . .

Cool. Blessedly cool. Zach felt something cool and wet on his face, as if he had dove into a mountain spring and the water was running over his fevered flesh. He opened his eyes to a vision—a beautiful woman with thick russet hair and soft gray eyes. Smoke Eyes. He managed a small smile, and when she smiled back, every muscle in his body tightened.

"He's coming to," a man said from somewhere over him, and Zach's smile broadened. Coming to was right, he thought. All over. He stared up at the barn rafters and drew a breath, then coughed. His throat was raw and parched. And then—abruptly—he remembered.

"Drink this," Katherine said softly, and held a dipper of water to his lips. He drank thirstily, though it hurt his throat. He lay his head back down. "Did he make it?" he asked hoarsely.

She smiled again and sponged his forehead. "He did. He got some second-degree burns, but he's going to be fine."

Zach frowned. He sat up abruptly, and cursed at the pain that shot through various parts of his body.

"Zach!" Katherine pushed at his chest. "You must rest!"

He hoisted his body up to a sitting position, and propped himself against the barn wall. Christ, he ached. His face throbbed, the back of his head pounded, and his body was sore as hell.

"Zach," Katherine said softly. "Please—"

Jake Duggan, who'd been standing over Zach, laid a hand on Zach's shoulder. "You saved my sons' lives, mister," he said, his voice breaking. "An' I owe you mine."

"You don't owe me anything," Zach said roughly.

Katherine was surprised by his tone, but as she watched him rub the back of his neck, she realized that he was embarrassed. Big, arrogant Zach Fletcher was embarrassed.

"You even saved my little Nan's whelp," Jake went on, tears oozing from his eyes. He shook his head, awed. "Not a common man'd do that. Sir, name anything, *anything* I can do for ya, and call it done."

Zach looked at Katherine, and she felt something lock in her throat. His eyes were bloodshot, his face alternately red from burns and black from soot, his hair singed. She knew what he was thinking, that there was nothing Jake Duggan could do for his own son who lay in his sickbed hundreds of miles away. But there was something, perhaps, she could do.

Still, she fought it, as she fought the swift yearning to touch him, to put her hands to his face and ease his pain. She lowered her eyes and saw the line of muscle in his long thigh. He was big and awesome and brave. He'd risked his life for strangers, and would do it again in a flash. He'd always had that reckless courage, as much a part of him as his skin. But now he was self-effacing as he nodded toward the family gathered at the other end of the barn. Mrs. Duggan was surrounded by her children, two of them on the floor, bandaged and moaning softly, but alive. Neighborhood women comforted them, and offered the Duggans use of their own homes.

"Go to them," Zach said quietly to Jake. "They need you now."

"They needed me then. I was in town, gettin' supplies. Thank the Lord my neighbors saw the house. Thank the Lord." Jake shook his head and shuffled back to his wife and children.

Katherine reached to take Zach's hand. She felt a strange dampness and roughness, and lifted his hand to peer at it. "I guess you cut it on some glass," she murmured. "More stitches."

He made a grim face. "Maybe I ought to get out of this town before I kill myself."

She tried to laugh, but as she looked at his bruised, soot-streaked face she had to bite her lip to keep it from trembling. She'd been terrified, watching him go into that flaming house. It had staggered her that he, so strong, so powerful, had been completely vulnerable in that ocean of flame. With her heart in her throat she'd watched the two little Duggan boys climb down the ladder, then waited . . . waited for Zach. And then he'd been there, hurrying down the ladder. Then he'd stopped, jerked, and she'd watched in horror as he fell backward, off the ladder, and slammed onto the ground. He was so lucky he hadn't been seriously hurt, and she was still stunned from the realization that even Zach could be vulnerable to the whims of fate. Yet looking at him now, though injured and hurting, he still radiated authority and unquestionable power.

Fearful of letting too much of her emotions show, she turned to search for instruments in her medical bag. "Your coat got badly burned," she said, her voice weak. "But it saved you from being burned." She glanced at him. "Perhaps it saved your life."

He smiled faintly. "Is that a nice way of telling me I need to buy a new coat?"

She grinned back at him. His humor was infectious. "I'd lend you one of mine, but I know it wouldn't fit."

He gave a short, husky laugh, and her blood quickened at the roguish gleam in his eyes. "I can think of other ways for you to warm me up, sugar."

Shock raced through her. That he could even consider *that* now! But seduction was as natural to Zach as breathing. He was a rake through and through.

Unnerved, she turned back to her medical bag. When she started to thread her needle, he made a face. "I think you take perverse pleasure in threading that needle," he said, and she stifled a giggle.

Suddenly the puppy broke loose from Nan's arms and wiggled his way across the room to Zach. He leapt up on Zach's lap and Zach laughed, allowing the puppy to lick his face. Nan came giggling up to them, watching the dog with glee.

"He's thanking you," she told Zach.

Zach lifted the pup in one hand and grinned. "Couldn't you teach him a more polite way to thank a person?"

Nan only laughed again.

"Why weren't you in school today, Nan?" Katherine asked as she sponged the blood from Zach's hand.

"Mama let me stay home because of the blizzard," Nan said, taking the puppy from Zach. "She needed extra help." She glanced over at her mother and younger siblings. "Good thing I did." She skipped lightly, unable to stay still for more than an instant. "I was playing with Terry and Timothy outdoors when the fire started." She lowered her head and whispered, "They say Grandpa started it. He was smoking a cheroot and fell asleep, but they won't tell him." She tapped a finger to her head. "They say he can't remember anything anymore. It saddens Mama." She rubbed her cheek along the puppy's singed fur and grinned at Zach and Katherine. "I'm changing his name to Lucky," she said, and skipped back off to her folks.

Katherine met Zach's eyes before she bent her head over his hand. "You were always every kind of fool for a dog," she said, trying to tease, but her voice shook.

"Mmmm. Maybe," he said.

As she sutured his cuts she felt his gaze on her and glanced up. "Drew had one," he said harshly.

A frown knit her brows. "One what?"

"A puppy." He glanced away from her, to Nan. "I brought it home to him one day after we got to Marblehead. Drew loved it. The dog cheered him, and he took it with him everywhere." He laughed shortly. "That dog made me think of you."

Katherine squared up her shoulders, insulted. "I beg your pardon?"

He gazed at her. "It was your hair," he explained, a faint smile warming his eyes. "Irish-setter hair." He reached out to take a silky strand of it between his fingers, and she trembled. But then he frowned and lowered his hand. "The dog died." He clenched his fist. "It got kicked by a horse. While it was dying Drew begged me to have you come out and look at it, heal it. I'd told him how good you were with animals and somehow he got it into his mind that you could save his dog. But I told him you couldn't come, that you lived too far away. He didn't want to believe that. But his dog died and after that Drew didn't believe in anything anymore." His lips tightened. "Still doesn't."

Katherine didn't know what to say, but Zach didn't give her a chance anyway. He glanced at his hand, turning it to examine the sutures, then looked at her. His expression was bland, as if he just hadn't tore at her heart with his story. "Finished?" he asked.

She sat back on her heels, but before she could respond he rolled to his feet, standing over her. She tilted her head back to look at him and caught the grimace of pain that flashed across his face. She stood and rested a hand on his forearm.

"Zach, you must rest. Your body has taken a beating and it craves rest." Though he still looked strong and robust, she knew he could collapse later—and with Drew as a perpetual worry, his health could suffer too. "Sit for a while," she said. "You took quite a fall. You were unconscious for several minutes and got the wind knocked out of you. It's a wonder you're on your feet now. Later we'll get some fortifying soup into you, and bathe your skin with tea. It's the best thing in the world for burns. I need to tend to these folk and get them in wagons so they can settle into the neighbors' houses, and it will take a few hours."

"I can help," he said, but his voice was weary.

"You can help by resting." He hesitated, then gave in and lay down on a pile of straw. She tossed a plaid saddle blanket over him. "Please," she said, "if you're in pain, let me know."

He only smiled at her.

She sighed and touched her fingertips to his jaw. His eyes narrowed but she kept her hand there. "What was his name, Zach?"

"Whose name?"

"The dog's. What was Drew's dog's name?"

In the weak afternoon light, Zach's eyes glittered with an odd intensity. "Arapaho. He called the dog Arapaho."

She drew her hand back. "Oh, Zach," she murmured, and a hot ache filled her throat. She felt his pain, and his son's pain, as if they were her own. Stepping away from him, she asked Nan to bring him another dipperful of water, then she turned to the others. Drew, she realized, was never far from Zach's thoughts, or his heart. She could see the torment in his eyes, hear it in his voice. His pain was beginning to torment her, too, but now she must tend to this family. She pressed her lips together and began her task.

By late afternoon the Duggan family was settled in their neighbors' homes and Katherine had left instructions for Mr. and Mrs. Duggan to administer to their two burned sons. She told them to call on her in the night if the need arose, and after she left them she and Zach rode directly to Fish Walker's house where she checked on his son. Then they drove to the dry goods store to purchase a jacket for Zach.

Katherine waited for him in the sleigh, noting that he moved more slowly than usual, that he winced once or twice before he even opened the door. His strength was fading, she thought. When he came out again, though, the sight of him in a thick sheepskin jacket was breath-stopping. The jacket hugged his great shoulders, making him appear even more formidable in the blue evening light. He'd turned the big collar high, and the wind whipped his hair. He glanced at her and smiled, just a little, as if to reassure her. For he was moving stiffly. She frowned as he settled beside her in the sleigh, then forgot her concern when his solid thigh pressed against hers. She tried to ignore the delicious little thrill that coursed through her at the intoxicating nearness of him. But she could smell the leather jacket, felt its warmth against her, and a longing surged deep in her belly.

She watched him pick up the reins, and had to close her eyes as she remembered his big hands cupping her breasts that morning, plying her flesh, stroking her. Banishing the image, she opened her eyes again, only to see that Zach had been watching her.

"Well?" he asked, grinning as if he'd been reading her mind.

She bristled and looked straight ahead. "Well, what?"

He rubbed his jaw, considering her. "Well now," he drawled, "if I can't even get a measly comment out of you about this jacket, maybe I should turn it back in."

She blushed and gave him a quick once-over. "It looks fine." But how distracting was his sturdy thigh nestled against hers!

He grunted and set the sleigh in motion. "I'm not sure I can handle such a lavish compliment."

Men! They were so much more fragile than women. Did he want a written statement on how absolutely riveting he was? Did he need to be told that he was so sinfully handsome he could tempt a saint? Didn't he realize how just a glance from his black eyes could send her pulses pounding, her blood boiling? She stared straight ahead and tried to keep her voice steady. "I said the jacket looks fine! What more do you want to hear? That you're the most handsome man that ever crossed my path?"

He laughed as he steered the sleigh toward her house. "That'll do," he said mildly.

Flustered, she let out a little huffy breath. "I wasn't *saying* you were the most handsome man that ever crossed my path! You really are a conceited cur, Zach Fletcher." But she said it lightly. "Actually," she went on, "I wasn't really looking at the jacket. I was watching the way you move."

One of his eyebrows lifted, and he smiled that devilish smile. Hot color flooded her cheeks.

"That's not what I—" she began, but stopped. Unnerved, she bit off an explanation. "You're stiff."

The glint in his eyes was wicked. "You noticed?"

"I *mean,* you're moving stiffly!"

"With damn good reason."

"Zach!" She swallowed a giggle, though her face was flaming hot. "Be serious! Is your back hurting?"

"Among other things."

She punched him playfully on his hard shoulder. "I'm serious!"

"So am I, sugar. More serious than you could ever imagine."

The husky tone of his voice sent shivers through her. Glancing up, she saw a sudden flare in his eyes, like tiny flames, and her heart seemed stuck in her throat. Quickly she looked away and saw her white frame house coming into view. Her brows drew together in a frown. "Where are we going?"

"Your place. Obviously."

"But the hotel is in the opposite direction!"

He looked at her, amused. "I'm not as dense as you might think."

"You're confused," she told him. "Turn the sleigh around."

But he was aiming it toward the stables where Shadow awaited them. When Zach caught her glare, he grinned at her. "I can't think of a better place for tea or soup."

Katherine counted slowly to five. If he thought she was going to play nurse for him— "The hotel serves both," she said between gritted teeth, "and I'm sure in enormous quantities."

With a lazy grace that surprised her, given his injuries, he swung out of the cutter. "I don't think anyone over there is going to be willing to bathe my skin with tea."

"Oh, I don't know about that," she said, a little snidely. "I'm sure one of those chambermaids would be eager to lend you a hand." She ignored his laughter as she climbed out of the sleigh. Shadow scampered around the horse, eager to help. "If you'd like," she added, "Shadow can drive you to the hotel."

Zach laughed again and came around the sleigh to take hold of her arm. "I don't like," he said.

She set her jaw and glared at him. She could not bear to be so close to him for another night! Already her nerves were stretched to the breaking point. And judging by the glow of deviltry in his eyes, he cared nothing for her reputation!

She tried, without success, to wriggle her arm free of his grip, but his fingers were like steel. As he escorted her to her front porch he poured on the charm, as thick and sweet as cool honey. "You aren't so heartless as to send me back to the hotel after all I've been through today, are you, honey?" He laughed when she glowered at him. "Please, don't shatter my illusion of you."

"You're paying for the hotel room," she said as they climbed the steps. "I'd think you'd want to stay there and not waste your money."

"I can afford it."

Yes, she thought, and felt an odd pang in her chest. She was sure Zach could afford plenty . . . and any woman he desired. They reached the front door and she rested her hand on the knob. "I want you to know," she said in her brisk, most professional tone, "that I am not letting you in out of the goodness of my heart. I plan to give you a thorough examination and then send you on your way."

"How thorough?"

Despite her annoyance with him, Katherine had to smile. She didn't even think he was aware of how naturally seduction came to him. Even now her hand trembled on the doorknob as all her feminine parts surged with life, aching for contact with him. All she had to do was turn and she'd be in his arms. She went hot, just thinking about it. Letting out her pent-up breath, she pushed the door open and stepped over the threshold.

The house was warm. Shadow had kept the fire stoked throughout the day, and it crackled and snapped in the hearth. "I'm going to brew some tea," she said, setting her black bag by the sofa and hanging her coat on the peg by the door. "Why don't you take off your coat and I'll be back in a minute." She hesitated, watching him shrug gingerly out of his heavy jacket. How badly hurt was he? She had just given him a quick check in the Duggans' barn, for his clothes had protected him, and his face and hands only slightly burned. But he could be badly bruised from his fall.

"And remove your shirt," she added briskly.

"Smoke Eyes," he said with obvious amusement, "is this what I think—"

She cut him off. "My motives are strictly professional," she said, and flounced into the kitchen.

When she returned with a tray of tea and soup she stopped short, stunned by the sight of him, bare from the waist up. He was beautiful. No other word fit the perfection of his body. The firelight reflected off planes of hard muscle, danced across his smooth, tanned skin. Dark curly hair covered his chest, and his shoulders looked to be a yard across. He had a flat, washboard stomach, and rippling muscles banded his lean waistline.

Her gaze followed the narrow line of hair that ran down his belly to the waistband of his trousers. She ached to run her hands over him, feel his hardness and strength. Her gaze drifted down his long, muscled legs, then slowly back up again to meet his eyes. She felt deep muscles pull tight inside her, and a warm weakness washed through her. Even across the room she could feel his burning energy. Knowing that he was forbidden to her, she marveled at the power of the attraction she felt for him, and let that power shimmer over her.

A slow smile swept across his face and her stomach dipped. "What's your next order, Doc?" His voice, still hoarse from the smoke, sounded incredibly intimate.

She stared at him and thought, *I order you to stand there in the firelight and let me watch the shadows touch your magnificent body, then let my hands follow where they lead.* She wanted to explore every hard, muscled inch of him, let her fingers ride over the various scars that marked him, press her palms to the solid swell of muscles. Her body was thrumming with strange pulsing urges, and with great effort she forced them away.

"I want you to lie down," she said, her tone businesslike again.

"Well, now, honey," he drawled. "This is starting to get interesting."

A tiny smile tugging at her lips, she set the tray on the table beside the sofa and took his arm, tugging him toward the sofa. "Lie down," she repeated. "I have to look at your back."

"What else do you *have* to look at, darlin'?"

"For heaven's sake, Zach, even when you're feeling under the weather you're thinking of—" She broke off as she saw a warm sensuality gleam in his eyes. She fought the bombardment of feelings within her and put her hands on his shoulders, urging him to take a seat. When he grinned lasciviously, she snatched her hands back as if stung. "Down, Zach! My actions are strictly professional, and you must remember that as I'm examining your back."

He nodded. "Oh, I will."

He lay stomach-down on the sofa, and for a moment Katherine just stared. His shoulders and back were powerfully muscled, and gleamed like copper in the firelight. She wanted to touch him, and *not* in a professional manner. But she frowned when she saw the faint discoloration of numerous new bruises. No wonder he'd been moving gingerly. She imagined every bone, muscle, and tendon in his back ached.

She reached out to touch him, and he jumped reflexively. She tested the bruised areas, her fingers probing expertly, and heard his indrawn hiss of breath. "Zach," she said, "I'm going to rub some liniment into your skin and massage your muscles. It will help ease the pain."

He only grunted, and she saw that his eyes were closed, his head pillowed on his arms. She reached into her medical bag for the liniment, then straightened and eyed him warily. The best way to do this, of course, would be to straddle him, but this was Zach. Just that morning he had pinned her under him on this sofa, and he had taken full advantage of his position. She shut her eyes against the explicit image that flashed across her mind of his big brown hand upon her breast, his dark head bent over her. Shaking off the tingling sensation, she turned and grabbed a chair. She may be attracted to the man, but that didn't mean she had to act foolishly.

"Just lie there and relax," she said, pouring some liniment onto her palm.

Relax? Zach thought. That was impossible when he was around Katherine. And now . . . He almost groaned when he felt her hands on his bare skin again, smoothing a cool lotion over his back. He couldn't stop the provocative image of her slim, naked body beneath his from forming in his mind. He envisioned the wild, vibrant flame of her hair spread out over a pillow, the nipples of her firm, rounded breasts straining toward him, begging for his mouth. And he saw himself moving in and out of her.

His muscles tightened involuntarily, and she murmured for him to relax. Her touch was both gentle and firm, her palms running over his skin and muscles expertly, almost erotically. As she leaned close to him, her sweet female fragrance surrounded him, making hot, wild things beat inside his body, his loins stir to life. He made a rough sound, too deliciously indulged to form words.

Katherine smiled as she felt his taut muscles begin to relax. She smoothed the liniment over his shoulders and upper arms. There was no give beneath his smooth skin; he was hard as oak. She probed his supple flesh with her skilled fingers, kneading muscles, feeling his heat and awesome strength. Never had her hands trembled upon a patient, or stumbled in examination, but never had she treated such a dangerous man, who made her dizzy with excitement.

A quiet heat burned deep inside her, flickering hot. Every stroke of her palms upon his warm flesh made her breath quicken, her blood race. A fine film of sweat had broken out over his body, and she watched the firelight dance upon him, glistening gold. She was captivated by the magical patterns that kissed his flesh. And she was seized with the mad longing to kiss his flesh too. She wanted to massage all of him, his perfect backside, his steely thighs, his sinewed arms, his brawny chest, even his face and his hands.

Flowing, sweeping, soothing, her touch, she knew, had become more caressing than therapeutic. Her hands lingered where they should not, just above the waistband of his snug-fitting trousers.

"Honey," he said, his voice slow and guttural, "if you doctor all your patients with such intimate care, it's no wonder they're beating down your door." He sounded amused, but stricken, Katherine drew her hands back, her fingers curling into her palms.

"Don't stop," he said.

Swallowing hard, she placed her palms upon him again and, more carefully now, continued her clinical massage.

"Are you going to the reservation tomorrow?"

"Yes." Her voice sounded odd, tight and small. She used her thumbs to massage his neck . . . and studied the soft thick hair at the back of his head. With effort she restrained the urge to touch it, to thread her fingers through the night-black strands and watch the light delve into the dense shadows.

"I'll be ready," he said, his voice becoming sleepy.

"You should be resting," she said, "not traveling."

"I'll be ready," he repeated, and even in his drowsy state his rumbling voice held that steely note of authority.

"Are you hungry?" It seemed an inane question, but they'd only eaten a piece of bread and butter at one of the neighbors' homes, and by now the soup on the tray had cooled.

"More sore than hungry."

She continued her massage, working the tension and soreness from his muscles. The only sound in the room was the low-crackling fire. Soon she would have to get up and stoke it, she thought, but now he needed her.

"You know," he said after a few minutes, "I'm too beat up to get off this sofa, angel? I'll have to stay the night."

A fluttery feeling drifted low in Katherine's stomach. She hardened herself against it and said, "You are so arrogant to assume! I suppose you think you've duped me."

She caught a glimpse of his smile as he said, "I promise to keep my pants on."

Warm blood surged into her face, and she heard his low laughter. He could guess her reaction without even looking at her!

"You're tensing up, darlin'. Maybe *I* should be giving *you* a rubdown."

"Zach Fletcher, stop teasing! If you don't be quiet, I'll stop this service right this moment!"

He laughed again, and she had to close her eyes against the beauty of his solid muscles rising and swelling under her hands. And his voice, rich, dark, held a seductive quality that threatened to undo her.

"If I need a doctor in the middle of the night," he said, "this is the most convenient place for me to be. Don't you agree that I'm safest on your sofa, Smoke Eyes?"

Her eyes flew open as her heart shot to her throat. "I don't agree that *I'm* safest with you on my sofa!"

Ah, God, what spirit she had! Zach thought. It took every shred of will power he had not to turn over and grab her and pull her beneath him. He wanted to show her how good love could be for them—yet he couldn't ignore the warnings from his conscience. Smoke Eyes wasn't a woman to be used that way. He had never wanted a woman so fiercely, had never felt this maddening desire to brand her, possess her. So he fought it, and it was torture. Zach was a man used to taking what came his way.

"If I was *really* doing a good job," she said, "you'd be asleep by now."

He grunted. "It's because you really *are* doing a good job that a certain part of my body refuses to go to sleep." He turned his head to look at her. "I want you, honey. And as a man, I can't make a secret of it."

"Don't," she whispered. "You mustn't, Zach."

"I mustn't what? Want you?" He paused, letting his words hang in the air as the silence stretched taut and swollen between them. When he spoke again, his voice was rough with new emotion. "How does a man stop such a thing, Smoke Eyes? Do you have a remedy for that?"

Katherine sat still as stone, letting his vibrant words wash sweetly through her, caressing her, rousing powerful sensations. Her heart raced so swiftly, it was actually painful. *She wanted him too.* But she didn't want to want him. He would be gone soon, and it was unfair that he made her feel this way, unfair that he held this power over her. Did he think he could just take her and leave her as he had every other woman in his past? How many hearts had he broken over the years? She was certain Laura hadn't been the only woman.

A sudden anger slashed through her, and she shot off the chair and back away from him as if she'd been catapulted. "Actually," she said, her voice trembling with her fury, "the best remedy for your 'problem' is a cold bath!"

He was silent for a moment, looking at her, then he asked, "Are you offering me a cold bath, sweetheart?"

She gritted her teeth, hating the endearment he'd probably used countless times on a hundred other women. She was suddenly so unaccountably furious with him, she was near tears. Arrogant wretch! Lying on *her* sofa, talking this way to her as if he'd earned the right! "No bath!" she shouted. "But if you'd like I can find a sleeping powder for you that will put you out till noon tomorrow! That will help you forget your 'want,' won't it, Zach Fletcher?"

"Noon tomorrow?" In contrast to her rage, he sounded amused. "That means you and Shadow will have to carry me on the sleigh to the reservation. Otherwise I'll still be here on your sofa when you come back."

"Stop it!"

He pushed himself up on his elbows and studied her. "What the hell are you snapping about, woman?" Suddenly, as if enlightened, he grinned. His gaze ran lazily down her body and came back up to meet her blazing eyes. "You just want a good-night kiss and are too shy to ask for it, aren't you, sugar?"

Heat simmered to the boiling point. "You, sir, are the most arrogant, conceited—" She couldn't even finish. She whirled, thick braid flying, and ignored his soft chuckling as she fled to the kitchen. But there was no ignoring his bellowing voice.

"How long are you going to pretend there's nothing between us, Smoke Eyes?"

Her only response was the tinny whack of pots and pans. Zach heard Clarabelle's loud shriek and smiled, then drifted into a deep, healing sleep.

He woke later to see her at her desk, head bent over a journal. Her hair shimmered with coppery highlights in the fire's glow, and her long lashes cast fanned shadows on her cheeks. She'd drawn one foot under her and she was immersed in what she was reading. He had always admired her intelligence, and it gave him immense pleasure to observe her secretly in the private act of feeding that intelligence. He watched her for a long time, feeling the familiar arousal of his body and an unfamiliar rush of emotion.

"Do you know," he said finally, "that your hair looks like flame by the firelight?"

She jumped at the unexpected sound of his voice, then turned to him. Their eyes met, and both felt the jolting impact of the other's gaze. With effort, Zach rolled onto his back, then said, "C'mere, darlin'."

She shook her head.

"C'mon, sugar," he coaxed, his gaze still fixed on her.

Katherine's pulses thundered. The soft light in his eyes captured her, making her feel, absurdly, like a rabbit hypnotized by a snake. "Go back to sleep," she said huskily.

"I'm in pain," he said, uttering the word *pain* with such intensity, he made her feel pain too. In her breasts, her belly, in the most intimate part of her body. She didn't understand it, was terrified of her want. He was danger, he was excitement. And for all her life, she could not turn away.

"I need to study," she said, yet she couldn't keep her gaze from dropping to his torso. She stared at him, helplessly fascinated. His large body was stretched out in a deceptively lazy sprawl. Deceptive, for there was still something wild about him, something untamed. He radiated heat and sexual promises too difficult to fight. The vibrancy of his presence was an assault on her senses, and she had become so acutely affected by him, it seemed even her hair quivered.

"What are you studying?" he asked suddenly.

She blushed as her gaze flew to his. She had been studying *him,* and wanted to continue.

"Work," she said tersely, but she was not telling him the whole truth. After she had cleaned the kitchen, she'd come back into the front room to make sure he was asleep. As she'd stood over him she'd begun to think of his son, and conflict had risen in her. She was certain she could not go home with him. It was impractical to expect it of her, though she understood his desperation.

More than that, though, she was terrified of her fierce pull toward him. She had never felt this way about *any* man before. Men were just . . . men! She had worked and studied with them for years and found them to be arrogant nuisances with unlimited privileges. To be attracted to Zach was dangerous. Never before had she crossed the line between personal and professional involvement, and if she were to travel to Marblehead with him, she would undoubtedly be crossing that forbidden line. She would not jeopardize herself for a man who would leave her in the end anyway.

Still, she could not shake the image of his ailing boy. She'd felt driven to take down her medical texts and research all the material she had on abdominal surgery. She pored over the books, studying illustrations of the abdomen, imagining what she would do if she were to operate on such a case. But she did not want Zach to know that. She stood and stepped in front of her desk, hiding the books from his view.

"It's time I retired," she said, forcing a bright smile to her lips. "It's late and I need to rise early."

"Before you do," he said softly, and she wondered if there was any other man in the world who could give her goose bumps just by speaking. "How 'bout the tea bath you promised me?"

"I don't remember promising any such thing."

He laughed. "Aw, c'mon, darlin'. Would you deny an injured man such a pleasure?"

She eyed him warily. "You've already been indulged this evening. And," she added, "you didn't behave."

He laughed again, his eyes crinkling at the corners. "I thought only schoolteachers punished for misbehaving." He let his gaze travel to her breasts. "Not doctors."

"Stop looking there!"

Grinning, he met her eyes again. "Where?"

Katherine's irritation was rising once more. She was all set to tell him just what he could do with his tea bath when he suddenly sobered.

"I'll behave," he promised.

He looked so sincere she went to him, sitting on the edge of the sofa. There was just enough room, and her hip pressed intimately against his thigh. She couldn't stop or deny the immediate, turbulent stirrings inside her. But she hoped to keep him from noticing.

Pressing her lips together, she began her ministrations, gently swabbing his face with the cool tea she'd left on the table. Her gaze followed the cloth's path, and she frowned as she laid the back of her hand against his cheek. His skin felt warm and she worried about fever. But she forgot about it instantly when his long fingers curled around her wrist.

"I feel like I've been out in the sun too long," he said.

She looked down at his fingers, so dark and powerful around her slight wrist. "You were extraordinarily lucky not to have been hurt worse."

Her breath caught as he brought her hand to his mouth and pressed his lips to her palm. She tried to jerk her hand back, but he held tight, touching his tongue to her skin. A thrill ripped through her.

"You mustn't!" she said, dropping the cloth on his chest.

"I must."

Katherine was terrified. Her heart beat wildly, and she tugged on her hand again, but he would not let go. Worse, he touched his tongue to the pulse beating under the delicate skin of her inner wrist. Fiery sensations soared within her, sensations she could not squelch. "This is not part of the ministrations," she said, her voice strained.

He kissed her knuckles. "I'm making this part of them."

Katherine felt on fire, every nerve alive. She tried to

resist him, tried to ignore what he was doing to her. "No . . . no . . ."

He lifted his head to look at her. "What are you afraid of?" he asked tenderly.

Your touch. She didn't say the words. Desire was tugging her toward him, and suddenly he reached up and traced her smooth cheek with his rough fingertips.

"Just one kiss," he whispered.

"You promised you'd behave." She heard the plea in her voice, but didn't know what she was pleading for.

"I am behaving," he said. "I haven't done anything you haven't liked." His long fingers slid into the hair at the nape of her neck, then caressed her skin in lazy, sensual circles as he urged her mouth down to his. Tears of fury sprang to her eyes, and she tried to pull back.

"Wrong!" she cried on a choked breath. "I don't like this at all!"

"Little liar," he murmured against her lips, and Katherine closed her eyes. She both fought it and welcomed it, this unleashed flash of longing that surged through her, making her ache for him. She could smell him—smoke and heat and male musk—and she heard his groan, rumbling low. There seemed to be no help for it. She sank into him, her hands pressed to his powerful chest, her lips opening to his. His tongue slid into her mouth, taking, stroking, arousing. She made a soft little cry and started to pull away, alarmed by the sensations whipping through her. He held her close, though, his big hand cupping the back of her head, his kiss penetrating deep. His tongue thrust slow and hot into her mouth, demanding her response with its commanding, sensual rhythm. She melted into him, her body turning to sweet honey. He made another rough sound, pressing her hips against his, forcing her to feel his throbbing want. Violent shudders ran through her, and she panicked. She broke away from the kiss and pushed against his chest, feeling the heavy slam of his heart under her palms. She was panting, and there was a hard glitter in his black-fire eyes.

"Stop fighting it," he said hoarsely. "What you and I have shared today is—"

She sprang to her feet, fighting for breath, her eyes blazing down at him. "Sheer foolishness!" she exclaimed. Her breath quickened as he scowled at her, eyes spearing her.

"There's not a damn foolish thing about it!"

"Oh? Would your son agree? Do you think he enjoyed his life without his father all these years?"

His savage curse chilled her heated flesh. He thrust his fingers through his hair, and his eyes narrowed dangerously.

"That's not fair and you know it, Smoke Eyes! It's a different situation entirely, and friends don't fling past mistakes at each other."

She was beyond caring, trembling with both fear and fury. "It's not a different situation at all! I don't want to become pregnant with your child, and I have every right not to want that, Zach."

His face was set and still. If she hadn't known him, she would have run in the opposite direction. Instead her own gaze softened, and she reached to touch his arm. "I'm sorry, Zach, if my words have hurt you. But that is the reality."

Before she could pull away he caught her wrist. "But this," he said, boldly reaching up to cup her breast, "is reality too." His eyes were so dark, and she was drowning in his gaze. He continued, and his voice was like cream pouring over her skin. "And sugar, you of all people know just what a realist I am."

She touched her fingertips to her mouth, her lips

still throbbing and tingling from his kiss. "Yes," she whispered. He smiled. Then she added, "All the more reason to make certain it does not happen again."

She easily twisted her arm free of his hold, then turned and walked away. She was still unable to work up enough courage to tell him she could not go east with him.

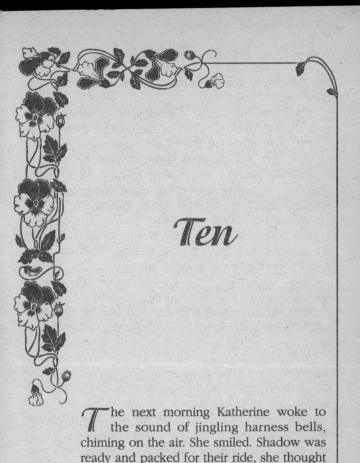

Ten

The next morning Katherine woke to the sound of jingling harness bells, chiming on the air. She smiled. Shadow was ready and packed for their ride, she thought as she rolled out of bed. Dressing quickly in warm woolen clothing and moccasin boots, she rushed out the front door. Her eagerness was dampened at the sight of Zach in the driver's seat. He flashed his breathtaking smile and lifted the string of tiny silver harness bells, jingling them. "C'mon, woman! Stop dragging your tail!"

Her cheeks flamed scarlet, and she glanced around for Shadow as she made her way down the porch steps. "What have you done with Shadow?"

Zach gave her a look of mock affront. "What makes you always think the worst of me, Smoke Eyes?"

She stopped at the side of the sleigh and looked up at him. "I'm not thinking badly of you, Zach. I just know your nature." She looked toward the barn but Shadow was nowhere in sight. "Have you gagged and hog-tied him? Did you stuff him in a corner of the stable so he wouldn't give you any trouble? He knew he was to drive with me to the reservation today. I didn't tell him that you planned on coming. Did you bribe him? How exactly did you do it?"

Zach smiled his sexy, lopsided smile. He studied her, rubbing his jaw. "Well, now," he drawled, "there's nothing like a woman with spit and vinegar to heat a man's blood in the morning. And, darlin', I'm heatin' up fast."

With that crooked smile tipping up one side of his mouth and his bold black eyes dancing, she remembered the night before with explicit clarity. She flushed to the roots of her hair.

"You seem to be in fine form this morning," she said, banishing all sensual memories. She could see he had bathed and shaved and changed into clean clothing. She hadn't even heard him leave her house. His apparently boundless energy amazed her. After such a trauma to the body, most folks would have been laid up at least a few days.

He grinned rakishly at her. "I'm always in fine form, darlin'. And I'm ready to go. What about you?"

"I'm ready," she said, though she took one last look around for Shadow.

"Then get up here and let's enjoy each other before the morning's gone."

She made a small, choked sound. His words

implied—intentionally she was sure—that they were going off to indulge in a romantic tryst. The air sizzled with sexual tension, and Zach had the look of a man who was far too confident, much too sure of his power over her. The last thing on earth she desired was to get anywhere near him. Despite that rational thought of self-protection, a thrill of excitement flared down her spine at the prospect of spending more time with him.

He lifted the buffalo robe beside him, making room for her. "Hop in, sugar. It's a long ride."

"But where's Shadow? I can't just leave—"

"I'm right here, Doctor."

She jumped nearly a foot and clapped a hand to her heart. He was so quiet she hadn't even heard him come up behind her. "Goodness, Shadow! You startled me!"

He was grinning, and she wondered just how much he'd heard. Though she and he usually communicated in Arapaho, he had no trouble understanding English. He made a small gesture to Zach and spoke in Arapaho now. "Your man has offered to take you to the reservation. Do you agree with his offer, Doctor?"

She eyed Shadow speculatively. "Has he offered *you* anything? Money? New clothes? A horse by any chance?"

When Shadow gave her a curious look, she waved her words away. "Never mind. Yes, I agree with his offer. We are old friends, Zach and I, and he wants to see the reservation."

A shadow darkened the boy's lean face. "There is nothing to 'see,' is there, Doctor?"

The two were silent for a moment as they thought of the sadness of their people, forced to live where the United States government ordered them.

"There's plenty of food in the larder," Katherine said, shaking off the momentary gloom. "Make sure Clarabelle is fed, and just keep an eye on the place while I'm gone. I'll be a couple of days, weather and no emergencies provided."

Shadow grinned again, forgetting his dark mood also. "I'm going to do some ice fishing. And some trapping."

"Catch something for me," she said as the boy gave her a hand into the sleigh. Within moments she was tucked under the lap robe, right up against Zach's solid body. She ignored him and waved to Shadow as the cutter sped off, its runners squeaking in the snow.

"What was that all about?" Zach asked, raising his voice over the wind as it rushed past them.

"Shadow is more than happy to let you ride me to the reservation. He has an irrational fear of the government officials capturing him and forcing him to live there. When I first brought him home from there, he said he would rather kill himself than be penned in again like an animal."

Zach's lips tightened. "Well, damn" was all he said, but it sounded somehow eloquent.

A few miles outside of town she ordered him to stop the sleigh. She climbed out of the sleigh and went to brush the snow off a tree stump. "Hmm." She stared at the stump. "The O'Tooles and the Brumbakers want me to stop at their places. Looks like Grandma Brumbaker is suffering from angina again and Mousey O'Toole has a terrible toothache."

Zach stared at her. "How in the hell . . . ?"

She brushed the snow off her mittens and grinned. "Witchcraft," she teased, and flashed him such an alluring smile that Zach felt an abrupt tightening in his loins. "We doctors are trained to read tree stumps and people's minds with such accuracy, it's eerie."

"Hmm." He rubbed his jaw as he eyed her carefully. "I don't doubt it, minx. Tell me, what's on my mind now."

Heat flooded Katherine's face. "*It's* never *off* your mind!" she said as she climbed back into the sleigh. She heard his soft laughter and glared at him. "Keep going straight and we'll find Grandma Brumbaker."

They did, and as Katherine examined her, the big German woman told Zach in broken English that she had all sorts of remedies for various ailments, but only the doc could treat her angina successfully. When she caught sight of the burn on his hand, she slapped wet tea leaves on it, then went on to tell him that the sure cure for a headache was to tie a rope used in a hanging around his neck. Though Zach could not imagine himself resorting to such drastic measures, he was fascinated by her repertoire of folk remedies. It seemed she had a cure for everything. Katherine had to drag him out of Grandma's house, and as they made their way down the front steps he was shaking his head. "I never would have thought that liquid a skunk ejects is worth a damn. But that old granny said it has supreme medicinal value."

Katherine rolled her eyes. "For the love of Pete, Zach! Did you believe any of that?"

He gave her a hand up into the sleigh. "Well, she sure sounded like she knew what she was talking about."

Katherine almost laughed. "Don't tell me you're superstitious, Zach. I thought you had more sense than to listen to an old woman."

He raised his eyebrows as he swung himself into the sleigh. "I know when we were young you used to whisper Arapaho words over injured animals." His mouth curled at one corner. "You used to tell me they were magical chants, and with your touch, I could see they worked magic. Can you deny this granny has the same faith in her own abilities?"

Katherine smiled too. "But honestly, Zach, those

were old Arapaho medicine chants. Can you really give much credence to touching a ringworm nine times with a thimble to make it go away?"

He shrugged. "You never know. She told me that if I want to head off a wound all I have to do is fasten the right eye of a wolf inside my right sleeve."

"I don't know," Katherine murmured. "That just seems to be a surefire way of keeping women at bay."

Zach laughed, his gaze moving over her lovely face, examining her as if she were a treasure. Strange, but he hadn't laughed much with women before. Smoke Eyes was different, had always been different. Scrappy and courageous, she glowed with high spirits, laughter and light. Her own laughter somehow eased all the knots of tension inside him, chased away shadows he didn't even realize he still carried. He wanted her, and the yearning increased with every moment. She delighted him, captivated him, and made him burn. He didn't want to leave her, couldn't leave her, and the reasons were purely selfish, not for Drew. He hadn't had anywhere near his fill of her yet, had only just begun to know the wild sweet taste of her.

His gaze fastened on her breath-stopping eyes, and his throat locked. He couldn't dismiss the fierce pang of wanting her—the need was in his muscles, his blood, the pit of his belly. They didn't have much more time together, and knowing it tore at him. He didn't understand it; he'd always managed to stay aloof from his women. But she was Smoke Eyes, and it pained him to know that she was not, would never be, "his woman." They had different lives, she and he, on opposite sides of the country. And she made it clear just how much she valued her independence. Still, he believed they belonged together, and knowing this only gripped him with intense frustration. No, it wasn't fair of him to drag her across the country with the very determined intention of bedding her. Yet he burned for her, ached for her, needed to be inside her, surrounded by her silky, soft depths, her essence.

Zach swallowed heavily. His eyes lowered to her lush, provocative mouth, and he had to steel himself against covering it with his own. *Smoke Eyes, Smoke Eyes,* he thought, *what are you doing to me?* He felt the same odd need to protect and possess her as he had years ago when he'd caught a boy, Sid Chase, roughing her up, telling her his pa had said squaws were only good for one thing. He'd lit into Sid, and to this day he wondered how far the fight would have gone if Tessa Amesbury hadn't stopped it. He had been a hard, tough boy then, hadn't thought anyone was worth much more than a damn—until that day when he'd seen Smoke Eyes's fear, anger, and courage, and recognized her as someone like himself. None of the local bullies had ever tormented her again, and a deep bond had formed between the two outcasts. A bond, Zach realized, that was still intact, and the depth of it shook him.

Katherine's breath caught as Zach's eyes filled with a sudden piercing intensity. His lighthearted mood had changed entirely. A quiver passed through her as their eyes locked and held. She could hardly breathe, yet forced herself to flash him a smile. "Granny also believes a steaming cup of cockroach tea will cure lock-jaw."

Her comment broke the tension. Zach smiled faintly, his dark gaze warmed, and she relaxed. As they made their way to Mousey's house, she regaled him with doctoring stories, letting him see both the humor and the despair in her chosen profession. By the time they reached the O'Tooles', Mousey was raving drunk. He'd guzzled a whole bottle of whiskey to deaden the pain of the toothache, but it hadn't helped. The tooth,

Katherine told him after examining it, would have to come out.

With a kind of stunned amazement Zach watched her yank out the howling man's tooth and present it to him, grinning. "It won't bother you anymore," she promised, and left him a tincture of paregoric to soothe the remaining ache away.

Was there nothing she couldn't handle? Zach wondered as they made their way down the front steps. She was beautiful and capable and, Zach decided as he watched the provocative sway of her shapely backside, infinitely desirable. He caught her around the waist and pulled her back against his hard body. Lowering his head, he whispered into her ear, "If Mousey had been wearing a rabbit's tooth around his neck he could have warded off that toothache."

Katherine laughed, even as she fought the keen yearning to melt into him, to feel his mouth open over hers and take it in a hot, deep kiss. But Zach released her and gave her a hand up into the sleigh. "Another one of Grandma's cures?" she asked.

"Well, I think it beats her other cure for a toothache."

"What's that?"

"Rinsing his mouth every morning with his own urine."

"That is vile!"

He laughed. "I know."

They started off again, the sleigh gliding swiftly over the snowy rolling land. Sunshine sparkled, and long streaks of yellow light darted between tree trunks. Katherine pointed out the tracks of wild creatures— rabbits and mice and foxes—in the snow.

"Remember how you used to trap antelopes?" she asked him.

He glanced at her. "I remember," he said softly, and looked ahead again.

"Tess and Cody thought that's where you were when you left to go to sea."

The note of wistfulness in her voice startled him, and he looked sharply at her. He searched her face with searing intensity, then said tersely, "I had to go."

He glanced out again over the land and she saw a muscle tense in the strong angle of his jaw. And then, surprising her, he changed the subject completely. "You like doctoring?"

"There's nothing else I'd rather do."

He grunted. "And you like doctoring out here on the frontier?"

She shrugged. "Well, I'd like practicing anywhere, I suppose. But the reason I settled in Newberry, as you know, is because of its proximity to the reservation."

He grunted again.

"But actually," she continued, looking out to the horizon, "I have a wonderful assistant on the reservation and he's taken over a good deal of my duties. He's Arapaho and knows the people's ways."

When Zach grunted a third time, she turned to him in bewilderment. A flash of red caught her eye, though, and she suddenly pointed to the right.

"Turn up that path," she said. "There's a red rag tied to that tree."

"What of it?"

"I'm sure you've guessed that folks leave signs for me along the way if they want me to stop at their homes."

"I figured it was something like that."

This time she tended to a boy with a fever and cough, then they were on their way again, the sleigh skipping over the damp smooth snow. The air was growing warmer, and Katherine thought the snow wouldn't last through the week. She settled back, warmed by Zach's body heat.

"Now, Captain Fletcher," she said, "I want to hear some sea stories."

Zach gladly obliged her. He told her about the shipyard he'd bought in Marblehead, just north of Boston. He regaled her with stories of his sea-roving days, describing ports so vividly that Katherine could imagine all of it. As the cutter skimmed over the white, glittering countryside, she found herself in other lands—the Orient, Africa, Europe. Zach's rich, deep voice sent shivers over her skin as he told her of countries with castles and palaces, of royalty and squalor, of tropical beaches with sand as white as sugar and dazzling lagoons, of sunrises red as fire.

"Sounds like heaven to travel like that," she murmured. "How lucky you've been, Zach."

"We make our own luck, Smoke Eyes," he said, and smiled at the way she wrinkled her nose at him.

"I know that," she said firmly. "But you've done a dazzling job of making your own luck."

His smile broadened as he felt a startling flash of satisfaction at her words. It pleased him that she saw him as a success. "Let's hope my luck holds out."

She looked away, reading the double entendre of his words. "Up ahead," she said, "is a cabin. I want to stop there."

Reluctantly, he turned his attention to where she pointed, a small cabin with blue smoke curling from its chimney.

"This is old Ethan Wright's place," she explained, reaching under the seat for her medical bag. "He used to be a trapper and, remarkably, won the respect of many of my mother's people." She braced herself as Zach stopped the sleigh in front of the cabin, and a shadow darkened her eyes. "And he's dying."

She hopped out of the sleigh, hauling her bag along with her. "I won't be long," she called as she started for the cabin.

Zach frowned. She'd let him join her all along the way, allowing him to watch as she tended to her patients. Why did she shut him out now?

"How long are you going to be?"

Katherine heard the odd, rough note in his voice, and hesitated on the front step. When she turned to look at him, his gaze drilled into her from across the yard. Ethan knew her better than anyone else in the vicinity, and he was likely to say things she did not want Zach to hear. She gave him a fleeting smile and shrugged. "Not long," she repeated.

She felt his hard stare on her back as Ethan's ranch hand, Mike, let her in. Mike was nearly as old as Ethan, and he lived several miles away. He helped out with odd chores, and looked in on Ethan every day. He smiled at Katherine, his lips cracking in his weather-burned, seasoned face. "Hello, Doc."

She nodded and smiled. "Mike. How are you?"

"Oh, well's can be expected. Lookin' forward to spring."

Her gaze sought out Ethan, in his bed across the rustic two-room cabin. As always, he missed nothing, and he was blunt about it. "Who's that feller ya got with ya, little one?"

She strode toward him. "An old friend, Ethan."

He grunted. "You could've invited him in."

"I can't stay for long, Ethan. And he doesn't mind waiting," she lied, setting her bag on the bedside table. "How are you feeling?"

"Same as always, little girl. So frail a strong wind could break me in half."

She smiled at him. "Ethan, you exaggerate." She set

a paper sack of candy and dried fruit on the table. "I brought you some licorice."

His eyes lit up with delight. He took a piece and offered one to Mike, who slipped out the front door to talk with Zach. As Ethan sucked on the licorice Katherine began to rub liniment into his crippled limbs. "If you moved closer to town," she scolded him gently, "I could tend to you more often."

"Aach!" he barked. "Too many folks. I like the company of wild critters, as you know."

"Recluse," she teased.

"It's good of you to come up and see me. Mike don't rub these old bones half as well as you do." A smile came into his faded old eyes. "I'm gonna be passin' on soon anyhow."

"Don't say that!"

The old man chuckled. "Ah, little one, you should know of all people. You should know."

She didn't answer, just kept her eyes on her work. In a very short time she and Ethan had shared so much—he tales of his past, she, her heart. Of all the people in and around Newberry, only Ethan knew her name, Smoke Eyes.

Ethan watched her bent head for a moment, then looked out the window, where he could see Zach on the porch. "So, he's an old friend, eh?"

Katherine's head snapped up. She caught the direction of Ethan's gaze and glanced out the window too. Her hands stilled on Ethan's gnarled leg, and her mouth went dry. How, she wondered, could just the sight of Zach make everything leap inside her? She ran the back of her hand over her forehead, and her skin felt hot, feverish. He was looking out at the mountains with one shoulder propped against a porch post, hands shoved into the back pockets of his jeans. She could see his breath mist in the sharp air, and remembered the warmth of it on her bare skin. She shivered.

"And how long have you known this 'old friend'?"

She glanced sharply at Ethan. Was it her imagination, or had his tone been slightly mocking when he'd said "old friend"? "I've known him since I was thirteen, but we haven't seen each other in eleven years."

"Ah. So it's a reunion, is it?"

She pressed her lips together tightly as she snapped the lid on the tin of salve. "That's right," she said, reaching into her bag to give him two more tins.

"Hmm, seems to me you'd want me to meet an old friend of yours, Smoke Eyes. In fact, I'm insulted that you haven't introduced us."

Their eyes met and parried. "You must eat more, Ethan. You're fading away." She ran her wrist across her forehead again. "And you wily old fox! You're not insulted at all."

"Oh, but I am!" he crowed. He waved a feeble hand toward the window. "Now don't disappoint me, miss. Open that door and bring him in to me!"

Sighing, Katherine went to the door and swung it open. Zach looked over his shoulder at her, and it seemed a long time before she let out her breath. She saw his gaze lower to her hands, and until then she did not realize she had been twisting them. She stopped, clasping them behind her back. "Ethan wants to meet you," she said, and her voice came out sharper than she had intended.

He eased away from the porch post and started toward her. For a moment she stood mesmerized by the sight of his thigh muscles rippling beneath the fabric of his snug trousers, and she had to banish the burning image of him naked, the memory of those hard muscles and warm bare skin against hers.

He strode into the cabin, all shoulders and muscles

and rugged masculinity. She watched as his gaze flicked around the cabin, making a quick study. He dominated the room with his powerful height and build, captivating both Ethan and Katherine for a moment. Then he suddenly smiled, his eyes crinkling, his white teeth flashing. He leaned to shake Ethan's hand as Katherine introduced them.

"So, what is it that you do for a living, young man?" Ethan asked with his typical bluntness.

Zach glanced at Katherine, but she was busy ignoring the men as she rearranged items in her medical bag. "I'm a sea captain," he told Ethan.

Ethan raised his brows. "Not much ocean in these parts."

Zach laughed. "Naw. I'm here for a visit." As if there was no help for it, his gaze strayed once again toward Katherine. "To see Smoke Eyes."

Katherine's spine stiffened. To call her that in front of Ethan. How dare he! And how dare he lie about coming out to Colorado to visit *her,* when he'd come to request her services for his son! Something caught in her chest, and it hurt. He hadn't come to see *her* at all . . . and probably never would have if not for Drew.

As the men talked about sailing and trapping, she kept busy, straightening the place, putting on some coffee, slicing bread and spreading it with creamy butter. Still feeling hurt, she avoided looking at Zach as she served the men the small meal. When they had finished she suggested to Zach that it was time for them to leave.

"Well, now," Ethan said, looking more pleased than Katherine had ever seen him. "You take care of this little girl, son. She's a mighty precious one, you know."

Zach's gaze drifted her way, but Katherine kept her own averted as she slipped into her coat. "I know," he said, and his voice sent shivers up her spine.

She leaned down to kiss Ethan's cheek, and whispered a few words of encouragement and advice before she straightened. "Good-bye, Ethan, till next time."

"An' you take care of him too, missy. One good turn deserves another."

"Usually," Katherine murmured. She headed toward the door, Zach following close behind.

"I'm glad to see you've finally found someone," the old man went on. "Anyone can see the two of you are a perfect match. When you get around to marry—"

Mortified, Katherine whirled around. Wicked amusement was dancing in Zach's eyes, and before Ethan could say another word, she grabbed Zach's hand and tugged him out the door.

Zach was laughing outright by the time they settled in the sleigh. When he spoke, though, all he said was, "Nice man."

But Katherine had gone from hurt to anger, and glowered at him. "You lied to him!"

He frowned, heavy brows lowering.

"You told him you'd come out to visit me!" she continued, her voice rising. "You lied! You came out because of Drew!"

Zach cursed under his breath. "Dammit, Smoke Eyes—"

"And you called me Smoke Eyes in front of Ethan! You had no right!"

Zach rubbed his eyes. What the hell was wrong with her? It was impossible to keep pace with her mercurial moods. She changed them faster than a person could blink. And then he actually did blink. He thought he was seeing things when Katherine made a move to jump from the moving sleigh. His hand lashed out and caught her, and she gave a startled cry as the sleigh lurched sideways. "What the hell—are you crazy?" he snapped.

Tears spurted from Katherine's eyes, but she made sure he didn't see them. "Let me go!"

Zach gripped her arm so tightly, she could feel the bite of his fingers through her coat. He halted the sleigh and jerked her to him, pulling her head against his chest, stroking her hair. Still she struggled, pushing at his hard shoulders with her fists. "Let me go," she said again, but quieter.

"I can't," he whispered, and turned her face up to him. He caught the diamond glitter of tears in her eyes, and his heart jerked. "Damn you, Smoke Eyes," he said hoarsely before his lips came down on hers. His tongue slipped into her soft mouth, and Katherine whimpered, pushing against him, hating the drugging effect of his kiss. But there was no fighting the rush of throbbing excitement that spiraled through her body, dripping honeyed sweetness into a pool of moist warmth low in her loins. Zach's tongue stroked hard and deep, searching her mouth almost savagely, even as she fought him, trying to twist her head away. But he cradled her face in his big hands, scalding her with the intensity of his kiss.

He made a rough, guttural sound as he tore his lips from hers, and she gasped, the cold wind hitting her lungs as if it were her first breath. He pulled her close again and kissed her mouth hard.

"You're right," he muttered when he released her, his voice as ragged as his breathing. "I came out to see you for Drew's sake, but if I'd had a whit of sense, darlin', I would have come to see you before now."

She struggled out of his arms. "Only because you desire me!"

He frowned. "And what's wrong with that?"

She fought to regain her senses while every nerve in her body reached for him, yearning. "I'm just one of a very long string of women!" she cried, unable to bear the way he was looking at her, so intensely, so passionately.

As if he understood that, his expression softened. "Is that what you think?"

"How can I not?"

He couldn't deny that there had been plenty of women. He lifted his hand and ran his knuckles over the delicate line of her cheekbone. "Darlin'," he said gently, "I want you more than I've ever wanted any other woman."

She glared furiously at him. "How many other women have you told that to?"

His lips compressed tightly. Obviously, he'd said the wrong thing—again. "Dammit, woman, you are the most exasperating—" He broke off, getting a handle on his rising temper. "Can't you tell what you and I have is different?"

No, she couldn't. *This* had never happened before with any other man. And it would be worse if what he said was true, because they would part very soon. And she would be a fool if she became his mistress.

"Nothing's different," she said. "It's all the same to you, isn't it, Zach? Another conquest in another land. I won't be your conquest! I am not such a fool!"

His face darkened formidably. "Is that what you think? Dammit, honey, I wasn't conquering you—I was *enjoying* you."

She drew in a swift breath, his words settling low in the pit of her belly. But Zach said no more. He picked up the reins, slapping them lightly against Hippocrates. As the sleigh started off, Katherine's gaze locked on his hard profile, harsh, forbidding. She felt a quick jab under her ribs. Odd, but it seemed she had hurt him. Impossible! Zach Fletcher was a hard, arrogant, confident man, and she was certain she had just knocked him down a peg or two. Still, it left her with a queer sensation, one she could not squelch as they rode in tension-filled silence toward the reservation.

It was near dusk when they coasted over a small rise and the reservation came into view. Katherine could see the low buildings, the dispensary, the front gate that kept her mother's people herded inside like cattle. Sorrow seeped through her at the sight. Even when the sun was shining the reservation looked gray, forlorn, as if all of this country had forgotten these people. With a swift pang she remembered her mother, her soft brown eyes, and remembered that when she, Katherine, was very young she had vowed to doctor her mother's people, as if it might help their plight. She smiled sadly now. Such a childish fancy! The Arapaho were destined to live almost as prisoners, and her doctoring relieved them only as it would relieve any person in pain—very temporarily.

She suddenly wanted to break the uneasy tension between her and Zach. She turned to him, reaching out to rest a hand on his forearm. "Zach—"

Her words locked in her throat and her fingers bit into his arm as a scream, a terrible scream, rent the air. And then another. Katherine wanted to put her hands over her ears, to cover them from the horrendous, blood-chilling sound of a man in agony.

Before she could move or speak, Zach was turning the sleigh toward the screams, toward the frozen pond by the woods. There they saw a man writhing in agony, clutching his leg. He had collapsed on the ice, near a hole he'd obviously cut for ice fishing, and Katherine could see as they drew closer that a steel trap had snapped around his ankle. His screams echoed horribly in the late afternoon. Zach stopped the sleigh and she leapt out, racing toward the man, unable to think of anything but ending his agony.

"Don't go out on the ice!" Zach shouted, swinging out of the sleigh.

Was he insane? Katherine wondered, even as she halted. She knew the ice by the shore could break off easily and such cold water could paralyze a person almost immediately, but the man was in torture. Already she could see that he was a ghastly white and bleeding, his blood staining the ice. He was twisting on the ice like a snake, bending toward the trap, trying frantically to pry it off. But it was rusted and he was fast losing strength.

She couldn't bear to hear his weakening cries and jerked her gaze to Zach. He was winding rope around the man's horse's saddle horn, swearing viciously and shouting instructions to the man who could only groan in agony.

"I'm going to throw you the rope!" Zach yelled. "Grab it and put it over your head and under your arms! We'll pull you off the ice, understand?"

The man's eyes were glazed with pain, though, and he didn't answer.

Zach swore and threw the rope at him. It wiggled across the ice. The man couldn't even muster the strength to reach for it. "Grab the rope, man!" Zach called hoarsely, and Katherine could feel the panic swelling within her. Her heart was slamming against her rib cage. She had to get that man off the ice *now*. She made a sudden dash for the pond.

"Goddammit, Smoke Eyes," Zach shouted. "Get the hell—"

"I need to help him!" she yelled back. "I'll put the rope around him!"

She was already making her way across the pond on her belly. She could hear the ice cracking beneath her and held her breath, trying to shut out the man's miserable tormented groans. "I'm coming," she whispered. Just a few more feet, she told herself, and all sound—his choked-off sobs, Zach's lurid curses, the wind in the trees—were muffled by the torrential thunder of blood in her ears. A sharp wind blew across the pond, driving snow before it. The icy flecks stung her face, but she ignored it as she reached the man. Grabbing hold of the rope, she slipped it over his head and shoulders. But the ice could not hold them both. Just as the horse began dragging the man toward the bank the ice broke and Katherine went under, dropping straight downward into the water. She lost her breath and her limbs went numb, and suddenly the world was nothing but dark, suffocating, paralyzing depth. She knew she would sink even deeper and be drawn under the solid ice, where no one would ever find her. Odd, but she didn't care. A numbing lethargy swept over her, through her, pulling her under. From above she heard a terrible crash, a hoarse shout, and felt a rough hand jerk her by her hair, pulling her to the surface. It was Zach. Big, solid, warm Zach. He'd tied the rope around himself, and now he crushed her to him in his powerful arms, the heat of his body surrounding her as the horse hauled them both off the ice and up on the bank.

Vaguely, she heard his rough swearing and a strange, droning moan, like a wounded animal. She shook her head, feeling a faint tingling upon her scalp where Zach had tugged her hair, but little else. Her thoughts were sluggish, and all she wanted was to sleep.

Zach shook her roughly. She frowned and grumbled, her eyelids fluttering as she tried to focus on his face. He looked fierce, furious. Hmm, she thought, what's got his back up now? His back, his back . . . there was something to remember about his back . . .

Zach shook her again. "Dammit, Smoke Eyes, wake up!" He ran to the sleigh for the buffalo robe, then began peeling off her wet clothes, knowing he had to get rid of them fast, for they only leeched the heat from her body. She fought him, amazingly, giving him a weak push. Good. If she could still fight, she wasn't too far gone. But her lips were blue and she wasn't shivering, and that was a damn bad sign.

"Christ!" he swore, and tore at her clothes, ignoring her whimpered protest and the man who lay on the snow beside them, passed out from his pain.

When she was naked, Zach wrapped the buffalo robe around her and roughly rubbed her arms and legs, hoping to increase her circulation. She watched him drowsily, and he swore softly, wishing he could do more. But the man beside them might be bleeding to death. He ordered her to stay awake, then turned to the unconscious man. Fastening his hands on either side of the rusted trap, he tried to pry it open. The man cried out, but Zach ignored him and strained his muscles. The trap would not unhinge. He swore roughly, applied more strength, but blood leaked over his hands and the trap didn't budge. Then he saw the lever behind the man's foot and pushed down hard on it. The spring lock sprang free, releasing the man's leg, and he groaned deeply in his unconsciousness. Zach raced back to the sleigh and pulled out one of the clean shirts he'd brought with him. He tied it around the man's leg in a rough bandage, hoping it would slow the bleeding.

Wiping the sweat off his brow, he glanced toward Katherine. She was half asleep.

"Smoke Eyes!" he shouted, and she jumped. "Don't you dare go to sleep, woman!"

She glowered at him and he almost laughed, but his heart was slamming against his chest like a sledgehammer. If she fell asleep she might never wake up. He left the two of them long enough to gather some wood, and managed to build a small fire. He made a pot of coffee and set it on the fire to boil, then returned to her. Setting her right next to the fire, he slid his hands under the lap robe and started to rub her body again. She made a little hissing sound, then began to curse—words he'd bet she hadn't used since she was a wild little hoyden running free over the Kansas prairies.

"Dammit, Zach, will you stop at nothing to take my clothes off!"

A rough laugh burst from him, and all he could do was circle a hand around her neck and pull her head against his chest. He held her to him, still rubbing her legs, his face buried in her hair. She shuddered, then gasped as sensation started tingling in her limbs. He released her enough to pour coffee into a cup, and held the cup to her lips.

"Drink," he ordered.

She did. When she'd finished that cup, he poured her another. She'd regained enough awareness that she was able to hold the cup herself this time. He held her still-icy feet in his hands, chafing them and looking at her with both relief and exasperation.

"Woman," he said, "don't you have better sense than to go crashing across the ice like that?"

Her teeth began to chatter violently. "Y-you m-m-make me s-sound about as g-graceful as an an-antelope."

He laughed again and pulled her onto his lap, feeling the fragility of her slender body. Closing his eyes, he locked his arms around her and breathed in her scent. Her skin was still cold, and he stroked his hands up and down her back. She made soft, sighing sounds that pulled at him, made his chest grow so tight he could hardly breathe.

"I'm naked," she mumbled.

He pulled away to look at her face. Oh God, he couldn't, wouldn't, let her go. "And I wish I was," he whispered.

Katherine was too sleepy to reprimand him. She could only smile sleepily and nuzzle her face into his warm throat. His hands continued caressing her, and she melted against him. The heat of his own body and the robe seeped into her, making her even more drowsy. Abruptly Zach stood, setting her on her feet, startling her. The robe protected her bare feet but standing made her more alert.

"I'm tired," she complained.

"I know, honey. But you have to stay awake for a while yet."

Katherine's sleepy gaze drifted toward the still-unconscious man. A little jolt knifed through her as she remembered his trauma. His breathing was shallow, and she could see where Zach had wrapped a bandage around his leg; a bandage that was swiftly growing red.

"Zach!" she said. "We need to get him to the reservation. I need to look at his leg." She swallowed, remembering the man's wretched screams. She was too tired to stand, though, and sank slowly back down to the ground. "You'll have to help me."

"What do I do?"

"Tell me. Did the trap cut through the muscle—the bone?"

Zach went quickly to the man and crouched down to examine him. He glanced at Katherine. "I think he was lucky. The boot saved him from that."

But Katherine knew the risks were still great. He had suffered a horrible shock and there was the danger of gangrene. "It's important to get him out of the cold. Lift him gently into the sleigh. We'll all have to squeeze in."

She watched sleepily as Zach carried the groaning man to the cutter. Then Zach was before her, a worried expression in his eyes. Muttering something she did not hear, he bent down to slide his arms under her legs and shoulders. She grabbed him around his neck as he lifted her and strode toward the sleigh. Surrounded by his strength and warmth, she snuggled into his hard body, letting the subtle musk-warm scent of him wash over her.

He tucked her into the sleigh and set it in motion.

"I don't have any clothes on," she murmured against his shoulder.

"That, honey, is the least of our troubles," Zach said. And he drove hell-bent-for-leather into the reservation with a bleeding, unconscious man, and a woman dressed only in a buffalo robe.

Eleven

They created quite a stir as they coasted up to the sentry at the gate, with Zach barking that he had the doctor with him and a man in a dire situation. Recognizing Katherine, the sentry paled and quickly directed Zach to the dispensary. Zach halted the sleigh there with a violent jolt, leapt out, and shook Katherine, who groused and mumbled. He was shouting for help as he continued to shake her, but Katherine had run out of energy and she slumped to one side, leaning on the injured man.

Exasperated, Zach scooped her from the cutter and stood her on the frozen ground. She was alert enough to clutch the robe around her as Zach reached past her for the man in the sleigh. He slung the man over one shoulder and walked toward the front door of the dispensary. He'd made enough noise to draw a small crowd, and as Katherine sank to the front steps two men spilled out the door. Zach brushed past them, still carrying the unconscious man. He swept down the corridor, finding a sterile white operating room where a tall, wiry, sharp-faced Arapaho man turned to face him. This, Zach guessed, must be Smoke Eyes's apprentice. But there was no time for introductions.

He dumped the man on the table. "Trap. Get the boot off. I'll bring Smoke Eyes in to look at it."

The Arapaho man stiffened, and his dark eyes narrowed. "You know Smoke Eyes?"

The two men quickly—almost fleetingly—sized each other up, and both could feel the immediate tension that sprang between them.

"I know her," Zach said tightly, and wondered just how well this man knew his darling. He felt an odd jerk in his chest as the endearment surged through him. How natural it seemed to think of her as *his*. "Get the boot off," he repeated, and left the room.

Something burned inside Zach as he strode back down the corridor, ignoring the curious stares of government officials and orderlies. Dammit, that man was interested in Smoke Eyes! Why hadn't she told him? Then a sudden thought gripped him, searing his gut. Was she in love with him?

He swung the door open more forcefully than he had intended, and it slammed back against the building with a violent bang. On the steps below Katherine jumped. She muttered something, and he saw that she was listing, one hand propped under her jaw, her eyelids fluttering in a desperate attempt to stay open.

He shook her shoulder. "Wake up."

She opened her eyes unnaturally wide and blinked at him. Zach felt his stomach muscles tighten. Knowing she was naked under that lap robe didn't cool his pounding blood any. He clamped back on the powerful surge of desire that washed through him and scooped her up in his arms. Ignoring the tittering of the women who watched them, he took the steps two at a time. "Your assistant needs direction."

"You met White Owl?" she asked.

Zach's arms tightened around her. So that was his name. "I met him."

Katherine clung tightly to him, her arms looped around his neck. She was oblivious to the gawks she and Zach earned as he strode down the corridor with her to the operating room.

White Owl had removed the man's boot, and his foot was more than double its normal size, and bruised a deep plum-blue. He was still bleeding from numerous gashes, and it was too early to tell if poison had set in. But already White Owl was heating a poultice and measuring drops of a clear fluid into a dish.

"White Owl," Katherine said. Zach tensed as he watched the other man turn, a smile of delight spreading over his red-brown face. Katherine slid out of his arms, and reluctantly he let her go. "You've met Zach?" she asked, then introduced them anyhow. "White Owl, meet Zach. Zach, James White Owl."

White Owl dismissed Zach by turning a shoulder to him and facing Katherine. "We shall keep poultices on him, watch the fever, monitor him closely."

She nodded and moved closer to the table where the wounded man lay. "Very good." She examined the wound, then drew back, frowning. "We still may have to amputate."

James White Owl cleansed the wound, not looking

at her as he asked, "Why are you unclothed, Smoke Eyes?"

Katherine blushed. She had forgotten. Glancing across the room, she saw Zach watching them intently. "I fell into the pond," she said. "Zach pulled me out."

What was this strange hostility she sensed between the two men? she wondered. She had hoped they would like each other, but they seemed to have gotten off on the wrong foot. She could feel the tension emanating from White Owl beside her, and Zach's dark face had gone tight. He looked as though he wanted to knock White Owl's teeth down his throat.

She shrugged, deciding to ignore the simmering tension between the two. She instructed White Owl to wrap disinfectant-soaked bandages around the man's shin and ankle. He would need suturing, but she was too weary to do that now.

"Smoke Eyes."

She turned at the sound of Zach's voice, wavering slightly.

"We have to get you some more coffee," he said, "and some clothes."

"You noticed," she said dryly, and caught White Owl's little smirk. She leaned toward her assistant, noting that Zach clenched his fists as she did so. "Can you suture him, White Owl? I need to get warm and alert, then we can discuss our patient in greater detail later."

White Owl nodded. Katherine left the operating room, feeling Zach put his hand to the small of her back. His touch burned through the robe and into her blood, pulsing warmly through her body.

She led him to a private room. Inside was a cot, a chair, and a washstand with a basin of water.

"I'll bring you some coffee and your clothes," he said, his big hands on her shoulders, pressing her to sit on the cot. "Keep your eyes open, darlin'. I'll only be a minute."

Odd, she thought as she watched him disappear through the doorway, how comfortable he was in the position of authority. He snapped orders as if he expected everyone to obey him, and they did. She was smiling dreamily when he returned with her bag and a cup of steaming coffee. "Drink," he said, pushing it into her hands.

"You like to give orders."

Zach ignored that. He was going through her bag, searching for warm dry clothing. "One of the young men took your horse and the sleigh to shelter. Said he'd take care of it for us."

"Mmm." She sipped the coffee and it burned a trail to the pit of her belly, glowing there like a warm flame.

"Dammit, Smoke Eyes, haven't you got anything *practical* in this bag?" He was flinging her lacy, silky undergarments over his shoulder in his search for some woolen or flannel underwear. "What th—" He held up a gossamer-thin chemise and gazed speculatively at her, as if envisioning her in it. Her face turned the color of a tomato. She slapped the coffee cup down on the washstand, the hot liquid splashing over the rim, and surged to her feet, clutching the buffalo robe around her.

"Put that back!" she said. "I can find my own clothes, Zach."

He dropped the chemise back into the bag and took one long step toward her. He stood so close, she had to tilt her head far back to see his face.

"I'm trying to help," he said, his voice mild though a fierce emotion glittered in his eyes. "But you don't seem to appreciate anyone helping you, Smoke Eyes. You haven't even thanked me for saving your life."

She looked down, embarrassed. He was right, she

hadn't. "Thank you," she murmured, then looked up at him again. "Thank you," she repeated in a stronger voice. "You were very brave too . . . and quick-thinking . . . and . . ."

He smiled that endearing lopsided smile. "I accept your thanks," he said, and his smile turned wicked. "Though perhaps you could show me your appreciation in another, more . . . enticing way."

She took a step back, instantly understanding him. "Zach . . ."

"Smoke Eyes." He followed her, trapping her between the cot and his body. "Just one kiss, darlin'. Just one."

She was about to retort that he'd never be satisfied with just one kiss but wisely held her tongue. No sense in inciting him further. "Zach," she said in a reasonable tone, "this isn't a very private place. White Owl might need me any minute, and if anyone were to come in and find you and me here alone, they'd think—"

"Yes?" His brows rose. "They'd think . . . ?"

She tried to sidle past him, but he was too quick and blocked her escape to the door. "I have to get dressed, Zach."

"Yes?"

"So you have to leave."

He grinned, obviously enjoying himself. "Not until I get my kiss."

She studied him, weighing her options. But she knew Zach, and he could be as stubborn as . . . well, as herself. "All right," she said. "One kiss."

That now familiar fire leapt into his eyes. He slowly slid his arms around her, slowly pulled her to him, slowly lowered his head. "Smoke Eyes," he murmured just before his lips touched hers.

Instantly, Katherine knew one kiss would not be enough for her either. It too felt good. Deep inside her a heat began to curl, lapping up, outward, flushing her skin. She was lost in the taste and feel of him as the kiss quickly became wild, hungry, staggering her senses. A primal need burned in him—she could feel it throb in the fierce heat of his hard body. Groaning, he pulled her up flush against him, fitting her softer body to his long, muscular frame. She shuddered and clung to him, her fingers digging into his shoulders. He pushed his tongue deep into her mouth, withdrew, and plunged again, tasting, searching. His kiss possessed her, and she shuddered with exquisite pleasure, wanting to fight it but feeling swept along, as she had in the icy pond water, dragged under, out of control, breathless.

He whispered things against her mouth, the words blurring as his tongue stroked hers. He was hard against her, his manhood pushing against her softness, and she felt a delicious shock. What was happening to her? She was helpless to restrain her response to him. Her body felt as though it were empty, and thirsted with a need so great she feared it could never be quenched. She wanted to pull free, to douse her desire, but Zach was kneading her hips . . . palming her buttocks so that she was forced once again into the thick, hard bulge that strained against the front of his trousers.

She pulled her mouth free, gasping. "No more, Zach, no more."

He wouldn't release her, though, but let his lips trail a burning path down her throat. "Soft . . . soft . . ." he murmured as his mouth slid lower. With one hand he pushed aside the buffalo robe and found her breast. He cupped it, lifted it, and his mouth locked hotly upon her hard, turgid nipple.

"Ohh—ohh—" Her fingers tangled in his thick hair, holding him closer, until she heard footsteps outside the door. Brought back abruptly to the reality of where they were and what they were doing, she wrenched herself out of his arms, clutching the robe closed.

"Please, get out," she whispered, and almost flinched when Zach narrowed his eyes on her. He stood with his legs apart, rubbing his jaw, his eyes glittering with a savage kind of hunger—and anger.

"Dammit, Smoke Eyes." His voice was hoarse, as if he were having trouble catching his breath. "Don't you pull that martyred act with me! You enjoyed that kiss—and my mouth on you—every bit as much as I did!"

"Martyred!" she exclaimed. "I'm not acting martyred—I'm furious! And how dare you tell me what I enjoy, you conceited, arrogant wretch!"

He laughed. "You did enjoy it," he said, more arrogant than usual. "So don't bother denying it."

She drew in a sharp breath. "I told you to get out, and I meant it." She looked away from his handsome face, his eloquent black eyes. She hated him in that moment, hated the mocking elusive smile that tipped up one corner of his sensual mouth. But she could not seem to stop her gaze from returning to his, and she narrowed her eyes.

"If you won't leave, then I will."

She marched past him to the door, but he pounced, slamming the door shut before she'd opened it an inch. She hissed and turned toward him, but he caught her upper arms in his hands and hauled her up against him so they were almost nose to nose.

He bent his head and took her mouth fiercely, but quickly, as if it was enough for the moment. She gasped, and her lips tingled after he'd lifted his mouth. Staring at him, she couldn't breathe, couldn't think. He was breathing raggedly, as if his body would never cool, and when he spoke his voice was raw and husky.

"I told myself I could wait for you, Smoke Eyes. But

I can't wait. I want you. I want you now . . . and for a long time."

Katherine felt the swelling of tears in her throat, her eyes. "What about what I want, Zach?"

His fingers tightened on her arms. She winced, and he loosened his grip, but only slightly. "You want it too."

She shook her head. "Not the same things. We don't want the same things."

He stared at her for a moment longer, then let her go. Swearing, he dragged a hand through his hair. "You don't know that, dammit!"

"Yes, I do." Her voice was even, almost imploring, almost as if she wished he would see her way, then let this all-consuming fire between them flicker out. "You want a mistress. I cannot be your mistress, Zach. How absurd even to consider it."

"Absurd!" he barked, and once again tore a hand through his hair. "There's not a damn absurd thing about this!"

She shrugged. "Well, certainly impractical."

He looked at her, astounded. She was discussing lovemaking as if it were a business transaction. She went on in that aloof way of hers as she began sorting through the clothes he'd tossed onto the cot. "If you gave it any thought, which I know men aren't prone to do, you would see for yourself that it is probably the most absurd notion you've ever had. And the most unfair." Across the room her calm gray eyes met his. "You have asked me to come east with you to help your son, and yet you pursue this—this—"

"Burning desire?"

She blinked, then reached for a woolen skirt. "As if we can just merrily go on about our lives." She picked up a blouse. "Well I, for one, Zach, find that a conflict."

"I've already told you one thing has nothing to do with the other."

"I beg to differ."

Their gazes clashed—biting black and stormy gray. "Are you telling me," he said between clenched teeth, "that you will not come home with me because we *desire* each other?"

Her chin edged up. "Speak for yourself."

Zach growled and stepped toward her, then thought better of it and stopped. "The hell I will. I'm speaking for both of us, since you are not going to be honest about it."

"Honest about what?"

"You want me and I want you. Are you going to ignore that?"

Katherine smoothed her blouse over the cot, carefully keeping her face averted from his penetrating stare. "We have choices to make. In medical school we are taught never to cross the line between a professional matter and a personal one. I am not about to start now."

She dared a swift sidelong glance at him, then quickly turned away. He looked so formidable, she felt some of her courage fade. "So what you are trying to say," he said, "and do not seem to be able to say, is that you are not coming east to help my son."

She whirled on him, clutching her skirt. "That's unfair! To phrase it that way makes me sound coldhearted and spiteful!"

He merely looked at her.

How dare he put her in this position! she thought. Suddenly she felt a dull throbbing ache behind her temples. She put a hand to her forehead and closed her eyes, feeling again the ache of tears in her throat. She wanted to cry with both confusion and frustration, but instead just sank to the edge of the cot and stared through tear-blurred eyes at the floor. "I will not," she said tonelessly, "become another Laura."

Hearing his savage curse, she looked up. There was such fury in his expression, she shuddered. "Are you going to continue to fling the sins of my past in my face? Now who's being unfair, Smoke Eyes? I was just a kid when I took up with Laura. I'd treat you different."

"I don't want to be your mistress," she said in a low, strained voice. "I don't want your jewels and silks. I will not be a fool for a man. Least of all you, Zach, who will set sail without a thought to those you leave behind!"

Zach frowned. What the hell did she want? He realized abruptly that he ached all over. He was bone-tired and worn-out from this woman who could make his blood flow hotly with both anger and desire. As if she sensed that, she made a gesture toward the door.

"You need to lie down," she said. "Your back must be hurting you and I'm sure it needs to be massaged. Why don't you settle into the room next door? I have some things to tend to and I'll be a while yet."

She was going to that damned assistant, he thought savagely. Damned if he could find any humor in this night at all. Well, fine, let her go to him. Let White Owl take her off his hands. He left the room, left her, and flung himself down on the cot in the adjacent room. Almost instantly he sank into the sweet oblivious world of sleep.

He awoke some time later to soft light shining into his eyes. He saw the fuzzy shape of James White Owl standing over him and he frowned, raising himself on one elbow. "What do you want?"

The Arapaho man gave him a small smile. "It's well past midnight. Smoke Eyes told me you needed your back massaged."

Zach shot up like a Fourth of July rocket. Pain seared along the bruised muscles in his back, making him grit his teeth. He swung his long legs off the bed and braced his elbows on his knees, staring at his boots. He was furious that Katherine had sent her lackey to him. When he felt under control, he lifted his gaze and caught the ironic humor in James White Owl's eyes. "I'll be damned if I let you lay a hand on my back," he said. "So you may as well just get the hell out."

White Owl only looked amused. "It seems you are in much pain."

Zach's eyes narrowed. Why did that casual statement seem to speak volumes?

White Owl reached for a tin of liniment, but his hands stilled when Zach gave him a warning look. White Owl let his gaze wander over Zach's face, then his hands, noting the stitches and burns. "It seems you've had a rough stay here in Colorado."

"And why does that fact seem to give you immense pleasure?"

"She is an obstinate woman, our Smoke Eyes."

Zach gritted his teeth so hard, his jaw muscles ached. Jealousy stabbed hotly through his gut, and its intensity stunned him. He felt the most overwhelming, unreasonable urge to crash his fist into White Owl's face, but he held on to his temper. "Funny," he said in a drawling, sarcastic tone, "I don't remember Smoke Eyes mentioning you owned her."

James White Owl leaned back against a table and folded his arms across his chest. "She has told me who you are and what you want from her. You must not take her east with you."

"Don't you think it's best if *she* decides that?"

"I think she has already made that decision."

Every muscle in Zach's body tightened, and it took

all his control to remain seated. "What you think and what she tells me are two different things." Though they weren't, he admitted. Not really.

James White Owl seemed to measure him carefully. "I have great love for her."

Zach gave a small, cynical laugh. "Yeah, she inspires that in people. Every man in that town she doctors is in love with Smoke Eyes."

White Owl was angry now; it showed in his taut face. "You make love sound cheap and tawdry."

"Love," Zach said bitterly, "between a man and a woman is very rare."

"You do not love her. You only want her."

His expression turned granite-hard. "And I find it amazing that you presume to know what I feel." An intense possessiveness gripped him, so intense his hands began to shake. Was it fury, jealousy? Zach did not know, for he had never felt this way about any woman before. In just a few days Smoke Eyes had seeped under his skin, into his blood, becoming such a vibrant force and need in him, he didn't think he'd ever be able to shake free of her. She was right—he was selfish and footloose, and perhaps vastly unfair to press her. But he wanted her. And he was a man used to taking whatever came his way. What was so damn wrong with that?

Suddenly he badly needed some fresh air. He stood up and walked to the door, smiling sardonically at James White Owl. "It's been nice talking to you. But I think we've said all there is to say to each other. In the time that I'm here stay clear of me, 'cause I've always had a real short fuse where Smoke Eyes is concerned."

With that he strode out of the room, and nearly collided with Katherine, who had been on her way in.

"Oh!" She put her hands up to steady herself, and he caught her by the wrists.

"Next time," he said, "don't send your lovestruck assistant to me, Smoke Eyes. I'm likely to take him apart by my bare hands."

He released her and strode off, before Katherine could say a word. She watched him stride down the hall and out the door, and a curious desolate feeling welled inside her.

They stayed at the reservation for three days, and during those three days tension simmered between Katherine and Zach, even though Zach took excruciating pains to keep his distance. Katherine felt oddly bereft, oddly—and unjustly—abandoned by him, and she wished it could all be different. She missed his teasing, their easy rapport. She didn't understand why he wouldn't accept that she couldn't become his mistress. She had a life to lead while he returned to his own with his son. Or maybe not, she thought with a surge of guilt. Maybe Drew would die. Would Zach blame her if he did?

Oh, it was all so confusing! She felt stung by his cold rejection, but perhaps, she thought sadly, it was best this way. Best not to make a miserable mess of the situation.

It had already become complicated, though, she realized the second afternoon, as she watched him from a window in the dispensary. He was out on the front lawn with several of the children, building them a huge, majestic ship out of snow. The children were delighted, scampering around him, calling to him, helping him slap on blocks of packed snow when he didn't need any help at all. He had infinite patience with them—rare in a man. He even carried one little tyke on his back for a quarter of an hour, talking to the boy who clung like a monkey, thrilled by the special attention Zach gave him. His back must be healing, Katherine thought, smiling at the sight. He appeared to have a natural affinity for children, and she wondered how he could have stayed away from his son for so long. Perhaps he just hadn't been ready for a child of his own, and though it was hard to understand, she *could* understand.

She saw him laugh at something one of the children said, his white teeth gleaming. But then he looked up and spied her. Her heart stilled. She could not move, frozen by his stare. His eyes narrowed, squinting against the sun's glare, and his smile faded before he turned back to the children. She felt stricken, as if he'd caught her in some indecent act, when all she'd been doing was watching him.

They had become too close, too familiar. It seemed impossible in the short time they had spent with each other, but it was true. She felt things for Zach she did not want to feel. It disturbed her that she found so much to admire in him, even if he was a commanding, arrogant man. He was courageous—almost recklessly so—and though he burned with a powerful sexual intensity and unconquerable strength, there was a haunting tenderness about him that drew her inexorably to him. He would be an easy man to love. No! The notion whipped through her with real pain, making her heart pound heavily with alarm. It would be dangerous to love Zach. Instead, she knew, she must get him out of town, out of her life as soon as possible. It was certainly the wisest choice.

She was glad she had the distraction of her patients—coughs and colds, a woman in labor, and most especially, the man they had rescued on the pond. His name was Buttons McCormick, and he had eyes like bright brown buttons, and scads of wispy hair that stuck out crazily around his head. He was charming despite the pain he still suffered, and had no fear of finding himself on the Arapaho reservation. He was lucky in that they did not have to amputate, and his wife was sent for—the best medicine of all, Katherine thought, for she nursed him night and day. With such good care he would be on his way home in a week or so.

She and Zach left the reservation on a clear, cold morning, Zach with a pair of moccasins one of the elders had given him for Drew, and Katherine with a heavy heart, as James White Owl stared after them with censuring eyes.

They rode home in virtual silence, stopping only once, at the Duggans' to see how they were getting on. Nan and her puppy greeted Zach with great excitement, Nan jabbering animatedly and Lucky waggling in circles.

"He wants to kiss you!" Nan cried with glee. "He wants to kiss you!"

Obligingly, Zach lifted the pup and let it lick his face. All the Duggans laughed.

Close to dusk they coasted up to Katherine's stable, and Zach stopped the sleigh with an abrupt jolt. "I'll walk to the hotel," he said, his eyes only briefly meeting hers.

Katherine's chest tightened with a piercing ache. She reached a hand toward him in supplication, touching the sleeve of his coat. "Zach, I—"

"I'm leaving in two days," he said grimly, swinging out of the sleigh. He glanced up to her, and his eyes bored deeply into hers, mercilessly, as if they were penetrating her very soul. She clenched her fists, fighting his power. "I take it you've decided not to come with me."

"I didn't say that—exactly."

An ironic smile touched the corners of his mouth.

"You've said it," he told her. "In many ways, many times."

She was stricken. If only he had kept his hands off her, she might have considered coming with him. But this—*this* situation was impossible! She swallowed, but an ache resurfaced at the back of her throat. "If only—"

He cut her off, and his half-smile was soft, almost wistful. "No ifs, no excuses. It always comes down to yes or no. Simple as that, Smoke Eyes."

"No!" she cried. She was protesting his statement, not giving him her reply, but the word hung in the air between them. She thought—erratically, irrationally— how breathtaking the harsh planes of his face looked brushed by the blue light of dusk. "You haven't made this simple at all, Zach!" She saw his self-deprecating smile and wanted to say something—anything—to comfort him. "Zach, I—listen. I'll send James White Owl with you. He knows my—"

Zach frowned darkly. "You don't get it, do you, Smoke Eyes? Drew wants *you* to come—you, the fantasy, you the miracle worker. You know and I know you're not, but Drew does not know. My son wants you to be there."

Zach fought the swift dart of desperation that lanced through his vitals. How could he bear to go back without her? She had been like a ray of light in his life when it had been dark and somber for so long. Her laughter could make him feel young and lighthearted; it soothed him as no medicine could. The thought of leaving her tore at him, and he didn't want to face it, not yet. But, dammit, he needed her for Drew too. What would happen when he walked into his home and Smoke Eyes was not with him? *What would happen to Drew?*

Katherine was staring at him, her eyes huge in the purple shadows. Bracing his hands on the seat back on either side of her, he leaned close to her. He searched her gaze for a long moment.

"Don't you know it haunts me every day, every night?" he asked, his voice tormented. "I wake up thinking about Drew, I go to sleep wondering how I'm going to save his life. And many nights I don't sleep at all. But it's out of my hands, isn't it, Smoke Eyes—a cruel trick of fate. At least you have the power—the skills—to act, to help. Even if he does die you'd know you'd done everything possible to save him."

He stopped to draw in a breath, and when he spoke again, it was more calmly.

"The only relief in all this time has been you, Smoke Eyes." He lifted his hand to run his knuckles over her soft cheek. When she trembled, he smiled. "You, darlin'."

Tears stung her eyes, and Katherine wanted to close them against his harsh face, against the stark pain she read in his eyes. But she stiffened her jaw and kept her gaze upon him, trying to reason with him. "Drew's a child, Zach, and children are resilient. He'll forget all about me if I send White Owl with you. He knows the Arapaho ways." Her words, she realized, sounded too close to a plea. She was trying to ease her own conscience. What would happen if the boy went into a decline when Zach returned home without her? She frowned. Zach had made her responsible for Drew's health either way. She sighed, rubbing her forehead. If only he had never pursued her! God, didn't he know she had to guard her heart as well as he had to help his boy?

But Zach was tired now too. He straightened wearily, and his face was hard and unreadable as he looked down at her. For a fleeting moment she thought his black gaze was condemning her. "If you change your mind in the next day or so you know where to find me." He turned away.

He couldn't just leave! "I—" She swallowed, and he stopped to look at her. "Your stitches," she said lamely. "I might need to see how you're healing."

His somber gaze flickered over her, dismissing her. "I'll be fine." But he lingered now, a faint smile warming his eyes. "You'll say good-bye at least," he stated flatly.

Her heart thumped and she felt a stirring in her very depths, hot with emotion. "Of course," she said softly.

Without another word he left her. She sat for a long time in the sleigh, staring into the deepening blue-black shadows, almost expecting his tall, broad-shouldered frame to materialize so she might have a better chance to explain. But only the darkness closed in to embrace her.

Twelve

During the night, while Katherine was poring over her medical texts, a warm wind sprang up, and she could hear the melting snow dripping from the eaves. She hadn't *wanted* to look at her books, but after coming in from the stable and eating a light supper, she'd felt compelled to study her notes on abdominal surgery.

"I don't know why I'm doing this," she muttered halfway through the night, even after her eyes became sleep-blurred. She fell asleep at her desk, the image of Zach's harsh, troubled features, his somber gaze burning into her brain. She thought she could imagine his son, too, with the same dark hair and intense gaze. Silly, she knew, but she woke at dawn with the same images intertwined in her mind. She shook her head to clear it and shifted her gaze to the window, where shadowy gray light seeped in through the slatted wooden shutters.

He helped me, she thought with a twinge of guilt. Zach had helped her with the Duggans, had saved those children when she knew she never would have been able to reach them in time. And he'd helped her save Buttons McCormick. He had even saved *her* life. He never once had hesitated to act in the teeth of tragedy; he would have braved anything to rescue anyone—man, woman, or child—from a crisis. He only asked the same of her.

But, clearly, her professional and personal motivations had become blurred in Drew's case. Certainly there were competent doctors in Marblehead—even Zach had admitted as much—but she knew how important a patient's mental state was before going into an operation. And a child such as Drew, so depressed and having suffered great losses in his young life, was certainly not a good candidate for so serious an operation.

She sighed and rose from her desk, rubbing the small of her back which ached from sleeping in her slumped position. She didn't do that often and her brow furrowed as she thought of what had caused her condition. *He* had made this difficult! Why had he touched her in the first place? There was no future for them. Hadn't Zach made it clear that he did not want to be tied down? And didn't she fear her loss of freedom just as much, not to mention her reputation?

"Ah, Lord, Clarabelle," she murmured to the for-once silent bird, as she dragged the tub from the lean-to, "why do things have to be so complicated?

Why can't Zach, just once, accept no from a woman?" But she had to smile as she thought of his wicked black eyes, his perfect physique, his dark, erotic nature. He burned with passion as hot as fire, and every woman that crossed his path would likely—no, undeniably— get burned.

She shuddered and began to heat the water for her bath. It was best to get her mind off things, and a bath was the best way to do it. After that she would call Shadow in and they would share a huge breakfast of fried potatoes, buckwheat pancakes with butter and maple syrup, sausages and gravy, and spicy apple pie—Shadow's favorite. Unless, of course, he had eaten it in her absence. Then Katherine would drink a quart of tea before she headed off for the jail.

What's the status on the Waters murder? she wondered. Had the sheriff investigated it more thoroughly? She wrinkled her brow in consternation. She didn't know what drove her to defend Toby. Handling the murder was really the sheriff's territory, but something gnawed at her, a sense of injustice. Toby was disliked by so many and provided the sheriff with a convenient scapegoat. He was sixteen years old and truly without a friend. The sheriff had jailed Zach without any evidence, just glad to have had *someone* in jail, and now Bates was doing the same thing with Toby. True, Toby's knife was the murder weapon, but at least he deserved a fair trial. In any case, Katherine was sure Toby could use a visitor. And perhaps she would take a hamper of food to him.

At the jail, however, Toby was more surly and withdrawn than ever. His mother had come to visit him several times, he said to Katherine, had told him that she had dismissed the servants, and when the trial was over, would be leaving town. Even now she had left the house where she claimed the ghost of her husband haunted her. She was living in a boardinghouse.

"It isn't fair," Toby said, clenching a fist on his bony leg as he sat on the cot. "It isn't fair that she has to throw her whole life away because of *him.*"

"But, Toby," Katherine said gently, "perhaps this is just a way for her to start a new life, a happier one."

His head snapped up and his pale eyes blazed, narrowing on her. "Doc, there isn't any such thing as *happy*! Don't you see that?"

An uneasy notion slithered through Katherine. What if Toby's mother had murdered her husband? Almost as soon as she thought it, Toby surged to his feet and grabbed hold of the steel bars. "She didn't do it."

Katherine drew back, her heart pounding. For all the torment in the boy's face she could almost understand how Francine, his mother, could have killed her husband. She forced herself to speak in a low, soothing tone. "Toby, you still have some time. I'm going to talk to the sheriff now—"

Toby snorted and returned to the cot. "I'm gonna hang and it's time to face up to it. Why don't you let it be, Doc?"

But moments later she was speaking earnestly to the sheriff. "Did you learn where he was the night of the murder?"

Sheriff Bates looked exasperated. He began to steer her out of the back room toward the front door. "Doc, put your mind at ease, will you? Rumor has it the kid was outside of Murphy's saloon in a brawl with two wastrels. God knows where he went after that."

They passed Toby's cell and the boy pointedly turned his back on the sheriff. Bates bent near to Katherine and said, "Rude little brat, ain't he?"

Katherine eased herself from the sheriff and spoke

past him to Toby. "Toby, did Miss Harris send you your lessons?"

Toby looked at her. He smiled coldly—a mere lift of his lip. "Naw." He laughed shortly. "Why would she?"

Hot anger flooded Katherine. Would it have been so much for the schoolteacher to have complied? She drew a deep breath and turned back to the sheriff, but before she could speak the door opened and in walked Toby's mother.

She was beautiful. Even the sheriff, who seemed to disdain everything about Toby Waters, stared at her. Her golden hair was swept back from her elegant face and there was something extraordinarily exquisite and gentle about her.

Francine glanced at Katherine and Bates, then turned to her son. Toby stood immediately and walked to the door of his cell. Katherine saw his whole face change, caught the raw emotion, the love, in his eyes, and something tightened in her throat.

"Ma," he said hoarsely, then cleared his throat. "Ma, did you bring my books, my knives?"

Francine looked again at Katherine and the sheriff, then cast her son an apologetic look. "I'm sorry, Toby. I wanted to see you first."

The boy grasped the bars on the cell doors, almost as if clinging to them would bring him closer to her. "That's all right, Ma. I just don't want anyone to steal them. You know . . ." His voice cracked and drifted off.

Bates cleared his own throat. "Well now, Mrs. Waters, I ain't rightly sure we should remove them knives from the premises. I mean after all—"

Toby's harsh laugh cut him off. "Aw, c'mon, Sheriff. What harm can there be if I bring 'em to my grave? Who can object if I want to be buried with my knife collection and my books?"

The sheriff looked ill. He backed up a step under

the piercing and disconcerting gazes of the two women facing him. "Well, I, uh, suppose I could hold the knives for you till the trial is over."

"Gee, thanks, Sheriff," Toby said. "I'll remember that favor once I'm dead."

"Doctor," Francine said, her voice soft and refined, in contrast to her son's. "May I ask you a favor? Would you mind fetching Toby's books and his knife collection? I'd appreciate it greatly and would give you some coins for your time and trouble."

Katherine was astounded. "I don't want money for a favor. I would be happy to help out any way I can." She ignored the sheriff's scowl. Francine did not smile, but her eyes lightened as she handed Katherine the key to her house.

"Thank you so much. You will find three of his treasured books in his bedroom upstairs, on the night table. You may bring them here at your convenience. I'll be here most of the day."

Katherine nodded. She bade good-bye to the three of them and left the jail. She got no farther than the top step, for across from the jailhouse, in front of the general store, was Zach astride a huge black horse. That aura of carefully restrained strength emanated from him, and she caught her breath. She could almost smell the horse and leather, as well as *his* lusty scent, from the jailhouse steps. He was wearing a dark blue chamois shirt that made his tan look darker and his eyes and hair deeper than the midnight hour. He saw her, and she stood impaled by his slightly censuring gaze. Why was he looking at her like that? she wondered, then she understood. He was annoyed that she had been with Toby. He was annoyed that she apparently hadn't given his own son half as much consideration as she gave a stranger. What he didn't know was how many hours she had spent studying cases similar to Drew's. He couldn't know how making this decision tormented her.

Just as she was going to ask him where he was headed, Jake Duggan rattled up in his wagon, filled with lumber and nails and crates of goods with which he would build a new house. He called out a "Hullo!" to her and rumbled past. Zach wheeled his hired mount and trotted after Jake. Katherine watched him go, a hand pressed to her stomach to quell the riotous feelings he stirred up in her—the rush of tenderness, the desperate yearning, the terrifying physical desire.

As she started down the steps she was filled with an overwhelming melancholy that he would leave her. They had never had enough time with each other—not eleven years ago, not now. But she knew where more time might lead. There was no denying the combustible passion that flared between them. They were naturally drawn to each other—because of their past, because of their passion. It was dangerous, risky, for her to travel to his home with him. She was terrified that he could make her lose control of her senses, her wits, her body, with just a touch.

Was she falling in love with him! Had she already?

Alarm surged through her at the thought. Even her vision blurred as she walked down slushy Main Street. She *couldn't* fall in love with Zach. He would leave her in the end. He always left those who loved him. She could not trust her heart to such a man. She had learned to live her life with a shortage of trust, and with Zach she harbored no delusions.

She turned down Mulberry Street, where the Waterses' house was, feeling shaken by the myriad emotions pouring through her. She had to work hard to control the intense feelings as they beat inside her, like the throbbing of a drum.

She stopped suddenly, her gaze turning up to the

azure sky, as a startlingly clear realization swept through her. She *wanted* to go with Zach. She *wanted* to see his son, his home. She *wanted* to help him.

A huge weight seemed to lift from her chest. "I'll go up to the Duggans and tell him there," she said aloud, buoyed by her decision. Of course he would have to promise her that he would not force his attentions upon her. He would have to keep his hands to himself. Well, she could make him swear it! She would make him stick to the deal. She had managed to hold him at arm's length thus far, had she not? Well ... maybe a hand's length.

There was a skip in her step as she continued on to the Waterses' home, gleaming in the sunshine like a bright jewel. Yet as she stopped in front of the house, a cloud passed over the sun, casting the house in shadow. She shivered as she stared up at the house, its eaves dripping, one patch of melting snow sitting like a big gray toad in the center of the front lawn. She was oblivious to the horses clip-clopping through the muddy street, a wagon rolling past. But she jumped when a cackling voice called out, vibrating with the jolts of a hack as it made its precarious way down the street.

"Hey, missy! Haven't you anything better to do than stand daydreamin' at a house?"

Katherine whirled and grinned, waving to Birdie McDowell, who'd poked her orange head out of the hired rig.

"Poker tonight, lassie! My house. Will you be comin'?"

Katherine laughed. "Yes."

Then Birdie was gone, the rig pulling around the corner and splattering mud and slush everywhere.

Her heart pounding, Katherine walked up to the front and fitted the key into the lock. She turned it, stepped into the house, and was instantly surrounded by wood smells, beeswax, dust, and well-oiled leather. She closed the door, shutting out the sunshine, and stood in the foyer a moment, wondering where to start. She didn't know where Toby kept his knife collection, but she'd look downstairs first, then up.

The house was stately, tastefully furnished with rich damask curtains and Aubusson carpets. Crystal and china dazzled her as she passed the dining room, and the library was well stocked with leather volumes. She turned into the parlor and saw a display case by the window. She crossed over to it and stared down into the case, seeing immediately the empty pocket where the Viking knife had been. A cold chill raced over her. She glanced around for an empty box, something with which to carry the knives. There was nothing in sight. Perhaps upstairs she would find a crate of some sort.

Almost reverently she opened the case. There were at least two dozen knives in his collection, some ivory-handled, some crude and dull. But it was obvious that Toby had taken great care of them, for they were all labeled and almost lovingly displayed. There were knives centuries old, from England, Spain, Africa. She took them out one by one, careful to avoid the blades. She was so fascinated by each knife's history, she didn't notice the darkening sky, the wind picking up, the spatters of rain upon the roof. But she did hear the creaking above her.

She froze. Glancing out the nearest window, she saw the heavy rain and forced her shoulders to relax. It's only the wind in the trees, she told herself. Lord, she was jumpy!

But she had spent too much time there already. She went upstairs, peering into rooms until she found what was obviously Toby's. She was astounded at its glory. He possessed everything a boy could want, and more.

She started toward the night table, then stopped as she heard another creak, as of someone walking across a loose floorboard. She darted out of the bedroom and saw Emilee Harris standing in the hallway, clutching something that looked like a jewel box to her thin chest.

"Emilee!"

The teacher stared at Katherine, her lips pressed tight. "You! I should have known, Miss Busybody."

Emilee flew at her, dropping the jewel box, her hands outstretched. Her eyes blazed with feverish intent; her face was twisted with hatred and outrage. Katherine cried out just before the teacher fastened her hands around her neck and squeezed. Katherine made a startled choked-off sound, unable to believe the pain that crushed her throat as the schoolteacher's talonlike nails dug into her skin. She raised both hands, trying to pry Emilee's from her throat, but the woman was fierce, crazed. Gripped with a furious rage, she shook Katherine, pressing her perspiring face up close.

"Couldn't have left things alone, could you? You just *had* to come snooping where you didn't belong."

White pinpricks of light swam before Katherine's eyes. She couldn't breathe! She could hardly see. She began to go limp, sliding slowly into darkness as Emilee's hands kept their relentless grip around her throat. In a last desperate attempt, she shot her foot out, catching the inside of Emilee's ankle. It was an Arapaho trick she had learned from her grandfather, and it worked. Caught off guard by the sudden move, Emilee went down, floundering.

Katherine collapsed on her knees, clutching her throat, gasping for breath. She felt as though Emilee had crushed her windpipe. And the schoolteacher was coming at her again, on her knees, scrambling for both the jewel box and Katherine. Fighting for breath and clarity of mind, Katherine rolled away from Emilee, into Toby's bedroom, and knocked over the jewel box. A dazzling diamond and emerald pin spilled out, and she could only stare, stunned. She had never seen anything so beautiful in all her life.

"It's mine!" Emilee screeched, charging into the bedroom. But Katherine was on her feet now. She kicked the pin under Toby's bed and lifted her arms to fend off Emilee's blows. "He gave it to me, then took it back!"

"Emilee, stop! Stop!" Her words were only a faint rasp, and Emilee kept hitting her. She sidestepped, and Emilee stumbled against a chair. Katherine seized the opportunity to push her to the floor. Before Emilee could gather her wits, Katherine's foot was planted squarely in the center of her chest, pinning her down. It was another trick her grandfather had taught her.

"Do not move," Katherine panted, each word tearing like fire in her throat. She touched her burning skin and felt the stickiness of blood on her fingers. When Emilee bucked under her foot, she increased the pressure. She stared down at the glaring teacher.

"The sheriff is on his way here," she lied, and Emilee quieted, her eyes widening at the realization of her actions. "You killed Richard Waters and you were going to let Toby hang."

Emilee made a strange garbled sound. "He told me he loved me!" she wailed, and Katherine knew that she spoke of Richard. "He told me I was beautiful—he gave me things. He told me he would never love anyone as he loved me." She gave another pitiful sob. "But he was laughing at me all the while. Laughing while I wrote love letters to him and filled my journal with memories of our trysts! When I learned about those *whores* he was seeing it broke my heart—broke me! When I told him I loved him he laughed. Laughed!"

Tears streamed from her eyes, and she gasped for breath. "He enjoyed hurting people. He told me the only reason he'd bothered with me in the first place was because he enjoyed watching a skinny, pinched-up schoolteacher become undone. And still I loved him," she said miserably. "Loved and hated him. And I couldn't bear to look at him anymore. Couldn't bear to see him walk into that whorehouse and know he was giving those other women pleasure. So I drove that knife into his back. Killed the whore too."

"But Toby . . ." Katherine said.

A feral light burned in Emilee's eyes. "That boy! If it weren't for him Richard and I could have married. Toby is incorrigible! Why shouldn't he suffer for some of his sins? It was easy to get into this house. I stole the key off Richard once and he thought he had misplaced it. It was all very easy—very quick."

Seeing Katherine's stunned state, she grabbed her ankle and yanked. Katherine hit the floor. Emilee scrambled for the box and the pin. Pressing her palm to her painfully throbbing tailbone, Katherine reached for a book and hurled it at the teacher. Emilee threw an arm up to block the blow, but the book glanced off her head, knocking her spectacles to the floor. She groped aimlessly for an instant, and Katherine grabbed her ankle, but Emilee shook free and stumbled toward the front stairs.

"Emilee, wait!"

The teacher was already out of the house and across the lawn before Katherine reached the front door. She saw Emilee running in an awkward, stumbling gait toward the road . . . and into the path of a speeding dray. Unable to stop, the vehicle careened sideways. The horse missed her, but not the dray itself. It struck her hard, tossing her like a broken doll. Horrified, Katherine started toward her as other people raced over, but she felt as though she were moving through water. She ached everywhere, and her throat was thick and swollen, as if a band were tightening around it. When she reached the road, she could see Emilee lying in a crumpled heap, a thin trickle of blood seeping from the corner of her mouth.

Katherine fell to her knees beside the woman and felt frantically for a pulse. Nothing. Emilee Harris was dead.

She looked up at the people standing around her. "She's dead," she said hoarsely. Seeing something glittering in the mud beside Emilee's body, she reached over. The diamond-and-emerald pin. She held it up as if it were proof, as if it could explain. "She killed . . . she killed Richard Waters. They were lovers. Tell . . ." She swayed, a black haze falling over her mind. "Tell the sheriff." And she fainted.

Someone had carried her home. Distantly Katherine heard a fire crackling in the grate, soft murmuring voices, Clarabelle's occasional squawk. She opened her eyes to see Lisa Gormen standing over her with a tray of soup. Katherine swallowed. Her throat hurt. She lifted her head and it ached dully.

"What . . . ?"

"Don't speak." Lisa set the tray on a table. "You've had a rough time of it, Katherine. The deputy carried you home. Said to make sure we keep you rested and fed." Her brow wrinkled and she turned to look over her shoulder. "Cynthia!" she bellowed toward the kitchen. "Where's that tea?"

Katherine struggled up on one elbow. "What time is it?"

"Now, now, lie down," Lisa scolded gently, but Katherine had already propped herself up against the pillows. She was in her front room on the sofa, and she stared blankly into the fire. Only a pale light crept in the window, and she guessed it was late afternoon. Everything—Emilee's crazed attack, her confession, her broken body lying in the road—came back to her in a rush. She moaned and held her throbbing head with both hands.

"There, there," Lisa said, fluttering to her side. She patted Katherine's hand and once more darted a swift glance toward the kitchen. Cynthia came around the corner just then with three cups of steaming tea and a pot of honey.

"The teacher killed Richard . . ." Katherine mumbled, still trying to clear her mind.

"We know, we know. And you were so brave to chase her out of that house."

Katherine looked at her with disbelief. "*I* didn't chase her anywhere, Lisa. She ran out on her own."

Lisa shrugged daintily, sipping her tea. "Doesn't matter who did what. We have our murderer."

"She's dead," Katherine mumbled, staring into the fire again. Lunatic or simply a scorned woman, Emilee had been a lonely, heartbroken person, and Katherine felt a pang of pity for her.

"Yes, but she would have hanged anyway," Cynthia said, oblivious to the two startled expressions cast her way. "Best this is over and done with and everyone can get on with their lives."

Katherine sat up straighter, but lots of places hurt. Her tailbone ached, even her arms. Lord, she was weary. "Has the sheriff let Toby go?"

"Yes," Cynthia said. "With great reluctance."

"He was wrong again," added Lisa. "I wonder about the men we have keeping order in this town."

"I heard him mutter to Tom he was glad he didn't have to face your I-told-you-so look," Cynthia informed Katherine.

"Have I ever given that look to the sheriff?" Katherine asked with mock indignation.

They all laughed, then Katherine sobered. "I have never fainted in my life."

"You didn't faint," Cynthia said, pooh-poohing the very idea. "You were only taking a short nap."

They laughed again, and Katherine thought how good it was to have her friends with her now. Indeed laughter was the best medicine.

"But where are Toby and his mother now?" she asked.

"They wanted to come see you, but Sheriff's orders are 'leave the doc alone till morning.'" Lisa shrugged. "Guess they'll have to wait. But Toby is forever grateful."

Katherine stared into her cup of tea. "It was pure luck and happenstance that I stumbled upon Emilee. How different it could have turned out."

Rain pitter-pattered against the windowpane, and she watched the diamondlike patterns it made across the glass. She remembered the decision she had made before her episode with Emilee, and she knew she had to speak with Zach. She had to tell him that she was coming with him, and she had to tell him soon. He would be leaving tomorrow.

What if he were to leave early in the morning? she worried. He had wanted her to say good-bye, but she hadn't the strength to walk across town to the hotel.

"Lisa, Cynthia," she said. She sat up higher and winced as pain shot up her hip. "I need you to do me a favor. Get Johnny Baker next door—you know, he's that twelve-year-old blond-headed boy—and send him to the hotel to get Zach Fletcher. Tell Johnny I'll give him a dollar for helping me. If Zach's not there he could still be up at the Duggans'. Would you do that for me?"

The sisters glanced at each other. Katherine caught the look and sighed. "It's not what you think. I'll tell you after you send Johnny off. Oh," she added as Lisa started for the door, "tell him to stop off at Birdie McDowell's afterward and tell her I just can't make it there tonight." When both women raised their brows, Katherine blushed and said, "She was having a party. Actually, a poker party."

The Gormen sisters hooted.

"I'm sure she would have dealt you in."

"We don't know how to play poker."

Katherine grinned. "I'll just have to teach you."

When Johnny was on his way, Katherine explained to her friends about Drew. Lisa and Cynthia were round-eyed, then caught up in the romance of the story.

"Oh, this is wonderful!" Lisa said. Under Katherine's disapproving scowl, she added quickly, "Not about the boy, that's sad and frightening. But wonderful that you can help your old friend this way. Though anyone can see that you are much more than old friends. Not that," she went on, "that means there is anything *improper* happening between you."

"Oh, pooh!" Cynthia waved off her words. "Each one of us knows we don't care a hoot for proper."

They babbled on excitedly about Katherine's trip, and how she must write down all her impressions of the east coast so she could relate them upon her return. They kept the fire blazing, refilled their teacups, and waited for Johnny to appear with Zach. But two hours later Johnny was knocking on the door with the news that Zach was nowhere to be found.

Long past midnight the women fell asleep. Katherine had argued with Lisa and Cynthia about their staying, but the Gormens insisted, worried about their friend.

First thing in the morning, they promised, they would all go to the depot and see if Zach had already gone. But that didn't soothe Katherine. She slept fitfully. If Zach had already gone, she reasoned, there wasn't a thing she could do about it. Still she tossed and turned, and somewhere between sleep and consciousness she heard someone knock at her door.

Before she could rise from her bed, she heard Cynthia call, "Who is it?"

"Doc, that you?"

"What does it matter who *I* am?" Cynthia asked. "*Who* are *you?*"

"Ah, I need the doc."

"I'm here!" Katherine said, hurrying down the hall before Cynthia had a chance to lose her patience.

"Well, Doc, we need you down at Murphy's saloon," the man said through the door. "Another Red Berry brawl—"

"I'll come right away," Katherine said, and turned back to her bedroom to dress.

"No!" Cynthia said. She scowled at the closed door. "Red Berry's a brawling, drunken fool! It's time he patched himself up."

"But it ain't only Red that needs patchin' up," the man said. "It's that there stranger in town—Fletcher. He's drunk as a skunk but he beat Red . . . no one's ever beat Red in a bout before. They both need attention . . . an' about half a dozen other men do too."

Katherine needed to hear no more. She pulled on her clothes and coat, and opened the door to see Mr. Epson, owner of the dry goods store. She was down the rain-slick steps before either Gormen sister could open her mouth, calling over her shoulder, "Be back soon!"

Though her head and various body parts ached, she kept pace with Epson, picking her way over puddles of mud, her skirt gathered in one hand, her black bag in the other. Up ahead the saloon's gas lamp gleamed soft yellow in the misty night against the boardwalk, the saloon doors, and the hitching post, making everything look like an oil painting.

The saloon smelled of sweat, sawdust, and beer. It was warm and crowded with men—some shirtless, most of them drunk. There were a few women there, too, draped over the barstools or around the necks of some of the men. The strumpets, too, drank beer. The center of the saloon had been cleared for boxing, and as Katherine scanned the crowd, men called out to her drunkenly.

"Me first, Doc!" one of the men yelled, and a loud guffaw broke through the crowd. Katherine ignored all that, looking almost frantically for Zach.

And then she saw him. He was slouched in a chair, long legs stretched out before him, booted feet crossed at the ankles. He was shirtless, his magnificent bronze chest gleaming with sweat in the blazing light, and he was looking at her out of one eye. The other one was swollen shut and purple. He sat with a beer balanced on his thigh and was obviously drunk. He lifted his glass to her in salute.

Katherine was torn between anger and laughter. She pressed her lips together and strode purposely toward him, despite the hoots from the other men. She passed big Red Berry, the local blacksmith and—until that night—the best boxer in the region. He stopped her, taking hold of her arm with his thick, sausagelike fingers. He grinned down at her; two of his teeth were missing.

"Your man there packs quite a punch, Doc. He didn't tell me he boxed as a kid."

Katherine eyed Red's bruised, puffy face. His skin, his hair, even the freckles that dotted his face and thick arms were all tinged with red. He had well deserved the title of boxing champion, and he was also renowned for his drinking and his wenching.

"Zach," she said, "was boxing in the streets of New York at five years old." She raised her eyebrows. "Did you learn anything, Red?"

Red threw back his head and roared.

Katherine shook her head and walked on to Zach, who watched her with a cool, cynical expression. As she stopped in front of him, she immediately saw the damage. "Dammit, Zach! You popped your stitches!" Blood trickled from that opened wound, and new ones. "And now you'll need more."

"And what happened to you, pretty one?"

Her eyes widened in surprise. Even drunk he noticed the smallest details about a person. Her hand went to her throat where he stared with his one good eye. "It's a long story."

"I have all night," he drawled.

"You're very drunk." The fumes were rolling off him.

Zach ignored that. He watched her crouch down to open her bag and thought how beautifully her hair shone in this bright light. Like sun and fire, he thought, and smiled ironically at his own poetic notion. He reached down to touch her nape, where gossamer hairs brushed her golden skin, and felt her stiffen.

"We are in a room full of spectators," she whispered.

He smiled. "You know that never bothered me."

"Zach," she said, not looking at him, "I cannot do a proper job of patching you up if you continue to distract me so."

She bent her head lower and dug in her bag for her instruments. "Why'd you do something so foolish right before you go home?"

"Because I felt like slugging someone."

She lifted her head and their eyes met. Katherine felt the pulse kick in her throat. She wanted to say, "I'm coming with you," but the words would not form. She scanned his bruised, cut face and thought he looked much like the sardonic rebel he'd been at fifteen. Oh, yes, he'd used his fists plenty then. Though Big Red was broader and beefier than Zach, Red couldn't come close to Zach in skill or experience. Zach was a born fighter.

And he was grinning at her again. She dabbed disinfectant on his open cuts, and when he scowled she smiled sweetly at him. She took a salve and rubbed it into her palms before smoothing it over the big red welt that marked his muscled ribs. He sucked in a breath between his teeth.

"Men," she said, *tsk-tsk*ing as she shook her head. "I don't understand why you have to take out your frustrations with your fists."

"It feels good," he said, and held his breath as she touched the needle to his chin.

"Does this feel good?" she asked, and proceeded to place four neat stitches along his chin. He was endlessly brave, she thought, but decided not to speak again until she was finished. As it was he drunkenly slung an arm around her neck, pulling her in close for a kiss. She reeled back.

"Zach Fletcher, I can't tolerate a drinking man!"

He grinned drunkenly at her. "I want him to know you're mine."

Puzzled, she frowned, trying to ignore the hot pins and needles that prickled her skin at his possessive statement. "Who?"

"That dandy."

She turned and saw Jim Lowell standing against one wall, scowling at them. She offered him a weak smile and turned her attention back to Zach. "He's not a dandy. Now, Zach, remove your arm from around my neck so I can continue." Though her words were wry and calm, her heart hammered. She rested her hand upon his solid chest, and she could feel crisp hair, damp with sweat. She went weak all over. "I'm coming with you," she murmured, and smiled as his one good eye widened.

He sat up straighter, as if he hadn't heard right. "Say that again, darlin'."

She backed up an inch, feeling the potency of his power like a hot imprint upon her skin. Was she insane? How could she fight him? He was overwhelming, the sheer force of his personality leaving her breathless. Even now her body yearned toward his, and a thought jolted through her mind. She wanted, despite every warning she gave herself, to be his.

She backed up another inch. "There will be certain conditions I will discuss with you when you are sober. Zach? Zach—"

She gasped as he lowered his head and claimed her mouth with his. His heat scorched her and the men whooped as she struggled against him. He tore his lips from hers, and she could taste the beer on her mouth and feel her breasts tingle as he laughed hoarsely.

"It's a damn good thing you decided to come with me." Looping a hard arm around her neck, he brought her in close for another quick, hard kiss that made even her toes tingle.

"Why's that?" she asked in a breathless whisper.

"Because otherwise"—he grinned wolfishly—"I would've had to kidnap you."

With that he slammed down his beer glass, scooped her up in his powerful arms, and walked out of the saloon with her, ignoring her protests and the whistles of the other men.

Thirteen

"I will never be able to show my face to those men again!" Katherine exclaimed, but Zach continued to carry her toward her home, his strides long and weaving.

"Aw, they know it was all in fun," he assured her.

"Zach, you must put me down. I take it your back is much better?"

"Much," he said. "But my ribs hurt like hell."

Her laughter floated out on the damp night air, and every muscle in Zach's body tightened. He skidded a little and she clung to him, holding her breath, but he righted himself and dug his boot heels into the wet earth.

"Zach, you are thoroughly drunk."

He grunted.

"Put me down before you get us both killed."

He turned down Fisher Road. She wiggled in his arms and he let out a soft curse.

"Zach, I left all those men back there cut and bruised."

Noting her troubled frown in the glow of a street lamp, he said, "Aw, they're all right. Just a little beat up is all. Besides," he added with a grin, "they'll just have to get used to your absence and some other doc's services for a while, won't they?"

"You must not act smug or arrogant about my coming with you."

His white teeth flashed in the dark, and Katherine sighed inwardly. Zach would act any way he darn well pleased and the world be damned.

Her house was in sight now, and when he spoke again, his voice was quiet and he sounded remarkably sober. "What happened to you?" he asked. He bent his head and nuzzled his lips against her throat, touching his tongue to the welts that Emilee's fingernails had left on her skin. Katherine made a purring sound, but turned away from his delicious caress.

"Don't," she said hoarsely, then told him what had happened. She felt his arms tighten around her when she related Emilee's attack. "It's over now," she murmured.

He cursed. "I was drinking and brawling while you were fighting off a crazed woman."

She smiled teasingly up at him. "You can't be the hero *all* the time."

He stopped to kiss her, and she gasped, arching against him as his tongue pushed slowly into her mouth. It twined with hers in a seductive dance that made lush sensuality wash through her. When he finally released her mouth she was shaking.

"I wouldn't *have* to be a hero all the time, little minx, if you would just stay out of trouble."

She made a muffled sound of protest as he reached her house and took the porch steps two at a time.

"Careful!" she whispered, giggling as he slipped and grabbed a post with one hand.

He found the door with his foot and gave it a hard kick.

"Zach, I have—"

The Gormen sisters squealed and shrieked as the door swung back against the wall with a mighty crash.

"Guests," Katherine finished. She scrambled out of Zach's arms and rushed forward to reassure Lisa and Cynthia. They were staring at Zach as if he were some Viking warrior come to rape and plunder.

"For heaven's sake," Katherine said, whisking toward the table to light a lantern. The sisters were clutching their blankets to their chests, though they were fully dressed. Katherine did have to admit that Zach looked mighty intimidating. He filled the doorway, and his bruised, stitched face made him look as if he had been in a street fight. "Zach, you remember my friends, Lisa and Cynthia Gormen." She looked at the women with an expression that was partly pleading, partly amused. "They've been very dear to watch over me this afternoon."

Zach nodded to the women, and they made mewing noises before they caught Katherine's exasperated look and composed themselves.

"How do you do?" Cynthia said. "Katherine has told us *so* much about you."

Zach lifted a brow and let his gaze drift toward Katherine. She blushed and pretended to busy herself with collecting the teacups. "I told them only the truth. Now, do you think you can find your way back to the hotel or shall I have Shadow drive you?"

Zach scowled. He had hoped to sleep there, but even with his fuzzy vision he could see the Gormen sisters were acting rather possessive toward their friend. He knew there was no chance of *them* leaving the premises. Slowly, his mind absorbed what Katherine had said about Shadow, and he rubbed his stubbled jaw. "I think you have just insulted me," he said.

"Insulted? Hardly. Zach, you have to get up first thing in the morning and telegraph Drew and change our train tickets! And I need to pack and make arrangements." But she wondered if Zach would even be able to open his eyes in the morning.

He grunted and ran a hand through his hair, and they all held their breath as they watched him turn and make his precarious way down the front steps. They crowded at the door to assure themselves he'd get to the hotel all right, then Cynthia slammed the door and fell back against it. She fluttered her eyelashes, her hand over her heart. "Oh!" she said breathlessly. "I think I'm going to swoon."

"He is absolutely devastating," Lisa announced. "And I, for one, would be scared to death to travel with such a potent male creature for all that way."

Katherine leveled a steady gaze on her friend. "Thank you," she said dryly, "for that reassuring thought."

The sisters laughed. None of them felt like going back to sleep, so they began to pack for Katherine's trip. By dawn Cynthia had become melancholy, and when Katherine had returned home after telegraphing to Denver for a replacement doctor, Cynthia was dabbing at her eyes.

"Heavens, Cynthia, I'll only be gone a little while!"

Cynthia looked doubtful, and by the time Zach showed up handsome and freshly shaven—though still battered and with one eye swollen—with the news that everything was settled, Cynthia was in a definite sulk. Everyone ignored her, even Toby and his mother and the sheriff when they came by to thank Katherine. Francine and Toby were still leaving town, heading west to where Francine's sister lived in California.

"I'll never forget what you did for me, Doc," Toby said, his eyes glittering with unshed tears. "And I'll never forget that you believed in me."

She hugged him. "Write to me," she said. "I will be sorely disappointed if you do not."

He smiled a real smile. "As often as I can."

When the sheriff learned that Zach was leaving town, he immediately brightened.

"But you can bet you'll be hearing from my attorney," Zach said, still enjoying the threat of a lawsuit that he held over the sheriff.

Bates scratched his head as Zach left Katherine's to return to the hotel. "Well, now," he said to Katherine. "Seems to me that boy holds a grudge."

By five o'clock Katherine was ready to go. She had even packed her special herbs, kept in airtight containers to prevent deterioration. She hoped they would have a beneficial effect on Drew. She tried not to dwell on the sick boy, instead looking forward to their brief stop in Kansas to visit Cody and Tessa.

While preparing a light supper for herself and the Gormen sisters—who wanted to spend every last minute that they could with Katherine—a knock sounded on the front door. She opened it to a tall, good-looking man with straight blond hair and hazel eyes. He smiled at her, and behind her Katherine heard Cynthia gasp. "Hello," he said. "I'm Dr. Brian Guest, your temporary replacement."

Out of the corner of her eye she saw Cynthia sink onto the sofa. Katherine hid her smile. "Why, yes, come in, Dr. Guest."

He strode in, hat in hand, and glanced about the place. "I'm Dr. Benton's new partner. He felt it wise to send me in his place—learn how to doctor in a small town. I'm looking forward to it." His eyes lit on Cynthia, and she jumped to her feet. Katherine made the introductions, then showed the doctor her operating room, office, and lab.

"I understand you'll be staying in a room at the hotel," she said. "But I'll give you a key to my home, of course, for your use. My stableboy will take care of the bird, but if you find her an annoyance I have another friend who will take her."

Dr. Guest smiled. "I'm sure I will find her delightful."

He glanced at Cynthia, who flushed.

"If you'd like," Cynthia said as Lisa strolled into the room, "I could show you around town tomorrow."

He smiled and nodded. "I would like that very much."

"In fact," Cynthia suggested, slipping her arm through his and widening her pretty blue eyes up at him, "I could walk with you to the hotel now. I was on my way home anyhow."

"My pleasure." He looked at Lisa. "What about your sister?"

"Oh, not to worry about her. She has her own escort."

Lisa leaned close to Katherine and murmured, "I do?"

"Bye, Katherine!" Cynthia called as she led Dr. Guest to the door. "Have a wonderful trip. And write if you have a chance."

"I will," Katherine promised as Cynthia sailed out the door with Dr. Guest.

"I think," Lisa said, shutting the door after her sister, "Cynthia is finally smitten."

Katherine smiled, knowing she was leaving her home and her friends in good hands. Especially Cynthia!

On the train ride to Kansas Katherine reiterated her conditions to Zach for traveling east with him. She wanted to make certain, she told him, that he was sober when she informed him that if he tried to seduce her, she would take the next train home.

"Now promise me you won't," she said, as they rocked gently against each other with every sway of the train. They were seated together in a first-class coach on a fine plush seat. Zach lounged lazily, his long legs stretched out before him, his fingers laced across his stomach. His good eye was at half-mast, drooping slightly at the corner, giving him a deceptively nonchalant expression that hardly fooled Katherine. Even when idle Zach emanated a pulsating sexuality. She gave him a little nudge. "Promise me."

He looked amused. "I promise I won't *try* to seduce you."

She frowned, feeling duped somehow. Then her face cleared and she pushed her knuckles into his hard shoulder. "No, that's not good enough. I know you, Zach. You won't *try* to seduce me—you just will!"

Zach laughed softly and rested his head against the comfortable seat, closing his eyes. Katherine was proving a delightful companion after all, and a wonderful distraction. He did not make promises lightly—and he never broke them. That was why, he thought, a smile curling a corner of his mouth, Katherine should have made him promise *before* they had left Newberry. She had entered *his* territory now, and on his territory he ruled supreme.

Katherine frowned, watching him feign sleep. Since they had left Newberry Zach had seemed edgy, anxious to get home to Drew. Even as they boarded the train he had emphasized that they were only spending one night in Harper City and leaving the following day. Though Katherine was thrilled to visit Cody and Tessa she, too, was eager to get to Marblehead and treat Drew.

It was afternoon when the train screeched into the Harper City station, and Katherine caught sight of Cody waiting for them under the gabled depot. Tall and broad-shouldered, he held his youngest child—a two-year-old girl with his dark hair—and she was squirming to get out of his arms. When the train stopped he let her go, and she scampered down the platform, her three brothers racing after her.

Katherine laughed. "There they are, Zach!" She tugged on his hand, ignoring his grunt, and waited impatiently for him to shift his big body out of the seat. He must still be in pain, she thought, watching him rise with some caution. His face was bruised and his eye was still swollen, but he could open it if he squinted. Some of the passengers had turned their noses up at her as if she were indecorous for traveling with such a ruffian. "Was that boxing rout worth it after all?" she asked with reproach.

Zach looked down at her. "Yup" was all he said, and he urged her forward with his hand at the small of her back.

"The captain's back! The captain's back!" five-year-old Trey shouted as Katherine and Zach came down the steps. Katherine quickly looked around, then realized the captain's identity as she met Zach's amused eyes.

"He calls you Captain?" she asked.

Zach grinned. "He seems much intrigued by the title." He then swung Cody's youngest son up in his arms without regard to the pain shooting through his ribs. There was much chattering and shouting as Cody gathered Katherine close and murmured, "Welcome home, little one."

Laughing, she hugged him hard, then turned to hug each child.

"How you've grown!" she exclaimed to Jesse, Cody's oldest son.

"I'm almost as tall as you," he said. He was eleven years old and proud of it.

"That ain't so much to brag about, is it, sugar?" Zach whispered to Katherine.

She glared at him.

"What the hell happened to you?" Cody asked Zach as they carried the luggage to the fine carriage awaiting them, the children scampering ahead. "Smoke Eyes still putting up her dukes?"

Both men laughed as Katherine turned her nose up at them. "It happened to be Zach's own 'dukes' that turned his face such a pretty shade of blue."

Cody laughed. "Ah," he said knowingly, and Katherine was baffled by the thoroughly male look the two men gave each other.

"You were in a fight?" Cody's middle son, Cole, asked. With his large deep brown eyes, tawny hair, and lean, sensitive face, Cole looked much like Tessa, Katherine thought, but had the rough and tumble qualities that all Cody's sons possessed. The boy never missed a trick, even though he appeared to be only mildly interested.

Grinning, Zach reached out and mussed the boy's hair. "Boxing. Your father taught you how yet?"

"I'm the best boxer in Harper City!" nine-year-old Cole bragged.

"No better than me!" Jesse cried, and began to jab the air with his fists.

"I'm better!" Trey declared, and accidentally popped Jesse one in the stomach. Jesse spun on him.

"If you touch him," Cody warned, "you'll sleep in the stable tonight."

"And eat hay!" Trey put in bravely as he hid behind his father's long legs.

They all laughed, then settled into the carriage, two-year-old Rachel promptly plopping down on Katherine's lap. Katherine tucked her arms around the child's waist, relishing the clean, sweet scent of her glossy black curls, marveling at the long lashes that shielded her huge blue eyes. Cody and Tessa had such beautiful children. She stroked Rachel's hair as the boys bounced on the high-sprung seats and chattered like monkeys, full of lively energy.

As the fine red-and-black carriage rolled through town Zach leaned back in his seat and watched Katherine. He studied her fingers, capable and elegant, as she stroked Rachel's hair, and remembered them upon his own skin. She was beautiful and radiant and so damned desirable, his hands shook just from looking at her. He felt an overwhelming urge to pull the pins from her lustrous hair and feel the satiny mass pour over his fingers. In seconds his body had grown so uncomfortably hard, he had to shift in his seat. Still he continued to watch her, feeling his muscles tighten as she smiled down at Rachel. She would never have children of her own. She had said as much in her office back in Newberry. "No room in my life for a husband and babies." A damn waste. She was playful and loving and imparted information naturally as she chatted with them.

Sometimes she was too independent for her own good. Yet in an odd way he understood her need for independence. She'd acquired it young, and it had become her way of survival. Most women had been brought up to learn how to be a good wife and mother. Smoke Eyes had had no such upbringing. She'd been wild and free, and now that freedom was as deeply ingrained in her soul as her doctoring. To rob her of either would be a sin she would never forgive.

She looked up and caught his gaze, and he felt a quick tug in his gut, that intense reaction she always provoked in him. Her brow puckered in a puzzled expression, and he smiled faintly at her—a mere lift of his lips. She offered him a tiny smile of her own, then turned her attention to Rachel again as the little girl pointed to the ice-cream parlor.

Still, Zach could not keep his eyes off her. He buried a growl in his throat and fought the surge of pure lust that washed through him in a hot, thundering wave. His gaze slid down the front of the snug-fitting bodice of her yellow chintz traveling dress, fastened with tiny pearl buttons. He wanted to tear it open and feel her warm, firm breasts fill his hands. He wanted to touch her bare, satiny skin, to taste it, to slowly build her tension and pleasure to the breaking point, then watch her explode beneath him. He wanted to fill her, take her, feel her hot, sleek flesh clasp him tightly.

Zach locked his jaws, clamping back the tormenting images that crowded his mind. But the ache in him grew. Even though the bouncing children provided a welcome distraction he could feel—and he knew Katherine could feel too—the vibrant tension between them pulse.

The carriage veered left, and they rode a couple of miles out into the country to a rambling white two-story house with a sprawling yard and stables. Katherine caught sight of the visibly pregnant Tessa standing on the front porch, and she waved. As soon as the carriage stopped, she was out and flying up the porch stairs to hug her dear friend.

"Goodness, Tessa, it feels as if it's been centuries instead of months since I've seen you!" she said, leaning back and taking Tessa's hands in hers. She smiled at the woman who was her mentor, friend, and older sister all rolled into one. "You look wonderful!"

"And you," Tessa said. "Honestly, Smoke Eyes, you grow more beautiful every time I see you."

Katherine felt Zach come up behind her, his commanding presence and his heat. He was so tall and broad-shouldered, he always overwhelmed her, until she could heardly breathe. But she could smell him, that indelible scent that encompassed everything male—spice and leather and fecund earth, racy, pungent, and dangerous.

"How come no one warned me just how beautiful she was?" he said to Tessa. His hand came up to caress her shoulder, and Katherine's heart began to race. "When I first laid eyes on her in that jailhouse I felt like I'd been kicked in the head by a mule."

Tessa's eyes widened. "Jail . . . Zach Fletcher, what kind of trouble landed you in jail? And what in the name of heaven happened to your face?"

Katherine stifled a giggle as she glanced back at Zach. "It's a long story," she said, and caught her breath as his eyes burned into her like a dark flame.

Cody came up to Tessa, slipped an arm around her expanded waist, and kissed her. They were still a striking couple, Katherine thought, Cody as handsome as ever with his silver-templed dark hair, sun-darkened skin, and laugh lines around his teasing blue-green eyes, and Tessa lovely with her honey hair and large chocolate-brown eyes sparkling with gold glints.

"You can tell us the story indoors," Tessa said as the children danced and tussled around them. "The cook prepared tea and refreshments for us in the kitchen, and Mary and Tim Lyndon are here to see you, Katherine."

Katherine started to speak, but was drowned out by the excited yips of the children, each wanting to hear the story about the jail. Tessa led them inside, through the big, cool house with its polished floors and rich mahogany furniture, the white-and-gold china lamps and pretty wallpaper with fine stripes and tiny flowers.

The Lyndons, Katherine's adoptive parents, were waiting for her in the huge, sun-warmed kitchen, fragrant with the smell of freshly baked bread and clove tea. Katherine hugged them both, then they all sat down at the long trestle table to reminisce. They laughed about Katherine's and Zach's deviltry as youths, and spoke warmly of the days when Katherine worked as Cody's apprentice. He had found her one day, when she was twelve, peering into his lab. Intrigued by the little tyke with such a keen mind, he took her under his wing. When Tessa taught her to read Cody loaned her his medical books and she devoured every word. Cody taught her how to mix drugs, compound salves, and use a scalpel with skillful dexterity. He took her on his rounds with him and she learned by watching him administer to folks.

As Zach listened, he was sorry he had missed all that, Smoke Eyes growing into the woman she had become. He wondered what she had looked like at fifteen, at seventeen. He wondered when her face had begun to change, become so beautiful, the delicate bone structure emphasizing her large eyes, making them all the more mesmerizing. Again she caught him studying her, and he cast her a brief, lopsided grin, but this time she did not return the smile.

Katherine had been aware of the predatory gleam in Zach's eyes that made her feel she were his prey. His hungry, wolfish look started a fire in her, and she had to resist the compulsion to fan her face. She felt he was touching her, stroking her, reaching straight into her soul. Risking another glance at him, she knew the pull of his sexuality was too strong to fight. How would she make it through the next few weeks without touching him?

"It's time we let Katherine and Zach refresh themselves," Tessa said, interrupting Katherine's worried thoughts. Glancing at the older woman, she suspected Tessa needed a rest just as much. Her baby was due any day and faint shadows had appeared under her eyes. "I'll have the maid draw you a bath," she said to Katherine, "and we'll have supper later."

"And popcorn," Jesse added.

"And tell more stories," Cole put in.

"Yes, yes." Tessa laughed and made to rise, but Katherine stopped her with a hand on her arm.

"I can find my own room, Tess," she said. "You must rest. There's no need for you to exert yourself."

Aware that Zach's hawk stare followed her, she left the kitchen and climbed the stairs to the guest bedroom where she always stayed.

It was a blessed relief to be out of Zach's sizzling presence and in the sanctuary of the large, comfortable room. As the maid filled her bath with steaming water Katherine sat on the edge of the four-poster and began to undress. She was weary and distressed, and she felt her eyelids prickle with the threat of tears. Her emotions were in a turmoil. Zach had to stop this. Couldn't he understand that she could not become his mistress? Didn't he know that she couldn't stand the pain of his leaving her once he had possessed her? He would saturate her with his black fire, the force of his passion, and then she would never be free of him.

She could not allow that to happen.

Sighing, she finished undressing, wound her thick hair on top of her head, and went to her bath. A low fire crackled in the grate of the marble fireplace, and the room was cast with a dusky rose glow. The heat of the water soothed her and she washed with a fragrant gardenia-scented soap. Tilting her head back against the rim of the brass tub, she basked in the luscious heat. She could hear faint sounds from the household below her, maybe even out in the yard . . . and other muffled but closer noises: soft whistling, the chink of a belt buckle, water splashing. Her brow wrinkled in consternation. She cocked her head in the direction from where she heard a low male voice dismissing the maid, then her eyes grew wide with alarm. Zach was on the other side of the door that connected the two guest bedrooms. Her heart lurched in her chest, and suddenly, desperately, she wished Tessa had put her in the room with Rachel.

Of course a gentleman wouldn't even consider opening that connecting door, but Zach was no gentleman. She knew the delight he would take in feasting his eyes on her as she was now.

She hissed a little swear under her breath and eyed the fluffy white towel that the maid had placed on the footstool a few feet away. She eased her body from the tub, but the water still slapped against its sides. All sound from Zach's room ceased. Quickly she stepped from the tub and wrapped the towel around herself just as Zach pushed open the door.

Katherine froze. He stood with one shoulder propped against the door frame, his arms crossed over his wide chest. The fiery colors of the fading sun poured in through the windows behind him, spilling over his gorgeously sculpted body. Katherine could scarcely breathe as she looked at him. He wore nothing more than trousers, and the top two buttons were undone. A tantalizing line of silky black hair funneled down beneath the buttons, down to where the long, thick bulge of his full arousal strained against his trousers. The heart-pounding sight begged for the touch of her fingers.

"I told you before I couldn't hide that I want you."

His voice was raw and raspy, incredibly arousing. She shivered and lifted her gaze to his. He was looking at her with such hunger, she felt her skin was on fire. His eyes—she had never confronted such eyes. They touched hers with a shimmering need, and little tremors shuddered in her belly. His gaze scorched her as it made a slow trail down her body, touching her everywhere, all the way down to her bare, curling toes. She stood paralyzed as that gaze took even more time to make its way back up her body, settling at last upon her flushed face.

He said one word. "Don't."

Still unable to move, she gazed quizzically at him.

"Do not," Zach explained, his voice dropping even lower, "hide your body from me." The room was fragrant with the sweet scent of gardenia, and Katherine was unspeakably, stunningly beautiful. Her hair was piled like a color-cloud atop her head, and her lush body glowed like gold. A powerful hunger roared through him, and he knew then that Katherine would be the only woman who would ever brand him with *her* mark, her irresistible, haunting essence. The thought twisted in his belly, but he knew, too, that the elemental pull he felt for her could not be ignored. He did not want to think of the future, though. He was selfish and hungry, and his body craved her now.

"Take down the towel, darlin'."

She shook her head, clutching the towel tighter between her breasts. "I will not," she said shakily, lifting her quivering chin at him. "I will not play slave for you, Zach."

"I'm not asking you to play slave, honey," he said softly. "No one, not even me, could be your master. Except, perhaps"—his gaze dropped to her breasts, where the light spilled into the valley between them—"in bed."

"Your arrogance astounds me."

He smiled. "Arrogance? Hardly. Just fact. And I intend to prove my word."

He eased away from the door frame and began to walk toward her. He was stalking her, Katherine thought, feeling again as though she were his prey. She tightened her grip on the towel. "Zach," she whispered tautly, "we had a deal. You were not to put your hands on me if I came with you. Those were the rules."

Her words did not stop him. "That was your deal, not mine, sugar. And besides." He halted in front of her. "Rules are meant to be broken."

He towered over her, shadowing her, and the flickering light danced over his hard cheekbones, his chiseled, sensual lips, the bold, strong nose. He looked like a marble sculpture of masculine beauty—only he was real, warm and vibrant. He stood close enough for her to reach up and press the solid rise of muscles in his chest. She could feel the sultry heat of his body and was mesmerized by the ardent intensity in his eyes.

He lifted a hand and stroked one finger down her body, from the hollow in her throat to between her breasts, beneath the towel. She felt a rush of arousal so intense it was painful, spilling through her veins, scalding her blood, and settling in a low, throbbing ache deep inside her. He caressed the inner curves of her breasts with the lazy, errant finger, and she felt her nipples harden, aching sweetly for his touch.

"Take the towel down," he murmured.

She shook her head again, and he hooked his finger over the towel and tugged.

She bolted toward the door. She had her hand on the knob when he reached her, capturing her with his hard body, pinning her against the wood.

"Smoke Eyes," he whispered as she tried to shove back, tried to push him off her. "I can't promise not to touch you. I need you too badly. And if you were honest with yourself and me, you'd admit you want me just as much. You want me to touch you." He paused, his breath hot against her ear. "Want me to make love to you."

"No," she said, but even she could hear the weakness in her voice. She did want him, regardless of the pain when he left her. "Zach, I—"

Her words were cut off as he began to caress her, sliding his hands down her bare shoulders and arms, then back up and down her chest, pushing the towel away until he could stroke her bare breasts. Her back arched, and she instinctively pressed against him, feeling his hard arousal nudge insistently against her buttocks. She was melting from the inside out, and she knew she could resist him no longer. She was his.

"Zach—"

She stiffened at a sudden knocking at the door. The knock vibrated through her aroused body, and she gasped as if she'd been struck. Zach released her, and they both backed away from the door, staring at it warily.

"Who is it?" Zach asked, his voice harsh with frustrated passion. He saw Katherine scramble under the bedcovers, her cheeks burning, and knew she was already swamped with regrets.

"Captain?" Trey's small voice called from the other side of the door. Zach and Katherine glanced at each other. Katherine wanted, in the worst way, to dart behind the silk dressing screen as Zach let out a tense breath and strode toward the door. He opened it just enough to see the little boy looking way up at him with huge brown eyes. "I thought this was Miss Katherine's room."

Zach smiled wryly. "It is."

Trey scratched his head. "Well, are you visiting her?" He leaned to take a peek into the room, but Zach shifted to block his view.

"Could say that. What do you want, Trey?"

"I want Miss Katherine," he said.

You aren't the only one, Zach thought. "She's not dressed." He almost laughed as he heard Katherine hiss behind him. And Trey looked thoroughly confused.

"Then why are *you* in her room?"

"Uh, I was helping her find something."

More puzzled than ever Trey tried again to get a better look. "Well, when you find it could you tell her I need her to mix a magic potion for me?"

Zach raised his brows. "Potion?"

"Yeah. I want Pumpkin to hurry up and have her kittens. Miss Katherine makes magic happen."

An odd emotion tightened Zach's chest. "She sure as hell does," he said. He patted the boy's head. "I'll send her to you as soon as she's ready," he promised, and Trey trotted happily down the hall.

Zach closed the door and rested his back against it. Katherine was sitting up straight in her bed, clutching the quilt to her breasts. But the firelight glowed upon the honey-colored skin of her face and her bare shoulders. "You are," he said quietly, "the most intoxicating woman I have ever known."

Katherine swallowed, her heart wrenching with

both wild joy and an ache so raw she had to close her eyes against the pain.

When she opened them again, they were filled with tears. As Zach came to the edge of the bed, she lifted her gaze to his face and the tears slipped down her cheeks. He brushed them away with his callused thumb, then his wide palm cupped her chin. There was such poignant tenderness in his gaze, she went weak. "No tears, darlin'." His thumb continued to caress her cheek. "Are you afraid?"

She caught his wrist. "I have never been with a man before."

His face hardened with primitive satisfaction. His long fingers slid into the hair at the nape of her neck, making her skin tingle. "You will be," he promised her. "Soon."

He leaned over and took her mouth in a deep, passionate kiss, his tongue twining with hers, thrusting slow and hot. With just a kiss he possessed her. She was his, would always be his, even after they parted.

When he straightened, he stared at her for a long moment, then without another word, turned and left.

After dinner the Lyndons left and Rachel was put to bed as the rest of them retired to the parlor to pop corn, crack nuts, and tell stories. After a while Cody played the harmonica, and the poignant music actually brought tears to Katherine's eyes.

Though Zach told his share of stories to the eager boys, he sat apart from the others, brooding as he stared into the fire. He was surrounded by these happy, healthy children and could only think of his own son, and his pain. How unfair it was that Drew had to suffer so. How unfair that he, Zach, had abandoned him for so many years.

He gritted his teeth, fingers tightening around his

glass of brandy. He'd make it up to him, dammit, if the boy lived. He'd bring Drew everywhere with him, give him the gift of travel, of an education, of love. He'd bring him to Kansas to visit these boys. He'd teach him to ride, to swim, to sail. He prayed—he who never prayed—that God would grant him the chance to share his life with his son.

His sober gaze flicked Katherine's way. He knew he pinned a lot of hope on her, knew it was unreasonable. Yet she was his only hope. He knew, too, that he wasn't playing fair with her, but he must have her or die from wanting. Just looking at her made his heart lift with hope, with an odd sense of peace. She was far more to him than just a beautiful, desirable woman. He almost felt as if he'd been lost a long time and had come home. Yet she had told him she would not stay with him.

When it was time for the children to go to bed, Zach stood, offering to settle them. He swung Trey up on his shoulders, ruffled Cole's hair, and told Cody, Tessa, and Katherine good night.

Katherine watched him leave. The room became quiet, the only sound the softly crackling fire.

"You look troubled," Tessa said softly.

Katherine turned to the older woman. "I'm afraid Zach has built me up as some sort of mythical creature to Drew and he'll be sorely disappointed." Her lashes lowered and she stared into her hot toddy, fingering the edge of her glass. "Zach has invested a great deal of hope in me."

Cody smiled at her. "I don't know about that, Smoke Eyes. Zach is a sensible man. He just doesn't want to give up."

Katherine turned her troubled gaze to the fire and stared into the flames. "I don't know if I can save Drew. The tumor might kill him . . . the surgery might."

"And might not." Cody drew Tessa onto his lap, ignoring her protest that she was too heavy, and stroked her shoulder idly as he spoke. It somehow comforted Katherine to witness their love. "God's hand will guide you," Cody said.

Still she fretted. Gnawing her bottom lip she glanced again to the flames. "I even thought of you going in my stead." She glanced again at Cody's face.

"The way I hear it," he said, "Drew wants only you."

Katherine sighed. It was hopeless to wish for any other circumstances. If she was going to fail, it would be miserably.

Cody smiled reassuringly at her. "Chin up, little one. Zach understands the risks." He lifted Tessa's hand and kissed her knuckles. "If you want, we can go over some books tonight and discuss the operation."

Katherine's eyes lit up. "Oh, Cody, would you?"

"My pleasure, little one."

Later, as she started to follow Cody out of the room, Tessa stopped her with a hand on her arm. "You love Zach, don't you, Katherine?"

Katherine's eyes widened. She stared helplessly at Tessa for a moment, then nodded. "I—I do. But I don't want to," she added softly.

Tessa smiled at her. "You and Zach were destined to be together. I've felt it for years. I always thought he'd come back for you."

"But he hasn't!" Katherine cried. "He's come back for his son's sake!"

"Don't be so sure. I think he would have come back anyway."

"I could have been married."

"Perhaps you knew too that you had to wait for him."

Katherine felt a sharp ache in her chest. "Tess, there

is no future for us. We have separate lives. He's left women behind always. Look what happened with his son's mother. I don't want that for me. Zach's footloose, restless."

"Cody was too."

They looked at each other. Tessa didn't understand, Katherine thought. She and Zach could never have what Cody and Tessa had. She smiled anyway and squeezed Tessa's hand. "Be sure you telegraph us when you have the baby."

Tessa smiled radiantly. "Of course. And you, about Drew's operation."

Katherine nodded, praying once more that all would go well.

Fourteen

Zach had reserved a sumptuous, private Pullman coach for their trip to Boston, complete with elegant wing chairs, rich hangings, and a massive bed. Damask curtains graced the windows and the floor was carpeted with the most costly Brussels. Fragrant damask roses were placed in crystal vases throughout the coach—vibrant splashes of pink against the plush emerald background. Thunderstruck, Katherine turned in a slow circle, taking in a huge gilded walnut-framed mirror on one wall, the marble washstand, the ornate brass tub. Hand-carved inlaid paneling of oiled walnut added an ele-

gant touch, and the ceiling was frescoed in mosaics of
gold, emerald, crimson, and varying shades of blue.

Her gaze strayed to the bed again. It dominated the
entire coach, its luxurious deep green coverlet turned
down invitingly, several plump satin-covered pillows at
its head. One bed. Obviously it was Zach's intention
that she and he share this coach, that bed. She could
feel him watching her, as if trying to gauge her reaction. She lifted her gaze to his and stifled a shiver. Sizzling awareness crackled in the perfumed air between
them, and Katherine felt the quick leap of her heart.
She forced herself to take a deep breath and turned
away from him, her pulse still erratic.

She patted the seat of the settee. "This is finely
sprung," she said, straightening again to smile at him.
"I'm sure I will enjoy a good night's sleep here."

A flicker of humor lit his gaze, but he said nothing.
Instead he turned to the tray of decanters to pour himself a brandy. His facility with the crystal glasses and
decanters, the fine liquors, and the opulent surroundings proved the extent of his wealth, which was far
greater than she had realized. He glanced over his
shoulder at her and offered her a brandy.

"No, thank you," she said. "I think I'll just read by
this light over here."

But she could not concentrate at all. Tension coiled
tightly inside her as the afternoon wore on. She pretended to read, her head bent over her book, but she
was keenly aware of Zach's gaze from across the coach:
it resembled a caress, tingling on her skin. She had the
uncanny sense that she was riding fast into territory
where she would retain only a thread of control.

By dinnertime she had convinced herself she was
famished, and in the magnificent dining car she examined each course with relish and dove in. But as she
waded through the poached salmon and new potatoes

garnished with parsley, the grilled fillet steak and stewed tomatoes, the coconut pudding with wine sauce, and the selection of cheeses and fresh fruit, she downed several glasses of fragrant champagne too. Perhaps, she thought as Zach watched her knowingly from across the table, she would be so sated she would fall into a heavy sleep and be able to ignore his potent magnetism.

Her efforts were to no avail, though. Zach ordered a second magnum of champagne and brought it with them back to their coach, where he lit a candle, casting the compartment into blushing rosiness.

"I really shouldn't drink anymore," Katherine protested as he handed her a glass brimming with the bubbling gold liquid.

"Sit" was his answer, and he lowered himself into a plush wing chair. Katherine stared at his tanned fingers, such a powerful contrast to the delicate crystal glass he held. Her gaze drifted over him—so handsome in impeccably tailored black trousers, a crisp white shirt, and a brocade waistcoat of rich wine-red. He stared right back at her, making her think of a wildcat, sleek and muscled, waiting to pounce.

Her vision suddenly went fuzzy, and she tilted her head as if to straighten out the edges. She knew if she sat down it would put her at a disadvantage, that she might not be able to rise and he would have to help her. And she did not want Zach's hands on her—not tonight.

The champagne bubbles tickled her nose as she took a sip. She averted her eyes from him and turned her attention to her surroundings, pretending interest in the lavish fittings. "This is all so lovely," she said, and reached to touch a pink rose. "Pink roses are my favorite." And she plucked one from the vase, closed her eyes, and inhaled its sweet fragrance. "They grow in my front yard, cascades of them over the white picket fence."

Enchanted, Zach watched her. She looked so irresistible, a rose in one hand, a glass of champagne in the other. He reached for her, his hand clasping her fragile wrist. He pulled her in close, between his knees, and he could feel her warmth. She stared down at their hands—his so large and masculine, hers slim and delicate. He gave her a little tug so that she would look at him. "Are you drunk?" he asked.

She blinked. "Drunk?"

He smiled slowly. "Yes. You know." He traced his fingers over the delicate skin of her inner wrist, where the pulse rapped frantically. "Inebriated."

"No . . ." She answered carefully, but he could tell she had some trouble forming the word.

"Good. Because I want you to remember every detail of what I am going to do with you tonight."

She watched him set his drink down. "Do?" she echoed vaguely.

"Do," he affirmed, and lifted her hand to kiss her knuckles. "With you," he went on, his voice growing husky, "to you, for you. Now." He tugged her closer, ignoring her little gasp. "There will be nothing left unfinished, no interruptions—"

"Zach, I—"

"And no," he continued as he took her glass from her and brought it to his lips, "protests."

Watching him drink from her glass released such an erotic sensation in Katherine that she could not take her eyes from his sensual mouth upon the rim, remembering it upon her own skin. Her heart knocked against the walls of her chest as he lifted the glass to her lips and urged her to drink from where his mouth had warmed the glass. Her gaze locked with his, and a breathlessness assailed her as she took his offering and wet her lips with the heady wine. *Was* she drunk? Or just drunk on him—his face, his scent, those mesmerizing, thick-lashed eyes that held hers and burned with dark passion?

"You look beautiful, darling. You were meant to drink champagne." He took the glass from her weakening fingers and set it on the small table beside him. "To wear silks, to grace elegant ballrooms with your beauty . . ." He grinned crookedly, teasing her. "See? You even bring out the poet in me."

A treacherous heat began to seep through her as his words poured seductively over her. He spanned his large hands around her small waist, and she stared down at them. He pulled her closer, so that her skirt brushed his inner thighs, and she went light-headed. She tried to jerk back but her body was slow in reacting. Frowning, she met his eyes.

Zach smiled as he looked at her. Her eyes sparkled with strange lights from the candle—tiny white flames leaping in the purest gray depths. Cat's eyes. "Kat," he said huskily. "I should call you Kat."

She touched his jaw with her fingertips, shaking her head. "My name," she whispered over the clackety-clack of the train as it sped over the tracks, "is Smoke Eyes."

Zach swallowed thickly. The rose-gold candlelight illuminated her face, and he knew that for the first time since they had reunited, she was trusting him. As she stared at him, he thought of how small, how delicately made she was, and he, well . . . he would have to take extreme care with her, so he would not hurt her. How could he go slow with her, though, when he wanted her so desperately, so deeply? His entire body was one big ache. He wanted to pull her astride him, bury himself in her, hard and fast and deep. It was a colossal effort to stay seated when all his muscles strained toward her.

He took her hand and turned it so he could kiss her palm. Touching his tongue to the center of her hand, he felt her shudder. *Gentle,* he told himself, his breathing becoming labored as he kept his lips on her palm. He closed his eyes, the taste of her lingering upon his mouth, and placed her hand against his neck, under his collar.

Katherine watched his eyes as Zach lifted his head, and almost gasped at the naked, vulnerable need he revealed to her. She traced an idle pattern over his neck, wiping away the fine film of sweat with her fingers.

"Undress me," he said.

She drew her hand back as if stricken. Dazed, she shook her head. "I—I can't—"

"Yes, you can, darlin'." And he began to help her, shrugging out of his waistcoat, then bringing her hand to the top button of his white shirt. Her fingers fumbled under his, then freed the button at his throat, then the next one, and the next. She stopped at the center of his chest where she could feel the crisp curls of his chest hair against the backs of her trembling fingers. The ache had become so thick in her throat, she could not swallow.

"Zach, I can't—please."

He ignored her entreaty and guided her hand down his shirt till all the buttons were undone. Then he pulled the shirttails out of his trousers, and his bare skin gleamed in the faint light. "Now touch me," he said, his eyes scorching hers.

The rose she held dropped to his lap, resting intimately against his arousal. He took her hands and placed them on his shoulders, and her fingers tightened reflexively upon his sinewy flesh. She hesitated, then began her exploration. Her hands skimmed over his massive shoulders, riding the ripples of granite muscle that shifted under her tingling palms and shaking fingers. As she continued her slow descent down his perfect body, a languorous heat began to spill through her veins, scalding her from the inside out.

"You're beautiful," she breathed, and her heart leapt as she saw him smile that lazy, sensual smile that always captivated her.

"No one has ever called me beautiful before," he said with a laugh. "And I think I would have knocked anyone out who might dare—" He sucked in a sharp breath as her hands drifted lower, smoothing over the hard planes of his belly. His body ached with restrained passion. He thought he would burst under her touch . . . but then she ran her hands up his arms, testing, squeezing the muscles, trying to circle his bulging biceps but unable to. Her palms slid up his shoulders again, his neck, then she was touching his face, fingers skimming his faint bruises, concern flickering in her eyes as she avoided the sutures in his forehead and chin.

I love your face, she ached to tell him. *I love all your rugged angles and planes, the strength, the scars, the crinkles at the corners of your eyes.* But of course she could not tell him. Even in her slightly inebriated state Katherine knew she must stanch the words of love that trembled upon her lips. She would love him forever. Even when the time came for her to leave him, she knew her love would not recede. Stricken by the soul-wrenching truth, she fought the powerful emotions pouring through her. Zach didn't want a woman to love him; he'd made that clear when he'd told her about Laura.

It didn't matter, she told herself as her fingers lovingly caressed his face. She had never been in love before. Zach had given her a gift, bittersweet as it was.

She knew her love was one-sided, but she would enjoy whatever time she had left with him.

She placed a palm on his cheek and felt a muscle jump under her hand. "I've wanted to touch you like this for the longest time," she confessed, "and have been so afraid to."

At her candid words, Zach felt an ache hit his loins like a gunshot. His body was throbbing, pounding for her. Sweat broke out on his brow. He wanted to taste her, touch her, bury himself inside her. Now.

She traced a finger over his sweeping black brows, first one, then the other, then brought her gaze back to his. "Even your eyebrows are so . . . masculine . . ."

He caught her wrist, his hand shaking. He caught the puzzled expression that flashed into her eyes and said raggedly, "When you touch me like that I want to take you and take you and take you, until we are so buried in each other we can't breathe." His voice was hoarse and thick and acutely arousing, making Katherine weak with the pictures his erotic words painted. "I want to die inside you, honey. I want to fill you, feel your sweet flesh take me until it can't take one inch more—"

She was gasping, her eyes sliding shut at the impact of his words. Her breasts had grown taut and full, her nipples tight and puckered, her body melting, wet and warm and waiting for him. And he hadn't even touched her. He sat with her between his legs, his face etched with tension and hunger. Her body was strung taut as a bow, and just looking at him ignited such piercing physical pleasure, she already felt his possession. It was shattering—terrifying—to realize that she would never be free of him, that something in her would die when she left him, that the memory of him—so intensely masterful—would forever numb her to loving any other man.

Masterful. She shuddered. She would never have believed it just days ago, before he came into her life again, that any man could be so. He had promised her he would be her master in bed. Now she believed it. And wanted it. Heady, intoxicating thought. But, she knew, she possessed power too. Passionately female, she was keenly attuned to her own seductive nature. She knew men wanted her. To give the fact any attention had never suited her, but to know that *this* potent, devastatingly sexual man desired her, *ached* for her, flushed her with pride, and a need to wield that power.

She plunged her fingers into his thick, black hair, taking handfuls of it, the silk strands slipping through her fingers. She leaned down to breathe in its clean scent, swearing she could smell the sun in it. Yes, she thought, like the sun in a night sky.

"You have the hair of an Arapaho," she whispered, and felt him shudder as her hands moved over his back. "And the body of a stallion." His low growl fired her nerves, created another rush of moisture between her thighs. She saw the fine film of sweat glistening on his skin and became drunker still on his rich, musk-warm scent. "You're so hot," she told him.

"You make me burn," Zach whispered hoarsely, and, unable to tolerate one more instant of the excruciating tension, he lifted his hand to her bodice. Quickly he released all the tiny buttons that shielded her from his view. He spread the dress open to reveal her lacy camisole, and under it, her round, ripe breasts quivering for his touch.

Blood roared in a torrent through Zach's body. He tugged her sleeves down till they lay tight just above her elbows, trapping her, but jutting her breasts upward. Groaning, he captured one taut, apricot-colored nipple through the material of her camisole, pulling the aroused flesh into his hot, open mouth. Katherine arched and cried out at the delicious torment, her fingers twining through his hair. He moved to the other breast, and the rasp of his tongue on her throbbing nipple aroused her to the point of near insanity. She pressed her thighs together in an effort to ease the empty ache between them. Her head fell back as he tasted her, tugging on her rosy flesh.

"Zach—Zach!"

He growled low, moving his head from side to side, teasing her nipple between his teeth as he fondled the other breast with his hand, squeezing, kneading the firm flesh. Desire splintered through her in hot shards of pleasure, and she moaned as he licked a nipple through the wet fabric. It was frustrating—maddening— that he had not removed her camisole, and she arched against his mouth, her hands digging into his hair to press his head to her breasts. He buried his face between, squeezing them, pushing them up and out, straining the fabric of her camisole.

"Umm," Katherine murmured at the delicious pleasure of his hands and mouth upon her flesh. He lifted his head and slid his warm hand inside her chemise to cup her bare breast. A soft sound of pleasure erupted in her throat, and she moved her shoulders sinuously, begging him to free her.

"Not yet," he whispered hotly, leaning back to look at her. But she made another frustrated move, causing her breasts to tremble, and the erotic sight aroused him to the point of agony. Heat erupted in him, a fierce pounding heat that slammed into his loins with the force of a gale wind. He couldn't wait any longer.

Zach grasped her camisole in both hands and tore it in two. It came apart in his hands, and her breasts spilled free. He groaned, pulling her close so he could fasten his mouth upon her distended nipple.

Katherine gasped as shafts of wet heat spiraled down her body to the juncture of her thighs. Staggering pleasure gripped her loins as his tongue licked and sucked, sliding over and around the tingling flesh. She fell against him, but he was ready for her, pulling her down on his lap and covering her mouth with his own, hot and fierce. Her arms were still trapped and he freed them, slightly, then stopped to press her breast upward with the heel of his hand. He rubbed her hard nipple with his callused palm, making her moan softly and squirm to be out of her dress.

"I've been waiting only a few days," he said against her trembling lips, "but I feel like I've waited a lifetime for you."

He slanted his mouth across hers in one direction, then another, his tongue plunging into her mouth, seductively withdrawing, only to penetrate again. As he kissed her he eased her arms free so she could at last, thankfully, put them around his neck. He slid his hand to her ribs, rasping her skin with his rough, practiced fingers.

"Your skin is like honey, darlin'—smooth and sweet and golden."

She smiled dreamily, closing her eyes as she let him explore her breasts. He brushed his fingers over her nipples, then tugged until they ached sweetly, a surging rapture intensifying throughout her heated body. "Oh, Zach . . ."

"You like that?" he asked huskily, but she didn't have to answer. Her skin was like a sheet of flame, her body swollen and lush as she pressed it willingly against his. He kissed her again, and her lips parted, her breath mingling with his. His tongue slowly entered her mouth, twining with hers, filling the velvety interior with slow, deep strokes. She clung to his shoulders, sinking into his delicious male heat.

She could feel his rigid length against her bottom, ready for her. Instinctively she moved against it. He made a gruff sound, and his tongue drove deeper, demanding she follow his lusty rhythm. She did, taking all that she could of him. She felt as though a volcano had erupted inside her, moisture pulsing out in soft bursts, drowning her in need. How could she have known it would feel so good? She could understand now why violent acts were committed in the name of passion. Passion *was* violent—savage-hot and wildly sweet.

"Let's get you undressed, honey," Zach muttered against her mouth.

He picked her up and carried her to the bed, where he laid her down carefully as if she were a china doll. He ran his tongue lightly around her trembling lips, lingering on the surprisingly full upper one before he lifted his head. A wave of unbearable longing surged through her, and she reached blindly for him. *I love you,* she whispered inside herself.

He became lost in her, lowering his head to spread feverish kisses across her burning skin. "God, darlin'—"

She could feel him shudder as he slid down the length of her, his hands following the scorching trail of his lips. Somehow he still had the rose, and he plucked a few velvety petals, crushing them into her skin. Back up his lips went to taste the perfume upon her quivering flesh, his tongue licking her nipples, then sucking them till they were hard and wet and reddened. She writhed under his hands, his mouth, the ardent words he pressed against her acutely aroused body.

"Look at that," he whispered hotly, and touched each nipple with a fingertip. "Look at you." He let the backs of his fingers drift tantalizingly over the taut peaks of her breasts. "If you're not the most beautiful . . . Look at yourself, darlin'."

When she shook her head, her dazed eyes locking on his, he smiled tenderly at her. "You're softer even than the petal of a rose." He laid his hand on her stomach, and felt her body tauten. "Are you afraid, sugar?"

"Yes." Her voice sounded tiny over the rattling-clack of the train wheels.

Zach's eyes softened. He cupped her face, his thumb running over her bottom lip. "Don't be," he murmured, and lowered his head to brush her mouth with his—just a whispering, champagne-scented kiss. Katherine forgot all her fears as her desire heightened. She should be more afraid—for so many reasons—but she wanted him so intensely, with a yearning so extreme that her love and need shut out her fears. She could only feel. In the warm, sheltered cocoon of this lavish coach there was only man and woman, want and need.

But then he left her, standing to tug off his boots, then unfasten his trousers. He kept his gaze on her, but she watched his hand. Her breath stalled in her throat as his fingers brushed his bulging manhood. She couldn't look away. Even as his trousers came undone and he pulled them off, she stared at his magnificent, throbbing manhood, vibrant and pulsing with need. He was big and strong, undeniably male, and she suddenly felt remarkably small and vulnerable. Stricken by the size of him, she lifted her gaze slowly to his. "You can't . . ."

He stroked her cheek. "I can," he said. "Don't worry, darlin'. I'll go easy with you."

His hands were gentle as he quickly stripped away her dress and undergarments, shoes and stockings, and she was suddenly bare, her flushed skin glowing in the soft light. But she shrank from the consuming heat in his eyes, the passion in his face.

"Zach, I—".

"Hush."

He was over her, covering her body with his, with his heat and his power. She almost cried out from the intense pleasure of feeling his solid weight upon her. He took her mouth in a kiss both tender and passionate. When he pulled away their eyes met.

"What do I do?" she asked softly, her fingers tangling in the thick hair at the back of his neck. "I know nothing about this—nothing at all. You have to teach me, Zach."

Zach tamped down the surge of primitive pleasure. She was so sweet, so sensual, so giving. He wanted her more than he wanted his next breath. He could feel their hearts pounding, pounding, almost in rhythm with the train. The golden candlelight and gaslight spilled over her hair, which fell in rich cascades over her bare shoulders and breasts. He touched his mouth to hers and felt the shudder of her breath.

"There'll be plenty of time for lessons later, darlin'. I'll teach you everything you want to know. But first"— his voice lowered huskily—"I want you to know this." He brought her hand down to his rigid arousal, showing her how to caress the hard, pulsating flesh. She was an adept learner, and he groaned as violent shudders ran through him. He kissed her, ravaging her mouth with savage thrusts of his tongue. Then he tore his lips away and pressed them to her ear, where his breath beat hot and fast, much like the wild rhythm that pulsed in Katherine's blood.

"I think," he said as he took her slim hand away and twined her fingers with his, "you have proved a good pupil already. Christ, Smoke Eyes, your touch . . ."

But then he was touching her, his hand sliding over her bare stomach, fingers spreading to tease her silky triangle of curls. Her pulses beat harder and faster, especially where his long fingers touched her. He was watching her with a fierce, heated expression, and her body jerked as his hand moved lower.

"Open your legs, darlin'." She couldn't seem to move, though, so he eased her legs apart, his fingers combing through her auburn curls. Then he covered her with his palm, pressing, making her moan and arch under his magic touch.

"Zach—"

"Shh, baby, I won't hurt you." His voice was so warm with tenderness, she began to relax as his fingers trailed lower to where the moistness beckoned. Tingles of pleasure lit her nerves. His expert fingers brushed against her honeyed sweetness, slid inside her, and he groaned deeply as she cried out, straining toward him. His fingers stroked her, sliding in and out of her in a slow, bewitching rhythm that shattered her. Quick, darting rushes of sensations burst within her, racing wildly up her spine, spreading heat and fire throughout her body. She was twisting under his hands, his exquisite fingers sculpting her delicate flesh and taking her from mounting pleasure to agonizing ecstasy. Breathy whimpers escaped her lips as she trembled again and again, and Zach's tongue came into her mouth, stroking with the same delicious rhythm as his fingers.

Katherine arched higher and higher. Sensation built in her like an inferno. She had never felt anything so rapturous! It was frightening, yet freeing, making her feel like one of the high-soaring eagles she often spotted against the blue Colorado skies. She was soaring now to a quivering peak of need. Pleasure spasms raced downward to pulse in the velvety softness where Zach caressed. His mouth was magic—upon her breasts now, wet and achingly tight. She throbbed everywhere, though most intensely in her deepest hot core, which surged with undulating excitement as he kept his hand against her. Tiny inner convulsions tugged at her, the delight swelling unbearably—and then bursting at last in shattering waves that engulfed her in blistering, shimmering heat.

"Zach!"

He caught her cry in his mouth, then moved swiftly over her, settling between her parted thighs. He could feel her sweet pulsations against his hard abdomen, and clamped back on the ferocious urge to thrust himself into her silky hot sweetness. She stared up at him with wet, smoky eyes, and his breath caught.

"I didn't know . . .," she whispered as he leaned down to touch his tongue to the tear that traced her cheek.

He lifted his head and smiled down at her. "You still don't know," he said. "Are you ready for me, darlin'?" His loins were heavy and throbbing, his aching body needing relief. When she nodded, her huge eyes trusting, he felt an ache so great he had to close his eyes.

"Little angel," he breathed, kissing her mouth, her eyelids, her nose. He braced himself above her, and his hot hardness touched her, making her body jump convulsively. Damn, he didn't want to hurt her. She was so soft . . . and so small. He opened his eyes to see hers pinched shut. "Open your eyes," he whispered, and she did. Her gray eyes were misty with passion, and his control slipped. His swollen flesh pulsed at her throbbing entrance.

"You're mine," he growled, as he tightened his buttocks and began entering her. She cried out, a soft and wild sound. He covered her mouth with his own, his body sinking slowly, slowly into her. "Tell me," he said in a racked whisper.

Katherine watched his face, tight with passion, his burning eyes pure flame, consuming her. "I'm yours," she whispered. Oh, yes, she was his, would always be his. But *he* was not *hers*. She felt his burning body enter her by slow degrees. Alarm shot through her as she was inexorably stretched, her delicate skin unfolding to accommodate him. Panicked she pushed her fists against his shoulders. "Zach! I can't take you—"

"Shh, shh," he soothed, stroking her hair as he looked deep into her eyes. "You are taking me, sweetheart. I'm inside you now." He paused, his body shuddering as he exerted iron control not to plunge into her. She was so tormentingly warm and female. Desperately he sank deeper into her, wanting to absorb her through his own flesh. Her cries were sending him over the edge—clouding his mind with dizzying silvery mists.

Deeper and deeper he pushed into her tight, velvety heat. His need was so urgent it drew him into mindless dark depths, a sweet, succulent insanity. And still her untaught body resisted.

He was hot and solid like steel. How much, Katherine wondered dazedly, could there be of his magnificent manhood? He gentled her with words and kisses, as he would a skittish colt, then exerted more pressure. She felt an instant of pain as Zach groaned, his hard flesh impaling her.

He stayed buried in her, the deep penetration staggering Katherine's senses. She whispered his name, but her eyes were closed. Zach waited, letting her get used to the fullness inside her. He dared not move, fearing that if he did it would soon be over. He gritted his teeth, sweat beading his brow as he fought for control. She was meltingly hot, wet with lavish sensuality, and so tight around him he could feel the gentle hugging sensations as her body adjusted to him. A pulsing ache shunted up his spine, and at last he began to move inside her. He pulled back, almost all the way out of her, keeping just the swollen crest of his manhood tantalized by her delicious heat. Then with a long, slow stroke he pushed back in, wringing new degrees of ecstasy for them both. When he drew away from her again, she instinctively tried to hold on to him, sleek inner muscles tightening around him. His arms trembled violently on either side of her, and he thrust once more. The penetration was rapturous, and Katherine purred low in the back of her throat. On the next thrust their eyes met, and hers were so deep and bright, they made Zach think of all the different ways light could fall on the ocean—scintillating on the clear surface to find variegated shades below . . . and below . . . till there was only mystery and depth.

He had to close his own eyes as a different kind of ache flooded his chest. He steadily increased his tempo, delving into the sweet center of her body, filling her as he burned with fever at the sound of her pleasured cries. "Tell me you want me," he rasped in her ear.

"I want you," she whispered, kissing his neck.

He groaned and buried himself deep inside her.

It was too much, too fast. Screaming heat roared up and down his body. He slid his hands beneath her bottom, lifting her up to receive his deep, urgent thrusts. Searing waves of passion undulated through her, rushing dark torrents that flooded her senses, then light, blinding white, as she was flung to the highest pinnacle where everything fell away but the pure sensation, so brilliantly intense it was almost unbearable. She cried out, the wave tossing her high, then abruptly tumbled down again, drowning, shuddering, clenching, till Zach's slamming thrusts sent her high again, higher than before. She arched and he took her, both melting into the violent intoxication of blistering wanton need.

Zach cried out hoarsely as she shattered around

him, tugging him off the edge of the world. Heat fogged his mind as he poured himself into her, then they spun away in ecstasy, their cries of delight funneling away down the length of the rails.

Katherine awoke wrapped in the peaceful rocking rhythm of the grand coach. Behind the drawn fringed pull-shade she could see the stain of gold-orange sunlight and knew that it was near noon. She didn't want to stir, though. Her limbs were heavy, totally relaxed. So she remembered the rapture of last night.

Zach. Nothing, she thought, could compare to the wild glory of belonging to him. They had been one last night, their joining soul deep, and she wondered if he felt it too. She could understand now how Laura had shared her bed with him, had born his illegitimate child. To love Zach was to give all, and even if Laura could not have all of him, she could have a part of him, through his child. It might have been unfair to Drew, but Katherine could understand Laura's selfish act.

She wondered—without alarm—if Zach had given her a baby too. Even if they could not have a future together they could share a child. She was used to living with rejection—she had been an outcast for much of her life—and if she returned home only to discover she carried his baby, then for the child's sake she could lie about Zach, tell folks he had died or had become lost at sea. She knew she would be strong enough to handle the situation, knew that she would have to go live somewhere outside of Newberry, perhaps even the reservation. And she knew that Cody and Tess would at least understand. But she had also learned that love could hurt.

She stared up at the frescoed ceiling, thinking of all the ways he had touched her in the night. She had dissolved under and around him, had let her body take over under the pure possessiveness of his. Even now she could feel the slight soreness in her thighs and deep inside herself where she had received Zach's full hard thrusts. A flush burned her cheeks as she remembered how wildly her body had responded to his. And she knew she would let him in again, for his lovemaking was nothing short of exquisite—and addictive.

She stretched her limbs and wriggled down into the luxurious covers. She felt lazy and sated. The coach smelled of candle wax and the fragrant bouquet of champagne and roses, of man and woman . . . She remembered how she and Zach had talked for a while after their lovemaking—murmured endearments, breathless sounds—and how he had bathed her all over with a soft sponge, most gently the delicate flesh between her thighs. She had wanted to stay awake, to talk about the wonder of it all, but the gentle rock and sway of the train and Zach's strong arms around her had lulled her into a deep, dreamless sleep. The last she remembered before drifting off was the flickering candlelight upon their bare skin, his kiss in her tangled hair.

Her gaze drifted from the sumptuous hangings to the inlaid paneling to the flower-decked tables. How far he'd come! From a lonely, sullen, pugilistic youth to a compelling, sophisticated, wealthy man. As she continued to study the rich furnishings her nostrils prickled with the faint scent of tobacco. She saw the curling smoke before she caught sight of Zach sprawled in a wing chair. His rugged, disheveled appearance was an almost violent contrast against the elegant backdrop. He was bare-chested and bare-footed, wearing only trousers. Her gaze flew to his face and she found he was staring at her.

"You look," he said, his voice deep and sensual in the close, fragrant air, "like an angel when you sleep."

She sat up suddenly, and pink rose petals floated to the satin sheets. She saw Zach's eyes focus on her bare breasts, then lift again to hers.

"I wanted to take you again in the night," he said. "But I know your body needs time to get used to lovemaking."

Heat singed her face. He seemed to assume that their lovemaking would continue, and she knew that once couldn't be enough, would never be enough. As she watched him through wisps of smoke, she wondered at the contrasts in him. Despite his vast experience and sexual appetite he had been achingly tender and considerate with her. He had held back when she sensed another man might have just climbed atop her and satisfied his need. But Zach had been concerned with her satisfaction. He had seemed to enjoy it all, too, despite her lack of experience. And he wanted her again.

But she could see by the harsh, tired lines around his eyes that he had more than just lovemaking on his mind. "You're thinking about Drew."

He stood suddenly and crushed out the cheroot, then shed his trousers. She gasped at the beauty of his magnificent body gilded in the sunlight. *Oh, God,* she thought, the ache of love clogging her throat, *I will never get over this man.*

He came to her and lay down beside her. The joy of feeling his warm, solid body again made her cry out. He kissed her, hard at first, then gently, coaxingly.

"Help me forget for now, darlin'," he begged hoarsely, and lowered his head to suck on her nipple.

"Oh—Zach! Zach!" She reached blindly for him as his avid mouth tugged at her puckered nipple. Zigzags of heat ripped down her body to that place where he was heading, spreading torrid kisses over her flesh. Lower, lower he moved, pressing his mouth to her abdomen, which quivered under his magic touch. He murmured erotic words against her, and at last sank his tongue into her lush heat. Ecstasy hurtled through her. What was he doing? What . . . *Oh* . . .

The pleasure was overwhelming as Zach's tongue danced in and out of her with a silky, sliding rhythm. *I love you,* she thought, as flame licked over her body. *Oh, I love you.* Afraid she might say the words aloud, she let him take her over the edge of the earth, into a shimmering pearl-white lake of pure sensation.

Fifteen

*I*t was a cool, gray, dank day as the carriage wound up the hills to Zach's home in Marblehead. From time to time Katherine glanced out the window to see the rugged beauty of the northeast coast, the storm-gray ocean whipped with frothing whitecaps. She shivered and settled back against the plush seat, nibbling on her bottom lip as she glanced at Zach's dark, brooding face. He was tense, his eyes bloodshot. As far as she could tell he hadn't slept the entire journey. She always woke to find him sprawled in that same wing chair, smoking and nursing a whiskey. Sometimes she'd waken to the sound of his pacing, and she'd watch him for a while, watch him tear a hand through his hair, then toss another shot of whiskey back.

"That won't help," she'd said one night, and he'd spun on her, eyes narrowed. Then his gaze had softened and he'd come to the bed and kissed her, making her purr with pleasure.

"No," he'd said, "but you will." And he'd taught her new ways to love a man, and told her there would always be more.

Now she knew he thought only of Drew. His body was coiled tightly, and he looked as though he would leap out of the carriage and race it home. She reached out and placed her hand on his. He looked up, his eyes filled with desperate worry and hope. After a moment he visibly relaxed. Twining his fingers with hers, he tugged her onto his lap.

"Don't worry," she whispered, burying her face against his warm neck. He cupped the back of her head, stroking her silky hair with his fingers.

"I wish I could take you now, right here in the coach," he muttered. "The only release I crave is your sweet body, darlin', and you make me forget—for a little while at least. But the house is up ahead."

She sat up and looked out the window, then gasped when she saw a magnificent estate, set like a jewel among rugged seaside cliffs. Her gaze swept over the immense three-storied house with its double porches, balconies, decorative balustrades and gingerbread trim. Many large multipaned windows caught the sea breezes, and the front steps swept up to a wide, graceful veranda where four Corinthian columns supported the portico above. Acres of emerald-green lawn sprawled and rolled in gentle undulations, merging with the jagged cliffs. And as the black-lacquered carriage came to a halt in front of the house, she caught sight of several outbuildings and stables. Gracing one side of the house was the beginning of an extensive garden that curved around the back, hidden from view. The entire estate maintained an air of pride and dignity, and to her it was nothing short of majestic.

"Oh, Zach," she breathed, and thought at once of the little boy who awaited them indoors. How lonely he must be in such a grand home, with no mother, no siblings, and so ill. As the footmen rushed forward to assist them, she wondered how Drew would receive her. Would he be spoiled, demanding, and sullen? Would he be too ill to acknowledge her? Would his depression swamp all his other emotions?

The air was brisk and tangy as Zach led her to the wide front steps, his large hand nestled to the small of her back.

"Good afternoon, Norton," Zach said, greeting the butler. The dignified, ruddy-faced man was careful to keep a sober expression, but his eyes gleamed at the arrival of his master and his companion. "Sir."

"This is Dr. Flynn."

Norton's eyes slid to Katherine, then quickly away. "Miss."

Katherine hid her smile at the man's carefully blank expression. "Sir," she said, and thought she caught a flicker of surprise in Norton's gray-blue eyes. The servants welcomed Zach home, and though he flashed them a warm smile, she could see that smile did not reach his eyes. He introduced her to the staff, and she could hear their whisperings in her wake. "She's come! Oh, he'll be healin' now, he will!" And, "She's beautiful. The master can't be avoiding gossip with such a beauty under his roof!"

She had never expected such grandeur, though the extravagant Pullman coach should have given her a clue. She watched as Zach strode into the entrance hall, which was larger than her entire home. A wide, curving mahogany staircase swept up to the next two floors and a great domed skylight drenched the area in soft light from high above. The scent of beeswax and lemon oil tinged the air, and she gazed with awe at the splendor of her surroundings.

"Zach, I never—"

But he had strode to the center of the foyer as if he owned the very seas. "I'm home!" he boomed, and her heart caught with love for this bold man with flashing dark eyes.

Katherine's attention was drawn from him, by the appearance of a small, plump woman on the second-floor landing. A ruffled cap was perched atop her blond-white curls and she wore a comical expression, seeming to be torn between wanting to scold Zach for interrupting the quiet of the house, and wanting to smile broadly at his arrival. She waddled down the polished flight of stairs, shaking her finger at the rangy sea captain, who stood with feet braced wide apart as if against a hearty wind.

"Hush, now! Don't you realize, Captain, that the boy is sleeping?"

"Ah." Zach grinned, the long vertical line running deep into his cheek. "Surely he'll want to waken for the woman who has come all this way to help him."

Dorrie, Drew's nanny, almost tumbled down the rest of the stairs in her haste to reach Katherine. When she did, Katherine was delighted to find the woman at eye level, her cheeks as red as autumn apples, her eyes blueberry blue. "So," Dorrie said, peering close, "*you're* the one who's come to fix the mite."

Katherine glanced to Zach, then back to Dorrie. Lord, what would she do if Drew died? She offered Dorrie a weak smile. "I'm going to try."

"And that's all a soul can ask for," Dorrie assured

her, patting Katherine's hand. "He's better already since
he heard you were coming. He's been sipping soup
and nibbling on bread and the like. Even a bit of beef
at noon today."

"Has he spoken yet?" Zach asked.

Dorrie glanced at her feet. "No, sir."

Tense silence fell between them.

"And have the Kingstons been looking in on him?"

Dorrie's face cleared and she looked up again.
"Faithfully ... every day, sir. Those two tykes—the
twins—do him more harm than good, I think, with all
their cavorting—" Suddenly Dorrie broke off and
moved a step closer to Zach. "Why, Lordy Lord! What
happened to your face, Captain?"

Zach smiled, his gaze flicking to Katherine. "I was
in a boxing rout, Dorrie."

"And a fire," Katherine put in as Zach took her by
the elbow and began to lead her to the staircase.

"And a jailhouse," he added for good measure.

They were halfway up the stairs now, two footmen
behind them, carrying their trunks. Dorrie put her
hands on her hips and drew in a huffed breath. "Captain, sir, don't you dare leave me wondering—Captain!
You mustn't disturb Drew—"

Zach and Katherine had already reached the bal-
cony of the second-floor landing, though, and Zach
was guiding Katherine down a hallway carpeted in
deep blue and gold. She felt as though she were walking on a cloud.

"Zach," she said, feeling as though she should
speak in hushed tones. "You're ignoring Drew's nanny.
Don't you think she knows what's best for him?"

Zach grinned down at her. "She forgets who's boss
sometimes." He sobered suddenly, his eyes becoming
shadowed as they stopped outside Drew's bedroom. "I
can't wait any longer for you to see him, Smoke Eyes.

I need to hear your diagnosis. Tomorrow morning—or even later today if you want—we can go into town and visit Dr. Langley, the doctor who has been caring for him until now."

He stopped the footman who was carrying Katherine's black medical bag, as well as the bag that held the moccasins Zach had brought home for his son. The footman brought the bags into Drew's bedchamber, and Zach and Katherine followed him in.

The room, of course, was stunning. Katherine's first thought had been that *six* children could have fit quite comfortably in the enormous chamber. A massive fireplace of cream marble was at one end of the room where a pair of cream-and-blue striped silk settees faced each other. Along one wall were shelves filled with toy soldiers, sketch pads, paintboxes and books, miniature wooden trains. Zach had not spared his son one luxury.

She abruptly interrupted her study of the room to glance toward the massive four-poster where Drew reclined against the pillows. Even from the doorway she could see how the solemn little boy with the dark curly hair bore a remarkable resemblance to Zach. He looked minute in the enormous silk-covered bed, and as she approached him she saw that he had not been asleep at all. He turned his gaze on her and her heart jolted. He had Zach's eyes, the same slightly drooping corners and thick sable lashes, but Drew's eyes were a penetrating indigo blue. Katherine was instantly captivated.

Zach was already at his side, and he tenderly lay his hand against his son's cheek. "Hello, son. I've missed you." As he said the words, Zach was stunned to realize he *had* missed the boy as he had never missed anyone but Smoke Eyes.

Drew scarcely afforded his father a glance, though,

keeping his intent gaze fixed instead upon the woman he had yearned to know.

"I've brought Smoke Eyes home, Drew."

Katherine could hear the distant pounding of the surf far below the closed window. She stepped closer, and could see the smudge of dark rings under the boy's eyes. He was wan, sallow, hollow-cheeked. She smiled at him. "Hello, Drew. I've heard a good deal about you. Your father tells me you are the bravest boy in all the world." He hadn't, but she doubted he'd dispute her. "And Dorrie tells me you've been eating. That's good, Drew. You must eat so you can get better."

As the boy simply looked at her, she got a sense of just how lethargic and listless he was. Her heartbeat quickened with alarm. He was even more ill than she had imagined. Just from looking at him she could see the depression that crushed his spirit. Only a glimpse of life remained in his eyes.

She placed her hand on his brow. It was cool and dry. "I hear," she went on, lifting her bag up on the table by the bed, "that your father has been telling tales about me." Still the boy did not look Zach's way. Katherine frowned but forced a lightness into her tone. "Well, now it's my turn to tell some tales about your father!"

She did so as she examined him, regaling the boy with the pranks Zach had pulled as a youth—how he had jumped a train once and found himself sharing a car with a gang of bandits, how he had built a small boathouse on the edge of Gullet's Pond and would let only Smoke Eyes near it.

"Of course," she added, "there were no boats, but it was a superb little boathouse. Even then your father was thinking of the sea."

Drew's face remained expressionless. As Katherine continued her examination, her fingers skimming his swollen, distended abdomen, a sick sensation rose within her. Judging by the size of the tumor the boy would not live more than a year. There was no option but to operate.

She pulled his shirt down and smiled at him. It disturbed her that he had not shown any reaction to Zach's presence. He had not revealed even the slightest bit of curiosity about his father's sutures and bruises. Zach was standing at a nearby window, and she could almost feel his tension.

"You know, Drew," she said calmly, "that you must have an operation." She saw a flicker of what could be fear in the eight-year-old's eyes. "And you must help me if I am to help you. Will you do that?"

Slowly, almost imperceptibly, the boy nodded.

"Good. You must eat—"

He shook his head.

"I know you can't be very hungry, but you must try. When the weather warms up a bit, I'll open that window and let in the lovely sea air. That will certainly give you an appetite." When he glanced away from her, she took his hand and squeezed it. "If you don't, I won't let you watch me make my secret potion. It strengthens little boys when they're feeling poorly."

Interest sparked in the depths of his eyes.

"Now do you promise to nibble on the meal Dorrie will bring you tonight?"

Again, a slight inclination of his dark head.

"Good. Now your father has brought you something."

Zach had almost forgotten. He crouched down to pull out the moccasins he'd brought Drew from the reservation. He placed them in the boy's hands, and Drew stared at them. His fingers traced the silver buttons on the sides, then he lay them beside him on the bed.

Katherine glanced at Zach, glimpsing the odd glitter

in his eyes. He *must* understand, she thought, that the boy was deeply depressed, that it was too much effort for him to speak, to thank his father for the gift. She wanted to force the thank-you from his son, but Drew's eyes had fluttered shut now.

"He's tired," she said to Zach by way of explanation. But Zach was already on his way out of the room, and she followed him.

In the hallway, he looked skeptically at her. "Potions?" he drawled.

Striving for lightness she grinned up at him. "Yes," she said blithely. "There *are* certain herbal concoctions passed down from my ancestors that truly can fortify an ill person. Some of these herbs strengthen tissues and improve the nervous system. They will also aid in recovery."

He frowned as they headed downstairs. "And your diagnosis, Doc?"

Her cheerfulness faded. "You know the prognosis is not good, don't you, Zach?" She stopped two steps higher than he, and as he turned to look at her, she caressed his cheek. "I know how difficult this is for you. It was enough of an adjustment to bring the boy home, though I do think you should have visited him many more times in his short life." She hurried on as his expression darkened. "But my judgments matter naught. We are dealing with the here and now, and your son is very ill. I will be spending hours with him, trying to perk him up, to make him ready for the operation. I think we should go now to Dr. Langley while Drew sleeps. But I warn you, Zach, this is a very risky operation."

She saw him swallow hard. "Kiss me," he said, and as she turned her mouth up to his she began to wonder if her kisses, her touch, were only a form of consolation for his pain.

• • •

The following days, from dawn until Drew fell asleep at night, Katherine sat with him, read to him, tried in vain to involve him in conversation. She made every effort to build up his strength, and at each meal, and sometimes in between, she practically force-fed him. She had Zach order Cook to buy fresh oranges every day, and she made sure Drew ate at least two. She was adamant, too, that he take daily doses of beef and a bit of red wine to build up his body and blood. And Drew began to shudder when she presented his daily dose of cod-liver oil.

At night when the boy slept she continued to study her medical texts, and made notes in her journal. Often she would hear Zach pacing if she passed the library, or his suite of rooms in the south wing. She could say nothing to reassure him. He didn't sleep, hardly ate, and had actually become a nuisance hanging around Drew's room and pacing the floor there too. With some amusement Katherine suggested he spend some time down at his shipyard, that his tension was only making *her* feel tense. He did disappear, but only for brief spurts. Always he came home with something—wood carvings, more fruit or oysters—for Drew. Once, to Katherine's delight, he brought home a perfect red rose, and she was absurdly touched. A man, she thought, could not know the joy a woman feels when presented with flowers from her lover. She touched the velvety petals and, under Zach's close perusal, her color heightened. She was thinking of the roses in the coach, of how he had crushed the petals upon her skin. And she knew he was thinking the same.

Since they'd arrived in his home, though, Zach had not come to her. In a sense she was relieved, but she was also thoroughly disappointed. Was this to be the way then? A brief period of lovemaking, then they would part ways? Well, perhaps it was best to keep a distance. She loved him so much it hurt, but she had no illusions. Zach had never loved a woman in his life; why should she be any different?

Only once had they been alone together. Two evenings after they had arrived she had gone to his library to remove his sutures. He had been standing by the window staring out at the black sea, and she had watched him for a moment.

"Zach," she said softly, and he turned around. "Are you ready?"

He smiled slowly, the first hint of teasing she'd seen in him for days. "Always ready for you, honey."

His light words oddly pained her. It was just habit with him to flirt with any woman within walking distance, she told herself. With her emotions churning, she walked to the desk, put down her bag, and briskly set about her task. She made Zach sit while she removed his stitches, remarking casually upon each scar. In the end she was left holding his hand, examining the fingers and palm where various other scars nicked his skin. Quickly he turned the tables on her and caught her hand in his, rubbing his thumb over her knuckles. Katherine's breath caught.

"Zach." Only then did she realize the tempting way they were positioned, he sprawled in a chair and she standing between his legs. She could feel his heat, and when she moved back a step he tightened his hold. Her eyes flashed to his and he smiled again.

"C'mere." He tugged her forward and she ended up on his lap. She tried to fight him, but she was dazzled by his utterly gorgeous smile. "What's the matter, little one? Shy suddenly?"

"No." She wriggled, then stopped when she felt his arousal beneath her hips. "Just cautious."

He chuckled. "Ah," he murmured, nuzzling the sweet hollow behind her ear.

She could not stop the quivering in her body as he slid his hands up her arms. She was melting beneath his touch, and miserable that he could have such an intense effect on her. In self-defense she turned her face away from his lips.

"There is no place for caution in lovemaking, darlin'," he said. "Haven't I taught you that at least? You showed no caution in the coach—"

"Please!" She jumped off his lap, and he did not move to stop her. "No," she said. "I'm not your woman, Zach."

A keen pang of possessiveness lanced through Zach. He stood up, towering over her. "Yes, you are," he said, even as he tried to fight his own response to her. For she was making it clear that she didn't want to be in his life. Perhaps she considered the incredible force and splendor of their torrid lovemaking nothing more than a mistake. Dammit, he knew they had to part, that she valued her freedom and profession above all else, but he wanted her to be his, and only his. For the first time in his life he knew he couldn't just take what he wanted, and frustration clawed at his insides. She was his now, couldn't she see that? He had branded her, and just looking at her reminded him of how she felt naked beneath him, her arms and legs wrapped around him as he spent himself inside her.

He wanted her now. He wanted to crush her to him, blot out the fear and alarm in her big eyes. Never had he felt such hunger for a woman, yet he should have guessed it would have been like this with Smoke Eyes, his first love. Something kicked in his gut at the mere *thought* of love, and he immediately shut it out. She wouldn't want him to love her, for God's sake! As it was she had resisted him all the way, trying to keep him at a distance, keep their relations on a friendly level. And as irritating as that was he understood. At least he knew she wanted him. That would have to be enough for now.

She was almost at the door.

"Do not walk away from me," he said, and started toward her.

Katherine turned, her back against the door. Anger began to creep through her as she watched Zach come after her, as if she were a wild creature he was determined to capture. She lifted her chin and stood her ground. "I will not be a kept woman."

"I don't want to *keep* you, sugar."

"No, you only want to use me."

His eyes softened. "Is that what you think, darlin'?"

He was too close now, his warm masculine scent invading her nostrils. His gaze seemed to stroke her, caress her, and she felt a damnable weakness in her middle.

"Well, hell, Smoke Eyes, I thought we were sharing."

She wanted to melt into the door behind her. The urge to let Zach touch her was a torment, and she knew she was every kind of fool for letting him get close to her.

He reached out and touched her cheek, and she cursed herself for trembling.

"You will let me leave this room," she said, managing to hold his gaze.

"You're free to go," he said, and braced his hands against the door on either side of her shoulders. The heat between them was searing.

"You have just very effectively trapped me against this door."

His smile mocked her. "I'm not touching you at all."

Oh, but he was! With his dark voice, his smoldering

gaze. . . . Her voice was faintly pleading when she spoke. "Why do you continue with this—this foolish pursuit, Zach?"

"There's nothing foolish about this, darlin'," he said, and lowered his head to kiss her with absolute possession.

Katherine moaned as his tongue penetrated her mouth with a deep, slow push. She clung to him as he gathered her close. His arms tightened around her, and his kiss became hot, forceful, and drugging. Unable to bear the wild currents of desire ripping through her, she pulled her mouth free and rested her forehead on his chest.

"Bully," she whispered.

"I want you," he said, and pressed his rigid erection against her stomach. He kissed her hard again when she moaned. "Tell me you don't want me too."

Already he had pulled her blouse free from her skirt and was untying the ribbon of her chemise, sliding his palms up her bare ribs, and finally, *finally*, cupping her breasts. He circled her nipples with his thumbs, and they grew hard and aroused against his palms.

She gasped and fell against him. He slid one arm behind her back, making her breasts arch upward, as if begging for his mouth. He bent his head and sucked a nipple greedily, wringing a throaty sound of pleasure from her. Pulling her up tighter, he rasped his tongue over the sweet rosy flesh. Her soft female sounds over the muffled crash of the surf drove him mad. She was sweet and fresh and perfect for him, and he knew he would never get enough of her. Her skin felt like satin and her husky voice was that of a seductress. And her scent, oh, God, he would never be able to forget her fragrance, lush and spicy, as haunting as the woman herself.

He sucked and pulled, sucked and pulled, on her

nipples, and Katherine felt the same rhythm tugging in her depths. He was hard against her, and already she was empty and aching for him, warm and wet. His touch was torture, torture she knew that would never, never leave her.

"Miss Katherine!"

Dorrie was calling softly from the hallway. Katherine and Zach froze, their ragged breathing and thundering hearts the only sign of life from them both.

Dorrie knocked.

"She's out on the porch, Dorrie!" Zach barked, letting Katherine out of his arms with great regret. He watched her button her bodice, covering her pretty breasts from his eyes. "What do you want?"

"Sorry to disturb you, Captain," Dorrie said. "But Drew is wanting the doctor to be tucking him in."

Zach gritted his teeth in frustration. Mention of his son made the hot throb of desire wane from his body. "I'll tell her," he said wearily, and both listened to Dorrie's receding footsteps.

"I have to go," Katherine whispered hoarsely. And Zach let her pass, finding grim humor in the fact that their lovemaking had been thwarted by the demands of his own son. And, dammit, he thought, how come the boy never asked for him? And why in the hell did it even matter?

When the Kingstons first came to visit, Katherine knew them immediately. She had heard Dorrie's tales of the twins, and hoped their antics would shake Drew from his lethargy. One afternoon she heard a commotion in the hall downstairs. Moments later a vivacious blond woman and a set of towheaded twins—a rosy-faced boy and a girl—came tumbling into Drew's room. Katherine looked up from the book she had been reading to Drew, blinked, and asked, "The Kingstons?"

Trish Kingston smiled at her, her blue eyes glittering. "Ah, our reputation precedes us." She was elegant in a royal blue silk dress, with diamonds flashing at her ears and throat. And she was, Katherine learned after an extended visit, delightful company. Her children were so lively and energetic, Katherine wished they could infuse their vitality into Drew. They seemed to feel it was their duty to entertain their young friend, and they somersaulted about the room, which was long enough for them to roll along quite a distance before turning in the opposite direction; played checkers on the small bedside table so Drew could watch every move, though he didn't; and pitted his soldiers on opposing sides in a vicious battle. Drew showed a mild interest in their antics, almost as if he were humoring them, but his attention was often drawn toward the open window where the sea beckoned.

"I'm glad it's warm enough for you to open the window," Trish said. "It's wonderful for him to get fresh air." The sea breeze was a cool, salty tang that swept into the room. Trish glanced at Drew from where she sat with Katherine on the settee before the fireplace. "Poor little mite, I do so hope he'll pull through."

Katherine smiled at her. "You've certainly offered plenty of support for Zach. Knowing that Drew had companionship while Zach traveled to Colorado eased his mind."

"Hmm. It's the least we could do." She glanced at the twins. "And it gives them a change. They do so hope he'll become a steady companion. My little Rose is enamored of him."

Katherine laughed as they both looked at the dimpled Rose, who was doing everything in her power to gain Drew's attention. "Twins!" Katherine exclaimed softly. "What a blessing."

Trish sent her a curious glance. "Strange," she murmured. "Many folks have extended their sympathies over my plight."

Katherine laughed. "Well, I think you are blessed indeed."

Trish's eyebrows rose, but she only asked, "So you and Zach have known each other since childhood?"

Katherine glanced away toward the window, watching a sea gull drift lazily on the wind. "Yes. He left for sea when he was almost sixteen."

As if summoned, Zach appeared in the doorway with a burly blond man Katherine surmised to be Trish's husband. But Katherine had eyes only for Zach. She noticed his lean features were more sharply honed, all jutting angles and stonelike planes in a face etched with lines of tension. His waist seemed leaner beneath the cobalt-blue work shirt he wore, his trousers riding lower on his straight, narrow hips. But his keen eyes radiated warmth as he looked across the room at her. Her throat grew tight. He was as ruggedly virile as ever and still seemed indomitable, even standing beside tall, muscular Joe Kingston.

Joe strode into the room to greet Drew and ruffled his hair. "He's put on weight," he said, turning to look at Katherine over his shoulder. He was a good-looking man, with brown eyes and the same tanned, weathered face of a seasoned sailor that Zach had. "Eh, what say he'll be working down his father's shipyard as a stevedore in a matter of weeks!" He winked at Katherine and she grinned back at him, thinking that friends like this would certainly speed the boy's recovery—if he came through the operation.

"We're going down to the yard," Joe told his wife, leaning down for a kiss, then hugging his children. "It's been neglected of late and the boss"—he winked in Zach's direction—"is to blame. We should be late—past dinner perhaps, for there is a good deal that needs our attention."

As they left Katherine cast a grateful glance at Joe's receding back. "Thank goodness for your husband," she murmured to Trish. "Zach has been making himself ill. All he does is pace the floor, up and down, in and out, daily, nightly, as if he doesn't know what to do with himself. He needs to be busy, doing physical work, but nothing I say changes his mind. He wants to help with Drew, but he doesn't know how. Working at the shipyard will surely release some of his tension."

"Hmm, yes." Trish studied Katherine's face for a long moment, then she said, "You're in love with him."

Startled, Katherine stiffened. "No—I—"

Trish smiled. "I can understand why," she said, not listening to Katherine's weak protests. "Zach is a fine man, honorable and brave. Not to mention *exceedingly* male. He is absolutely the most potent creature—" She broke off and leaned toward Katherine so Drew and her children, playing by his bed on the far side of the room, would not hear her. "Joe would be jealous if he heard me talking about Zach like that, but facts are, every single woman in town has been pining after Zach ever since he built this magnificent mansion and moved here a year ago. He's always managed to stay elusive. But the way he looks at you!" Trish laughed. "Like a hungry wolf."

Katherine laughed, too, though she shivered inside at Trish's accurate observation. "How fanciful you sound!" Again the sea gulls, gliding gracefully across the cerulean sky, drew her gaze. "Zach hasn't the inclination to fall in love," she said. "Oh, he loves women, all right." She smiled ruefully, bringing her gaze back to Trish. "But only for what they can give him."

"Don't underestimate the man. We've known him for years and he is one of strong character—"

"And lusty appetites," Katherine finished wryly, making Trish laugh. Katherine grew serious, though. "It's impossibly hopeless to love Zach. Nothing can come of it. I have a home and profession to return to, and Zach, well . . ." Her gaze drifted away again. "The sea calls to him. It always has."

"And?"

Katherine studied her new, shrewd friend. How refreshing it was not to have to hide the truth. "And he'll be leaving again, for years perhaps." She shrugged, flipping her hands up in a casual gesture, though she didn't feel casual at all. "So my love for him is foolish."

"And do you think mine is for Joe? He's a sea captain too."

"Oh, no, I didn't mean—"

Trish waved her off. "Don't be ridiculous. I don't take offense. But to me, having Joe part of the time in my life—our lives—is infinitely better than not having him at all."

Katherine lowered her lashes. Having known Zach—the incredible beauty and power of him, when he held her in his arms and made love to her—she felt a slash of pain that he could share that with another woman. She didn't like the hot, seeping ache of jealousy, but it was there, and knowing he would leave her and go to another made her stomach clench in a sick knot. She forced herself to look at Trish once more. "He'll leave and keep other women in other ports." She glanced at Drew. "And perhaps, even, other children."

Trish shook her head. "Men! They have their needs. But I think your man will be careful in the future about other children. He is learning a very difficult lesson with that little cherub over there." She cast a quick glance at Drew. "Has he spoken at all?"

Katherine regarded the listless child who watched as the frisky twins arm-wrestled. "Not yet."

Just then Rose, with a quick lurching movement, toppled Robert. Crowing victoriously, she scrambled to her feet and smiled at Drew, lording it over her brother. Unable to resist the infectious charm of his golden-haired admirer, Drew smiled—an exact replica of his father's devastating smile.

Katherine's breath caught. That was the first sign of emotion she had seen Drew reveal. Yes, she thought, with a tiny burst of joy, there *was* hope. And she would draw on that.

Every day Drew became stronger. When Dr. Langley dropped by to check on his progress he was amazed. Though the boy still showed little interest in his surroundings, it was clear by the way his eyes lit up at the sight of Katherine that her presence had much improved his state of mind. He had put on weight and his color was healthier, and Dr. Langley agreed with Katherine that the time was fast approaching to operate.

Night after night she fell asleep in her huge, luxurious bed mentally rehearsing what she would do when it was time for the operation. Though she had always been emphatic about not tying her personal and professional relationships together, there was no way she could *not* have become emotionally involved with Drew. In order for her to fortify the boy, it was necessary to spend a good deal of time with him. Still, she left him to his own devices as often as she could. After a while he began to show a mild interest in his soldiers.

Sometimes she walked the beach alone. The sun and surf soothed her, the green-gray rush of water tumbling almost playfully to shore. Looking out to the sharp blue line where the sea met the sky, she could understand why Zach had been drawn to the sea's mysteries. Its roar surrounded her, and the endless waves were wild and free, with a dash of danger, like Zach.

One late afternoon she turned her gaze to the cliff beside her and the mansion that gleamed brilliantly atop it in the orange glow of the sunset. Her breath caught when she saw a tall, broad-shouldered man watching her from the porch. Apparently he had been staring at her for some time. Across the distance they stared at each other, both very still. And then Zach moved.

She watched him leave the porch and lope down to her, sure-footed and graceful as he made his way across the craggy boulders. Her senses suddenly seemed so acute, everything around her came into sharp, almost painful clarity. Gulls wheeled and screeched overhead. There was music in their cawing, vibrant on the wind. Salt stung her lips; the ocean spray cascaded in needles of ice that fragmented upon her sensitive skin. And she kept her gaze glued to him.

It would be heaven to spend my life with this man. The thought came quickly—a forbidden, desperate thought that she squelched instantly. Zach hadn't asked her to stay with him . . . and wouldn't. At least they had always been honest with each other. She refused to let love cloud her mind, though it was so easy to become dreamy and foolish over a man like Zach Fletcher.

He reached the beach and strode across the sand to her, stopping just two feet away. He smelled of fresh wood shavings and sweat and the sea. Katherine's heart turned over. He was hard and lean and honed as smooth oak. His tan had darkened during his days at the shipyard, and his skin was coppery dark, burnished in the light of the setting sun. With a faded blue bandana knotted loosely around his throat, and his hair whipping wildly in the wind, he looked like a hard-bitten brigand. Until he smiled. His heavy-lidded eyes crinkled at the corners and his white teeth were a startling flash in his rakish face.

"Hey, darlin'," he said.

"Hello, Zach," she managed to say, still mesmerized by the sight of him.

"Tess had the baby."

She gasped. "Well? That's all you're going to tell me?"

He laughed. "Tess is fine. A baby girl."

"Oh, how lovely."

"They're naming her Katherine—after you. And calling her Kate."

Zach watched her eyes go soft and dewy, and he felt his gut tighten. Wisps of her fiery hair had escaped the knot atop her head and feathery tendrils brushed her face. Her cheeks were flushed from the wind, her lips parted. He stared at her mouth, thinking of how he would like to catch her full upper lip between his teeth and suck on it.

His whole body tightened at the thought, and pure hot desire washed into his loins. Something was different between them now, though, and that something was his own son. They were both anxious about the impending operation, and the fact that Drew scarcely acknowledged Zach while he hung on Katherine's every word gnawed in Zach's gut. It was his own damn fault, he realized, for having been absent all those years. He couldn't blame the boy for not trusting him, but Christ, how he ached to be the father he had never been. He wanted desperately for Drew to give him that chance.

Realizing that Katherine was gazing curiously at him, he forced his pain over his son away. He ran the back of one hand across her cheek, smiling with affection at her. "You ought to feel honored."

"I do." She smiled, too, then ducked away from him and began walking back up to the house. His eyes narrowed speculatively, and in two long strides he caught up to her. "I'll be operating on Drew in a few days," she said quietly.

His heart jerked in his chest. "Is he ready?"

"Dr. Langley thinks so and so do I. Drew's state of mind has improved and it's time. I'm going to talk about it with him now."

She almost lost her footing on the rocky path, and he reached out and caught her under her elbow. His fingers were warm through the sleeve of her blouse. She fought her response to his touch, wanting only to turn into his arms and feel their strength surround her.

"Do you want me to come up?" he asked.

"I think your support is very much needed now, Zach," she said, wishing she could ease the concern in his eyes.

He frowned. "I don't know about that, sugar. Drew doesn't seem to know whether I'm in the room or not."

Tenderness filled Katherine's chest. She knew Zach felt excluded, and knew that hurt him. A proud, confident man, he would never admit to hurt—especially over a child's rejection—but she could detect that emotion in his face.

"He knows you're there," she assured him. Lacing her fingers with his, she tugged his hand, urging him to follow her to the house.

Minutes later, with the fiery red-bronze colors of sunset splashed across the sky beyond Drew's open window, she told him about the operation and what to expect. Zach stood just inside the room, his arms folded across his chest. He watched his son's face—so like his own—watched Drew's eyes fixed on Katherine.

"We have to help each other," she was telling him. "In the next few days I want you to think of yourself growing stronger, your body able to heal quickly after the operation. The sooner you heal the sooner we can swim and fish and ride horses."

Drew continued to stare blankly at her.

"I'm a better fisherman than your father," she went on. "And I can certainly swim better."

She cast a teasing look at Zach, but Drew did not follow her gaze. Zach's mouth twisted wryly. She was giving his son hope, something to look forward to, to live for. He thought of himself when he was young, of the wild, reckless boy he had been. Drew might never be wild or free, or ride or fish or swim, simply because of this gross injustice that might take his life. Zach's lips compressed grimly as he fought the crushing pressure in his chest. He was eager to set things right between him and his son, and was determined that he would never leave Drew again—if Drew survived.

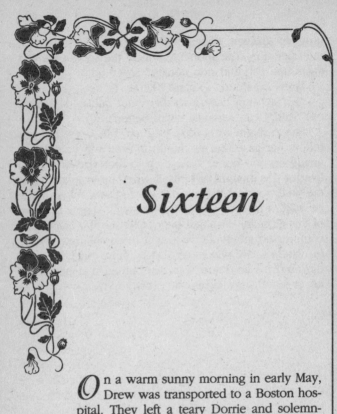

Sixteen

On a warm sunny morning in early May, Drew was transported to a Boston hospital. They left a teary Dorrie and solemn-faced servants behind, but Katherine held Drew's hand for the entire trip and chattered about her childhood. She told him of the time she stole a whole plate of doughnuts right out from under Mrs. Clayborn's nose, and ate them all up so fast that when the woman turned around again and found the empty plate, she wondered if she had even made the batch. She could tell by the glimmer of amusement in Drew's eyes that he liked the tale, and she searched her mind for another, hoping Zach's brooding countenance across from them would not sober Drew's spirits. She understood Zach's anguish and was certain he wasn't aware of the dark cloud he cast in the coach, but she needed to lighten the atmosphere as best she could for Drew's sake.

Both Katherine and Zach stayed at the hospital that evening—Zach in the waiting room and Katherine in a small room reserved for doctors. Dr. Langley was to assist her, and he arrived in the middle of the night looking tense and anxious.

Katherine slept little. She lay on her cot rehearsing the operation in her mind, repeating each delicate movement of the knife she would wield tomorrow. When she rose at dawn she went to the waiting room where Zach was pacing. Hot emotion clogged her throat as she watched the tall, indomitable man that she loved, lines of strain etched deeply into his features. He looked up and saw her.

"Can I see him before you operate?" he asked, his voice tight and thick.

She nodded, unable to speak, and led him to the corridor where Drew was lying on a cot, waiting to be transferred into the operating room. Zach went to him, resting a big hand on the boy's head.

"Son," he said hoarsely, "I know times have been tough for you." For the first time in a long time Drew looked at his father, into his eyes. "But things will get better, I promise you. I'll take you down to the shipyard when you're strong again. I'll—" He broke off as the boy looked away, clearly not believing him. Zach ran a hand down his face, and Katherine saw him swallow. He clamped his hand on the boy's shoulder, squeezed it gently, then turned and walked away, his boot heels making a hollow clunking sound.

Katherine walked over to the boy. "Drew," she said,

smoothing the curls off his brow, "I know you must be afraid, darling. But everything will be fine. I'll use secrets my grandfather taught me, all right? You'll be fine."

She watched his gaze shift down the hallway where Zach had disappeared, and as an orderly came to wheel him into the operating room, Drew reached up and tugged on her sleeve. He tugged harder, and she realized he wanted her to lean forward. She did, and was stunned to hear him speak.

"I'm not afraid," he whispered.

Somehow the words did not cheer her. They were the first he'd spoken in how long? Yet they were not words of hope or even courage, but of resignation. *What* didn't he fear? Death? In his eight-year-old mind had he decided that he would join his mother in death—that he missed her too much to stay alive?

The orderly rolled him toward the operating room. Katherine took a deep, steadying breath, then followed, determined to make this operation a success.

The operation was taking a damn long time. Zach sat hunched forward on a chair in the waiting room, his elbows braced on his knees as he stared morosely at the floor. Hours, dammit, hours. He rubbed a hand over his burning eyes, then the back of his neck, trying to ease the knot of tension in his muscles. He hadn't slept more than snatches for weeks now, and his body ached. He stood and went to look out a window, aware of the nurses and doctors whispering behind his back. He supposed he'd been somewhat of a nuisance, pacing like a caged tiger all morning, but what the hell, they should expect it of folks. Folks whose kids were getting cut open down the hall, who could be dying—

Damn! He jerked when someone touched him from

behind. The nurse squealed with fright when he spun around, glaring fiercely.

"Sir? I thought maybe you'd like me to bring you something to eat or drink? I'm going to the café down the street and—"

"No. Thank you," he said. As if he could eat, for crissake. He did decide to go outside for a smoke, though. He sat on the steps leading up to the hospital entrance and lit a hastily rolled cigarette. The harsh smoke tore a fiery path down his throat, searing his lungs, and it felt good. His eyes narrowed through the smoke and he thought back, way back, to when he had been eight years old on the streets of New York. Cold. He remembered feeling such aching cold, he just wanted to find sun and heat and clothes thick enough to stop the cruel ache that seeped into his very bones. And Ma. Another cruel constant ache. Why had she left? Where had she gone? Folks at the poorhouse had been hard on him, laughing about his pa who'd come around once in a while, more often drunk than not, and told him he was so bad even his ma had left him.

At eight he ran away. He slept in cellars and caves, then he found an old woman who let him live with her for almost a year since he helped out with the chores. But then she died. He found her one morning dead on the back stairs and it was the last time in his life he cried.

His father caught up to him when he was almost ten—a hard, rough boy with a wild reputation even in that tough city. He was a loner. Though most roughs traveled in packs, he had learned to stay so aloof, boys much older and bigger than he kept their distance. He didn't care, he told himself, didn't care about anyone or anything except survival. He was a hunter and a warrior. He even protected those much smaller than himself, bringing food to little ones who had no one to feed them, to fight for them.

His father took him out of the city, though. They drifted west until his father left him again a year later with a man who wanted to work the eleven-year-old Zach as a slave. Raze Sautter. The name tasted bitter on his tongue even now as Zach let himself remember the pitted face of the man who had beaten him and tied him to the bed at night. Finally Zach had stolen a knife and cut his ties by holding the knife between his teeth. He had run, with gunshots exploding in the air around him as Sautter stood on his porch and fired at him.

He went back to New York and started searching for his mother. He didn't find her. Anyone who knew him never guessed that he suffered a soul-wound that would not heal. His cold, remote facade was a mask to hide impenetrable feelings. He was too intense to feel lightly. His mother's betrayal had cut to the bone, and he made up his mind never to love a woman.

Unwilling to steal his food any longer, he went down to the wharves looking for work. At twelve he was big for his age and was hired on as a stevedore, to scrub decks and load ships with cargo. He was enthusiastic and strong, and worked long hours for little pay, and loved every moment of it. He was fascinated by the sights and sounds of the seaport, and vowed that someday he'd go to sea. The work, coupled with his visions of going to sea, dispelled the haunts of his past.

Women liked him. They called to him from doorways of bordellos, beckoning the twelve-year-old who looked fifteen. But it wasn't a prostitute who serviced his body for the first time soon after he turned thirteen. An older woman he met at the docks took him into her home. She was beautiful, in her twenties, recently widowed, and "kept" him for a year. By then he was hungry, searching for more, always more. She wanted him to love her, but he couldn't, so he left her. And until now he had left all his women. But he didn't want to leave Smoke Eyes, and he didn't want her to leave him. Or Drew. Drew, who had the color of his mother's eyes, haunting him still.

"Zach."

All his muscles tightened at the sound of Katherine's voice. It was husky-soft, soothing, like a cool drink of water on a broiling hot day. She touched his shoulder, and he stood. He exhaled a stream of smoke, then crushed the cigarette under his boot heel. His eyes searched hers, but his throat was so tight he couldn't speak.

She reached up and lightly caressed his cheek. "The operation was a success," she said. "I removed the tumor and sutured him. He's still unconscious but in recovery—"

Zach jerked her into his arms, crushing her to him, burying his face in her hair. "Christ," he said, his voice a raw ache. It was over. Smoke Eyes had saved his son and given him a second chance.

Drew's recovery in the hospital was as smooth as Katherine had hoped. For the first few days he slipped in and out of consciousness, and his pulse beat erratically. She hovered over him, alternating shifts with Dr. Langley, almost ill with worry that Drew would slip into a coma. Zach, too, was there often, uttering words of encouragement to his son, stroking his curly hair, promising him the world. Katherine fell in love with him a little bit more, seeing this big, rough man display such tenderness, and even the hospital staff bent the rules for him. At one point a nurse confided to Katherine that on the day of the operation, she'd thought for certain Zach was going to storm the operating room and demand they allow him to assist. Katherine had to smile. She'd never known a man like him—so sensitive, so deep, so strong.

It was Zach whom Drew first saw when he fully regained consciousness, three days after the operation. His eyes fluttered, and Zach held his breath, gripping the rails on either side of the boy's cot. Then he heard the first words from his son in more than two months.

"Where's Dr. Smoke Eyes?"

The request hit Zach with the force of a slap. He straightened, his lips tightening, but laid a gentle hand on his son's head. "She's right here, son." He nodded almost insolently at Katherine, then turned and strode out of the room.

Tears filled Katherine's eyes as she walked over to Drew. She didn't know if they were caused by this sign that Drew apparently was out of danger, or because of the hurt he had unwittingly inflicted on his father.

A few days later Drew was transported back to his home. Dorrie fussed over him to the point of annoyance, and Katherine sent her off on errands, gently stating that Drew still needed plenty of rest. Dorrie was back an hour and a half later with freshly baked gingerbread and other delicious treats that her "baby" had always loved. Drew could not eat them, though. He was only allowed soup and bread for the first week at home, but he did enjoy gazing at the sweets.

It was a delight for the household staff to hear his voice again, then to see him up and about after that first week home. He walked gingerly with a cane Katherine had provided for him, but he was tottering around his bedroom the first time the twins came for a visit.

"You *can* talk!" Rose exclaimed, and jabbed her brother in the chest with her finger. "I told you so, Robert!"

"Aw . . ." was all Robert could muster, embarrassed that he'd doubted it. Drew just grinned at his friends, and they chattered excitedly about when they would share a tutor, when they would horseback ride and play outdoors. The twins were delighted with Drew's British accent, and before the day was out they had both adopted one of their own.

Katherine still made sure he rested for half days and napped as often as he needed. She read to him, and indulged him with more childhood stories, often bringing Zach into them. But he showed no curiosity about his father. It was almost as if he didn't want to know about him, and she was deeply disturbed. When she left, Drew and Zach *must* get on. They only had each other.

Since Drew's return from the hospital, Zach had put in regular hours at the shipyard. He always stopped in to say good night to Drew, speaking politely, but distantly. One night, however, he issued a command, albeit in a gentle voice.

"Son, when I address you I want you to look at me."

Katherine saw the hurt and vulnerability in Zach's eyes, and prayed Drew would respond, ease some of Zach's hurt. The boy was motionless, though. Zach put his fingers under Drew's chin and lifted the little face up to meet his gaze.

"Do you understand me?"

Drew nodded.

"I want you to speak to me," Zach said.

"Yes, sir."

Zach ran his thumb down the boy's cheek. "Tomorrow," he said, "I will bring you a piece of wood and a knife, and I'll teach you how to whittle."

"Yes, sir."

When Zach came home early the next day, Katherine left them alone. She ordered the carriage for herself and rode into the town. She took her time, exploring various shops, making her way toward the docks where vendors sold everything from fruits and flowers to fresh cod and oysters. She noticed a young boy crouched by a crate, and coming closer saw a litter of brown and white puppies.

"How darling they are!" she exclaimed, kneeling too and scooping up one of the small balls of fur. She laughed when the puppy eagerly licked her face with a little pink tongue. Drew would love it.

"I'll give one to you for a good price," the boy said.

So it was that Katherine returned home with the little fluffy white puppy. Carrying the puppy, she circled around the house, heading for the sun porch along one side. She planned to summon Dorrie and have her fetch Drew. As she rounded the corner, though, she came up short at the sight of Zach. He was seated at one of the white wrought-iron tables, his long legs stretched out in front of him, a bottle of beer in one hand. He wore a denim shirt so faded it was almost white, and he'd rolled the sleeves up, baring his hard, muscular arms. Dark beard stubble shaded his face, and his smile was sardonic when he saw her.

"Zach—"

She got no further. Oblivious to the tension sizzling between the two humans, the wriggling puppy lapped at her face, making her laugh. She tried to control him, but he gave a sharp bark of protest, making her laugh again.

"You don't mind, do you?" she asked Zach as she walked up the steps to the porch.

Zach lifted the beer bottle and took a long swallow. When he set the bottle down between his thighs, his expression was blank, hiding all emotion. "I don't think puppies are Drew's favorite gift," he said flatly.

Katherine remembered, of course, that the dog Zach

had given Drew had died, but she hoped this one might fill that loss for the boy. The puppy was insistently squirming to be put down and she let him go. He immediately scampered over to Zach, clamped his small teeth on the hem of his trousers, and tugged. Though Zach looked bored with the puppy's antics, Katherine laughed and bent down to pull it away from Zach. The puppy yipped and began to explore his new home, sniffing the porch floor, its stubby tail wagging excitedly.

"I think Drew will love him," she said, watching it fondly. "Of course," she added, casting a glance at Zach's scowling face, "if you want, I'll take him back. I just couldn't resist him."

Zach drained the beer bottle, then set it down on a nearby table with a thump. He eyed the puppy with a look of such excruciating boredom that she knew he, too, found the little fluff ball irresistible. When he stood and faced her, though, she sensed he was tightly reining in some fierce emotion.

"I'm sure," he said, "that I wouldn't want to deprive Drew of some company. After all," he continued in a sarcastic tone, his gaze flicking dismissively over her, "you'll be leaving soon."

Katherine felt his words like a slap, and turned away to hide her pain. She leaned down to free the puppy, who had wedged itself behind a chair. "It's true," she said in a falsely bright tone, straightening with the puppy in her arms. "I thought I'd leave the beginning of next week. By then Drew won't need me anymore and Dr. Langley can—"

Zach's hand shot out, closing over her arm. Startled, she cried out. "I need you," he said as he pulled her close.

She felt a sharp pang of love and need as his mouth came down on hers. She moaned, the sound blurred by

the deep thrusts of his tongue. Her senses exploded
and she began to shake all over. His hand cupping the
back of her head was all that steadied her. But the
puppy, squeezed between them, yelped, and Zach
pulled back, breathing heavily. The icy hardness had
melted from his eyes, replaced by an almost reverent
intensity. He leaned down to brush his mouth over
hers, once, twice.

"Kat," he whispered. His warm tongue traced her
lips, then he pulled away again. "Buying the puppy for
Drew was very thoughtful of you, darlin'."

Zach cursed himself for hurting her, cursed himself
for his past. He released her and ran a finger down her
delicate jaw. He had only a few days left with this
beautiful, brave woman whose sunny nature and generous heart had turned his life upside down. His son
was enamored of her, too, and Zach suspected the boy
had substituted her for his mother. But she would
leave. He had tried to explain that to Drew just an hour
ago, but Drew had stubbornly set his jaw and refused
to discuss the matter. Now, ignoring the jab of pain he
felt, he smiled crookedly down at Katherine. "Bring it
up to him. I have to go over some paperwork before
dinner."

Katherine watched him walk into the house, her
gaze lingering on him until he was out of view. Her
mouth still tingled from his kiss. The taste of beer lingered seductively on her tongue . . . the taste of him.
And in the golden heat of the spring day she began to
shiver, feeling as though Zach had already walked out
of her life forever.

When Katherine brought the puppy up to Drew he
looked at it with interest, but held off from touching
it.

"Isn't he precious?" she said. She was down on her

knees in the center of the room, rolling a ball to the puppy, who only sniffed at it. She laughed, and Drew couldn't hide his grin either.

"Will this one die too?" he asked suddenly.

She glanced up at him. He was sitting on the settee, keeping a careful distance from the frisky animal. Dressed in dark trousers and a white shirt, he was a charming little dark-haired devil who would no doubt break as many hearts as his father had. "Every animal, every person dies sooner or later, sweetheart. Your other dog had an accident." The puppy licked her hand and she stroked his fur, but he scampered off again, wagging his tail. "But this one looks perfectly healthy and should have a long life."

Drew stared at the dog, his face expressionless. He turned his gaze to the window. "My mother died."

"I know," she whispered, and came to sit by him, taking his hand in hers. "You must miss her very much."

Drew stared at their entwined hands. "I wish she would come back." His mouth began to tremble, and he bit his lip. "She never will though." His little jaw worked back and forth as if he were trying to force back the emotion welling within him. His eyelashes, Katherine thought, were beautiful, as thick as an artist's brush, and she saw the dampness on them, like dew. He held back his tears, and his voice, with its charming British accent, sounded oddly mature when he spoke. "I have a tintype of her. Would you like to see it?"

He left the settee and walked over to his bed, pulling out a book from under his pillow. He opened the book and produced the photograph of his mother that had been stored between the pages. How often had he studied that picture before he went to sleep at night, or during the day? Katherine wondered. She felt like crying herself as he gazed lovingly at the picture, his fingertips stroking it. He brought it to her and she stared down at the pretty, soft-eyed woman who had borne him, who had loved Zach. She circled her arm around Drew and brought him close. "She was very beautiful."

He nodded. "I know. Great-grandfather said it was too unfortunate that she fell in love with a scoundrel like my—" He broke off and ducked his head. "Great-grandfather didn't like the captain."

Katherine hid her smile. So formal! Zach's own son called him the captain, as had Cody's young boy. She supposed Zach's authoritative air had something to do with it. "Why didn't your great-grandfather like Zach?"

Drew shrugged. "I don't know. They had arguments in the study last time the captain came around."

Katherine stroked his curls. "I suppose that's normal. Your great-grandfather probably thought Zach should have come to see you more often."

He nodded. "Yes, and I wish he had too. But now it doesn't matter."

"Why not?"

He shrugged, tracing his mother's face. "Because he'll just go away again."

Ah, Katherine thought, at last. She drew him closer and held him, cherishing the feel of his now sturdy body against her side. "I'm going away, too, you know."

He stiffened against her. "I know." He turned to look at her again. "You'll write to me, won't you?"

Ironic, she thought, that she would have to stay in touch with the boy when trying to forget his father. But she nodded. "Of course."

"My mother used to tell me stories about the captain. About his trips all around the world. I've read about those places," he added wistfully. "I think I would like to see some of them."

"Me too," she murmured, thinking of how deeply Laura must have loved Zach to hold no bitterness. She had glorified him to his son.

"But I would not like to be a sea captain," Drew added. "I would not want to leave *my* son behind." He suddenly broke free of her and strode to the window, staring out at the sea. "He might never come back, do you know that? One of those great big waves might swallow him and his ship right up, and then I would not have a mother *or* a father."

"Drew, you mustn't say such things."

He turned to look at her. He cocked one brow, and the expression was so like his father's, she almost laughed in spite of her pain. "Mustn't I?"

"No, darling, you're only hurting yourself."

He shrugged, pretending indifference. The puppy darted at him then, yipping and tugging on his trousers so insistently that Drew laughed and scooped him up. "I like him," he announced. "Thank you very much." He laughed as the puppy licked his face. "Does he need to go for a walk? He shouldn't be here in my room."

"Your father said I could bring him up."

At the mention of Zach Drew's happiness dimmed. "You can tell my father thank you for the moccasins. I have never owned anything so fine."

From a boy who owned many "fine" things this was a compliment of the highest form. Katherine rose, smiling at the little boy who had found a permanent place in her heart. "I think," she said, "I'll let you tell him yourself."

Katherine sat on the sun porch that night, sipping a cup of tea. The gas lanterns hanging from the porch cast a halo of yellow light around her. The rhythmic thump of the surf was soothing, and the air was thick and moist with an approaching storm. In a week she would be gone from here. She closed her eyes, trying to calm her nerves, her thudding heart. Certainly she would be returning home a different woman.

She was a woman who'd known a man. A man who was outrageously self-confident, incredibly arrogant, and utterly wonderful. But he was also incurably independent. He had no need for family, for love.

Suddenly she tensed, catching the faint scent of his spicy cologne. She looked over her shoulder to see him standing behind her, his weight slung on one hip, his hands in his trousers pockets. In the pale lamplight she could feel more than see his passionate gaze burn into her.

"Zach," she whispered. "What—what are you doing out here?"

"I came out to find you." His voice was deep with heat and sensuality. He stepped forward and took her teacup, setting it on a table. "I want to talk to you," he said. Before she could protest or question him, he'd taken her arm and urged her from the chair, then was leading her off the porch and deep into the formal garden.

She hadn't explored the garden yet, and lost track of her bearings as he strode along the paths, not stopping until he'd almost reached the woods on the far edge of his property. He stopped suddenly and whirled to face her.

"Drew will be lost without you," he said.

She looked away, unable to bear the pain in his voice, or her own pain. The wind was rising and clouds had blanketed the sky, smothering all light from the stars and moon.

Zach grabbed her arms, forcing her to face him. "He doesn't want a damn thing to do with me!"

The rough words tore at her. She reached up to cup

his face and saw him close his eyes as he turned her hand so he could press his warm mouth to her palm. She shuddered, fighting the enormity of her love for him.

"He's afraid you'll leave him, Zach."

"Sometimes I have to leave."

"Yes!" she cried, suddenly desperate to make him see how much his son needed him. A gust of wind whipped hair loose from her topknot, and she impatiently shoved the strands back. "And he harbors a deathly fear that you won't come back. He's refusing to let himself feel anything for you, Zach."

"Oh?" Zach's voice was hard and cynical. "And have you and my son discussed me at great length?"

He had every right to feel defensive, Katherine told herself, but she could not squelch the cold shiver that raced up her spine. "Zach, you've left him before! You saw him only three times in eight years, and—" He cursed harshly, and she forced herself to go on. "And it's only natural that he think you'll do it again."

The storm was upon them. The sky opened up and cold rain poured down. Zach grabbed her hand and pulled her along with him, toward the guest cottage on the far side of the garden. He kicked the door open and dragged her inside. Whirling, he slammed the door shut, then pinned her to it.

"Zach—" she began, but his mouth was on hers. She was tired of fighting him and wound her arms around his neck, taking all that she could of him. He groaned, drawing her tight against his body. He was iron hard—everywhere. She pressed into him, and he tore his lips from hers to trail burning kisses over her face.

"I can't change who I am, darlin'." He took her face between his palms, threading his fingers through her satin-soft hair. "Just like you can't change who you are." His mouth brushed hers. "And I wouldn't want you to." He kissed her feverishly again, then drew back. "I'm trying with Drew. And I can't do one damn bit better than that."

"I know." Her throat arched as he pressed his mouth to its hollow.

"You do know, don't you, Smoke Eyes?" His tongue swept over her lips, and she made a soft murmuring sound. "You understand everything, don't you?"

Not everything, she cried silently, but he was peeling off her sodden clothes, slipping her blouse off her shoulders and kissing her skin as he went downward. Then she was naked and he was kneeling before her. She moaned and fell against him, gripping his hard shoulders, her fingers digging in. He swirled his tongue in her navel, and she sucked in her breath sharply.

"You taste good," he said, and went lower parting her legs and finding the warm, throbbing need between them.

"Ohh . . . Zach . . ." Her fingers clutched his hair, pulling his head closer as his tongue slid in and out of her. Blood roared in a torrent through her head, sounding much like the torrent that beat around them. She shuddered as he drove into her, his tongue dancing like a stroking flame. She cried out with pure ecstasy as the almost unbearable waves of pleasure crashed over her, shattering her body into fragments of sensation, propelling her toward the sun. It burst and poured over her, bathing molten gold over her loins.

"Zach . . . Zach!"

She was trembling and shivering, so weak her legs gave out. He caught her, lifted her in his arms, and strode with her to one of the bedrooms. His clothing was wet, and it chilled her feverish skin. She shivered as he laid her on the bed and quickly stripped. A sudden flash of lightning lit the sky, lit him in splendid silver glory. He was beautiful, wild and hungry as a sleek stallion. His muscles were hard and powerful, and he was shaking with need. With a hoarse groan he came to her, and his mouth opened hungrily on her breast. He took one rigid nipple into his mouth, and she arched up to him. His hand played with her other breast, and desire leapt at her.

"I can't wait, darlin'," he muttered. "It's been too long. I need you . . . need you now."

She pressed her body to his, wordlessly offering it. She needed him, too, a need as elemental as the storm outside. He kissed her hard as he slid his fingers along her damp heat, seeking, finding her soft satiny folds, lush and wet and ready for him. His long fingers stretched her pliant flesh, and she shook wildly, drowning in pleasure. As his fingers stroked her his tongue plunged deep into her mouth. She felt violent shudders rack his powerful body, then he was spreading her thighs and coming into her, thrusting hard and deep. Her hips rose to meet him, and he pulled her even closer, a rough groan rumbling up from his throat as her sleek flesh tightly sheathed him. They were fused so tight it seemed they had melted into one.

Then Zach began to move. Katherine's eyes slid shut as his tormentingly erotic rhythm drove her mad with longing. The exquisite pressure built. She shoved her hand against her mouth to stifle her wild cries, but Zach pushed it away and replaced it with his own mouth. She made soft whimpering sounds into his open mouth as she began to peak, great ripples of pleasure tearing through her, starting at her throbbing center and radiating out. The spasms gripped her, saturating her in seething, pulsing waves of passion that carried her up, up to him, and still he drove into her, wanting her as hungry and obsessed as he was. Zach surged into her with one magnificent thrust, and his body gave a convulsive jump as he climaxed, hot and powerful and deep inside her. In that final, scalding shudder of release he felt he had poured his soul into her, felt that he had died a little, and knew that all he had ever wanted was Smoke Eyes.

Seventeen

Zach woke, roused by the sunlight streaming in through the small window over the bed. He smiled with pure satisfaction as he remembered the previous night. They had made love, napped, woke to make love again. He felt utterly sated, yet somehow still hungry, and he wondered if that hunger ran so deep it might never be sated.

His hand stroked up and down Katherine's back as he watched her sleep. Her skin felt like satin, and her hair was vibrant with all kinds of colors weaving through it—deep reds and golds and soft tangerine. How could he ever leave her again? He caressed her bare shoulder, marveling at the velvety softness of her skin. She was a woman of strength and humor and passion, and he loved her.

His throat tightened as the emotion surged through him, shaking him with its force. Had he always loved her? All those years at sea when he'd strolled foreign lands, lost himself in the arms of countless women, he had been like an animal on the prowl, fighting a gnawing restlessness, a sometimes overwhelming loneliness that could not be quenched. Until he'd found her again.

His hand shook. Zach had never been afraid of anything in his life, but now he was terrified. The need for her pervaded his senses. He felt it in his gut, his blood, the pit of his belly, and worse, his heart. He had never loved a woman before, but love for Smoke Eyes was inescapable.

He didn't know how to say the words, didn't know how to tell her. His entire body tensed as he realized she might not want to hear that he loved her. After all, what would it solve? They both had to get on with their separate lives.

She stirred, opening her eyes, captivating him with their pure gray depths. She blinked, a little disoriented, and he saw a misty light come into her gaze as she remembered. Pink color flushed her cheeks, and she turned her face into his neck. He caught her chin, urging her to face him, and kissed her lips.

There was no need for words. He kissed her deeply, thoroughly, and she pressed herself against him. His hands slipped over her bare, silky skin, and with one palm cupping her bottom he urged her against his full, hard arousal. The need to be inside her was suddenly too great. He rolled onto his back, taking her with him, and slid her over his rigid manhood. They both cried out as her sweet flesh clasped tightly around him. She gripped his awesome shoulders, and with his hands cradling her hips, he raised her, showing her the rhythm.

She moved as he'd taught her, taking him completely into her, so deep that he could feel her tiny shuddering pulsations. Joy filled him as he watched her, bathed in gold. Her cheeks were flushed, her lips parted, and he reached up to fondle her breasts, cupping them, rubbing their tips into tight, hard peaks. She moaned as her pleasure increased, and his eyes closed as he let her take him.

She moved like a dream upon him, lifting them both to the crest of pleasure, then holding them there, slowing the pounding, driving want and making him groan aloud. She rotated her hips, and he clenched his teeth, striving for restraint. But he could feel her heat tugging at him, pulling him close to the edge. His hunger for her was a fire, burning out of control. He felt her slender body tense, then tremble as her climax hit her with stunning force. Her muscles pulsated around him, and the wild intensity of it fogged his mind.

He swiftly rolled her to her back, needing to drive deep, deep, into her. He filled her to completeness and she screamed, as he locked her to him with steel-muscled thighs and arms and gave one final thrust, his body shuddering with the powerful explosion.

They lay limp, entangled, so weak and shaking they could not move. Tears streaked Katherine's face, and Zach's thumb idly stroked her damp cheek. Her head lay on his broad chest, and his fingers threaded through her silky hair. How, she wondered, would she ever find the courage to leave him? She belonged to him just as completely as he belonged to her. The rapture of their lovemaking was so intense, so awesome, she could not believe it was this way with every couple. To end it would be agonizing, devastating.

As if he were reading her mind he asked her, "Do you *want* to go back home, Smoke Eyes?"

She lifted her head, and her heart lodged in her throat as she met his eyes.

She swallowed hard, pushing down the lump of emotion that swelled inside her at his solemn question.

"What?" she teased lightly, though her heart ached. "Don't you think I miss Newberry—Birdie and Clarabelle and Sticks? I have patients counting on me to return soon, and don't forget I have my obligation to the folks at the reservation." His face hardened at that and she wondered why. "But I'll miss you," she added, closing her eyes against the tears that welled in them.

He grunted. "What do you feel for White Owl?"

Surprised, she sat up. "White Owl is a friend and my assistant."

"He's in love with you."

She smiled, understanding his gruffness. He looked like a ruffian, lounging back on the pillows, his dark skin and rough beard stubble adding to his rugged appearance. "Well, he's just going to have to fall in love with someone else. I like White Owl, but I'm certainly not in love with him."

"Are you in love with anyone?"

She jerked her gaze from his. "I don't have time to fall in love, Zach. Surely you of all people know and understand that."

"All too well," he said. She glanced at him again, surprised by his rough tone, but he was grinning roguishly at her. "Up, woman!"

"What—"

"You heard me!" He rolled off the bed and playfully swatted her bottom, making her squeal in protest. If he couldn't keep her with him, he told himself, then he'd make the most of the time he had with her. Knowing she didn't love him, *wouldn't* love him, shook him to the core, but still he wanted to take that wild, reckless ride of loving her. For as long as he could.

Katherine didn't let herself think of time in the golden days that followed. There was little of it left—even though she had agreed against her better judgment to stay an extra week—and she lived completely in the present, reveling in Zach's company as he spent more time with her and his son. As Drew began to trust his father, he included him in conversations, asking him questions about his travels and the shipyard, about anything and everything Zach had the patience to answer. And Zach's patience with the boy was infinite. Drew was a mature, precocious child with a keen intellect. On tour at the shipyard he asked questions of such a technical nature that one of Zach's men joked that Drew should be running the yard. Zach swung the little boy up into his arms and rubbed the sawdust out of his curls. "Maybe someday he will, Jack. Maybe someday he will."

Drew, however, seemed more fascinated by doctoring. He followed Katherine into the hills to collect herbs and flowers, and he wanted to know the medicinal use of each one. She showed him how to prepare them, and soon he had started his own herb garden. Once, on a picnic with the twins, she applied a mud poultice to Robert's wasp sting, and Drew gushed at his father, "Isn't she magic? Isn't she?"

Zach's gaze drifted lazily to her, and she felt the sizzling current of desire that ran between them. "She sure is, son," he drawled, and she lost her breath.

As Zach gained more of Drew's trust, Drew began to confide in him in a way that touched Katherine. "I'm calling my dog Max," he said one day as they all took a walk on the beach, "because my best friend in London was Max."

"You never told me that," Zach said.

Katherine smiled as she watched them, both for the way they were sharing and for how alike they were. They had the same long stride, the same habit of thrusting their hands into their pockets. Drew was looking healthier every day, his deep blue eyes contrasting beautifully against his tanned skin.

"Can he come visit?" Drew asked.

Zach smiled. "Sure. We have plenty of room. As long as his parents agree."

Drew lowered his gaze and kicked a rock out of his way. "Well, they don't have very much money, and . . ."

"We'll pay for his passage."

Drew brightened. "And Great-grandfather?"

"Great-grandfather?" Zach scowled, remembering that crotchety old man. "You want to have your great-grandfather come visit?"

Drew hesitated. "Or we can go there," he said hopefully.

Zach was silent.

"I left him all alone," Drew added. "He only had me and Mama and Dorrie. Great-grandmother died when I was three. You know that, sir."

"Yes." Zach let out a tense breath between his teeth. Seeing Drew's crestfallen face, he reached out to ruffle his hair. "Whatever you wish, son." He was sure the house was big enough that he could stay clear of the old curmudgeon. And it had been worth agreeing to, he felt, as he watched a slow smile dawn on his son's face.

"I'll go write a letter to him now!" Drew shouted, and raced Max back to the house.

"Drew—" But he was gone, and Zach looked helplessly at Katherine. Her eyes sparkled with amusement.

"I guess you better get his room ready," she said.

Zach's eyes took on a roguish gleam as his gaze drifted around the empty, secluded beach. It was a brilliantly hot May day, perfect for lovemaking. "And I guess," he drawled, "I better get your room ready too."

"Oh?" she asked, also looking around the beach. "Do we need a room?"

He laughed, the sound rich and full on the wind. "Whatever suits you, darlin'. Whatever suits you . . ." And he lowered her to the sand and stripped off their clothes, making a bed of them, then proceeded, with his mouth and his hands and at last his perfect body, to suit her very well.

"I don't want you to leave me again," Drew said to Zach.

They were in Drew's bedroom, and it was night. Drew had posted the letter to his great-grandfather that day and Katherine had just tucked him in. Zach sat on the side of his bed and looked at him, considering his statement.

"Well, now, son, and I don't want to leave you. But since I'm a sea captain, how do you propose we work this out?"

Drew lowered his eyes. He stared at his father's dark hand near his—so much larger and stronger. It seemed impossible that his tall father had ever been a boy. But he had been and he must know what boys feel. "Did your father go away too?"

Zach felt such a sharp pang in his chest, he lost his breath. His eyes narrowed, but Drew stared up at him with an open, dauntless expression. Then he lifted an eyebrow, and Zach almost smiled. Though he'd led a sheltered life, Drew had the same sound instincts that had kept Zach alive on the streets. "Yes," he finally answered.

Drew nodded sagely. "Was he a sea captain too?"

"No." He was a drifter, a drunkard. Zach didn't even realize that the boy had taken his hand, was holding it and trying to press some of his own strength into it. Didn't realize that Drew had understood the expression on his face, and knew that he had felt the same loss over *his* father that Drew had suffered.

"But you wanted to be with him just the same," Drew said.

Zach looked sharply at him, but still the boy met his gaze.

"I missed you dreadfully all those years, sir. If"—his mouth trembled, but he quickly firmed it—"if you'd rather not be with me, if you are going to leave for two or three more years, I'd rather be with my great-grandfather, sir. I'd like to go home."

Zach felt as though he'd been sucker-punched. Though Drew stared steadily at him, he saw the glint of tears in his son's eyes, the vulnerability. His own eyes began to sting, and he reached out to cup Drew's hand, to draw him against his solid chest and hold him there, against his heart.

"Drew," he said hoarsely, threading his fingers through his son's glossy curls, "there's no way in hell that stubborn old man is going to raise you." He looked out at the black night, hearing the sea that called him, called him . . . But his mind was made up. He hugged his son tight, knowing he could never leave this boy again. "You'll just have to come with me is all. We'll hire a tutor and you'll study on board, and we'll make a sailor out of you yet."

Drew clung to his father, feeling as though he had been lost a long time and had finally found home.

Like silver and gold threads woven into a tapestry, her days and nights with Zach were a thing of beauty to Katherine, treasures she would cherish the rest of her life. She dared not dream of paradise. Already she had conveniently forgotten why she had originally come there. The days had grown balmy and sun-splashed, and she luxuriated in every moment she spent with Zach.

He took her to the opera, the theater, and to several dinner parties, as if trying to cram every moment of living into the short time they had left together. He bought her luxurious silk gowns, showered her with glittering jewels, and though she considered them a loan he insisted she keep them.

She learned how women adored him, men respected him. Gossip abounded about the beautiful woman staying with the most eligible and elusive bachelor in town, but she didn't care. She was able to distance herself from the whispered speculations, for she knew she would be leaving soon, and she had never cared about what people wished to believe.

For his part Zach saw how people were enchanted by the unorthodox doctor from the West. She so effortlessly charmed people and made them feel charming too. Even in the glittering crowd of Boston society she stood out—a queen surrounded by a flock of ardent admirers. Insanely he wanted to shield her from every male that came within a hundred yards of her, but that was impossible, for those who did were enamored of her. She was a woman of mystery, but even more alluring was the glowing quality she emanated of a cherished woman, the telltale flush of color in her cheeks and the sparkle in her gorgeous eyes that no man could resist. Least of all Zach. He had never been so happy, so satisfied in his life, and the gossips put their heads together and whispered about that too.

"God's teeth!" Trish exclaimed the night Zach took Katherine to a ball. "The way he looks at you!"

Across the crowded ballroom Katherine cast a curi-

ous glance at her lover. He was standing with several
people who were speaking animatedly, and though he
had inclined his dark head toward them as if listening
to them, his eyes were searching the crowd for her.
When he found her those night-fire eyes burned a path
to her, scorching her with their power. She felt a shock
rip all the way down her spine, but managed a light
laugh for Trish.

"Zach *always* looks like that!"

"At you, yes," Trish said. "*Never* has he looked at
any other woman with such focused intensity. Like he
owns you . . . possesses you!" She shivered delicately,
and Katherine laughed again at her friend's dramatics.
"You laugh! I vow, I think the man is in love with you."

Katherine looked at Trish with wide, incredulous
eyes. "*Zach?* In love? Never, Trish, never! You know
Zach is renowned for his sexual conquests." How could
she sound so breezy, she wondered, when her insides
were knotted so tightly? Women flocked around Zach
even when she was on his arm, and Katherine knew it
was like that with him in other countries, other cities.
To think of him holding and kissing those women as he
had her scalded her with jealousy and hurt. But that's
what it would be like. Zach was a man with lusty appetites and to women he was irresistible.

"Yes," Trish said, "but he regarded *those* women
with amusement, perhaps some affection. But never
has he looked at them the way he looks at you."

Katherine shook her head. "Trish, you know I'll be
leaving soon. I can't stay and Zach will have to leave,
too, eventually. There can't possibly be a future for us."

Trish's gaze clouded. "I was so hoping you'd stay.
Drew adores you and he's already lost so many in his
young life."

"Drew understands that I have to go. For heaven's

sake, Trish, you know my staying is a preposterous idea."

Trish still looked disheartened. "You've become such a fun friend. There's no one else in town like you! I'm forced to suffer the company of *these* stuffy folks and with you, well, we can be so refreshingly honest with each other." Her gaze was drawn by a movement across the room, and she perked up. "Oh, here comes Zach."

Katherine's heart tripped in her throat as she watched Zach disengage himself from the group he'd been talking with. He wore a raven-black suit and a snowy white shirt that contrasted sharply with his deep tan. His brocade waistcoat was also black, and a striped silk cravat was knotted impeccably at his throat. By the time he reached her Katherine was weak in the knees. Of course, Trish's whispered comments did nothing to soothe her jumping nerves. How could she respond to, "Oh, he is one well-packed man! Watch the way he walks!" when the object of her comment was only a few feet from them? She sent Trish a half-laughing, half-exasperated look and turned to Zach.

"Katherine was just talking about you," Trish said blithely, ignoring Katherine's killing glance.

Dark amusement flickered in Zach's eyes. "A coincidence," he said, taking Katherine's arm and urging her close to him. He grinned crookedly down at her. "I was just talking about Kat."

Although Smoke Eyes was Zach's special name for her—a form of endearment—he had taken to calling her Kat in the presence of others, much to the delight of "society," and Katherine liked it every bit as much. Even Drew called her Kat on occasion, having dropped the formal "Dr. Smoke Eyes."

"You oughtn't leave her alone," Trish warned Zach. "The men are mad for her."

"I noticed," Zach said. He looked down at Katherine with such intensity, even Trish blushed. "Let's go," he murmured in Katherine's ear.

"But, Zach," she protested, "the party's not over yet."

A roguish gleam lit his eyes. "Lady, it's hardly just begun." His hard, warm body brushed intimately against hers. "And I want you."

They left as quickly as they could, and at home went directly to his spacious bedroom suite.

"Do you know," he asked, as he removed her emerald necklace and earrings, "that you were the most beautiful woman there tonight?"

"Oh, Zach," she said, "there were so many beautiful—"

"Yes," he said, cutting her off as he turned her around, his hands on her shoulders, bared by her low-cut gown. "And you were the loveliest of all." He stopped unfastening her ivory-silk gown to kiss her, putting his warm mouth to her neck and feeling the throb of her pulse. She shivered and he smiled. His fingers skimmed the silky curve of skin where her neck met her shoulder, and in the mirror above his bureau he watched her eyes flutter and close. She reached behind to cover his big hand with her slender one.

"Zach . . ." she whispered.

He held her necklace in one hand, the emeralds draped like a green waterfall between his long fingers. He held them up to her skin, and she jumped, the jewels cool against her heated flesh. "These," he said, "threw strange green-colored lights into your eyes all evening." He turned her around to face him. "You are mesmerizing."

As he kissed her, he pressed the emeralds into her skin, and they made tiny bites of pain-pleasure upon her back. Keenly aroused, Katherine lifted her arms and wound them around his neck, pressing her body ardently into his. He continued unfastening her gown, his hands sliding up and down her back, peeling the silk from her even silkier shoulders. The gown shimmied down into an ivory puddle at her feet. Zach groaned, his open mouth covering hers hungrily, feverishly, the thrusts of his tongue making her crave the thrust of his hard flesh inside her.

She stepped out of the gown but Zach continued to hold her, his hands cupping her face as if it were something holy, a chalice. His mouth moved up and down her throat, upon her cheeks, her parted lips, and he whispered hot, explicit words against her velvety skin. She tipped her head back, allowing him his fill, her heart beating in rhythm to his.

He lifted his head. "Undress me," he said, his breathing strident, ragged.

He was so tall. She had to reach way up to unknot his silk cravat. Her hands shook uncontrollably. There was nothing, she decided, more devastating to a woman than to feast her eyes on a man with a tie hanging loose around his neck. It spoke of such *intention.*

He had already shrugged out of his evening jacket, and she unbuttoned his waistcoat, her fingers tripping over the task. She could not unlatch her gaze from him, even as she pushed the waistcoat from his shoulders and it, too, fell to the floor.

His shirt now. He stood waiting, looking down at her. Her heart pounded, and beneath her fingers she could feel Zach's heart pounding too. Love burned in her, and to hide it she quickly undid the ruby shirt studs that lined his front and spread his shirt open. Her eyes slid closed when she pressed a kiss to his warm, firm flesh. She let the tip of her tongue brush his nipple, and felt the primal growl rumble up from his chest. He closed a hand around the nape of her neck, tilting her head back, forcing her to cease her tormenting caresses. She shivered as she caught the primitive gleam in his eyes. Then his mouth took hers with a quick and desperate savagery.

"My trousers," he whispered against her lips, taking her hand and pressing it against the hard masculine ridge that strained the front of his trousers. "Undo them."

She shook her head. "I can't," she whispered. "It's—" She gasped at the light sweep of his tongue upon her lower lip. "It's too much. I—I want you inside me."

Swiftly he bent and lifted her in his powerful arms, dropping the emeralds upon the bureau, then striding with her to his massive bed. He laid her down with exquisite gentleness, then shed his trousers, kicking them away. Coming to her, he gently lowered himself over her, covering her bare body with his own.

She arched up to him, the sheer pleasure of feeling his burning skin against hers almost unbearable. *I love you, love you, love you,* she cried inside herself, almost bursting with the need to tell him. The moonlight bathed him in white-gold, and he was a god, yes, the epitome of male beauty. And he was hers for tonight, and then no more. The thought sent such an acute stab of pain through her, she had to turn her face from his.

"Sweetheart, what is it?" He put his fingers under her chin and tipped her face up to his.

"I—" The words tried to force themselves out. *Don't be a fool!* she told herself. *This is Zach.* He'd left Laura behind as soon as she declared her love for him. This was no different. She refused to ruin these last hours with him, refused to succumb to her private pain. She could hear the surf thump on the shore, could feel the sea breeze sweeping into the room through the open french doors. She loved him, yes. She put her fingers to his jaw, stroking it as she struggled to speak. "You—"

"What, darlin'?"

She studied his face as if it were the last time she would ever see him. "You make me feel so alive, Zach. Like—like a fire is always burning inside me, like it will roar out of control when you touch me. And it does." She lowered her lashes, but he lifted her chin again and stared into her eyes.

"You make me feel the same," he said gruffly.

"I do?" She was stunned.

"You do." He bent his head and pulled a taut nipple into his mouth, sucking strongly. She gasped and arched, her fingers twining in his thick hair.

"Is it—is it this wonderful for everyone?"

He laughed, looking at her. He ran a hand down the length of her body, watching the way the moonlight pooled in all her curves and hollows, silvering the dark curls between her legs. Her beautiful body was like a vision, a dream beside him. "I don't know about others, and I don't want to know. All I *do* know, sugar, is that it has never been like this for me before."

"Me either," she whispered, and they both laughed, but a rush of emotion flooded Katherine's chest. "And I'm so afraid this feeling will never go away, even after I leave—"

His mouth came down hard on hers, crushing her words, her protests. Desire and hunger pounded through him, and love. Love was a great crushing pain in Zach's chest. He kissed her everywhere, the soft sounds of arousal she made driving him mad.

"Do you remember," he whispered, sliding back up her body, "the time we were in the shack?" He lightly flicked her pointed nipple with his tongue, and she writhed under him, impatient for him to be inside her. He parted her soft flesh and slid two fingers deep inside her, making her cry out. "When we made the pact, forever friends? We nicked ourselves with your knife and rubbed our blood together, blood brother, blood sister . . ." He positioned himself between her legs, and her body arched to him.

"I remember," she whispered, shaken to the core that he remembered too.

His face looked etched from stone in the moonlight, taut with passion. "Touch me before I come into you."

His words seared her skin. She obliged him— anything to hurry his entry—reaching down between them to grasp his hot, solid length. She'd barely started to caress him when he pushed her hand away. All his muscles were shaking as he began to enter her.

"Don't forget me, darlin'," he whispered.

She reached for him, her fingers trembling upon his face, and somehow she managed a shaky smile. "Don't be a fool. As if I ever could."

He groaned and surged against her, and she felt him deep inside her, touching her. She gave a high, thin cry and he took it away with his tongue, took her soul away with the hard, slamming thrusts of his loins. They strained together on the bed, the wind sifting over them, the sound of the surf rushing in their ears. Katherine crested abruptly, her inner quiverings clamping around him, and Zach succumbed to the black, hot pleasure. He could feel her shudder as he drove into her. He lost his breath, his sight, all but dizzying sensation as he spiraled down, down, crying out hoarsely, as if he were hurtling into a depthless chasm . . . as if he had just given her his soul.

In the night's deepest hour they lay spent, entwined on the tangled sheets, the salt breeze cooling their flesh. Katherine curled into Zach, her fingers stroking the back of his neck.

"When is your next voyage?" she asked. Her voice was husky, etched with pain she tried to disguise.

She felt him tense. "I don't know."

"But you do know where." His silence confirmed the fact. "So where?"

"Europe," he said shortly, then gritted his teeth as she swirled her hand through his chest hair.

Katherine tried for lightness, but her voice came out thin and reedy instead. "And you'll forget all about me."

He shut his eyes. "I never forgot about you, Smoke Eyes." *And I never will,* he added silently. His hand trailed through her hair, caressed her silky shoulder, but her body had stiffened. She knew, too, that it was almost over. Unbearable pain washed through him, and his fingers tightened on her flesh. She winced and he loosened his grip. "Drew," he said hoarsely, "will miss you."

"I know," she whispered. "And I will miss him."

"So stay."

Her breath caught in her throat. He wasn't asking for permanency, she told herself. Zach was not the marrying kind. And even if he were, she knew she could not bear the pain of him leaving for two or three years at a time. And what about her profession? Had he conveniently forgotten she had one? The last angered her and she frowned, rising up on her elbow to lean over him.

"How can I stay?" she asked. "How can I just drop my life and become your mistress? And when you sail off, do I just twiddle my thumbs and wait for you to come home?" She was working herself into a fine fury, but it felt infinitely better than desperate longing or sorrow. She sat up, glaring down at him.

"I guess that profession is mighty important to you, isn't it, Smoke Eyes?"

She couldn't believe her ears. If anyone knew how important it was, Zach did. She struck her jaw out at him. "It's my life."

They measured each other in the gloom. The moon had lowered, and there was little light to make out features. But she heard him swear softly, then in one quick, smooth motion, he rolled her over onto her back. "Zach!"

"Dammit," he swore again, stroking the hair off her temples. He kissed her mouth, hard, then he was entering her before she could speak, lifting her toward him, surging deep, filling her to completeness. He shuddered as she arched up to meet his thrusts, and he brought her to her peak quickly, watching her shatter in his arms. But his desire was unquenchable, because it was more, much more than physical need. Words of love dammed in his throat. He knew he should stop, but the wild sweetness of her body beneath him, clasping him tightly, drove him to the edge. And somehow it was infinitely easier to communicate with his body the words he could not speak.

She and Drew were pounding tinctures out on the side porch where the wind was blocked when he looked up from his task. "Will you come out to my father's island?"

"Drew," she said, touching his curls, "you know I have to be leaving soon."

He laid out some paper squares as she had taught him and sifted powder into each one. "Yes, but you could come out for a visit." He deftly folded the papers, sealing the powders inside. "You would like it, Kat. There's a beautiful blue lagoon, and lots of palm trees . . . and fish! So many fish you could eat them every day, every meal." He laughed. "If you can hook 'em, that is." He glanced up at her, then away again. "And there're plenty of natives who could use some doctoring."

She gazed at him, her heart breaking. She wished she could watch him grow into a man, watch all the stages in between. Written correspondence with him would only tear her in two. She loved this child, Zach's son, and wanted to share with him his joys and sorrows as he developed. He was such a special child, so bright and so brave, and how unfair it was that this joy was to be taken from her.

She smiled at him, determined to lighten her dampened spirits. "Maybe I will visit," she said casually, noncommittally. "And maybe I'll bring my talking parrot to keep Max company. A tropical island seems just the type of place where she would feel at home."

Drew was so astonished by this news, he dropped the china mortar. "You have a talking bird?"

"Oh, yes. And she tells secrets—sometimes very embarrassing ones."

Drew laughed at that, and he was begging her to tell some tales when Dorrie interrupted them. She had a man in tow, a Mr. Donnelly who looked sheepishly at Katherine, then at the boy.

"Says he's got a splinter in his big toe," Dorrie muttered. "Wanted to know if you'd take a look at it."

Katherine glanced at the man, recognizing him as one of the men who'd stuck to her like glue the night before at the ball. She smiled at him and extended her hand. "Why, yes, Mr. Donnelly."

He came forward, stammering and blushing, his hat in his hand. "If you're busy—"

"I'm not," she said cheerfully, and gestured to a chair. "Sit, and Drew and I will take a look at that toe."

Drew was so excited about examining a "real" patient, he was hopping up and down on one foot as Donnelly removed his shoe and stocking. The little boy peered close, one eye closed, and shared his opinion with Katherine.

"Well," he said, "I don't think we need to amputate yet . . ." He was oblivious to the shock on his patient's face. The man sank slowly in his chair, all the color draining from his naturally florid face. "But let's try soaking it first and see if we can nudge it out."

Katherine almost laughed out loud at the intense relief that flooded Donnelly's face, and she clasped her hands behind her back, smiling at Drew. "Good idea," she said. "Get the basin filled up and we'll get to work."

But it was a very stubborn splinter. Some time later, well into Donnelly's string of boring stories, the splinter came loose and Drew whooped, happy not only to succeed with the "surgery," but to put a stop to the impossibly loquacious Donnelly.

"Thank you so much," Donnelly gushed at Katherine, completely ignoring Drew. "I don't know *how* to repay you!"

"Try currency," came an icy suggestion from behind them. Katherine jumped up, whirling to face Zach who stood lounging in the doorway, arms crossed over his chest. He inclined his head at her, sardonic amusement flickering in his eyes.

"Zach!" she exclaimed. "You're home early."

He cocked an eyebrow. "Am I?"

Donnelly was stammering and stumbling and fumbling with his sock. Finally, totally undone by the hard, cold eyes that watched him from the doorway, he hopped from the porch with his sock half on, his hat and shoe jammed under his arm.

"He didn't pay you," Drew said, and Katherine and Zach shared a smile. Then Katherine frowned, noting an odd discomfort about Zach. Something was wrong.

"I thought we'd all take a ride into town," he said,

"go have dinner at the Grand Bay Hotel." And then he would tell her, Zach thought. Tell her about the telegram he had just received from Drew's great-grandfather informing him of a court date set in London. There seemed to be some question about custody, about Drew's parentage. He was illegitimate, after all, and had lived for eight years with Laura and her grandfather. And now Thaddeus Wells wanted him back.

Damn interfering old man! Zach had been livid when he'd read the telegram. He knew, since Drew's letter had been posted only a week ago, that the correspondence had crossed. Wells had no idea what had evolved in the past few months, that Drew belonged with his father.

He would straighten this thing out, but he would have to leave for England immediately. And he would have to tell Smoke Eyes. But later, alone.

After their oyster, caviar, and lobster dinner, though, they returned home to a small crowd of patients for Katherine—all men. The butler looked completely chagrined, and when Zach coldly questioned them all for not seeking their customary doctors, all answered they wanted to "try out" the new one. As if, Zach thought with disgust, she were a delectable dessert. They waited politely for Katherine on the front porch, and even after Drew had been tucked in bed she did not turn one of them away. At last, Zach's imposing presence scared the last of them off, and by then he was so annoyed he dragged her up to his bedroom, stripped her and himself, then laid her down on the bed.

He couldn't tell her, not then. If he said the words they would become real, and as the wild flame of their passion engulfed them, he wanted only *this* reality. He pulled her over him, lifting her upon his rigid tumescence, till they were welded as one, and she rode him, rode the stallion, wild and free, her hair streaming out behind her, pitched into a mind-sweeping tide that carried each into the pure, pulsating center of the other, blinded by love.

"Hurry up, missy!" Dorrie was urging one of the maids, her own arms piled high with folded laundry ready to be packed. Both were oblivious to Katherine who had just rounded the corner of the upstairs hallway. She watched with amusement as Dorrie snapped orders like a military officer.

"I'm hurrying, ma'am," Martha protested. "I can't see how the captain expects us to pack for an extended trip to Europe in just a day though!"

"Never you mind," Dorrie scolded, nudging her down the hall ahead of her. " 'Tisn't your duty to expect anything. You do what the captain orders, and do it well! Now, hurry. And don't forget to pack Master Drew's soldiers. He'll be lost without them."

Katherine stood frozen, watching them disappear into separate rooms. A sharp, hot pain sliced through her. *He was not going to tell me!* It had been his intention all along to leave for Europe and not say goodbye. The hurt spread through her, like a wound that would not stop aching.

She hurried to her room, not wanting anyone to find her. He was taking Drew too! Hadn't he wanted her to say good-bye to the boy? Oh, yes, she knew how Zach felt about a permanent woman in his life, and she was going to be leaving the day after tomorrow anyhow, but it appeared *he* had intended to leave first!

"Damn him!" she whispered, tears burning her eyes. She hugged her arms to her chest, feeling suddenly cold. Her gaze fell on the glittering sea beyond her window, and she suddenly knew *she* had to leave first.

She took her trunk down and began stuffing her clothes into it. It was best this way, she thought. They were both parting anyway. *That* had been inevitable from the start. But Drew. She pressed her fists to her eyes to stanch the flow of tears.

She stopped in the midst of packing to write him a long, tearful note, telling him she loved him. She wanted to invite him to Newberry but knew that she couldn't without Zach's interference. *If you ever need anything, Drew,* she finished, *please contact me. Here is my address, and I will write and send you notes.*

She wrote no good-bye note for Zach. He did not want one. She knew he'd understand. After all, he'd never bothered with a good-bye himself, and maybe, maybe, she could treat this as lightly as he seemed to be able to.

Her chin went up. She'd take the noon train out, be hours away before he even came home from the shipyard. She would make up her mind to chalk this all up as one very pleasant, though deeply disruptive, experience. Now it was time to go home, to forget the man who had changed her life.

Hours later, ensconced in the third-class coach of the train speeding west, Katherine was crying as though her heart would break.

Eighteen

*H*ow could she have gone? The question stabbed into Zach repeatedly in the following weeks. The voyage to England was miserable. Drew caught a cold he could not shake, which did not look good to the magistrate in court. As it was, the man looked more favorably upon Drew's great-grandfather's argument that a sea captain was not a fitting father, than Zach's argument that he had provided well for Drew since leaving England.

"Furthermore," the magistrate droned, looking down his nose at the Yankee captain, "I agree with Mr. Wells that you all but *wrenched* the boy from his London home, and without a thought to his welfare sailed to America with him." He said the word "America" as if it tasted bad.

Zach had never felt such cold, gut-twisting rage. He explained about Drew's operation, even had Drew show him the scar, and Dorrie testified that Zach had proved a fitting father indeed. She had torn loyalties, though, having worked for Wells for eight years, and it was finally Drew's testimony that he loved both men that determined the magistrate's ruling. He ordered Zach and Drew to live with Thaddeus Wells for the summer to see if they could work out a reasonable agreement.

Reasonable! Zach thought. The old man would be lucky to escape murder by September if he didn't keep out of Zach's way! Zach had never known a person more infuriating, more grating, more *un*reasonable in his life! Wells looked for every opportunity to undermine Zach's position as Drew's father, and he grumbled constantly about Zach's general habits, right down to the way he buttered his bread.

"The proper way to butter bread," Wells intoned one morning at breakfast, "is like so." As he proceeded to smooth butter across his bread, Zach slammed out of the room and Drew stared woefully after him. But Drew hadn't been much interested in food or anything in the past weeks. He wondered, miserably, why Katherine hadn't said good-bye. He had reread her note so many times it was too wrinkled and worn to make out all the words anymore. Still, he slept with it, along with his mother's photograph, under his pillow every night.

"She said she would visit our island," Drew told Zach with a hopeful note in his voice, deliberately leaving out Katherine's "maybe." Perhaps if he didn't think *maybe,* she really would come.

• • •

As he stared into the cold gray water of the Thames one day, listening to it splash on the shore, Zach found the sound haunting. He knew he would forever remember the times he and Smoke Eyes had made love on *his* shore, and he'd watch the sun bathe her bare skin, caress her body's golden hollows. He hardly slept—even less than when he'd been racked over Drew—and, keeping his identity a secret, he often went down to the docks before dawn to work—backbreaking, exhausting work—so he could drive the memory of her from his mind. Even physically exhausted, he still lay awake nights remembering her scent, the feel of her thick, silky hair, her sweet, responsive body, the satiny texture of her skin. He wanted her and damned her at once. She was in his heart, his blood, his soul. The need for her ate at him, like a poison that permeated his senses and settled in his gut. He saw her everywhere, in every woman. It was like a sickness he could not shake.

But he'd better shake it if he wanted his life back. It was ridiculous that a woman could do this to him! He had been a fool to love her. And he was glad he'd never told her. Who was he to expect good-byes anyway? He had never been any good at it.

But he'd thought she might have spoken with Drew before she'd left. The kid was hurting, and she ought to know that. Yet even when he wanted to hate her he couldn't. She had been honest with him from the beginning. Her profession and her freedom had been priorities for her, which, he thought grimly, is understandable. He would just have to forget her.

But how could he when Drew spoke constantly of her? "Kat would like this!" he would say. And, "Kat told me she would like to see the world." And, finally, "Did you love her? Why did you let her leave?"

Zach had no answers.

As tough as the days were for Zach, the nights were far worse. To escape the memory of her in his bed, he visited private gentlemen's clubs, drank and transacted business and played cards, losing and acquiring small fortunes, and none of it meant anything. When he went to the theater or to parties, he was surrounded by beautiful, elegant women, and none of them even tempted him. He missed Smoke Eyes, wanted only Smoke Eyes. He missed her beautiful face, her passion, her insatiable spirit, her haunting eyes.

By August he was sure he was going mad. And the old man! Damn, the magistrate could not have conjured up a more horrifying torture than for all of them to live together. It felt like an incarceration, and there was no way out if he wanted to keep Drew. His temper was shot to hell and it got to the point where the staff ran for cover when he came in at night. And the old man grumbled, " 'Tisn't *anything* pleases that ogre!"

Only Drew offered Zach comfort. Only Drew seemed to understand that his father wanted nothing and no one more than Smoke Eyes.

The roses were blooming when Katherine came home. They burst in cascades of pink over her white picket fence, perfuming the yard with their sweet scent. The sight of them filled her with an overwhelming depression. She stopped in the path as Shadow unloaded her bags and trunk from the carriage, and closed her eyes while myriad emotions tumbled through her. She would never, she knew, be able to look at a rose without thinking of Zach.

But she had to go on. She put her chin up and went into the house, finding everything in order and Dr. Guest in her examining room. It felt odd to see a virtual stranger so at home in her own house, but when she entered the room he looked up and smiled, stepping forward to take both her hands.

"Katherine!" he said. "How good to have you home."

Home, she thought. How disheartening that she would never share it with Zach. But she returned Dr. Guest's warm smile and thanked him.

He scooted around the room, packing up his instruments. "I trust the operation went well?"

"Yes, very well."

He gave her an odd look. She imagined she didn't sound as though the operation had gone "very well."

"I'd like to hear about it," he said, "when you have the chance. I'll be staying in town—"

"Katherine!"

Katherine whirled to see Cynthia Gormen, all blond curls and laughing blue eyes, sweeping forward to hug her. "When did you get back? I thought you'd notify us or write—"

"I just got in," Katherine said. "I sent a telegram to Shadow to let him know when to pick me up. And I actually didn't have time to write."

Cynthia searched Katherine's face. "No time? You've been gone for weeks!" She squeezed Katherine's hands. "You must have been mighty busy!"

"I was."

"And your captain? Where is he?"

Suddenly Katherine felt unutterably weary. She pressed her fingers to the bridge of her nose to relieve it of sudden pressure. She didn't want to answer questions about Zach, didn't even want to think of him. She knew, in order to live a reasonably happy life, she would have to forget him, empty her mind of all memories, her heart of all love.

"My captain," she said dryly, "is in England right now—or somewhere in Europe . . ."

"You don't know where?"

She shrugged and pretended to busy herself with checking the medicines in her cabinet. "Hmm? Oh, well, last I *heard* he was going to England." She forced a smile. "And what have you been up to?"

Cynthia, easily distracted, glanced up at Dr. Guest. She slipped her arm through his and smiled. "Brian and I are getting married!"

Stunned, Katherine looked at her, then she broke into a genuine smile. "Married! Why, that's wonderful!" She hugged Cynthia, and Brian too. "We have to celebrate!" she exclaimed, immediately enchanted with the idea of *not* spending her first night home alone.

"Sounds wonderful to me!" Cynthia said.

"We should have a poker party," Katherine went on. "Birdie would love it."

"Hmm," Brian said. "I think this sounds like a 'women only' affair."

"No," Cynthia said. "Birdie would love to have you, wouldn't she, Katherine?"

Katherine laughed. "Birdie loves men of all types and ages."

In the end, though, only women gathered at Birdie's that night, and it was a celebration indeed. Not only did they celebrate Cynthia's engagement and Katherine's return home, but there was news of Lisa's engagement to Jim Lowell too.

"Jim!" Katherine exclaimed, when she heard the news after the women had set up tables for playing poker.

Lisa cast her a wary look and gnawed on her bottom lip. "You don't mind, do you, Katherine? He asked me to the social after you left and since then it's been—"

"Like a house afire!" Birdie said, and the women laughed.

Katherine smiled, actually relieved Jim had found someone else. "I'm thrilled for you, Lisa. You and Jim make a perfect match."

There was much gaiety that evening. When it was time to deal cards Birdie rolled up her sleeves, offered Katherine a cigarette made of the 'finest' tobacco, and peered at her over the table. "Let's see what Adonis taught you, missy."

Katherine had to look away to hide the tears that welled in her eyes. "He taught me a lot," she choked out, and the Gormen sisters and Birdie exchanged surreptitious glances.

Katherine's pleasure in the celebration faded after that. Oh, she laughed with the others and smoked and popped back a few swigs of whiskey, but her enjoyment was forced, and she knew her friends knew it. When she left the room to get some water, the sisters found her with her back toward them, leaning her forehead against the kitchen wall.

"Katherine."

She jumped when Lisa put a hand on her arm, then turned to face them.

"We're sorry," Cynthia murmured. "We didn't mean to make it worse."

She laughed shakily. "Don't be ridiculous."

"You fell in love with him, didn't you?"

"Yes," she said softly. "I did."

"And he didn't?" Cynthia shouted, suddenly outraged.

"Shh—shh!" Lisa scolded, looking exasperated. "My goodness, Cynthia, have you no tact?"

Cynthia looped her arm through Katherine's. "Well, he is nothing more than a scoundrel, and you are better off without him."

Katherine smiled at her well-meaning friends. "I'd

really rather not talk about him. It doesn't do any good. And I'm so very happy for both of you."

They walked her home, and it was worse, much worse when she went to bed that night. She instinctively listened for the sound of the sea outside her window; it had become so familiar to her, but there was nothing, not even a breeze. Only the fragrant scent of roses. She yearned for Zach, his arms around her, his hands on her body, quickening her blood. She *needed* to hear his hauntingly sensual voice whispering love words in the dark. But he was gone.

She had been foolish to hope. She'd only been a dalliance to him, that was all. She had gone with him knowing the risk, and had come home with no part of her intact. She had convinced herself before going that she would be able to separate her professional involvement with Zach and his son from personal involvement, but she'd failed utterly at that.

It was best this way, she told herself, wrapping her arms around her waist, holding on to herself as if to ease the ache. Zach was footloose, had never tied himself to anyone. Why should she be any different? Why should she even have been surprised that he hadn't informed her of his plans? But all those nights!

As she lay alone in the dark she was plagued by fragmented images of Zach—the way his eyes softened and crinkled at the corners when he teased her, the way he looked in expertly tailored evening clothes, the way he felt waltzing her down the length of a ballroom while he whispered to her what he was going to do with her later.

She thought of his hands—broad and masculine—how he'd shown Drew how to whittle ... how he'd slid those hands over her skin. She craved him now. In the warm summer night with nothing but cricket sounds and the rustle of grass outside her window to soothe her, she ached for him to fill her. *Don't forget me,* he'd said. And now she whispered her own plea into the night.

"Don't forget *me,* Zach."

And she rolled onto her stomach and cried into her pillow, despising her weakness, her need, and her love.

The only way to forget Zach, Katherine decided, was to throw herself into her work. When she wasn't seeing patients in her office she went on rounds. She rode alone into the hills to gather herbs, and she worked late into the night writing notes in her medical journals, which she later expanded into lectures that she gave in Denver.

She filled every moment of every day, making certain she was never idle. She helped the Gormen sisters plan their double wedding. She helped Mrs. Duggan pick fabric for curtains for their new house. But the Duggans asked after Zach, as did so many other people who'd met him during his short visit. Even the sheriff, stopping by her office for a visit one afternoon, inquired after him.

"Is he coming back?"

"No." Katherine kept her eyes downcast as she worked on bottling some pills.

"So, uh, nothin' about that lawsuit?"

She looked up at him and couldn't resist prolonging the joke. "Oh, I don't know about that. Just because Zach is gone doesn't mean he can't sue you. He still has a scar, you know."

"What? A little itty-bitty mark over his right brow?"

Katherine tsked him. "Do you think it's wise to declare over *which* brow Zach is scarred?"

The sheriff narrowed his gaze on her, uncertain whether or not she was joshing him. Katherine went back to her pills, and she was relieved when the sheriff left a few minutes later.

Katherine could not even find refuge at the reservation. White Owl immediately saw the change in her—her lusterless eyes, her bland smile, her face strained and thin.

When he was alone with her his dark eyes burned with fury. "I knew he would hurt you."

"White Owl, please—"

"No!" He took her by both arms and forced her to look into his face. "Look what you have allowed him to do to you—Arapaho!"

She frowned. "I'm tired, that's all. I've been busy—"

"Yes!" White Owl hissed. "Busy because of him—to erase the pain of him from your soul!" He tightened his lips when her eyes darkened. "Hate me if you must, but I speak the truth! And perhaps your mixed blood had more to do with his leaving you than anything else!"

"No!" she cried, refusing to believe that of Zach. Then she remembered what Zach had told her about White Owl, that he loved her. She shook herself free of his grip. "I am over Zach. And you," she added, "will not speak of him to me ever again." Her demeanor softened. "Please, White Owl, I ask this of you as a friend."

He stared at her for a long moment. "I will never mention him again," he said quietly. "But you must promise me, as a fellow doctor, that you will take care of yourself."

"I will," she promised. And tried.

But even when she was able to push Zach out of her mind during the day, she would lie awake at night and could almost feel his hands and mouth upon her, could smell his distinctive scent. Her skin craved the touch of his. She hadn't known anyone could love as deeply and all-consumingly as she loved Zach.

August came and went. She didn't hear from him, not a word. She ached with loneliness and didn't know how to change her condition. The heat was blistering, shimmering in ripples over the dry, dusty town. It had been an extraordinarily hot summer, and September rolled in on a wave of the same unbearable heat.

One sultry afternoon she decided to go to the hills and visit old Ethan. She'd seen him only once since she'd come home and he was becoming weaker all the time. It did her heart good to talk with him, to listen to his tales of the old days.

By the time she reached his home her throat was parched and perspiration splotched her clothing. Dust coated her outfit—a pair of worn-out boy's breeches and a baggy white shirt that was missing a couple of buttons. She'd clubbed her thick auburn hair back into a braid and didn't care if the most proper folks in Newberry witnessed her appearance.

Ethan's yard looked unkempt with its tufts of over-grown grass yellowed by the dry weather. She frowned when she noticed the closed windows. He must be suffocating in the heat.

She swung down off Hippocrates and started for the house, which seemed to shimmer in the haze. She knocked on the door, waited a minute, then turned the knob and let herself in.

His place had been emptied out, and there was no sign of Ethan or Mike. A note was pinned to the wall, though, and she knew before she read it that Ethan had died.

Hot tears gushed from her eyes. She swayed and leaned against the wall, her cheek pressed to the panel which smelled faintly of cabbage and beef. "Ethan," she said quietly, "I wished I had known."

She heard the creaking of a floorboard and whirled, long braid flying. Mike, Ethan's ranch hand, stood in the doorway, gazing somberly down at her.

"Mike," she said, swiping at her eyes, "why didn't you come and tell me?"

He twirled his hat in his hands and looked at the floor. "He asked me not to, Doc. Said you were havin' some troubles of yer own right now and you'd find out soon enough about him." He smiled sadly. "Said din't want you blubberin' all over him like some blame fool female—"

She gave a snuffled sound of laughter through her tears. "Ornery old cuss! He knew I wasn't one to blubber—" But that sounded absurd because she was certainly blubbering now!

She and Mike walked out to the porch together and lingered, watching the late afternoon heat shimmer over the dry grasses. Hippocrates nickered softly, then Mike left her alone. She leaned back against the porch railing and let her gaze drift up to the hot white sky. "Ethan," she whispered, "Godspeed."

Then she was off like a shot, swinging herself up onto Hippocrates' back and urging him into a canter over the hills. She rode hard till the horse was lathered and she was drenched in sweat and tears. She was clinging to the horse's mane, her face buried in its silky mass.

"Zach, Zach . . ." She wept, terrified she would never get over him, terrified he would haunt her forever. Months had passed and still she could taste him, feel him, remember every detail about him. The pain was still fresh and jagged, cutting at her insides like shards of glass. All she wanted was to wash away the painful memories and get on with her life, to free her heart from the past forever.

•   •   •

At the stable Katherine slid off Hippocrates and handed his reins to Shadow. Seeing the boy's concerned expression, she offered him only a lame smile, then trudged wearily toward her house. Lemonade, she thought, smoothing strands of hair off her forehead and turning up the front path to the porch. Abruptly she halted. The breath deserted her body. Cast in sunlight and shadow, a tall, dark, harsh-faced man stood on her front porch.

"Zach . . ." She didn't so much speak his name as breathe it.

In the play of light the contours of his face were even more sharply chiseled, as if from stone. He radiated more power and heat than the blazing afternoon. Sweat darkened his shirt, making a diamond pattern of where his chest hair would be. She thought she could smell the musky scent of his skin, and her heart began a wild banging in her chest. He was raw and physical and riveting. He hadn't shaved and looked as if he hadn't slept, but his black eyes drilled her like two deadly pistols, aimed, cocked, and ready to be fired.

As she stood motionless, Zach let his gaze take a slow ride over her body. Her clothes were sweat-dampened and dust-caked, her shirt sleeves hanging past her hands, the worn-out breeches clinging to all her soft, firm curves. He felt an abrupt tightening in his loins, and quickly lifted his gaze back to her face. It was thin and streaked with dust and sticky paths that ran down her cheeks. Why tears? he wondered. Her fire-shot hair had unraveled from its thick braid, and even though she looked like a street urchin, her beauty and poise struck him forcibly. Still, she had left him without a good-bye, and before he touched her he wanted to set a few things straight.

"We have to talk," he said.

It seemed a ludicrous reaction, but Katherine

bolted. She hadn't the faintest idea where she was headed. All she knew was that she had to escape him, escape the pain of loving him. He was a heartbreaker, *her* heartbreaker, and she'd had enough heartbreak to last her a lifetime.

She wasn't three strides down the dusty road when he caught her, hooking her around the middle with one powerful arm. He swept her up, and she was running in place, her legs kicking air.

"Release me!" she yelled. She tried to kick him, but he held her at an angle that deemed her efforts futile. "Let me go!" When her heel whistled too comfortably close to his most precious parts, he became exasperated and slung her roughly over one broad shoulder.

He took the front porch steps two at a time, ignoring her squirming and flailing. He flung the screen door open and strode into her front room. Clarabelle squawked, and he swore at the bird as the screen door slammed behind him.

"Put me down!" Katherine demanded, and she grabbed fistfuls of Zach's trousers' seat and pinched hard. He only laughed.

"Dammit, Smoke Eyes," he muttered as he turned down the hall with her, "you smell good."

She stilled, his words washing through her in a scalding wave. How could his voice alone make her melt inside? But, of course, she must smell like a goat—or certainly like Hippocrates.

In answer to her startled silence he added, "You smell like woman."

And he smelled, oh, so much, like man.

He turned into her bedroom and dumped her unceremoniously upon her bed. Against the pale sheets her bright hair looked like an autumn leaf. She bounced slightly on the mattress, then scrambled to get up. His rapier gaze stilled her, though.

"Why'd you leave without saying good-bye?" he asked.

She stared at him, shocked to see that he was unbuttoning his shirt. He was breathing hard, as if he'd run a long distance, and suddenly she was breathing hard too.

"Why did *you* leave without saying good-bye?" she countered.

He stopped unbuttoning his shirt. "*You* left first."

"Yes, but *you* were going anyway. I overheard Dorrie speaking to one of the maids, and she said you were going to England—just after you told me you didn't *know* when you'd be leaving. Why would I want to wave you off when you so obviously wanted me out of your life?"

She gasped when he flung off his shirt. His skin, his damp, curly chest hair, glistened with sweat, and the perfect symmetry of his broad shoulders tapering down to his narrow waist was breathtaking. She ached to put her hands on him, to touch his beloved face.

But he was cursing fluently. "What the hell kind of logic is that? Dammit, Smoke Eyes, when you asked I *didn't* know when I was leaving. Then the next day I received a telegram from Drew's great-grandfather stating I had to be in England to settle a custody dispute. He wanted the boy back and I had to prove I was a fit father."

"Oh . . ."

"I had every goddamn intention of telling you, but when I came home that evening you were gone." He stabbed her with another look that made her feel a pang of guilt.

She was sitting up now, enthralled with the story, and fascinated by the play of muscles in Zach's hard bronze shoulders as he began to unfasten his trousers. "What happened?"

He tightened his lips. "What happened," he said with dark irony, "was a summer in hell. The magistrate forced me to live with that old—" He stopped himself. "We're all back now," he finished succinctly.

"We?"

He scowled. "We. All of us. Dorrie, Drew, me—and that old goat who has the audacity to call himself a great-grandfather!"

Katherine's eyes widened. "He's living in Marblehead—with you?"

Zach's scowl darkened, and she had to smother a giggle. He sat on the edge of the bed and yanked off his boots, then stood again. "It seemed the only solution. Dorrie said she couldn't bear another instant of my temper, Drew was miserable, and it didn't seem to solve anything staying in England. The magistrate agreed that if we could all live together peaceably, then he'd give us his blessing and send us on our way. I've legalized Drew's parentage through the English courts, and he's mine now. Not even that old man can take him away."

"Then why has he come to live with you?"

Zach shook his head as if in bewilderment. "Drew wanted him to. Says he's a sad and lonely old man, and that's what makes him grumpy. I tend to disagree, but Drew's happy and I figure the house is large enough so I don't ever have to see the old crank."

"Zach, you're a soft touch."

"Touched, all right, dammit." His trousers were open, spread to reveal the dark hair at his groin. He stood over her, and trickles of sweat ran down his face. "I cut that trip short and high-tailed it right out here for a woman who believes I want her out of my life. Now get undressed."

She caught her breath. What was he saying?

"Undress for me, Smoke Eyes."

She shook her head slowly, even as she watched him push his trousers to the floor. He reached out to stroke her face, tilting it up so he could look into her eyes.

"These eyes," he said, "have haunted me every night and day since you left. I was furious with you." Her mouth trembled as he ran his thumb across her bottom lip. "I had planned to talk with you about things I plan to talk about now."

"Now?" Her voice was hushed, shaken. His big hand was in her braid now, loosening it, letting it fall around her shoulders.

"You have beautiful hair, darlin'."

The heat in the room was stifling. So was the pain that crushed Katherine's chest. As always, he wanted to take her and leave her. But she would not be his port of call. "Zach, no. You can't do this."

"I want to talk."

"Then talk."

He smiled, his eyes crinkling at the corners, the long groove in his cheek deepening. He sobered, though, as his gaze followed the path of his thumb, running lightly down her cheek. "You've been crying."

"Yes . . ." Her eyes fluttered closed as she was both soothed and hurt by his caress, his gentle words.

"Why?"

"Ethan died," she choked out.

"The old man? The trapper?"

She opened her eyes as intense emotion washed through her. This was why she loved Zach. He was so hard, so rough, his life had been so depleted of love, yet he could remember someone like Ethan—just a brief encounter that would have meant nothing to most men. Behind his tough exterior was a haunting sweetness that ran soul-deep.

She nodded, and he leaned down to brush her lips

with his own. "This is not talking," she admonished him lightly, catching her breath as his callused fingers rasped against her skin.

"Yes, it is," he murmured. He deftly unbuttoned her shirt and pushed it from her shoulders so it fell to the mattress. His hand slid up her delicate ribs under her chemise, then he filled his palm with her breast. His thumb flicked the erect nipple, and she gasped. But his touch slipped away.

"I've been dying to put my hands on you again," he said, and pushed her back on the pillows. She let him pull off her breeches, then he stared down at her, her naked body dappled with sunlight, her nipples tight and eager. He held off a moment longer, then he did what he'd been hungering to do. He fell on her, his aching body needing relief, needing only Smoke Eyes. He ripped her chemise in two, baring her breasts to his mouth, which he fastened hungrily on her. She arched to him, holding his head to her as he caressed her nipples with his tongue until they were wet and straining and aching for more, more . . .

Katherine felt drugged. Her body was a seething, pulsing current flowing toward him, only him. She ached for him to come inside her, just once more—only once. Maybe then she could be rid of this terrible consuming hunger. But his hunger was just as raw. Their mouths met rapaciously, as if they had been long nights in the desert and now were quenching their thirst.

He lifted his head to gaze down at her, and his breath was hot and damp, beating fast upon her skin. "I'm in pain," he said, his voice guttural and thick. "Heal me." He brought her hand to his heated flesh and groaned when she closed her fingers around him, grasping him so tightly he thought he would die of the pleasure. He parted her thighs, looking down at her with his heart in his eyes. "Are you ready, angel? I need you now."

She *wanted* him now. She felt the tip of him against her sleek tightness, then he thrust into her, meltingly hot and lush and wet. She was so ready for him Zach almost lost control.

Katherine closed her eyes, pressing her hands to his warm hard back, pressing him into her so tightly she could feel the pulse beat of his hard flesh. "Oh, Zach, Zach . . ." she moaned, tears slipping unheeded from her eyes.

He began to move, slowly at first, drawing out the ecstasy with long, slow strokes. Ribbons of pleasure rippled through her, tingling her nipples, her loins, her silky inner flesh stretched by his magnificent manhood. His muscles rippled under her gripping fingers.

"I want you always," he whispered, and she wondered if she'd imagined the words, for he was driving harder now, deeper, as he took her with a desperate, savage need. She met the ardor of his mouth, his tongue filling her with a deep, lustful satisfaction. She was wild, shaking for him, taking all of him into her.

"Smoke Eyes." He smoothed the hair off her hot face, and the power of his thrusts made her consciousness dim. Still she clung to him, begging him not to stop. Zach couldn't. He was buried so deep inside her it was torment to pull back, but he did, then thrust even deeper.

Fiery white heat exploded through her, carrying her to him in seething hot waves of passion. He drove hard against her, the pleasure so sharp, so exquisite, he could not hold back. As his body erupted in powerful, shuddering release, he cried out the words that he'd kept locked inside him for what seemed an eternity.

"I love you, Smoke Eyes."

•   •   •

Slowly they stilled. The tiniest of breezes puffed into the room, cooling their flesh. Zach rested with his jaw against her temple, and Katherine's fingers stroked his chest. The words he'd uttered hung between them, stark, vibrant. The only sound in the room was their breathing.

Zach felt an incredible, overwhelming liberation within himself. The throbbing emptiness that had plagued him for months—years—was gone, replaced with incomparable peace.

He lifted his head and looked down at her. He saw the glint of tears in her eyes and cursed himself. But before he could jerk away she tightened her arms around his broad shoulders, cradling him close.

"You do?" she asked.

"You sound like you don't believe me."

She hesitated. "Men don't usually fall in love with their mistresses."

He cursed and rolled away from her, and the separation of their bodies was a cold shock. "I don't want you for my mistress," he growled.

"You don't?"

"No, goddamm it, I want you for my wife!"

She was stunned. Before she could even form a coherent thought he was above her again, gripping her arms, forcing her to meet his gaze.

"Think about it," he said. Her heart thumped crazily, but she let him speak the words she had craved for so long to hear from him. "You could doctor in Marblehead, and I wouldn't interfere at all. I promise you that. We could set up an office for you right outside. And Drew—Christ, Drew is following in your footsteps, I swear it, Smoke Eyes. He looks for herbs and flowers in the fields just like you taught him. I know how important your work is to you and I would never want to take that away from you."

He grinned crookedly, ruefully, and touched the corner of her mouth with his forefinger. "Somehow if you gave up doctoring you wouldn't be the same woman." He sobered again. "I know I'd be asking you to leave the reservation, but you can come back and visit anytime. We have plenty of money, and well, you left it when you took care of Drew and that seemed to work out fine." He dipped his head and his mouth grazed her. She sighed against his lips, savoring the feel of him against her and his words. "Drew needs you, Smoke Eyes. He's pining for you, sugar, wants to hear more stories—about the Arapaho, about the time you rode old man Cooter's pig."

She laughed and lightly punched him on the shoulder. "You didn't tell him about that, did you?"

He grinned again and she traced her finger down the long groove in his cheek. "You hung on," he said, "and Drew wants to know how."

She giggled, remembering back to that crazy ride. "He *was* a large pig."

He laughed again. "And Drew tells me he won't set foot on my ship again unless you're with us." He saw her eyes widen and he caught her to him, burying his face in her throat. "I love you," he said against her skin, breathing in her unique scent. "I won't be taking so many voyages in the future. It's the shipyard that needs my attention. I remember you saying how you wanted to travel, to see the world. Why not now, Smoke Eyes, with me?"

She thought she would explode with happiness. She eased back to look at his face, to give him her answer, but he kept talking, as if talking would convince her of their destiny. "And Dorrie says if I don't bring you back she will never fix scones for me again." And his voice became lower, hoarser. "I need you, sweetheart, don't you see that?"

"I see," she whispered. And though it pained her to say it, she had to. "There have been many women for you, Zach, many that you have needed—"

She stopped as he took her face in his big hands. "As if there could be any others after you, Smoke Eyes." The expression in his eyes grew soft, tender. "All these years I've been searching for something in all those women, and I didn't find it till I found you."

Hot tears washed into her eyes. "Oh, Zach," she breathed, but he was leaning over the side of the bed, searching his pants pockets.

"One more thing," he muttered, and came back up to drape the sparkling emerald necklace she'd worn in Marblehead around her throat. The beautiful green stones glittered against her peach-colored skin. She laughed, winding her arms around his neck and tugging him down to kiss him.

"No one wears 'em like you," he whispered, and locked her tightly to him. "What do you say?"

"I can't breathe," she gasped, and he eased his weight off her. But he stayed close, watching her with troubled eyes. What if she didn't want to marry him? Hell, she hadn't even told him she loved him. What if she still valued her freedom more than anything in the world? He'd so carefully thought out every angle, every possible problem, those nights he'd lain awake thinking of her. And now she looked so uncertain.

"You told me once you didn't want a woman to love you," she began.

He gritted his teeth. "That was Laura. I didn't want *her* to love me—a sin her grandfather is making me repent for now!"

Katherine laughed, and the sound was so beautiful, so intoxicating, he had to kiss her again. The more he took from her, the more he wanted. Would he ever have his fill of her?

When he released her, his breathing was ragged. "Well, dammit, how about an answer?" His pride was beginning to suffer. Weren't women supposed to swoon or something when a man proposed marriage? This one hadn't even blinked.

"I—"

"What?" He pounced.

"I want babies."

He grinned roguishly at her. "That won't be a problem. Especially the way you keep wriggling around under there."

She looked down, though, as if disturbed.

"What is it, darlin'?"

Her mouth trembled. "Our babies will have mixed blood."

He snorted. "Hell, *I'm* a mixed blood. Not Indian maybe, but there's a whole lot of mix in me." He grinned lopsidedly. "They'll be beautiful babies, sweetheart. You know I never gave a damn about your being part Arapaho. You should be proud of where you came from."

She met his gaze again. "I am."

"Then our children will be proud too."

She smiled lovingly at him. "And it will take me a while to pack."

His gaze traveled around her room, stopping when it touched on a silky undergarment hanging provocatively over the armoire door. He lifted his brows, his knowing gaze coming back to meet hers. He noted the delicate pink flush in her cheeks and started to smile. "I'll help," he said, then gave her a mock scowl. "Are you saying yes, woman?"

But Katherine was savoring her feminine power. "It depends."

"On what?"

"Can we take Shadow? And Clarabelle? I think Drew

would like them both. Heavens, Zach, must you be so impatient?"

"Yes. You know patience isn't my strong suit."

"No," she agreed, feeling his rigid length growing harder and fuller against her thigh. "It isn't." She moved her hips. "Are you always going to be so commanding?"

"That depends," he growled, giving her a taste of her own medicine.

"On what?"

"On whether or not you need to be commanded!" He covered her mouth before she could protest, and ground his hips against hers. When he eased back, he thought she looked like a fine painting—naked, with only emeralds draped around her throat.

"I love you," she said. "I've loved you for so long, Zach, and was so afraid." She hugged him tightly, tears running down her cheeks, unable to believe she could say the words, that he was with her. "More than anything I want to spend the rest of my life with you, have your children." Joy exploded through her. She knew he felt it too, this strange bond that had always been between them, as if they were destined to be together.

"Then let's do something about it," he said, shifting his body over her. The love in his eyes nourished her soul. "It's time I got you out of this town." He palmed her breast, his finger teasing her nipple. She moved sinuously beneath him, making him stare down at her reverently. "But I'm sure some folks are going to miss you." He ran his tongue along her bottom lip, then plunged it deep into her mouth. When she was whimpering and writhing beneath him, he lifted up, bracing his forearms on either side of her.

"I saw the sheriff while I was walking through town," he said.

Her eyes danced with amusement. "Was he surprised to see you?"

"He looked a little pale—as if he'd seen a ghost."

She laughed merrily. "What happened?"

That slow grin spread across Zach's face. "He sputtered for a few seconds and I growled and told him I was takin' you away. Marryin' you."

"But you didn't know!" she exclaimed. "You—" She stopped, reading the wicked light in his eyes. "You are, irrefutably, the most arrogant man I have ever known!" She was both laughing and indignant at once. "How could you be so sure I'd say yes?"

"I wasn't." Though he smiled, his eyes were like fiery brands that burned into her. He raised himself up and entered her, pressing deep, and she felt the solid heat of him inside her. Her eyes flickered, closed, then opened again as he began to move in and out of her with long, slow strokes. She felt he touched her soul with the passionate heat in his eyes.

"But," he added, "I do have great powers of persuasion."

And he set out to prove it.